The Arthuriad Volume Two:
The Madness of Maelgwn

Zane Newitt

First published 2018
by Rowanvale Books Ltd
The Gate
Keppoch Street
Roath
Cardiff
CF24 3JW
www.rowanvalebooks.com

A CIP catalogue record for this book is available from the British Library.
ISBN: 978-1-911569-62-6

Contents

Acknowledgments

The process by which the first book, *The Arthuriad Volume One: The Mystery of Merlin*, was completed was a life-changing experience and exercise in humility. Having first a third-party expert and then the world, evaluate one's art brings many 'blushes and bruises' to the pride and growth to the soul. For her guidance and support (and softening of my idiosyncrasy, sans diminishing or changing it) and humor over many late nights and early mornings, I am eternally and deeply grateful to Emma and the team at Rowanvale Publishing, without whom the book would still reside as an unfinished manuscript, waxing and fermenting since 2003, on my laptop.

To the Arthur-haters guised as 'experts', who start with the premise that the Silure King never was, or was an amalgamation of many, or was a children's story, to those 'academics' who mislead and misdirect in the cesspools of social media… thank you too. Thank you for exposing the fallacious logic that renders every other culture's history as that, history, and makes Welsh history 'guilty of fraud and forgery until proven innocent'. The double and triple standards only serve to alert thinking people to the fact that something is amiss, that the fix is in, and that the more they cover up, the more they expose themselves. There is an unbroken chain of evidence in manuscripts, epic poetry, kings' lists, charters, stones, hills, wells and streams that proclaim the veracity of the great King Arthur without controversy and beyond disputation. So again, thank you, doubters, for shedding light on your lies, for opposing yourselves. 'The Truth Against The World.'

I am thankful for Alec and Pam, shop owners of Awen Celtic Spirit in Caerleon, Cymru. By being living ensamples of ancient codes of druidic hospitality, for the biscuits and tea, the hours of poring over maps, and for the ongoing exchange of the Mysteries, these two, along with the dear late Dr. Russell Rhys (he was the Merlin), have most influenced my contribution to the Great Conversation concerning our Once and Future King.

Lastly, I wish to acknowledge my children. My everything. My Avery, Camden and Olivia.

To quote my favorite band, 'They are what my story is all about.'

On Linguistics Places
and Names

Ninth grade Creative Writing class.

With salivating anticipation, we had finally reached a segment on Arthurian Literature in the curriculum.

I was an Arthurian and 'Celtic' radical at the time. While the potheads would visit "Stoner Hill" and the jocks would cut class to eat amino acids like captive sharks at feeding time, the vice of my youth was stealing away to the library to ingest as much Arthur, Lancelot and Merlin as I could get my hands on.

When the teacher, reading from a poorly rendered textbook summary of Mallory's *Le Morte*, opened class with the words "Arthur, King of England," all at once feelings of isolation, betrayal and subject-matter-specific arrogance consumed me.

"How could Arthur be king of a country that did not exist?" I demanded.

An alligator's death roll rant followed.

"The defeat of the Angles, Jutes and Saxons are the primary focus of Arthur's military campaigns! England would not exist as such for some two centuries later than the Arthurian period!"

With one final gasp, I pronounced: "Calling

King Arthur the King of England would be tantamount to making Geronimo Chief of the United States! You have ascribed to the king of the Britons the very title of his enemies."

I learned that day that there are two distinct camps when it comes to students and fans of matters Arthurian:

1. Students/readers who care very much about Arthurian accuracy.
2. Students/readers who care very little about Arthurian accuracy.

Over the ensuing years, I have observed a great spectrum amongst readers in general, and Arthurian fans in particular.

Some, moved by the romance of Arthur, care little that the knightly and ecclesiastical orders described in medieval Arthurian literature did not exist in 6th century Britain.

Contrastingly, the opposite extreme exists. The contemporary obsession with Celtic primitivism, of long-haired naked warriors running to and fro in skirts screaming in mania, has no place in legitimate Arthurian history.

The ancient British culture was the most advanced, perhaps save Rome, of the Ancient World. Men, though styles were diverse, wore their hair 'high and tight' and, for functions of health and cleanliness, had no body hair. As for armor and attire, the Cymry worked in fine silks, decorative crests denoting tribe, cantref (similar to our 'county'), sub-kingdom and nation. They wore a diverse range of battle arms, depending upon the situation. The ancient British were sophisticated, and it was the Saxon who was bankrupt of culture, virtue, or God, in the Arthurian setting. That modern academia has turned this truth on its head is historical revisionism that would shock and anger any objective inquisitor.

As with the first volume, the author here has endeavored to have a balanced approach, combining fidelity to the linguistics, culture, places and names, while at the same time providing some minor synonyms and modernity for ease of reading. This is primarily found in the use of the word Cymru, which is now rendered 'Wales'. The term 'Walles' is a Saxon pejorative that means 'foreigner'. This crude, if not callous and ingenious, form of racial imperialism, whereby the invader renders the invaded as the 'foreigner', remains a grave national insult to the ancient and glorious people of Wales. Thus, Wales is rendered as Cymru.

Other terms, such as Britannia, the Isles of the Sea and the Blessed Isles, are also used. As for its people, 'the Cymry' or 'Britons' is used throughout the story.

The Vale of Glamorgan (South East Wales), named after King Arthur's son Morgan the Courteous, has been left in its modern form as such for ease of pronunciation by the reader.

With regard to personal names, it is important to understand that many Welsh names are titular, some are descriptive, and others are given at birth. To fully bring forth the rich and powerful names in the Matter of Britain, the book toggles back and forth between nomenclature.

For example, in history Morgana Le Fay is Arthur's sister, Gwyar (mother of both Gawaine and Mordred). In the book she is presented as either Gwyar or 'Morgaine', depending upon the circumstantial punch needed.

Bedivere has been rendered Bedwyr and Guinevere as Gwenhwyfar. Gawaine will be found as Gwalchamai. Arthur is unchanged.

As for the historical model, this piece is set against the skeletal framework of the Arthur of Glamorgan and Gwent position, of which the greater portion seems, in light of current scholarship, to be most accurate.

The Seeds of Civil War

Dr Zane Newitt

A Poetic Entry in the 2014 AmeriCymru
Eisteddfod
(Revised for publication, 2018)

Civil Wars are a garden, not a rose. Whose seeds are sown in the deepest soils, rich with not hatred and envy unaided, but rather as much with love.

The place of this Civil War was sown in the like manner that pricks all common men. Woe for Cymru that it smote Princes!

'Twas a contest of 'who saw her first', and by the smallest grain of time, 'twas Arthur whose eyes first met those of amatory Gwenhwyfar.

At school.

Perhaps, rather, it is the age and not the setting that makes the scholastic years so paramount. The music a man enjoys at fourteen, he enjoys at eighty. The scents that ignite his memories at forty and ten were first ponged at ten and four. His policy of strife and forgiveness, of style and disposition, all established at fourteen.

And so it is meet that Arthur should both be crowned at such an age and see her in school the same year; twin events to forever impact the Blessed Isles.

Maelgwn was sixteen. And again, he yielded to the young Pendragon from the South.

Controversy already and always surrounded the Bloodhound Prince of Gwynedd. Already two heads taller than any Briton, lean with muscles and sinew, strong from his toes to his eyebrows, he was more god than man.

Maelgwn slew his uncle to have his wife and was sent south for fostering, forbearance and schooling with the royal households of the Silures.

It was more a banishing to let the folly of his youth cool in the memories of his kinsmen in Gwynedd. But when he looked upon the Princess, dark and small as a Fae, yet begotten of Ogyrfan the Giant, he loved her in an instant, and forever.

And he loved Arthur.

For the King's part, he had to master the grace of ever being second.

Second pertaining comeliness.

Second with sword.

Second at dancing and dazzling.

Second at the hunt.

Second in grappling and fighting arts without steel.

Second in the sports of fleet of foot.

Second in all the things that mean all to a man, but maybe to the wise, ought not to.

Yet first at character, grace and kindness. These virtues seemed as vices when sharing a schoolroom, fighting, and being in the presence of a warrior to whom Achilles would beg quarter.

And for all this, he loved Maelgwn.

But this time! This one time, Arthur had been first!

Illtud, the King's cousin, though younger than Arthur, mentored the others, and brought teachers near and far to rear the minds of the children at a small chapel within the monastic college that bore his name. A place of learning envied all the way to Alexandria, it had every convention and accommodation to sneak away from the toil of learning at times of recess and master the art of falling in love.

Yes, Arthur had seen her first, and she was his for the taking, but the curse of the young King's character bit him. His humility and equity flowed him over with thoughts of 'let her decide.'

And though her words chose for Arthur, the lust of her eyes burned towards Maelgwn; and Arthur knew it as lust, but Maelgwn took it for love.

That same season, the Saxon Wars began in earnest and their schooling was cut short and unfinished. The young Princes knew not to speak of the matter, and the painted Gwenhwyfar returned to her father's lands.

Arthur was made King in Caerleon, crowned by pious Dubricious, and given for a wife a stately woman: powerful, strong, learned, warm and maternal. The type of woman the Lord places on earth to perform the greatest and most difficult of all enterprises: motherhood.

This was a red-headed, fair lady who bore the name, but not the unbridled eroticism, of the painted girl whom the Bards would call Gwen II, but whom for Maelgwn and Arthur, was really, and between them alone, Gwen I.

Through the military mastery of Merlin, Arthur won the Saxon Wars and helped re-establish Kings in the North. This allowed Maelgwn, two decades passed, to at last return home.

The greater in power had served the lesser for the sake of Nation, and at long last, he could enjoy being King over his own courts again.

As the Golden Age unfolded for the Common Man, enjoying plenty of harvest and even more liberty of thought and enterprise, Arthur was enduring dark hours, losing his wife and Queen to madness.

All the sons the King had given her had

perished in the Saxon Wars, and one even at his father's hand for the unpardonable sin against State – treachery.

A craze of sorrow struck at Gwenhwyfar. Too despondent to walk, let alone rule, she abdicated the crown for the simple black tunic, putting herself away in a primitive order for women similar to later nunneries.

Arthur demanded sons of Maelgwn come and reinforce the strength of his own plenary courts against the wishes of Arthur (and the duality of Maelgwn had manifested through reports of raiding Arthur's lands), and again, Maelgwn acquiesced to the greater good and the orders of the King.

The garden of hurts grew, as Maelgwn observed his youngest son grow to make all of the Bloodhound Prince's sins right through the greatness of his progeny.

His son shimmered wheresoever he walked, his promenade at once on and off the earth. He was better with sword than his father, rendering him, for one small season, the greatest warrior in the history of the world.

The counselors, both men and women, the Royal Clans and people of influence recommended with much force that Arthur, now not quite so young as Sovereigns go, marry again and gain sons. A rivalry was yet a-fester between the two eligible edlings, Gwalchmai and Medraut, the nephews of the King.

But Arthur favored the young son of Maelgwn.

Many eligible damsels of various pedigree, background and temperament were available to court the Pendragon.

The memories of being fourteen returned, and Arthur sought the hand of Gwenhwyfar, the painted Pictish-like Briton.

Thoroughly, this decision was bemoaned by all, and with Merlin now gone to his sleep of imprisoned exile, the King made his choice, alone and without support.

Gwen II's eyes were full of adultery, and the way of loyalty and fidelity she knew not. Her look could fracture a nation and her touch render it as apocalyptic rubble.

And her Persian eyes often found Maelgwn when he was visiting his son at court. Onlookers, needing not the history about their schooling, could see the love in his visage, matched with the intrigue in hers.

A great calamity from the skies fell upon the Isles in the Sea, destroying so much life of both man and creaturekind. Many felt that Maelgwn, ever so absent from his own court in Gwynedd and Arthur's courts in Caerleon, Gelliweg and Caermelyn, was helping make the great Sovereign a cuckold with Gwenhwyfar II.

The King fell sick, and much of the Isles became a Great Wasteland.

Maelgwn was innocent, save in heart. The new Merlin, Taliesin, approached him. Though all feared the Bloodhound Prince, he had no such effect on Taliesin, who cursed Maelgwn oft for his erratic behavior.

"Your son will achieve the Grail, and be the healing balm of this Land."

In the betwixt and between of dispensations, whereby magic and ways of Old blended with the Christian Faith, Maelgwn knew all too well what was being foretold.

When a King was no longer virile, he was sacrificed so that the Land might rejuvenate and live. The rites of Sacral Kings, though fading, were not fully retired to the realm of superstition.

When a King was desired by the Clans to yet live, though the Land was dying, a proxy was chosen.

"Not my son!" cried Maelgwn, with a cry heard through the corridors of history, for never was a human father so stricken with hurt.

But the greater in power served the lesser (who had no sons), and allowed Taliesin's prophecy to unfold. Maelgwn's son erected the sword, a proxy for Excalibur; he achieved the Grail in the stead of the ailing King and died too, too young, the Galahad, the Gilead, or healing balm of the Land.

To the forests went Maelgwn's body, to parts unknown went his mind; to his own assigned hell of grief went his soul.

The Garden grew.

Some time later, Maelgwn, who was bidden to visit Arthur's court and serve as Seneschal as was his station, could not.

The look of Gwen II in the arms of the man who had made a terminal borrowing of his glorious son and who now was coupled with such a dark and desirable companion nearly finished the remainder of so many decades of friendship, making it as vapor. Maelgwn could function neither as King in his own lands, nor as servant and fellow in Arthur's. Only the solitude of the forest gave him an uneasy, interrupted peace.

Through the process of time, partially because he had healed to a degree and partially for the purpose of seeing Gwen II, Maelgwn visited Caerleon, to great reception by the King's Fellowship. Yet Arthur was absent.

Gwen II sought to seduce Maelgwn without hesitation or reservation.

However, firmly planted in the double-minded and oh-so-troubled mind of Maelgwn were the words Merlin had given him ere the Old Wizard turned Christian had disappeared so long ago (and besides, Maelgwn had liked the original Merlin more than the latter):

"When it comes time to do that which you would do, Lancelot, I beg you, do it not!"

And though she pressed upon him, through

secret and shortly written messages, through contrived reasons fabricated for pernicious and carnal visits, though she pressed and pressed, Maelgwn yielded to her not (though for the score and seven of women he had known biblically, this harlot had poisoned his heart, and he loved her).

For all his failings, this treachery was not his. And to Medraut's bed Gwen II turned.

Maelgwn found them in the very act of their tryst at a field in Glamorgan that bears the name of the deed to this day. The King was undone by his second wife, and by his nephew.

Knowing Arthur's grace and temperance, Maelgwn carried a shaky comfort with the delivery that Arthur would divorce the Queen and kill the vermin Medraut, and that the Kingdom would be scarred of scandal, yet not broken.

However, Maelgwn's exile in the wilds of his own choosing left him derelict on current political events. Arthur was presently in Brittany, succoring his great ally and friend King Howell against the tyrant Mark.

Medraut had taken the Queen, quite willingly, and meant to have the throne. To have Cymru.

As the fleets and ships of the great King returned, Maelgwn begged Arthur to forgive the painted Gwenhwyfar her adultery, and Arthur committed to doing the same.

The traitors fled north, where Medraut had

lands, and yet further north, to the Pictish village of Perth.

Unrelenting was Arthur's pursuit, likened more unto a Bear made of iron than that of a Man. Arthur yielded to rage rare and unbridled, and made a Jezebel ensample of the Queen, throwing her to his war dogs.

Like unto a slimy and poisonous frog, Medraut slipped through Arthur's too-tight clasp.

In the confusion and calamity, Maelgwn, maneuvering to spare the Queen, mortally wounded Gwalchmai.

Three men died to Arthur that day, and yet lived. Gwalchmai, for his wounds inflicted by Maelgwn; Medraut, for his treachery; and Maelgwn, for his attempt to abort justice.

The woman Maelgwn had loved since the age of sixteen lay in pieces and chunks. More red than flesh-colored substance remained of her. It did not matter that Maelgwn was only capable of loving one who would not requite it. Nor did his periodic raiding of Arthur's lands, nor his seasons of corruption, give any balance to the loss of son that Arthur might live, or the loss of love that Arthur might have marital justice.

Though Medraut was a weasel, Maelgwn was to join him in Civil War against King Arthur. Yes, over an affair, but not as recorded by the Bards.

However, as the infamy of Camlan drew to its event horizon and Maelgwn knew Medraut's *advantage escalated, the Bloodhound signaled, and his men switched sides to support his friend and ally ancient, ensuring that King Arthur would win the day.*

"'Twas he who saw her first," thought Lancelot.

'In the son alone rested salvation for the father. Lancelot. A beautiful, brutish beast, whose eyes, though oft he plucked them out, only returned again and again, filled with adultery. Whose spirit warred in losing toil with his flesh; who could not cease from sinning.

When good, the good that was Lancelot was real. The burning in his lusts, the insatiable, satisfied like the kettle's bubble, relieved only briefly and so quickly renewed again. When evil, the evil that was Lancelot was real. So, like antiquity's David, Lancelot was a fragmented man of dual natures.

The dichotomy did not pass; the son did not bear sin of his father. Rather, his fruit was the healing balm. The Galahad. All the angels of Lancelot's virtue present; all the devils of Lancelot's failings not found. Galahad was the perfect knight, the best ingredients of angels and of men. When he was translated for the sake of the Cup, sacrificed for Arthur, the King's salvation was sure; as surely was Lancelot's damnation wrought.

And what brokenness was already present, now unmasked when Galahad died, madness became.'

Dr. Zane Newitt
Autumn, 2018

The three wives of Arthur, who were his chief three ladies: that is to say, Gwenhwyfar, daughter of Gawrwyd Ceint; and Gwenhwyfar, daughter of Ogyrfan Gawr...

PROLOGUE
Brutus versus Gogmagog

King Brutus, whose forebears had escaped the fated fall of fabled Troy, that glorious city that lost its candlestick – due not to defeat of arms but rather to treachery, adultery and the justified madness of an elite warrior – now had a Giant problem… literally.

For when his fleets came ashore *the Blessed Isles in the Sea,* they found the lands overrun by wild beasts and strange, mystical creatures.

Worse, governing all life were gargantuan Giants.

A Giant is neither fully human, being some part angel, nor divine, being some part man. The angelic parents of these Giants took the spirit form of great Dragons who circumambulated the heavens in fixed courses, covered by their stars. These were sinister, ancient and wise. And the greatest amongst them was Y Ddraig Du, *the Black Dragon.*

Brutus and his armies made war with the Giants, as they held all men in subjugation. Like Caleb and Joshua of the Hebrews, Brutus and his generals had to clear their own promised land of milk and honey of the monstrous occupants. The number of the dead mounted, becoming great losses for both Man and Titan. Brutus and the king of the Giants, Gogmagog ap Ddraig Du, parlayed to decide rule of the Isles through trial by combat.

Against hope, the champion of Brutus prevailed, hurling Gogmagog from a high hilltop. Violently, he plunged atop a great apple orchard, nestled in the shadows of the mount near the mouth of an enchanted lake below. The liquescent press of the fall ran into the Lake.

The orchard was tended by powerful water faeries, called the Korrigan, and their renowned queen, who bore only a title: *The Lady of the Lake.*

A faerie is neither fully human, being some part angel, nor divine, being some part man. Whereas Giants came from the male progeny of angels, the faeries came from the female line. And though the Fae distrust men, by ancient rivalry, they loathe Giants.

The contention grew to enmity on this day, as Gogmagog's massive carcass had compassed and compressed the whole of the orchard, producing a mashy elixir comprised of the pressed apple juices, oaky sap and the Giant's demigod essence.

The Korrigan, though jubilant over the fallen rival king, hastened, worried and enraged, to examine what was salvageable of their orchard, an unfortunate casualty of the war. Seeing the faeries celebrate, the spectral Black Dragon descended from the heavens as a bird of prey, diving in a rush upon the watery spirits.

Tribes on the Continent as far as Gaul saw the calamity, recording it in their histories and remembering it in their oral traditions as *a comet striking down from heaven, the fire of angry gods.* Their assessment was not wrong.

Brutus and his men, overcome, or bewitched,

by mortal curiosity, looked on from the hilltop, awe-stricken at the otherworldly battle.

A great cosmic fire came forth from the Black Dragon, making smoky cinders of the orchard trees, creating a protective ring about the Giant and killing a great company of faeries in the process. A dead faerie's animating principle hath nowhere to rest and, displaced, haunts the area where it was slain, becoming almost always a dark thing.

The barrage of brimstone and death activated the Lady of the Lake, who called upon a dragon of her own. Using enchanted words in the Language of Heaven, made she her imprecatory prayer. Soon the Y Ddraig Hanner Nos, the Dragon of Midnight Blue, appeared in the firmament, just above where the birds fly.

With increasingly velocity, he dove and dove until in range of the Black Dragon. The serpentine spirits clashed, ethereal fire setting alight apple, wood, faerie and lake alike.

Such was the illumination of the struggle that the mortals were temporarily blinded and scattered. Striving against the chaos, Brutus dispensed a small troop of men to cautiously descend the hilltop.

Upon reaching the base of the mount, the troop found that Gogmagog had vanished, and the Korrigan too gone as vapor. Signs of fire, smoke, or bloodshed were not found.

Beginning to feel that they were indeed bewitched, or perhaps under a temporary madness from too many days at sea, they began to turn and climb back whence they had come. Suddenly appeared but one great tree standing, and a white-clad, hooded damsel holding its produce: a large, seven-seeded apple.

At her feet were several flagons; the sole remnants of the epic encounter.

"Drink," said the damsel, her seductive arm sleeved in white samite.

The scrumpy sup was unlike to anything the Sons of Adam had ever consumed. The spirit brought health and danger, purity and darkness as it refreshed, captivated and captured them, causing them to call for Brutus himself to partake of the elixir. This pleased the damsel, whose eyes gleamed to hear that the king himself would come.

But such was the power of it that the men were taken by madness. However, it was not yet upon them ere Brutus arrived.

"Drink," said the damsel.

"Drink not, Brutus!" The Lady of the Lake appeared, hovering upon the waters, with crystal-blue eyes whose centers were ablaze with a little red flame, filled with vengeful sorrow over the countless dead faeries, her people.

Plucking an apple from the tree (for there was now but one), she explained to Brutus, "No man can manage this enchantment. This apple is now filled with the strength of Giants, the ancient knowledge of Dragons, the cunning of faeries and the mortality of men.

"To drink it," she continued, "is to be at once full of a false strength, a boastful knowledge, a cunning tongue, and the woes of men. Such a combination would render you like unto" – she pointed at the king's men and their sorry state – "*them*."

"But I must have it," said Brutus.

"You may not," rebuked the Lady.

Calling the Midnight Blue Dragon once more, she cleaved an apple into equal portions, taking a seed from each.

"You may enjoy any of the six seeds, in any combination, and in extreme moderation. But never at once." Now her voice was grave. "And never with the seventh seed."

Her serpentine protector clutched up the tree at the root and took flight, taking each apple and apportioning the seeds, spreading them to seven locations amongst the Blessed Isles and Brittany, desperately hoping that they would never be combined again.

"In moderation, and never seek the seventh." Brutus the Prudent brought captive his reason, and agreed. He and the Lady of the Lake sought to query the damsel whose offering had rendered the men with madness. But, like the Giant, and Y Ddraig Ddu, and the faeries before her, she had vanished.

And this was how Brutus, by right of combat of champions, earned the right to colonize the Isles with the sons of Troy. Through the uncanny and accidental confluence of gods and monsters, the national drink of the Isles was born as well, along with one of the earliest mysteries and quests (for the Isles were a place of treasure, of quest and of the Spirit).

Men lacked the temperance of Brutus, ever questing to find and combine the forbidden *Seventh Seed.*

It was rumored that centuries hence, the druids found each of the seeds and planted an orchard that grew in spite of impossible conditions, against contrary winds and treacherous currents pounding and undoing the soils. The place came to be known as the Isle of Apples.

CHAPTER 1
The First Lie but Not the Last

*Seed 2 – "You know I love her, and didn't even ask
me how I would feel."*

Merlin often taught that a partial truth equates a
full lie.

At the king's very first moment of reprieve
from the revelry and pomp of his crowning,
Arthur took his champion aside and bade him
convey all that had befallen the Merlin during
their absence from Mynydd Baeden.

Vivien and Maelgwn had rehearsed the
conversation, and all that remained was for
him to perform. Twenty years of friendship, of
brotherhood, some spent at school, the greater
part on the war campaigns; the mightiest of
bonds forged. Distrust or misuse was beyond
contemplation.

There was little to lie about, save the main thing.

That a secret society had guided events
that could render Arthur their puppet king
might be beyond the grasp of the plausible, but
necessitated no veil in the sharing. That these
men's efforts could turn to the Merovingians and
be atop Howel's doorstop *ought* to be shared.

That Merlin had experienced a conversion of faith and sought the Christian God likewise needed no cover, though the nature of his doctrine peculiar. Arthur's neutrality over the gods and radical defense of personal choice would surely extend unto his once druidic counselor.

That Roman soldiers had given chase and that Maelgwn had suffered injury need not be some secret.

But…

That Vivien had formed a regretful alliance with the vile old priest-king, Meirchion the Mad, that had contributed to Merlin's demise could never be shared.

Not for so long as the old crone drew breath.

Its discovery would result in execution for the Lady of the Lake, and provoke the tribes to revolt in favor of their patroness and goddess. Moreover, Meirchion's part in the plot could spark a civil war against the North with potential help from abroad.

The perception of a poisoned beginning for the fresh-born Summer Kingdom could not be, must not be. Instead, it must grow and flourish; the age of peace and freedom. A rest from the era of death, so needed by Cymru. Respite from a greater menace, an enemy she knew not was coming.

For his part, Meirchion must never be able to confirm whether Merlin be alive or perished, lest he take occasion to double-cross Vivien. Vivien must in turn never overly oppose the Roman Church, lest the dispossessed and desperate king give Emperor Arthur just enough information to reopen the wound and destroy all. Thus, the deceit a taut line must hold. And Maelgwn must ever provide hints and whispers of hope that Merlin yet lived.

And so, full truth save the Lady's involvement, along with Merlin's final fate (which Maelgwn assumed was the grave, and durst not ask his foster-mother detailed questions of for the sake of her fractured and broken heart), was his course.

The only course?

Or I could take his head and lop off the need for a lie, the Bloodhound Prince thought. *I am meet to be Pendragon as well.*

In the maze of complexity that ran its woven courses through Maelgwn's brain, burrowed into the heart, and stained his soul, murder was situationally acceptable, but for untrue words to leave the knight's lips – unacceptable.

Had not Arthur's fathers persecuted the Old North? Had not they made full advantage of the *Night of Long Knives,* later causing the Sons of Cunnedda to make more sons, yet from their own daughters of the Silures in the south?

Maelgwn was master of lust unmatched and bereft of love, excepting his foster-mother.

And he loved Arthur.

And he loved Gwenhywfar.

And was not the one love now betrothed by imposition to the other?

The winds picked up in the courtyard, the Londinium air filled with a confused aroma, combing the stench of commerce with the sweet savors of cakes and flowers. A gust lifted Maelgwn's curly black locks up and off his brow, fully revealing eyes as a skulking predator upon the king.

The aroma without, a mirror of the confused shards of mind and spirit within.

Maelgwn's thoughts were both stench and beauty.

He could not pause long as Arthur, full of

perception on loan from the Merlin himself, would soon note the rehearsal of speech. For this cause, and for love, Maelgwn followed a pattern wrought of thirty and five years of chaos and pain. He put away all and, speaking in his mechanical tenor that was a numbness confused for strength or intimidation, communicated that which had been agreed by he and the Lady of the Lake.

"Unbelievable tales are often those most true." King Arthur comforted his champion after carefully hearing all, having listened actively without interruption.

Then the statements and queries followed.

"If Merlin weighed the threat heavy enough to miss Baeden, then we must give it equal measure." Arthur rubbed his forehead hard for a moment and continued, "We have had peace for but one moon. Are we to make war with Rome?"

The Roman Empire was an empire no more. No longer a shadow of the shadow of her former glory, the Cymry would put her to waste quickly.

Arthur continued to work out his thoughts while Maelgwn stole a glance at Gwenhwyfar, now waving at throngs of people from a tapered balcony. Such was his height that there was no risk the shorter sovereign would see his wandering eyes.

"Our nation has never invaded another. We defend our soil; we do not take to the dirt of others. Moreover, this seems to be a powerful cabal within the State, and not the State herself. We cannot kill Italians to avenge the loss of our friend." Here the careful prudence and longsuffering of Arthur won out.

But his tenacity lessened not.

"When next we convene at Caermelyn,

embracing peacetime quests and sports, I shall declare this: that the twenty-four divide into troops of threes, and that they perpetually quest for Merlin. Those not on assigned rotation may quest whatever questing they will, at the pleasure of the knight and the Fellowship."

This verdict at once multiplied the risk of investigative knights, sharpened by recent war and fearing the impending dulling of tending to farm and wife, finding out the plot between Vivien and Mad Mark to murder the Wizard.

Maelgwn gave a counterproposal.

"Send only two, and when I am not attending to my lands, I swear to always be the third. Only that they report to me for continuity of purpose."

For Maelgwn, this ensured that the quest would never be fulfilled; a quest for a concealed corpse, led by the son of the very woman who had concealed it. With complete trust, Arthur's tone was thankful, and edifying.

"Your plan is even better than mine, friend. Thank you." At that moment they both looked upon Gwenhwyfar's balcony, gesturing that they should return to the celebratory crowds.

Arthur made a final, friendly clutch upon Maelgwn's arm, asking a conclusive question.

"Have you told me everything, Maelgwn?"

Maelgwn looked upon Gwen II yet again. A seed of offense here planted as Arthur asked only after his lost friend and made no mention of the *other business between the two great friends.* The prerogative belonged to the High King, but that not a sentence was uttered showing a kernel of wheat's measure over Maelgwn's feelings hurt the Round Table Knight. Oh, the simple recognition he coveted and received not!

"Yes, Lord Arthur." A forced, anguished

response; his first, but not last, lie to the King.

Just then a voice, a desperate phantom, was upon the northern prince's shoulders, howling its cry directly into his right ear (yet was heard by no other man).

"Lancelot. When it comes time to do that which you would do, for the sake of all free men, I beg you, do it not."

Arthur had outpaced the towering warrior, making his way back to the throngs.

Recovering from his lie and eschewing the voice upon his shoulder: "Iron Bear–"

Arthur stopped and turned, familiar with the gravity of tone. "Yes, friend."

"Before Merlin and I were separated by fog and by ambush, he beseeched me to give you a directive. There was no riddle in it, no enigmatic lesson. Just a directive. A desperate directive." Maelgwn's palms faced the firmament, shoulders giving a confused but sincere shrug, passing along the order. "Kill the Giants," he said. "Kill every one."

CHAPTER 2
The Merovingian

"Locate, awaken and unleash the Giants on the Isles in the Sea," Simon Magus bade the Wise Man of the Dynion Hysbys, a sort of dark anti-druid whose actual name was not known. Whispers and rumors amongst the Tribes, and especially the noble, harmless and friendly druids, rendered him simply *the Adder*. "See it done."

"After such a long time dormant, hiding or, where not extreme in appearance, innocuously blended amongst men, will the Nephilim really bring the Sons of Brutus to anger again?" the Wise Man asked, challenging the head of the octopus, whose Roman arms controlled all secret societies upon the earth.

Simon always preferred education over empty dictates. His lessons were honest and sincere, to a point. Where misdirection and fabrication was needed to manipulate and control, even his own truth would be slightly blended and blurred. This was how the Mystery Schools were able to reign over the very many with the very few. Thus, calmly, he condescended: "If we are to create an apocalypse to either delay" – he now looked upon a faction of his fellows – "or bring about" – they nodded – "the Apocalypse, we will need to bring about hell on earth." His tone now scratchy and blistering with coughing, he continued, "Fire and brimstone from above, signs and wonders from the heavens, mayhem and mayhem upon the earth. Let her be again a den of dragons and abominations walking about in the open light of the day, as it was in the Days of Noah."

The Wise Man bowed, and vowed, "I will obey, find and resurrect that old hatred amongst the Giants in the Blessed Isles, my lord."

"And Arddu bless thy effort." Simon took the man by the hand, shaking it in sincerity. His voice now eased to a whisper in Italian. "It will take you some time to find many of them, and more time to cause them to do their Great Work. Know that you are setting out on a long quest; be patient, and mind well the timing."

"What is my mark, lord?"

The answer, blunt and no less educational than the former discourse, gave the Adder great pause.

"Twenty years."

The Wise Man fell open at the mouth as he suddenly saw the final two decades of his dark path filled hourly, risking his life rousing monsters below the earth in hollow hills, marshy rushes and foul caves.

Simon Magus proactively stayed response. "Ensure that there are minor slayings as soon as you are able. Create whispers of *the Round Table Knights*" (here his tone mocked the honorable and just men) "themselves being defeated or even disappearing, along with petty kings and well-known Churchmen, meeting untimely ends in caves and crooks in the North. Create a little fear so that they appreciate all the more the safety of their great Pendragon. But it must be but minor complaints; it must be a whisper, not an urgent crisis." The education continued. "For twenty years the Briton's famed War King must reign, and peace and safety reign with him. After that we will find for him another great war and declare, if he be the One, Britannia as the New Jerusalem.

"For three years, merriment and more peace unfettered.

"Then we will draw down a great dragon and make calamity, fire and disease from heaven that will cause men's eyes to melt within the socket. A slow death, a death that is certain but delays, that will not come. Hell on the earth where the worm dieth not, and the fire shall not be quenched. And war. So much more war. At the median of the third year, all the kings round him must fall." Simon Magus paused, then delivered some humor to lighten the burden. "Be thankful, Cymry, that you are on Giant and not Dragon detail; we have the more miserable task."

Simon Magus breathed in the winter air of Broceliande, deeply inhaling the forest's enchantments, secrets and good wonder into his chest. The little Fae found it blasphemy that one such as he would take their air, spoiling this special place by his very presence. Oblivious to the protest of his hidden watchers, he continued. "And now we seek out our alternative actor. Now we leave the forest to look in upon Childebert." Making motions for the tabernacle in the wood to be broken down and packed, he concluded, "From the Sons of Troy to the city of Troy's most tragic son." Simon Magus loved irony. "To Paris."

The Italian called after the Wise Man. "Wait. I cannot believe, Arddu help me, that I forgot."

Dreading the additional edict from the Bishop

of Rome, the Dynion Hysbys sighed, audibly. "Yes, Simon Magus?"

"The contents of Merlin's robe. Go back to the site where the traitor met his just end and retrieve them."

"Surely the Lancelot or some other friend has already discovered and buried the body. Three days have now passed!"

"Then find a merchant and purchase thyself a shovel!" Simon Magus was not accustomed to disobedience. *These Cymry, even the traitors, have too much freedom coursing through their blood. Would that the Caesars had removed their candle forever from the earth, like so many other petty tribes.*

Through his uncanny switches, corners and turns in his mannerisms, Magus traded hubris for manipulative dramatist. "My friend, I am sorry." The armored finger-claws now grasped the cloak of the Briton, pulling him to an embrace. "If the body has been removed or the contents sealed, then you will be the first to embark on a great quest – not just for Giants or treasure," and now the fullness of satanic revelation illuminated the Leader of the Council of Nine, "but the first to set out to recover the Cup of Christ. The quest for the Holy Grail." The Bishop of Rome gave the Wise Man an unholy kiss upon his neck, then returned his face to shadow, adjusting his mask.

"And now I say" – the thick accent was most profound when jesting – "and this time I mean it" – followed by a great singular chortle – "to Paris!"

* * *

Childebert, the Merovingian King of Paris, was an ideal candidate for the Antichrist.

A heresy, that the Lord Himself had continued His generations through a marriage with Mary the Magdalene, had taken root among many sects. The Bishop of Rome had denounced it publicly and supported it financially and evangelically from the shadows.

Here again, the laity of the Catholic church were biblical in their understanding. The Scriptures were clear that Israel's long prophesied Messiah would have no continuing generation (for the prophet Isaiah had said as much in plain words), and they were victims, dupes of poor leadership. That their tithes unknowingly were apportioned to fund devilish schemes was a great sin against these hard-working, gentle and romantic people.

Nevertheless, like other heresies manifesting in the dawn of the burgeoning Church, this one had its actors: the long-haired Merovingians.

Esteeming themselves direct descendants of Jesus Christ, and lingering in ambience until the *times of restitution of all things*, they were simply waiting for the right time to wage holy war, with or without the aid of Rome, in the region, and then the world.

Crowned King of Paris five hundred and eleven years from the year of the Lord's passion, Childebert possessed unmatched charisma and reigned well. He now sought to conjure cause to take Orleans next. The kinsmen of the Cymry, the *Bretons*, had long established their kingdoms and sister-cities on the Continent, and a collision was far off... yet inevitable. Lancelot had warned Arthur of the Italian Band's potential collusion with the House of Merovee in some plot, and Arthur remained vigilant of the same. But without evidence, he would let the matter lie dormant.

Magus had placed a subversive within

the House of Merovee and seen to it that the king's own sister diverged from the family way, converting her to the orthodox Romanist faith. Chrotilda was radically devout to the Church of Rome, and she became the eyes and ears of Magus. She guided and supported and necessarily hassled Childebert in the like manner that Gwyar did for Arthur.

In addition to continued assessment of the liege who wore his hair in uncut locks as Sampson or John the Baptist, Simon sought ways in which the Merovingian's desire for expansion over the Franks could be leveraged to make alliances with a foe that could actually defeat the tribes of the Cymry. *And that was not Rome.*

Magus believed that a confederacy of Teutonic tribes, known as the *Visigoths*, could be his unwilling agent to do as the Saxons, Angles and Jutes had done for the Council of Nine for the generations before Arthur had spoiled them. Once again, Magus would raise up an invader, slowly, methodically.

That a Germanic people would covet and attack the Isles in the Sea was an old, tired story. But this time the differences were substantial.

Merlin was gone. Though filled with heroes and living legends, he was the strategic difference in war strategy and policy making.

The armies would grow fat and stale from peace. This was man's nature.

The Council determined it would take twenty years to weaken the Round Table from within. Or to let the process of time, and the flesh of man, do this for and with them.

The Saxon kings had not the pedigree to rival the Pendragon or the kings of the Old North. Childebert, if viewed as a Messiah, and with an army equal to the

Cymry under his standard, could undo and supplant King Arthur.

If Childebert the Christ-child possessed the Cup of Christ, would not even Rome accept him?

Indeed! Magus was convinced that this generation would yield a different outcome. Either Childebert would be the Antichrist and fall to the Messiah Arthur, or Arthur would be Antichrist and fall to Childebert. *And thus the Mystery of Iniquity continued its dark work.*

The Visigoths were called *The Wild Boar*, and their theology was Arianism. The Christology of this religion demoted Jesus to possessing the blood of God, but being a separate and subordinate being to God the Father. Moreover, it held that Christ did not exist prior to His incarnation, bastardizing the Scripture that reads *"for there be gods many"*. This doctrine fit as a glove with the notion of the Nazarene's children being enlightened beings, even demigods, not equal in rank, but sharing direct substance with God, ruling and reigning over the whole of mankind on the merits of their divine blood.

Simon would make his visit under the guise of an emissary expelled from Rome for rejecting the Trinity, finding safety in North Africa where the Visigoths ruled. He would further his shadowy work of seducing the king. *And hope that his anti-druid would soon secure the Cup.*

CHAPTER 3
Four Cords and a Princess Broken

Seed 1: "I saw her first."

The whole of the kingdom, from beggar to king, from youth to aged, from city-center merchant to remote northern village fisherman, all men, and especially all women (for women possess natural intuition about these things) in all places, knew that Gwen ferch Ogyrfan Gawr was a whore. A harlot of the highest estate.

Everyone… except for her betrothed, the discerning, wise and just king, Arthur Pendragon of Glamorgan. The blindness wrought by blood is cruel, and no respecter of persons.

He floated on clouds of happiness when around her, and a man with thirty-and-four winters was again as the year he had met her, again as a fourteen-year-old boy. Full of verve, unstoppable, ever jesting with, embracing, and actively seeking to serve and help his people with immeasurable resources powered by love.

A War King who had outsmarted, outlasted and out-willed the Saxon invaders for two decades was at once made captive to her will. In spite of this, he was not rumored or mocked as a fool. For the people perceived rightly that Arthur and his former queen might have been great friends, might have known love, but never *in love* was Arthur. Never like his parents, Queen Onbrawst and King Meurig.

Thus, a thankful people durst not snicker and prattle about so great a ruler. Rather, a quiet respect short of an endorsement was the national mood since the pronouncement of their engagement. He had given them their liberty. He had forged for them their Golden Age. He was the Sun that had risen and illuminated their Summer Kingdom.

We are so grateful. Let him alone. Let him have his whore. This was the public sentiment.

As a lad, Arthur had actually known his new queen-intended before he had known his first spouse, the honorable and stunning, redheaded Queen Gwenhwyfar ferch Cwyrd, his neighbor in Gwent.

O, but 'twas the Gwen of the raven's hair that forged him.

* * *

Their paths had met in the grey time betwixt and between boyhood and manhood, lass and woman. And not theirs alone.

Arthur and Gwen ferch Ogyrfan, along with Maelgwn Hir of Gwynedd and Gwyar ferch Meurig, were inseparable schoolmates. Three months of joy uninterrupted can be as a hundred years to the young.

For these are the sticky years.

Two boys, two girls, a foursome fierce.

The most popular, revered and feared troop, dominating and conquering all that they surveyed at the chapel college named after Illtud. Brilliant and fiery. Cymry royals at play, defending the southern beaches against imagined Saxons, frolicking in forests green and valleys grim, filling their time with song and food and daily enacting theatre; portraying the far-off dream of the Summer Kingdom.

Then the four cords were untwined, torn asunder most unwillingly.

Gwyar, older than the others, was first to leave.

Vivien had privily observed the lass's gaze upon her foster-son, seen her innocent adorations mixed with the flowering of unbridled love. Unbridled lust.

Knowing, even then, the shattered multiplicity within Maelgwn (for, after becoming well-drunken on cider he consumed during a revelry on Ynys Enlli, he had slain his very own uncle and lain with the dead man's wife), Vivien aborted the schoolyard love, painfully quieted in one direction (for as Gwyar looked upon Maelgwn, so did Maelgwn look upon another), promised the young priestess to a northern prince, and promptly returned her to her druidic training at Ynys Mon.

The political marriage worked as designed, resulting in the birth of Gwalchmai, the Hawk of May, whose birth was a blessing to both the North and the South. The cost of leaving school was Gwyar's heart. And more.

A week after she left, Maelgwn too was called away. He went to a campaign on the Continent, where his legend as a warrior burgeoned. Around this time, Maelgwn entered into fosterage under

Vivien. And thus, from time to time after this, Gwyar, at function, holy day or feast, would now layer unlawful lust atop indifferent rejection, being married and yet in love with her foster-brother.

Then King Meurig suffered a grievous wound, driving him into early abdication, and his heir, the would-be sandy-haired boy-king, was pried from school, and from Gwen ferch Ogyrfan, to participate in the king-making rites of Spring and wield Excalibur as Pendragon.

The band of four broken.

This left only the little princess; *small as a faerie, but daughter of a Giant.*

Back then, Gwen was known by her three ever-companions as charitable, kind, full of dash and spirit, of good report – her only vice being that she toyed overly with the boys. A lustful look seemed ever carved into her visage. She was a poor student and sought nothing of the knowledge of books and scrolls, but was thrice smarter than the three when it came to life's classroom – the real world. She cared not for Gwyar's goddesses, and even less for Arthur's bishops and Hebrew God. Her father had taught her that there were no gods and that man was a cosmic mistake, a thing of nature, a thing of flesh alone.

And fleshly she was.

Gwen II fancied fashion and commerce over religion, and held no particular spirituality. And no youthful love captured this future queen.

As Gwyar looked upon Maelgwn did Maelgwn to Gwen.

As Arthur looked upon Gwen did Gwen look upon no one.

Thus, two loved Gwen and one loved Maelgwn, while none loved the seed of the

Pendragon beyond the love of a brother, sister or great friend.

That the boys fancied her, she was aware. That Arthur would anger and cry "I saw her first" she heard of many times. But such troubles are supposed to fade as the season and dissolve as adulthood ensues. Not so here. The depth and intoxicating nature of the matter, none knew. For this claimant to love based upon the primacy of *seeing* by the boy-king placed a seed of discord in Maelgwn; a seed that would, when watered with other violations, grow and blossom, to the ruin of many.

Nay, none saw these things, for the lives of children are as a sealed vault, withheld from parents and all elders. None saw.

Save perhaps the Fae.

Small as the Fae…

Daughter of a Giant.

And one dark day, visited by the Fae.

An overgrown oak tree, whose roots were already old before the Flood, encroached on the northwest side of the chapel. This was a stone structure in the stead of timber, due to its proximity to the wetter climate of the shore (in a country already doubly wet) breaching through windows, creating the need for a side door to access, trim and maintain its active and intrusive arms, some of which scraped the tessellated paving of the floor, near the altar.

One evening, wearied and alone, her bishops and schoolmasters at supper, she exited the chapel through the 'tree door', hoping the burgeoning sunset mist would cease her weary melancholy.

The mist came, and she began to dance.

It was here that Gwen met him. Where he sought the child.

And so, not ten paces from the right hand of God (as was known the place of the bishop next to the altar in the church), did Gwen, the daughter of the Giant, meet the son of the Devil.

For she had been dancing round the Oak.

Once.

Twice.

Stopping short of the third circle with a terminating thud at his thighs, the top of her head jolted backwards, not reaching even unto his navel. Suddenly the silence was uncanny.

And there he towered.

Crowned with a circlet of ivory. Blood-red skin and eyes to match, save the sockets, which were black as pitch. Brutish and lean, and clearly a great lord or sovereign. A thousand thousand pairs of eyes suddenly accompanied them, behind, above, below and beside.

These were the Tylwyth Teg, an ancient and dangerous progeny of the damned. Often feigning allegiance to the most of corrupt men on the Blessed Isles, the Dynious Hysbys, their true loyalty was to ancient gods, or alternatively to Arddu (who is the Devil), or elsewise to none but themselves.

An unknown force of conduct compelled them inexplicably, and rarely, also to do good. Ever changing and spiraling in mysterious motives, they maneuvered and manipulated the Isles that had once been theirs.

"We like the way you dance."

Gwen recovered from the collision but could conjure no response outside of, "My thanks to you, lord."

"Will you dance with us?" the king of the Tylwyth Teg inquired.

"Dance with you?" The Fair Folk raised a

buzzing cheer of encouragement. "Yes, I will," said the princess.

The company of Fair Folk turned the Giant's daughter to exhaustion until at last she swooned, falling as doth a baby bird from its nest. Light as air, right into the mouth of a hungry barn cat waiting agape.

Holding her snug, the king of the Tylwyth Teg's true motive was unwrapped, along with his trouser. Dividing her soul asunder with his dark arts, he knew at once that her mother had died, bringing her forth as a babe into the world of men. This occurred more than not when the sire was a Giant. Having none but a father, she ever sought to please and manipulate men in order to feel the security denied her by her mam.

And beauty.

Such, such beauty.

"I bless you to have dominion with all men, using but these." His black nails, gentle on the lids of her eyes, which at once were changed from dark but common brown to large, bronze and golden-speckled spheroids, great lights of lust for any man. Next his hand found her youthful garden. "And this." Upon touching the flower of her young womanhood, markings of colored ink began to dry themselves on her skin; from mound to crown, a canvas of flesh, filled with lustful patterns.

He also rendered Gwenhwyfar barren.

Next, the Fae King decided to taste for himself the instrument of carnality and lust he had rendered.

After having her, the Lord of the Fair Folk was filled with dismay and anger that his creation had already known a man, and was no virgin.

CHAPTER 4
The Queen, the Witch and the Stable Boy

From that very day, Gwen II began to use and discard men. Sometimes strategically, oft just for its own sake; never carelessly.

Arthur only saw her in person at times random and passing during the Saxon Wars. Married away at fifteen, leading three endless campaigns in the north (and when not on campaign, engaged in battles on the Continent), one year became twenty. The Pendragon noted her markings, but felt that her melting eyes were just as they always had been. He loved their friendship, his very soul driven always and always to honor and protect her. But a romantic love he contained as the Deep under the Great Stone, withholding it for the sake of honor, and for his wife, Gwen I.

All encounters were innocent, but not within his heart, where he betrayed not Gwen I by loving Gwen II, but rather betrayed Gwen II by marrying Gwen I in the first place.

But Gwen II cared for none of these things.

With Llacheu buried and Amr reckoned dead by all, and with Queen Gwenhwyfar self-exiled to her own place, a too-soon rumbling for Arthur to get heirs rattled and drummed low beneath the celebrating shouts and merriment of the people. Arthur wanted Gwen II, and the people wanted Silure babies of the houses of Glamorgan and Gwent.

Meurig liked none of it.

But he relented, and met his obligation as king (and more, as father).

At the behest of King Meurig, Gwen II and her father, the chieftain Ogyrfan of Croesoswallt, were summonsed to Caer Bovum to be queried on the matter of an arranged marriage. Meurig's great manor was but a short walk from Illtud's school – *and the oak tree where she had congressed with the Faerie King.*

After that, Meurig departed to join with Arthur and his Round Table Companions for the second crowning (for Arthur had vanquished fully the Saxon hordes and was made *Emperor* over Cymru, Alba, Lloegyr, Little Britain and sundry smaller vassal kingdoms. The republican monarch wanted none of this, and passionately advocated, with immovable conviction, local rule. But he enjoyed the celebration and joy of the Clans, Tribes and Nations nonetheless. They could have their great emperor, who would build no empire but rather straightway return home to Caerleon or to Caermelyn, never to encroach or infringe on other kingdoms and to raise an army only at their request when in dire need of defense) in Londoninium, and Gwenhwyfar was asked to wait.

To wait for the Lancelot.

For Maelgwn.

The journey from Croesoswallt to Londoninium required travel south through the Cymry kingdom of Powys, with a planned stop for repose at Amwythig, then west through the Midlands, with a turn southeast to the great port city of Lludgate, where Saint Paul had preached to the heathen above four hundred and fifty years earlier, a gilded place of worship erected to celebrate the same.

The Battle of Mynydd Baeden had been less than a moon ago, and the policies of expulsion and resettling not yet implemented. The threat of scattered survivors or opportunists remained in the shadow of a rejoicing nation. Robbers and villains of Cymry blood might turn opportunist in the distraction of celebration as well.

For this cause, the Champion of the Round Table Fellowship was bidden to personally see the princess safely to her husband-to-be. It was the logical choice. Maelgwn could see from all directions; he could sense and flush out attackers in the fog, or at night. He was a manslayer unmatched and never required much sleep. The report alone of his being with her would greatly discourage would-be malefactors.

Arthur placed reason and fevered focus on Gwen's safety above even an eye's twinkling moment of consideration over Lancelot's feelings. Arthur had seen her first at school; he declared this and, contrary to every other decision and manner of life, that was that. She was Arthur's noonday sun, and the light of it blinded him to Maelgwn Gwynedd, hurting in the shadows.

Gwenhwyfar's servants traveled separately. She and Maelgwn shared a steed. The sum of the trip was two nights and three days.

"Have you a wife?"

Gwenhwyfar was very forward. Her head was pressed into the rippling sea of muscles that was Maelgwn's back as she held tight, and rested upon, the warrior as he managed the bridle and harness.

Blissfully comfortable, her only complaint was that she could not see his face blush.

"I've had many wives, but when betwixt their legs I am at rehearsal but for one."

If Gwenhwyfar's soul were not black as her hair, she here would have blushed as well. Instead, her lips, thick and lush, pressed into a comfortable, flattered grin. She let her hair fall without pin or plait, ensuring that aromatic strands would badger her travel companion, and slept until they arrived at the chapel and small lodgings provided by a young saint called Tydecho, who was Arthur's nephew.

The circular timber home had a hearth that formed the center (and singular) beam of the dwelling. There were two beds on opposing sides, and a tiny common area. The fire blazed, and the desire within Maelgwn was fanned as well.

A great battle raged within him, as it had when he was sixteen. A battle he had lost when he put the sword to his uncle and ravaged his wife, who had begged for the ravaging. This was before Vivien had taught Maelgwn the form of martial art she had inherited from Boudicca, then adapted and perfected for the Bretons and Britons. Thus, the kill had been sloppy; a crime of passion by a boy who was a bundle of nerve-endings with no brain. He had lost the battle; the battle of appetite, of self above others, of entitlement and hubris, of lust unrivaled. He had lost it with his uncle, *and one other time*, and then, as she had done with unwanted Morgaine, the Lady of the Lake had saved him.

Ironically, Vivien had directed Maelgwn towards the will-worship and temperance of the

Christian faith in an effort to help him control what she and he called *"the bubble."* She did not abuse or elevate guilt as a force when weaving in Christian mechanisms of morality with the young man. Instead, she taught Maelgwn to focus on the great focus of the spirit at the expense of the flesh, the distraction of prayer and outwardly directed vitality. Where her worldview encouraged enjoyment of the flesh to access the spirit, where it viewed carnal relations as enjoyable and, under love, without restriction or regulation, she discerned correctly that Christian temperance and not pagan excess might save Maelgwn from his torment – from the lust that 'bubbled' and, when burst, would at once release him, only to bubble at some unknown and random time again and again.

Here in Tydecho's quaint hut, where Gwenhwyfar ferch Ogyrfan Gawr, full of seductive pout and overtly contrived reluctance, took *the other bed* but disrobed slowly, letting the fire light all the comely and privy parts that should have been committed only to the future of Arthur's eyes, sleeping spread and without skin or blanket, the bubble appeared.

Now, Gwen did not try and seduce Maelgwn. For her part, she had simply been transported back to the times at Illtud's, where an extreme comfort had existed amongst the band of four. The ride had been difficult, and her clammed disposition against Maelgwn's torso had rendered her a sweaty woman without a bath. Nakedness was natural for Gwenhwyfar, modesty robbed so long ago by the encroaches of the Tylwyth Teg and his otherworldly companions, who had watched.

But all she did was seductive. Usually knowingly, sometimes not.

Maelgwn, privily, was praying the words the Apostle Paul had given to the preacher-boy Timotheus. "Flee, youthful lusts." And again. "Flee, youthful lusts."

It was not until he left the roundhouse the third time in an effort to outrun the bubble that Gwenhwyfar realized her nudity was maddening the stoic warrior.

She covered herself.

That which conceals is more appealing than that which reveals, so the problem was made rather worse.

Maelgwn was evaluating all who he would have to murder, should he take her here and now. In all the wandering of a temporarily corrupted mind, simply killing her was not an option.

Nor, he rightly reckoned, was gossip or chatter.

He had no gift for conversation. He was a lover, and a killer, not a bard. *Let Taliesin to the poetry, and let me to the ladies who moisten at his words.*

Gwenhwyfar was to be betrothed and then marry the Pendragon, the king of kings and lord of lords. From this position, provided she was calculated and eschewed carelessness, she could do *anything* she wanted. For the rest of her life. She could not endanger that here over a sticky fumbling with the lust-mad Lancelot.

He left. He walked. He returned.

He had two ciders.

He lay down.

He read Scripture.

As the bubble expanded in the rear lobe of his head, the pressure became excruciating. This, and no Saxon or Pict, was his only equal. Only Lancelot could defeat Lancelot.

And Lancelot was winning.

He rose, also naked.

Lancelot was nearly ten spans tall, with a member as that of a great tannish stallion. His hair was curly, short, and black as Gwen's. Though he had a neck, it was abridged by muscles that sat atop muscles, connecting shoulder to neck, neck to head. Where most men had one small ridge of muscles here, Lancelot had two. His forearms were immense, but the rest of his build lean.

He was naked.

And coming for her.

Memories of youth rushed upon Gwen as she looked at the Bloodhound Prince. She forgot her future and leapt from the small bed to meet him.

Two of history's most famous Britons, alone and naked after midnight in a tiny roundhouse in Powys.

Just two paces from taking her tiny hand in his great paw, the two were suddenly three.

Yet only he saw the Wizard.

Face to face was Maelgwn with the Merlin.

"You died." Maelgwn's erection shriveled, crinkling to match his brow as he questioned the phantom intruder.

"When it comes time to do that which you would do, do it not."

Beyond the understanding of this world, the Merlin had slammed the hilt of a dagger into Lancelot's hand, but spoke no further.

"I love Arthur. And I love Cymru," he said.

"Is there anyone, anything, else you love, Lancelot?" At this point, Gwen's arousal was as nearly dangerous as his own.

"You," he responded directly. "I shall ever revere you as my one true love, and whilst I live, I shall love no other. I shall love you as the queen.

I shall love you as the wife of the friend whom I love." As he finished this speech, he ran from the hut and plunged the dagger deep into the fleshy part of his thigh.

Merlin's dagger had burst the bubble, sending it back to its dark abode.

The journey continued. Maelgwn with bandaged, self-inflicted wound, Gwen burning between her legs, both legends rubbing each other, passionately repelling desire as they rode, speaking very little, focused solely on combating the lust that was consuming them.

But know each other, they did not.

Maelgwn delivered the Princess Gwen II unto Londoninium, and after the crowning, he made leave for repose in Camlan.

His bubble returned ferociously, and no ghost appeared to deter him. He privately forced his son, Rhun Hir, to bring him the wife of a man called Elphin, whose comely spouse roughly resembled Gwenhwyfar. Taliesin, the new Merlin, knew of the deed, and would discern the time to condemn Maelgwn.

Gwenhwyfar's burning continued as well.

On the very first night upon arriving to her new estates in Caerleon, she strolled through the stables, privily (for King Arthur had put her in her own apartment and, respectfully, sought not to bed her so soon in the courtship). Perchance, she found an attractive stable worker who was ensuring that the stables were warm and the horses, who were one half of the union of the equestrian contrivance that had been the decisive factor in defeating foot soldier invaders and winning the Saxon Wars, were spoiled, doted upon and of happy disposition. Indeed, many Cymry women jested, with no small measure of annoyance, that the horses were doted upon more than the wives.

Gwen II had no use for his name, and didn't bother with the asking.

She turned him around where he stood and whispered, with enlarged eyes, "Do you know who I am?"

Less than twenty winters had not given the young man the confidence to engage a painted goddess. *A painted devil.*

He stammered, but he managed a choppy, "Yes, my lady."

"I command you to *serve* your future queen."

She had his trousers untied and his cock in hand before he could muster the word "Arthur" in protest.

The events of the past few weeks were gestating in Princess Gywar, as she surveyed the stables on a walk, taking the longer route to Lodge Hill, where she would make a small fire and commune with her goddess (and cider) under a clear winter night. The Usk River would be her choir and the diverse birds her chorus.

A walk at night in the south east of Cymru opens the door to the mind. The angels, adored in their stars, sing jealous praises towards the land, the view of them better in Cymru than in any other place on earth.

The clear Cymru night, the heavenly hosts dancing, the calm. It also had the effect of bringing down the guarding gates of one's mind, letting too many unfiltered contemplations bounce to and fro, loose and untamed.

How will I keep Gwalchmai safe? Why does my brother ever put him in harm's way in one moment, and imply him heir in the next? How do I keep my vow to the put-away queen? When will I return to Ynys

Enlli? Have Cadfan and his pilgrims found any of the Treasures? Have they found Her? How will I manage to serve my brother with that other Gwenhwyfar here? I don't want to see her. When will I see her?

Just then, she saw her.

Or, rather, heard her.

Gwenhwyfar was finishing her adulterous session with the stable boy, and Gwyar, sister to the Pendragon, both heard and then witnessed her; but she herself was, by Gwenhwyfar, unseen.

Gwyar repositioned herself three stalls over and let the boy, probably now empty of pride and full of shame (and now officially a traitor to the Silure Royal Clan), finish, dress and scurry away, as a small dog does when it thinks none saw it take the table scraps.

Then she made her move to intercept Gwen's path.

"How long has it been, my mate from school, my friend!" Gwyar feigned friendship, long having known what Gwen was, trying to determine how to best protect her lovesick brother, falling short of any immediate answers.

If she told Arthur this very night, who would he believe? How would it affect his rule? Would Gwyar be bound to him forever if he fell into heartbreak, and the Tribe's god-king diminished and sad? Gwenhwyfar was hell to Gwyar, a canker with no cure.

Gwenhwyfar felt no compulsion to return fettered words, and openly adjusted her undergarments. "Far from your Isle of Apples and Merlin's trinkets, are you not, Lady?"

"I am, tonight, just where and when I was supposed to be," countered Gwyar. Remembering the worldly smarts of her opponent, she opted for brevity. "I hope you found what you needed in our stables tonight, and that you look forward to being a chaste, loyal and good queen to my brother." At this, Gwyar hastened away from Gwen II.

"Witch," Gwen hissed after her, unheard.

Gwyar, once achieving her destination, screamed a terrific scream; a frustrated scream, such that lightning flashed and crackled from Lodge Hill.

Gwenhwyfar angrily slammed the door of her chamber, causing her to send away inquisitive servants and even spend above half of an hour convincing vigilant Cai that there was no matter.

Her anger was self-directed. She had been clumsy in using the boy. The king's very own sister might have stumbled upon them. If her, then anyone. If her, then the king himself!

She had been half disciplined with Lancelot (and this was simply her release, a fantasizing of that incident) and would not soon repeat the same.

Never again will I be careless.

The next morning she traded her body (and enjoyed the act, as it was well-organized with no fear, this time, of discovery) for an assassin to contrive a hanging. A false suicide by the stable boy.

Two days later, she poisoned the assassin, clipping frayed ends that the garment of her rule would not run and unravel. With a clean slate in the perversity of her mind, she set about to rule and reign as the replacement queen to Arthur Pendragon.

CHAPTER 5
The Field of Malevolence

It is a curious thing how one year can be as a hundred, bursting with adventure, intrigue, peril, and change, but how other years pass as leaves upon a stream, peaceful and of no repute or distinction. Taliesin spake an adage that was true. *Not all years are special.*

And so it was that time gave green and gilded Cymru three such years.

Arthur Pendragon would court and marry Gwenhwyfar ferch Ogyrfan. And although he woefully missed his Wizard, never ceasing the search, the King's heart was finally happy.

The Round Table Knights quested.

Arthur was true to his word. There would be no overreaching, tyrannical central government. Freedom prospered. Local chieftains governed justly, and when they did not, the appeal and escalation to Caermelyn was careful and deliberate.

The Lady of Lake continued quietly in exile, remaining in Broceliande over on the Continent in the safety and solitude of her magical forest. Its founts and streams and ancient oaks and elemental water spirits her ever companions in the self-imposed imprisonment.

The bishops and the priests enjoyed relatively few conflicts in executing their policy of baptism and church membership for the remnants of the Angles, Saxons and Jutes (and the several divergent sub-groups of each, as there were over twenty and seven tribes still extant in the east of Lloegyr and the Midlands). No Germanic parent claimed fidelity to Odin or Thor, knowing they must declare for Christ. Their children were baptized by water into whatever sect of the faith the parent preferred. The bishops continued to favor the *believer's baptism,* but struggled with evangelism, as they would not sup, bathe or engage in sport or play with any Saxon. Some Saxons joined the Apostolic Britons' Church, as a result of hearing the good news preached in the streets and markets.

The Catholics, be they native born or immigrants from Rome, Greece or Eire, fared better. Not above getting their hands dirty to help the common man, they established schools amongst the Germans, rebuilt houses and stables, provided supplies and used charity to earn converts; then implemented their sacerdotal policies of infant baptism as new Saxons were born upon Britannia's soil.

At this quiet time, there was no perceived extension of the policy of compulsory Church membership and baptism inward to the cantrefs and tribes in Cymru. This made the heathen and local Christian alike very happy, and a general spiritual liberty and contentment prevailed.

Arthur's principle rival, Caw, was also peaceful during these, the early years of the Summer Kingdom. Many of his sons favored the Silure king over their own father philosophically, working under Arthur's employ where scout work was available, and even came to own small farms in the South. Other sons held their tongues or grumbled within themselves. King Urien Rheged and his powerful son, Owain, were Arthur's constant eyes but had little to report on the northern rebels save Hueil ap Caw, who continued to be a thorn.

As for Caw, his affections were drawn away from land disputes, vain genealogies and generational complaints, falling upon his youngest son. The infant Aneurin (who is also called Gildas) had given the aging Son of Cunedda pride and vigor. There was something special about the lad, and liberty and peace afforded Caw the time he had never enjoyed with his other sons and daughters; time to parent.

The political marriages seemed to be working for the Silure's other enemy (or at best, lukewarm and risky supporters) – the house of Meirchion. The radical Catholic had been evicted from his lands for his probable involvement in Merlin's vanishing. However, he was father to Cynfarch Oer, who was father to Llew, who was estranged husband to Gwyar, who was sister to King Arthur Pendragon. This made Gwyar's sons beloved by both north and south. Just as her aunt Marchell had mitigated war with the Emerald Isle, the daughters of Meurig gave their wombs to Cymru, doing much to keep the sons of Meurig off the battlefield against the other tribes. The women sacrificed personal happiness (for the local laws and customs, though diverse, all extended to women the right to marry whom they would, to divorce, to own land and trade) to prevent an undercurrent of civil war that had been brewing since so many northern sons had been lost at the Night of Long Knives.

As for Meirchion himself, there was neither corpse nor grave marker to prove or disprove that Merlin had perished. Exposing Vivien would do nothing, yet she dared not reveal his plot either. And Meirchion the Mad was old. Very old, and nigh death. His efforts turned to his son Mark, whom he would rear on the southeastern-most horn of the Isles. He would establish Mark slowly there, and in Eire, and on the Continent, creating a future triangle in which to trap and slay the Pendragon. One day, many years hence. But at this time, it was enough for Meirchion to have food and lodging and live out his purgatory, all the while knowing Illtud was enjoying his hearths, his halls, his possessions of art and scrolls, and his sheep and cattle.

In Alba, the precocious painted Picts along the borderlands in the Old North behaved, abstaining from raiding, provided that King Maelgwn Gwynedd would periodically bed their queens and grant them permission to nominate him their king. He enjoyed the distraction some, the women more, and the title amused him.

Marital alliances through the line of Arthur's aunt Marchell and her progeny kept the raiders of Eire in check. In the east of the Isles, Cedric was peaceful, cultivating the small kingdom in Lloegyr that the Britons had allotted him.

For all of the Blessed Isles in the Sea, art and trade thrived. Many sons were begotten, such that newborn children began to match in proportion to lambs and calves. All of Britannia, including creaturekind, was in season, indulging in happy peacetime procreation.

During the Summer Kingdom, the bards were able to transition from perpetual war planning to formalizing and advancing their system of spirituality. As a result, the *Barddas* reached the zenith of its development. The twenty and four forms and meters of Cymry poetry were established, and the language of Heaven was codified in written form and etchings as never before, resulting in countless stones containing parallel cyphers that included the trade languages amongst the nations, Latin, the Ogham of the Emerald Isle, alongside the Cymraeg.

Personal wealth swelled, as treasure and savings were laid up through frugality.

Bishop Cadfan did found his small chapel on Ynys Enlli, yet not without ongoing travail, shipwreck and sacrifice. Gwyar did her privy dark work, protesting, and working magick from afar to ensure the secrets of the Isle of Apples remained concealed. However, she was not ignorant of the winds of change, nor of the fact that winds and currents and fogs would not deter the devout forever. After all, the island was very small. Soon, someone was bound to discover something.

And she honored the decree of the High Queen, the *first Gwenhwyfar*. Gwyar succored the king from the shadows, gave him confidence, advice and encouragement where a door of utterance manifested. Many times, the royal siblings retreated from court to Lodge Hill, where real decisions could be made far from priest and bishop, land-lord, merchant or bard.

But Arthur's seeking of Gwyar for stately matters, family matters or any matters began to wane like the moon, becoming a sliver and then – gone. For so deeply in love with the *new Gwenhwyfar* was the great king that the importance of "older sister" was fading as the dusk. Even his nocturnal haunts ceased during these three years.

Gwyar had vowed to remain at Caerleon only until another woman came into Arthur's life to give him the support arrested by the first Gwenhwyfar's abdication. The circumstance now allowed the king's sister to soon make her leave, whether in return to her husband in the north or to her Glass Castle and apple orchards on Ynys Enlli.

What circumstance allowed, conscience forbade. She felt bound to stay. To combat the malaise of her plight, Gwyar invited her son, the northern prince Mordred ap Llew ap Cynfarch Oer, to live at court with her in Caerleon for a summer.

The loss of Amr ap Arthur ap Meurig to a murderous, filth-covered wretch deeply grieved Mordred. *A prince should have perished upon the sword of another prince or chieftain.* It was Mordred's twenty-and-first year, and he was still young enough to prefer *mother over father* when stricken with a broken heart.

His time here will be good for both of us, Gwyar surmised.

Mordred and his hosts arrived at the entrance into Caerleon on the Summer Solstice, three and a half years after victory at Mynydd Baeden. His attire differed greatly from the skins and furs donned when patrolling the coasts on Ynys Mon. Though young, there was a grit and hardness about him, perhaps a contrived persona for would-be invaders from the sea.

But here he was, covered in gold, seemingly from head to boot.

Arthur's deceased son Llacheu had also favored gold armor, whether as rivets or grout lines in his breastplate, or in cuffs and gauntlets of shimmering gold over soft copper. Llacheu's golden ensembles had been shiny, whimsical, and perceived as adorable by the maidens and light-hearted by the men. It had suited the shimmering son of the Pendragon. Mordred, it suited not, and shouted and screeched arrogance to onlookers on him.

His headdress was molded to look like the deity Mab, the Divine Child. No detail was spared. This was not a functional helmet, but rather a wearable piece of self-promoting pride-art; a hollow and tightly-fitted head of Zeus or a mask of Ares, including golden hair and cheekbones with finite precision. The message was not lost on even the most casual observer: the boy counted himself entitled to be viewed and treated as a god.

And there was more.

His crown was distastefully hefty, a major departure from the simple circlets of the kings, princes and chieftains of the Royal Clans. The forearm pieces, gold and black, were dramatically oversized, forming a winged look that extended from wrist well past his elbows. Mail was not worn by Cyrmu warriors, but the under-armor featured some metal. It was master-crafted black leather, with concentric and interlaced gold-covered steel knots and tiny spikes spanning his torso, back and shoulders.

Mordred's jeweled cape represented the Ravens of the North, but its design featured neither the Awen to honor the divine inspiration that spirited the land, a cruciform to give glory to the Christian God, nor the double chevron of his mother's people, the mighty Silures.

His mount was equally gilded; a massive stallion, black as night, heavily armored, heavily decorated.

The son of Llew was a spectacle, come to stay

with his mother, accompanied by twelve men.

"His own Round Table Fellowship," mocked an innkeeper, who resided on the port side of the bridge near a place later called Casnewydd, as he was sweeping his storefront.

"Naye, his own company of bards!" added a patron.

Mutterings aside, and in spite of the prince's excesses, the ancient codes of the Cymry demanded compulsory hospitality. Thus there were cheers and gifts, wine and water, as well as flattering salutations, as the golden knight crossed the bridge over the Usk River. A small parade developed and pressed upon him as he navigated the narrow streets, until at last he rode past the public bathhouses and finally came to the great amphitheater, the epicenter of the city.

Gwalchmai and Gwyar hid in the archways of the prodigious circular stadium, concealing themselves for the purpose of surprising Mordred at just the right moment.

Gwalchmai was younger than Mordred by eighteen full months, yet the elder nephew of Arthur was never rumored Edling, or *heir*, whilst the younger was – even before the death of Arthur's sons.

This was for no other cause than Gwalchmai's fosterage in the South and the quantity of his time with the Pendragon. The red-haired Gwalchmai possessed otherworldly charms, appeared to command the weather, warmed any room he entered and brought entire halls to laughter. He was the 'people's heir', whilst Mordred, for reasons not quite so clear, was subtly kept away from the Gelliwig, Caerleon and Caermelyn, having very little time with Arthur at any of these courts.

Gwyar wanted Mordred at court for reconnection, for redeeming the time, and for love. Mordred, as was abundantly clear by the pomp of his entry and grandeur of his armor, cared for none of these things.

He was at Caerleon to assert his claims before King Arthur. His opportunity was now.

Arthur had younger brothers who were, for diverse reasons, ineligible for the throne, and Mordred, with Arthur's sons dead, was the hereditary heir. However, clear descent was subject to being negated by the people, whose rulers only governed by the consent of the governed. By voicing their will through the local bards, major landowners, bishops and priests, many kings had been passed over for lesser royalties on the basis of character and competence.

Now was Mordred's time. *Does Arthur even know me? Would he know me to look upon me? No matter; he shall know me. My will shall bring me all I desire. And I desire the Summer Kingdom.*

Mordred dismounted the stallion, and gave half-friendly embraces to the residents who had come to welcome him. Illtud's choirs introduced wondrous melodies into the summer air as tapestries danced in the breeze, seemingly to the singing. Harps and deep drums joined, and the smell of smoked beef caused a happy hunger for the hundreds of people reveling in and around the coliseum.

Yet Mordred saw none of his kin, least of all the High King.

He spun around a few times, sweating in his heavy, pretentious skeleton of gold, and began to grumpily inquire about the whereabouts of his mother. Just at the right time, *Morgaine appeared.*

"Looking for someone, Raven?" Even a powerful sorceress is capable of humor.

"Mother!" Mordred suspended political ambition as the moment broke his sourness; a sincerity of giddy reminiscence ensued. Gwyar was disconnected from the world of men save her sons, for whom she was as a lass with a new puppy – warm, doting, with smothers of love.

Tiny, Gwyar had to 'hug up', and in so doing pulled at the back of Mordred's mask-helmet, revealing his face, which was cleanly shaven, youthful and strikingly fair. He was of average height, a little shorter than his uncle Arthur, and of leaner build. He was of authoritative and mean-spirited disposition, and carried himself taller than he was.

The Hawk of May mauled him as well. "It's been three years!"

"You are – well – huge, Gwalchmai!" Prince Mordred awed at the burl and mass and bulk of his brother, who had let his red hair grow well beneath the shoulders and left it to run its own wild and curly course.

"It's been *three years!*" chuckled Gwalchmai.

The reunion continued for several minutes, and then Mordred returned to his aim – the wooing of the king. Or assertively demanding. *Whatever sophistry works, so long as the end is the crown.*

"Oh, my dear, my brother is, alas, not at Caerleon." Gwyar delivered the disappointment.

Mordred was not overly troubled. It was peacetime, and Arthur was sure to be at one of his three plenary courts and not far from the realm of his beloved Glamorgan and Gwent.

"Ah, off resolving a cattle dispute in Ergyng, or helping to thatch a roof for a cleric in

Llandaff?" Here Mordred mocked that the king was a neighbor first and a sovereign second, ever helping his neighbor.

"Would that were so." Now Gwyar's tone was grave. "He has traveled north, near your father's lands. To the highlands of Eryri."

Mordred wished his helm was still covering his face so that he didn't have to hide his overt anger.

"Why to the mountains?!" he emoted, then endeavored to calm himself.

Gwalchmai answered carefully. "I do not know why word did not reach Ynys Mon, brother. But an urgent call for the Round Table Fellowship, the first of its kind in more than three years, has come forth, on account of reports that" – a cheerful man struggles to deliver morose tidings – "a Giant has emerged, slaying chieftains and warriors, killing without cause."

"A Giant?"

"Not a tall man, or a figure or type to describe a large man. An actual, otherworldly beast of intelligence and rage. A six-fingered colossus, with multiple rows of teeth and bright, carroty hair."

Mordred interrupted Gwyar's description. "Kings, chieftains? Father?"

"We know not who has fallen. Arthur himself has gone to scout and gather information on the matter." Gwyar offered a hopeful tone.

Mordred queried Gwalchmai as to why he hadn't joined the other knights.

"I appealed strenuously."

"Why?"

"I have not seen my brother in three years." Gwalchmai hugged Mordred tight.

"My husband, your uncle, will be back

before you know. Welcome. Rest with us, Prince Mordred." Enter Gwenhwyfar ferch Ogyrfan. "In his stead, I offer myself." False humility. "Come, eat some dinner with us."

Gwen had manifested from thin air, and Gwyar was actually thankful that she broke the tension as surely, elsewise, Mordred would have remounted and raced back north to the mountains Eryri (which would later be called Snowdonia).

The new queen had mastered covering her ceaseless infidelity over the past three years, never again coming near to being discovered.

But Gwyar knew.

And it drove her to hatred.

She often wondered if she was hurting Arthur more by concealing versus revealing the matter.

The four, Gwyar, Mordred, Gwalchmai, and Gwen II, parted for a time, and then assembled for an evening meal.

'Twas here that the course of history changed.

There are no 'types' where love is concerned, no compatibility measures, no guarantees of 'like things with like things', no requisite mutual interests, no builds or equity of shapes and forms.

Indeed, *you love who you love, and that is that.*

And for the first time in her life, the one who had been abused by the Fae and in turn had abused men, hundreds of times, felt love. Real and actual love. *Love in the fashion of Meurig and Onbrawst.*

It happened over one meal.

And Mordred, though married to Kwyllog ferch Caw, instantly, fully and equally reciprocated. *And this is the only time love works, when it is requited equally.*

What Arthur had wanted for the sum of his life, Gwenhwyfar freely gifted to Mordred in their first moment. Her whole heart was given, spoken for, and taken.

Gwyar had become blinded by Gwen's constant playing of the harlot. Though gods and men alike feared her power and perception and *Sight*, she couldn't see this: Gwen was changed.

The following morning, Gwen II rose early, Prince Mordred the preoccupation of her dawn, and glided about the city, repenting openly with great contrition to the many whom she had wronged. She was careful, however, to have no direct interaction with past lovers (those who had not met *accidental* deaths and still drew breath to speak of it) who could reveal *that part* of her iniquity. She stooped to gather up spilled baskets of eggs at the market, she played with children, dancing round the poles, actually holding children!

Mordred had made the monster into a woman. A soft, kind, powerful woman.

Gwen had made the monster into a man. A soft, kind, powerful man.

Battling nerves, they stole a 'hand-hold' the following day. The innocent intertwine was alone more pleasing than a life of carnal pleasures and material goods, which before had been constantly fed into a bottomless well of the soul.

And oh, the first kiss!

She delivered a peck on his cheek, just below the eye. He absorbed it as a sponge absorbs vinegar, and when he could contain no further, turned inward and brought her lips to his. All time seemed to stop, and the two villains were born again as saints, not to God, but to love itself. They knew that somehow, in the end, they would be together.

They must be together.

Over the following days (with reports that Arthur would soon return with his report), the leaven leavened the lump, and the two sought where they could make love.

When Gwenhwyfar and Arthur had been betrothed, he had placed her in a well-appointed apartment within a small but luxurious farm home. Near the farm resided a storehouse; beside that, a small cell for chieftains or princes who retired unto monasticism. Arthur had visited the woman he loved with such frequency that the small estate came to be called Llanilltern, or *the place of the king.*

Gwen II loved this place, especially the nearby grove. Its form and features were an impassable blockade to the outside world. To be in this little grove was to be in a Cymru within Cymru. The diversity of flora and fauna, the goliath trees, the accompaniment of legions of birds and friendly fowl singing at all times. *For even the birds are Cymreig in Cymru. And the Cymry are a people who sing.* The place itself hummed notes of innocence, romance, virtue and love.

Ironic and fitting that it was the spot of Gwenhywfar ferch Ogyrfan's liaisons with Mordred ap Llew.

The spot of forbidden love.

And many times a day they knew each other upon its ferns and soft brush, its heather finding its way into every part of their inseparable forms.

Arthur was delinquent in his return to Caerleon. Messengers indicated that there was now twofold the trouble, as another abominable creature had delayed the king's homecoming. This beast presided in South Cymru, magnifying the fears of those in the cantrefs.

Mordred's mother sat at tea, listening to

reports that both Giants lived, and that Arthur would need to reassemble some portion of the army from the Saxon Wars.

Insultingly, the messenger indicated that Arthur wanted Gwen II, and not Gwyar, to organize this with the counselors, advisors and bishops in his stead. (The new Merli,n Taliesin, was away, chastising Maelgwn at this time).

"Fine." Mature Gwyar gave a childish snort, causing recall of like memories of the four at school. "Where is she?" she asked plainly.

None knew.

Gwyar thrice drew her forefinger round the teacup and, barely in a whisper, uttered, "*Morgana.*" Her eyes found her attendants and she said, quietly and authoritatively, "Leave." And the teatime acquaintances and envoys left, an immediate shadow filling the hall just as rapidly as they scurried away.

The thing that was in Gwyar or part of Gwyar or *was Gwyar* now manifested, and as her *Sight* focused, a most surprising voice was heard, in the shadows, there but not there, yet so clear.

"The field of malevolence in the thicket beyond Llanilltern."

A rush of unstoppable tears had their way with Morgaine's face and hands, and then her hair as she pushed it off her forehead, hoping better to see what wasn't there.

"Merlin!" Her voiced cracked nine times to finish the two-syllable word.

Alas, there were none but she in the great hall where tea was enjoyed in the Silure capital of Caerleon.

Immediately to her horse she sprang, the journey not far, the place concealed but well-known.

Arriving quickly, she yanked up by his robe

a cleric, peacefully studying Scripture outside the cell on a warm yet windswept summer's day. Placing the reins in his hand, she commanded him: "Watch her." Not waiting for a response, she was off into the grove, swiftly, but now silent.

A manifold trauma blasted the sorceress at the privy viewing of the intercourse between her very own son and the harlot queen:

Mine son will die a traitor under our laws, in any cantref or realm.

Arthur's heart will burst asunder at being cuckolded by his own kin.

Another betrayal by his own house.

If I kill Gwen, will it break him more or less?

If only Merlin were here.

WHY MUST MEN AND WOMEN, PAGANS AND SAINTS, RICH AND POOR, BONDED AND FREE, BETRAY LOVE IN FAVOUR OF LUST? IS THERE NOT EVEN ONE WHO IS TRUE?

The terminal thought was pointed at herself as well as the wide-reaching audience that neither saw nor heard her. She had performed fertility and sacerdotal rites that involved union, or sacred fornication, with men portraying gods, with women portraying goddesses. *That it was religious made it no less adulterous.*

Morgaine of the Faeries was not high-minded; a moment of burden and sorrowful guilt for her husband, loveless marriage begotten of Statecraft or not – *how would he feel if I was in some field making love to another man? How would any spouse feel?*

Seeing the tryst crushed Gwyar, altering her. At utter loss for reason, and sickened to vomit by the relentless repetition in her busy mind of *what she had seen,* the subject overcame her. She took only one item from her chamber – a tattered, worn brown pouch – and fled Caerleon straight away, wanting greatly to unsee it, wanting greatly to know how best to serve Arthur and her son, knowing that to do one would be death to the other. In pain and distress that caused her eyes and left shoulder to twitch and her circulation to run unnatural courses, resulting in a hammering chest pounding, she sought out herbs, and rest.

The Field of Malevolence. The wood which would come to be called *Mordred's Thicket,* the pitch branded *The Field of Melwas.* It was right here, in this very moment, that the Isles were lost to the Saxons. Not to Aelle, nor to Hengest or Horsa or Octa. And not to the villains who had orchestrated waves of destruction that slayed hundreds of thousands of Cymry, hundreds of chieftains, adding even a Pendragon to their murderous account. Rather, 'twas lost to young Saxons yet suckling, not yet having seen enough winters to lift an axe or wield the infamous *Long Knife.* Cymru was lost. Only, none knew of it.

Full of rage, and blinded by a multitude of unsolvable problems, Morgaine of the Faeries exiled herself to Brocelainde, exorcising her condition by becoming a powerful enchantress in the forest, luring and punishing lovers unfaithful and untrue.

CHAPTER 6
King Arthur versus Itto Gawr

Seed 3 – "This was my chance to be Champion before my Tribes."

Centuries before the time of Arthur, the king of the Tylwyth Teg seduced and lay with a damsel that he mistook for a daughter of Adam.

Unbeknownst to him, she was a second-generation Nephilim. Her father was a Giant, and his father a Fallen One.

So few were these incursions in the present dispensation, on account of the protective and ongoing war in heavenly places, that the Fair Folk paid little heed to the possibility.

The accidental offspring of the Nephilim woman and the Fae king wrought a type of double abomination, for the babe was a crossbreed of not just one but two atrocities against God and nature, leaving very little remnant of the substance of man within it.

From the darkest and most fantastic, far-fetched yet true ancient history, this type of incident was the source and explanation for monsters and indescribably strange flesh (including when Fallen Ones would go after creaturekind).

In this peculiar case, the babe's eyes were crimson-filled like unto his father, massive and perfectly round instead of elliptical, with no pupils. Yet he could see, and was able to change forms and walk secretly between the world of men and the realms of the Fae.

The unnatural mutation was elsewise like unto the Giants. Three times the height of a man, sulfuric skin, contorted vertebrae protruding and curving as the horns of a ram all atop his upper back, in tattered rags, the red-eyed monster operated without brain, without mercy. Dormant for long consecutive years, he would wake, eat a grotesque number of stags and fowl, and then return to a stench-filled cave, undisturbed and unknown.

Because of his lustful indiscretion, the master of the Fair Folk replaced all food consumed by the beast three-fold to the village in Cernyw (which is Glamorgan) where dwelt the Red-Eyed Giant. Barns were swept clean, and charms and delights often found upon entries to homes and halls. Moreover, lost wanderers were protected by the otherworldly creatures of the forest, guiding and directing them through enchantments to safer paths.

Many treasures and not a few monsters are hidden in comely, mystical Cymru. And this monster was hidden and sleeping.

Until the Dynion Hysbys found and woke him.

Whereas some Giants were far superior to men in knowledge, in the Sacred Sciences, in masonry and smithing skills, in remembering and recording histories, in theology and many other diverse and sundry spheres of the life-experience, others were more akin to wild beasts or carnivorous fish; constant in hunger and thirst, ever at the hunt for blood and flesh. So dramatic was the spectrum of acumen and disposition amongst these otherworldly beings that men venerated some of them as highly enlightened gods, whilst others they reckoned lower than dogs; a thing to be killed upon encounter, destroyed upon discovery.

The Red-Eyed Giant was of the latter kind.

By contrast, the Giant who had nominated himself the upstart *King of Gwynedd* and set up a court in the high peaks of Eryri was of the former. His name was Itto Mawr. In outward appearance he was in every particular as a man, save his size. His six fingers were the only outward anomaly, his extra rows of teeth subtle and concealed. He was well-groomed, with a comely long, grey beard that was braided and beaded, falling well below his waistline. Handsome to scale, this self-proclaimed ruler was charismatic, with kind eyes, rosy, high-sitting cheeks and a snub, upturned nose. Itto also had an eccentric mania for collecting the beards of his foes.

While Lancelot was frolicking in distracted and blissful fornication, leaping from bed to bed, losing himself inside painted Pictish princesses way up in the highlands of Alba, this Giant had usurped and taken over swaths of his kingdom.

Thus, in the space of but a few weeks, King Arthur had seen two very, very different co-inhabitants of his Isles. The one a mighty man of the mountains, the other a wretched monster from a heretofore unknown rank, putrid-smelling cave too near to Arthur's own cantref in Glamorgan.

Arthur did not openly engage Itto. The objective of his mission was to scout and to study. Horrifically, Arthur and his company saw Itto kill twenty ravens with no more effort than a milking cow swats the flies from her tail on a sticky summer day. Utilizing his advanced arts of disguise, the High King became as a rank and file Raven; a soldier amongst those assembled under Maelgwn and Caw's sons to fell this mighty usurper.

For above the space of a week, Arthur studied the Giant.

He primarily killed through lowering his left shoulder and trampling a man, or several men at a time. Once they were knocked flat and unconscious, he would snap the neck and then, with the speed of an adder, sheer the beard and tuck it away into a bulging satchel stuffed with the hair and blood of fallen men of the North. The maneuvers were as the reaction of a loosed bull, yet more fluid. A creature ten times the size of a bull and as many times as quick with fist, hammer or club. Arthur judged that the top of his helm reached the kneecap of Itto, and that the Giant's hand could crush a head as effortlessly as squishing a plump grape.

The assembled warriors would attack Itto in groups of six or eight, or in singular combat. The nature of the opponent made it difficult for *many to attack one*. Arrows did not penetrate Itto's skin, the constitution of which, although in appearance as a mortal, was, at least in part, of some other substance; swords produced scratches and scrapes (and bellowing laughter) in the stead of gashes and gapes.

During one frantic flurry, Arthur stealthily unsheathed Carnwennan (the last time the Pendragon had used the enchanted blade was three and a half years earlier, also in the north, in execution of a traitor. The punch of the memory in Arthur's bowels was more grievous than a direct strike by Itto Mawr could ever be). The ensuing shadow caused by the legendary dagger enabled Arthur to engage Itto at the back of the ankle, wholly unseen.

A cut! A real cut!

Itto cried out and swung violently at the disguised king. Arthur ducked the cedar tree whipping towards his head and sprinted towards the safety of the encampment.

It takes otherworldly weaponry to slay an otherworldly enemy, Arthur had learned on his perilous and privy experiment.

Privy to Men; not so for wise and brave Itto Mawr.

"Arthur ap Meurig ap Tewdrig ap Teithfalt! I thought you more brave, whelp!" The voice alone could shake one's bones and shatter marble.

Stunned at his discovery, Arthur removed the helm of the Ravens of the Old North and tore off his black cloak, revealing the dark blues and reds of the Silure tribe. Bowing his chest, having his feet shod with bravery, the Iron Bear said a rapid prayer and whipped around.

The eruption of cheers that the sandy-haired, blue-eyed king was amongst the Ordivices, his Cymreig kinsmen in the north, was deafening. Their savior had come, and the plague would be handled swiftly.

Arthur's prudence intended elsewise.

"I am he," he said, and stood stoic. Then he walked right up to the Pretender King of Gwynedd and withstood him, face to face – or rather, *face to knee.*

"A little far from the golden fortress of Caerleon and the spoiled fatness of Cybbor, eh?" Itto goaded him. Itto rubbed at his ankle, the wound now angry. "Bring me your army or your beard, or I will make of your absent friend's kingdom a wasteland." His snub nose turned further upward as he delivered the deeply ugly words with deeply kind eyes.

Merlin's greatest achievement in his young pupil was that Arthur always filtered; *think before you do, in haste act not.*

"I will make my leave and return unto you. Until then, I beseech you to leave the people of Gwynedd alone, troubling neither bishop nor farmer nor artisan."

The bravery of the piece of iron dressed as a man impressed upon Itto that he wanted to befriend, and neither eat nor clip, the thirty-and-six-year-old War King. But some force was *causing* the Giant to lust for nothing else save to destroy and disrupt. "Hurry back, son of Meurig," was all he could muster.

Arthur and his companions had to consider many issues as he traveled south towards home. Raising an army and marching into Gwynedd, even with cause, might have negative perceptions, on account of old hurts. Even in the Summer Kingdom, currents of *South versus North* ran and raged as veins of discord beneath the crystal sea of peace.

Arthur's next necessary step was assembling the Round Table, all twenty-six of them, seeking counsel from Bishop Bedwini in order to hear the Church's perspective, find his new Merlin, the Bard Taliesin, who was ever at some quarrel or rivalry with Maelgwn; and find Maelgwn.

To this end, Arthur directed the youngest son of the *king of the Picts and the rightful King of Gwynedd* (Arthur laughed at this, as his

Champion, who preferred no titles, now had seemingly doubled his collection of kingdoms on account of the peculiar fascination the Picts held for the beautiful grandson of Cunedda). "Rhyvn, please do all to bring Maelgwn to Caermelyn. Seven nights or sooner, but no more." No compromise or latitude was present in Arthur's tone. Rhyvn, the ever companion of Arthur's deceased son Llacheau, was ready to the task, hugging his hero tightly (for Maelgwn's sons adored the Silure king).

Arthur, the Iron Bear, desired to make haste homeward.

The Red-Eyed Giant had other notions.

Cai, at the king's side since the days of his fosterage, and Bedwyr were chief amongst Arthur's company. The latter saw the thing appear first, in full sprint at the horses on the byway but a few hours north of Caerleon near the Cwmbran, which is by interpretation *the valley of Bran* (who was also a Giant).

Throwing itself into ten warriors and bouncing through and ultimately off a cluster of horses as a wildcat bounces from a herd of stags, it came again and again, clawing, biting and visiting much damage onto the Cymry host.

Then, through a fakery of retreat, it hastened away, its stench leading Cai, Bedwyr and the king to its cave.

"What sorcery is upon us?" Cai, ever grave.

"Well, you don't see that every day." Bedwyr was ever ready to calm with jest and lightheartedness. "Let me at him first." His humor followed always with whole commitment unto the good.

Upon seeing a second otherworldly being, the king instantly wondered at and began attempting to piece together the connections. The Red-Eyed Devil gave the Pendragon no luxury of contemplation, appearing again in an instant from his cave and attacking Bedwyr.

Now, Bedwyr was Arthur's best friend. Above Cai. Above Urien. Above Gwalchmai, his heir. Above even Maelgwn, whom he loved.

And his best friend was in the dire.

Excalibur, that blade forged on Ynys Enlli using steely shavings of a cherubic flaming sword, first wielded at a time when Lions *did* lay down with Lambs. Excalibur, *the Sword of Power*. Arthur looked at that power seething in his protective palms and gripped the hilt harder than at any time before. Excalibur, *The Giant Slayer*, he thought as he plunged into the fray but two seconds late.

Bedwyr ducked, he dodged, he rolled. Ranked just below Gwalchmai and Maelgwn (and his sons) for skill, Bedwyr was amongst the elite ranks of swordsman living at the time. *Or any time.* He had dealt several blows to the monster but, in a slight sliver of a moment, separated his hands. The left hand held the sword low and swung to shoulder height; torqueing his mid-section and pivoting hard to generate momentum, the blade circled to above his head, where his second hand was intended to clasp the first, delivering a fatal downward overhand strike.

The second hand never made it.

Now agape, the monster's mouth revealed an extra rung of teeth set within a pink, mucusy second jaw that dislocated from the first and could distend out past the external mouth and then expand. A second mouth. The teeth were flat and level and would be regarded as 'perfect', if within the handsome mouth of a comely lad.

Uniform. Shiny. But sharp as shears, as twenty-four little Excaliburs filed flat and designed for making effortless and surgical chops of flesh and bone.

The Red-Eyed Giant clamped down, cleanly severing Bedwyr's right hand well below the wrist. The twisted mixed offspring of Fae and Giant and angel and animal, and whatever else the Prince of Darkness had placed into its composition, this sin against nature most foul had swallowed the hand, glove, gauntlet and all, with satisfied eyes popping as a frog gulping a mosquito.

Then straightway his brawny, deformed neck came round to see the Pendragon rushing upon him.

Arthur, an elite counter-fighter, was in this instance on the offense. Excalibur cleaved three fingers quickly, exacting some recompense for loss of limb and appendage. The Red-Eyed Giant answered with a clumsy lunge that Arthur easily avoided. Then the King shuffled back out of range of four, then five, and soon, nine attempted strikes.

As the monster inhaled to recover and have another go, the Iron Bear now returned to form, making his countermoves, slashing hard at the thigh and then piercing Excalibur through the thing's throat from under the chin. The skull was so monstrously elongated that the legendary sword was absorbed to its cross-guard. A pungent, bloody, black brain matter flowed down, covering the hilt's infamous elvish inscription and down Arthur's arms.

Giving no thought to his stuck sword, nor the disgusting, viscous material glazed all over him, he kicked the beast to the ground. Dead.

Immediately, he knelt to tend upon Bedwyr.

"If I had an enchanted faerie druid sword from the Garden of Eden, I could've done the same thing." The good-spirited Bedwyr did all he could to lessen the trauma of his friend, though he was the one maimed. He made the jest, smiled warmly, then passed hard into unconsciousness.

Twelve battles; never so much blood from one man!
Sixty raids, never so much!
So much blood!
So, so much!

The serrated line's placement was not accidental. The beast instinctively knew how to kill in a myriad of ways, and here it had sought to create a dramatic fount of spraying blood that would soak Arthur's friend and ensure that he would die in a crimson pool of his own life essence.

And spray it did. Men had passed away from much less blood than Bedwyr had already let.

"We have to get him to Gwyar," the king exclaimed, tearing his shirt sleeve into strips, doing all to slow the spraying blood.

Cai rushed on ahead, and was already circling back to meet the king and his company as they approached the bridge into Caerleon.

"She is not here." Cai flung despairing and helpless hands towards the heavens.

"Gwyar gone. Vivien gone. Taliesin far, far away. I need a healer; I need a healer now," hollered Arthur, not at the men, but at the dismal situation.

Suddenly a hooded man of similar stature to the king manifested. Adorned in the sigils of the Ravens, but now abjured of the gold and pomp from his entry some days ago, the young man extended the right hand of fellowship to Arthur, unveiling his head from under hood with the left in one smooth and regal motion.

"My mother taught me several of her healing arts, and I have received training on the Isle of Apples."

"Your mother?"

"Yes, uncle."

Though a stranger, Arthur saw familiar eyes looking back at him.

"Nephew." He took the offered hand warmly, yet with heightened angst and haste. Arthur then placed his dying friend in the hands of the young stallion who had, without reservation or guilt, been bedding his wife the queen for a fortnight.

Mordred had no special regard for Bedwyr, nor any of his neighbors, for he was by nature devoid of natural affection. But by nursing the Round Table Knight, he had cause; cause to remain at Caerleon, and with Gwenhwyfar.

Bedwyr lived.

Arthur parted immediately for the short ride over to Caermelyn, where the Round Table Companions were already assembling to consider their course against Itto Mawr.

With her husband gone, Gwen redeemed the time with Mordred, and savored it. She did things for him she had done for no man.

She cooked.

He helped her.

She sang.

He strummed the harp, providing tune and melody to harmonize with her suddenly soft and nurturing voice.

They read and held hands at tea.

They sculpted.

They talked. *Men and women never truly talk, but these did.*

The jubilance brought up from the grave long-dead memories of youth, from before she had been ruined by the Fae. There had been one other time, as a lass, that she had felt a similitude of this happiness, this thankful joy. *It had been with Lancelot at school. Was that a memory, or a dream?*

Arthur gave space of a few days for the Five Royal Tribes to assemble. Usually Gwyar or Gwenhwyfar took charge of the hospitality, being far superior in organization and style to the brawny gender, but Gwyar had vanished and Gwen had remained in Caerleon to host the nephew of the king and continue to look upon the convalescing knight, Bedwyr.

None found this curious, save Gwalchmai, who observed an extended glance between queen and nephew and liked it not.

Cobbling together meat and Illtud's choirs for but a few songs, Bedwini prayed for the assembly and the retired king, and Meurig opened the discussions.

As a constant, immutable principle, all Round Table assemblies were open; a clear looking glass to the public. Nothing was done under a bushel, nothing in the closet. Murky politics are part of the fallen condition of man, and still ran their course amongst bishops, affluent landowners and local chieftains. But Arthur did all to combat this through his policies, hoping for, but never forcing, emulation.

The Round Table Companions met infrequently, save for sport or for quest, and the congregational spirit took every man, woman and child emotionally to a place of trauma and dread, reminding them too much of the Saxon Wars.

When the Saxons' presence had become a validated threat to the existence of the Cymry,

Merlin had recommended the architecture of their defeat begin with study.

"Know your enemy first, and once you know him, then will you know how to destroy him," the Wizard would say.

Meurig reminded the assembly of this, and credited the quote to Merlin.

"I have another citation from the Merlin to share."

That familiar, feared yet coveted, low, metallic and mannish whispery voice, the one that paralyzed friend and foe, suddenly filled every story of the little castle that housed the Round Table.

"Maelgwn!" Arthur sprang from his seat, knocking his simple wooden throne (for all chairs at the round table were without respect of persons with one exception, and that not Arthur's) to the white marble floor, creating an irritating scratch and *skik*. He delivered a running hug upon the tall Briton.

"It has been too long since the best of us has been in these special halls. Suffer us to cheer and shout, for the Lancelot is come!"

Maelgwn disliked accolade and doting before men. But he had missed Arthur deeply as well, and thus suffered the shouts and songs of praise.

Finding a natural pause opened amongst the cheers, the hall teeming with renewed hope and vigor, the Bloodhound continued.

"When ambushed by the Italian Band, Merlin bade me pass along a request." Maelgwn looked upon Arthur, and Arthur's face acknowledged and remembered. "Nay, a command."

"Give us the Counselor of Britannia's words, Lancelot," beseeched Arthur's father.

"'Kill the Giants! Kill them all.'"

Though the words had been uttered years ago, that there was some connection was clear to all.

"With respect..." Maelgwn's posture further commanded the ear of the room, his battle spike shimmering in dramatic symphony with his speech. "We have no time to figure out what these brutes are, neither have three months of theological committees to determine their origin." He looked at the bishops, and a few blushed at the imprecatory verbal arrow. "He has made his encampment at the base of Mallwyd in the shadow of Dinas Mawddwy. That means he is positioned to detain, to cut off, and to devastate from the very gateway into Gwynedd."

Opinions and worried grumblings here naturally flared. Maelgwn spoke authoritatively through the noise.

"Raise the armies, and by force of number, let us quickly remove this menace. I request of you," he said.

For King Arthur's part, he was still of a sore and vengeful disposition over Bedwyr's wicked wound, and wanted immediate and decisive action as well. Arthur added to Maelgwn's plea, and the Royal Tribes, Clans and Chieftains, already squabbling about feeding the confederacy and 'who would do what', gave a hasty consent.

The uplifting wave of Lancelot's entry had waned. Three years of peace were not enough; the collective soul of the Nation was yet war-torn, yet war-fatigued.

"We will resolve this quickly, kinsmen." The High King sought to comfort the people.

The twenty-six, less Bedwyr, plus forty thousand professional equestrian warriors, along with bards, choirs, carts of goods and every type of employ to the administering of war, hastened to Gwynedd.

A summer fog filled the field, yet the otherworldly being could apparently count swiftly and see all. Surveying the ranks, he mocked the Cymry.

"I see you are missing one."

Lancelot did not stand idle for pre-battle, verbal member-measuring matches. Already dismounted, and knowing that armor would be of no effect, he ran ahead of the army, shirtless with no helm and no covering save a small shield that was designed only to protect the hand and forearm. Besides this he had only his unique battle spike. Death was available from either end of it. It had the benefits of a spear with the length and ease of use of a sword, with a curved third blade as a fin, sheltering the leather-wrapped area where it was held.

Itto had gathered some followers of the sons of Adam, but they were servants (or slaves) and no warriors. Instead of giving cry for them to intercept the living instrument running upon them, the mighty man made a motion, pointing to where the wood opened at the base of the mount.

Another Giant appeared.

This one also had the features and appearance of a man, and was much shorter than Itto. Whether it was offspring or kin was unknown. The mortal mothers rarely survived giving birth to the gargantuan babes, who tore the womb apart and serrated the insides, culminating in unspeakable and horrific death.

The smaller Giant met Lancelot, and it did not fare well for the former.

Seeing the head of his own kind rolling as a great stone at his feet and the one and only

Lancelot before him, Itto gave a cry that gave terror to the armies, causing even deer and rabbits to appear from the forest and make haste for the higher hills.

At the same time as a showdown was developing between Lancelot (who fully believed he would perish under the great fists of the monster, and in falling, would motivate the armies to use numbers to fell the Giant) and Itto, conflicts were arising amongst the Tribes.

A battle standard was clumsily knocked down.

Dirt was accidentally kicked upon supplies.

The Cornovii protested their flanked position, and eleven sub-tribes of the Ordovices each had two minor complaints (summing twenty-two squabbles).

Owain ap Urien, an impatient and undisciplined young man ever ready to spring up and fight (and especially disdainful of the Silure rank and file, even though he loved Arthur) was rebel-rousing.

Arthur, seeing the debacle developing before and around him (for this army, even when sharpened by the iron of steady war, had its internal skirmish and distress in delicate knitting of north and south), realized in an instant the reason that Itto had begun his bewitched siege against the northern kingdom of Gwynedd.

"Think before you act."

Merlin was not there in the flesh, but his words lived. And as his words lived, thus did he.

"Maelgwn, please fall back – *fall back*, Maelgwn!" Arthur silenced the bards and the choirs, hushing music and song so the great knight could hear. "Maelgwn, fall back!"

Itto helped.

"I think the King of Kings calls you; go to

him. I'll be here." Itto spoke with half mockery, half respect, for even devils and gods are quickly enamored with King Arthur Pendragon.

Maelgwn was irritated as he returned to the restless battle camp. He wanted to fight, not hear Arthur's revelation. His head crooked under the entrance of the pavilion, where an anxious friend awaited.

"You see this army? The cost of food, the complaints of the locals, who are your very people, the damage to property, the politics that will surely follow? By us even being here, he wins!" Arthur was articulate; Arthur was right. No army of such a magnitude had been assembled in over three years. It was a Golden Age disrupted. And this was the plan by Itto. *By whoever or whatever was controlling Itto.*

"One battle begets another. We must find another way," Arthur continued.

Some back and forth ensued, and as he and Maelgwn spoke, the Iron Bear remembered another of his old Wizard's lessons. *"The past informs the present; NEVER forget your history."* At that moment, he knew his next steps.

Brutus and Gogmagog! Recalling how that ancient founder had spared thousands of men by challenging that Titan to single combat, the Pendragon knew his course. He would emulate his forefather and wrestle Itto Mawr, unarmed.

"No," said Maelgwn.

"It is the only way. No more war, Lancelot. We promised the people. We promised our children."

"Granted, but this is my land. Let me represent my people."

"He will only agree to terms with me. He wants my beard, not your locks." Lancelot never wore a beard. "He wants the High King." Arthur would not relent on his intents. The Round Table Champion continued to protest until at last, Arthur was forced to do something rare and contrary to his nature. He *ordered* Lancelot to cease contesting him. He *ordered* the Son of Cadwallon Lawhir to fall in and support the words of his High King.

And the men of the Son of Cadwallon heard the order delivered with the tone of rebuke.

Maelgwn's bubble returned. Anger welled, but he said no more. His head brooded low, and he 'fell in' and walked three paces behind Arthur as the two alone went out to speak with Itto Mawr.

Prior to this, they informed Gwalchmai that he would be Wledig (as he was not qualified to be a Pendragon, being not of the paternal line of the Silures), should Arthur perish.

Itto's cheeks were flushed red, and the curl of his smile made his great grey beard lift and bounce; a jolly beard.

"Do you come to offer me your beard and end this conflict, Lord Arthur?"

"I desire no protracted war with you or whatever army you might raise." As though Itto needed an army. Arthur scratched at his short beard, sand-colored and well formed. "Neither will I give you my beard, which would represent surrender to you. That is an untenable selection. I offer this instead. Do you remember Brutus?"

Itto fell to both knees, had wine brought for the three, and listened to Arthur's history lesson and proposition.

Meanwhile the confederacy of Britons, growing impatient by the moment, asked for scouts and reports. And finally, with the sun soon to go into his chamber, word came.

"King Arthur fully disarmed of sword and scabbard, of dagger, of shield, of spear and cloak. He has gone to the summit of a hill called Bwlch Y Groes," a messenger declared.

"To wrestle Itto Mawr," added another.

"To what end?!" the crowd charged.

"To the winner goes the binding and ultimate victory. If Arthur wins, the Giant shall return whence he came."

"And if the Titan prevails?" another asked.

Maelgwn interrupted the herald and finished the conversation. "Then Itto will have one more beard for his odd collection, and the Hawk of May will be our Battle Duke. There will be no fight today, no loss of life and no bloodshed. Because of Arthur, we have already won the day. Make ready to home."

Maelgwn's bubble stretched and stretched, as the seed of public slight and public offence found fertile soil in the complex man's soul. His only defense against the bubble was filling his mind with the debauchery and foul deeds he would commit to satisfy its demands. Then, he surmised, he would return to Camlan, or even visit the forests of Caledonia. He also planned then and there to found four churches and give gold to the bishops and to the bards.

Meanwhile, Arthur climbed the hill, talking to and getting acquainted with his opponent.

CHAPTER 7
The Cup is a Cup

Vivien looked over the mazer, of no comely or peculiar design; a simple wooden 'wide cup', the kind used by many cultures in Arabia and Palestine at the time of Christ. Its only distinguishing features were the many bite-marks and grooves where desperate partakers had surmised that, by biting bits of the cup, their chances of healing would increase.

The extraordinary Lady continued to abase herself for suppressing the Marian Mysteries. For so long had she fought the corruption and encroach of the Christian Church; she had forgotten the fundamental truth that Christ Himself would have nothing to do with it. And that the druids and the *real Christians* were *almost* on the same team.

Well, Merlin merged the teams, didn't he? she thought, looking at the Oak.

"You wanted this to come to me. How did you know Meirchion would compel Cadfan to break ground upon Enlli and put all these secrets at the shovel and plow of the Roman Church? You risked your mortal coil to learn the truth, to share your truth, and yet made a nonsensical trip north to get this, only to return south again to the ports.

And now I hold the Grail, far away from Cadfan and danger." She caressed the oaken prison where slept the Wizard. "If I survive those who did this to you, my love..." She continued her conversation with one who could neither hear her nor give response. "You thought Lancelot would be here, unscathed and stained with Latin blood, ready to encompass me with an impenetrable shield of protection."

A singular, and swift, tear formed, escaping quickly over the curvature of her chin.

"You didn't drag my son along for you. You brought him here for me." She looked at Lancelot, sleeping soundly, his head wound freshly dressed. "How did you know all?!"

The one tear gathered a hundred friends.

"You are the Merlin of Britain. And there was none like you. Of course you did all this; you are *you*."

The Lady of the Lake wept sorely.

* * *

To understand the Cup of Christ, it is imperative to understand dispensational truth. Israel was a nation gestated out of captivity and set apart with a specific purpose (namely, as God's agency for restitution and eviction of the current god of the world, the Devil), special covenants (amongst these being the Abrahamic, the Old and the New), and a promised inheritance (the earth), far different from the Gentile kingdoms.

God set apart this peculiar people to bring forth His word, His Son, His King. This required separation, contracts and perseverance. And, as an Israelite is a fallen man just as any other, God had to add The Law (over six hundred and twelve of them) to show them that they could not obtain right standing with Him on their own merits. The Law was not given to make them good, nor could it. Rather, it was made to stop their boastful mouths, showing them their need for a savior. For The Saviour. Though closest to the Creator of Heaven and earth, they were unbelieving and rebellious in their generations, always requiring signs and wonders. To this end, a longsuffering and patient God delivered the same. At sundry times and for specific purposes, to validate a Man, a Ministry or a Message, God either gave or allowed men to give signs. The benefit of these was not for those who believed, but as a witness to those weak of faith who believed not.

Nowhere did this aspect of the divine accord manifest more openly than in the manifold prophecies concerning the visitation of the long-awaited Messiah. When the Son of God arrived on the scene, His signature included casting out unclean spirits, causing the blind to see, and many other like miraculous manifestations, validating beyond disputation *who* He was, and *what* He was saying.

He came unto His own, and His own received Him not.

So great was to be the declaration of His Son's might and clarity of His arrival that the Father allowed one tenth of the disembodied spirits – the offspring of those Watchers who, in the Days of Noah, had lain with the daughters of men – to freely roam the earth, to gather in Jerusalem and, along with more recent ghosts from their kin slain by Joshua and Caleb, launch an attack on God's people. All for the express purpose of the Lord Jesus defeating them, casting thousands of them into the Deep, using only His word; a rehearsal for the epic conflict at the End of Days wherein all of them would fall to His sword.

And He healed the sick. In diverse ways and with diverse instruments, often to teach some great analogy or truth, not for the one being healed but, rather, for the unbelieving eyewitnesses.

Prior to going to His Cross to die for His people (for it was not known by men, angels or devils that the secret of the Cross contained the Son of Man becoming sin for all of mankind. This secret was well concealed for, had it been known, the enemy of God would have prevented, rather than caused, the Lord's death), the Lord supped with His twelve (after this pattern do the Cymry kings hold twelve elect men in close companionship with the king, and likewise do the greater kings keep twelve bards besides, for twelve is God's number for *governance*) in a patternistic feast which was a repeat of the meal the Lord had enjoyed with Melchizedek long millennia ago, and would be enjoyed again when the Lord joined His twelve Apostles in their City and their Kingdom in ages to come. The wine that the Lord blessed was symbolic of the blood of His New Covenant with Israel (which supplanted the Law of Moses, containing therein precious things it could not, having a better sacrifice, a better priesthood and a better hope). And thus the cup represented deep fellowship, healing and doctrine. To partake of one's cup is to partake of all that they are, all that they stand upon.

And Vivien, four hundred eighty and four years later, held that very cup.

After the Lord was crucified and received up into Heaven to sit at the right hand of the Father,

His message and promises to Israel continued for a time through the efficacy of His twelve apostles, whom He gifted with powers, by the Holy Spirit, like unto Himself. Through handkerchiefs, through oils, through rods or other tangible talismans did they heal and cast out remnant unclean spirits. As sayeth the Scriptures, seas of ink could not contain all the good deeds that Jesus and His twelve did, and there were countless healings during the short season between the time of the crucifixion and the stoning of the Preacher, Steven. Here again, the signature gifts and healings were in acquiescence to an unbelieving and untoward generation; one that had murdered their own Saviour, even begging the heavens for a divine curse to be put upon their own heads, and their children's heads, thirsting for the guilt of His blood to be on their accounts. Though evil through and through, a merciful and longsuffering God allowed healings and miracles to continue, looking for but a remnant few to grant residency in the glorious kingdom of Heaven He had prepared for them.

But in parallel, God started to do something different.

He saved the chief of the rebellion.

A young Benjamite Pharisee, a Roman citizen born under the sign and sigil of the Bull, a *Hebrew of Hebrews* and a *Gentile of Gentiles* melded in one body, a picture of the Antichrist whose career was on projection to qualify for being he.

A blasphemer of the Holy Ghost and hunter of Messianic believers from the Church of Jerusalem. This man persecuted the early Church, scattering and wasting it.

Outside of the reach of salvation under Israel's gospel, God made of His greatest enemy an example for all times of His undiluted grace. He saved Paul, ushering in a new dispensation. Grace.

As the believing Jews were sorely afraid of him and the unbelieving Jews hated and mocked their one time kinsman, leader and ally, and as many Jews scattered at his own hand knew little about Jesus, the Lord allowed the signature gifts to continue, in Paul. Proving to the unbelieving Jews his Apostleship by many infallible proofs, he went forth, also using tokens and relics, and *cups*, to heal the sick.

As Paul's mysteries were slowly revealed while the sun set on Israel (for God no longer reckoned them as special amongst the nations, instead saving individuals on the merit of Christ's blood alone) for a time (for surely God will restore His favored nation, surely they will inherit their kingdom), God began to fill Heaven with the souls of those who trusted Paul's gospel. Whereas the earthly message required works and covenants and rules, Paul's Mystery required none of these things. An era and long hour of grace ensued and the signature gifts ceased, having no further purpose.

But the cessation was not permanent.

The sign-gifts waxed old (as did the Law), diminishing over time rather than vanishing in an instant. Some Jews were scattered as far as the Blessed Isles or other remote areas. For this cause, some of the supernatural characteristics of the earthly kingdom offering carried on as a trickling, drying stream.

And besides this, the Devil, who is cunning and crafty beyond comprehension, employs his favorite wile; namely, using *yesterday's truth as today's lies*. If he can get man caught up in doing and seeing (things necessary in the accompaniment of faith in times past, but wholly unnecessary this side of the finished work of the Cross), rather than trusting and resting, then he can do his greatest harm. More effective to hide the open manifestation of evil and rather encourage the soft and lethal deception of man-made religion. To this end, Satan himself was permitted to *charge* relics that had a past use for good, and repurpose them for evil; beguiling men to place their trust in things and spectacles that bring awe, forgetting the Lord who bought them.

Thus the Grail, with its deep representations of doctrine and fellowship and, in times past, healing and power, became a venerated and worshipped idol. Grail cults sprang forth all over Britannia and in Eire. Cauldrons came to represent fellowship, doctrine and power, only inverted and attached to powerful false goddesses instead of the Lord.

Blessed Mary foresaw this and did all to hide the relics until her Son would come again in the clouds, clothed with glory and victory, once again to enjoy the supper ritual with His twelve (and although she was sure any cup would do, Mary's heart was softened over *this cup*, for she was still a mother above all things and could not destroy it, though many times she tried).

Not only did the religious seek the Grail, but the very bones of Mary herself.

Knowing first the emptiness of idolatry and the unpredictable perversion and drunkenness of power, and then later learning the Pauline Mysteries as to *why* times had changed, a certain sect of the druids from Glamorgan made a pact with sweet Mary to forever hide these things.

And now Vivien held it in her hands as Lancelot lay healing from his wounds and, surely, the villains not far from the scene.

* * *

A woman of the strongest constitution, Vivien allocated herself no further time for weeping. She kissed once more the natural tomb that housed her most cherished friend and returned to the guest house (the very one where Lancelot had stumbled). Knowing he was too big for her to move, the Lady opted for combat instead of concealment. She hastened to the chamber within the northern-most peak of her castle: her very own bedchamber. A far more sophisticated and gaudy apartment than her simple little cottage at Llyn Fawr (tunnels, nay, an underground and underwater city, connected the Castle of the Lady of the Lake to her sacred lake in the Rhondda Valley, and other lakes besides, allowing her to travel much faster than waterborne vessel or steed between Cymru and the Continent). She opened a large silver chest, the perfect box to house its matching silvery contents.

Tiny faeries, who were as fireflies, zipped in orbiting spirals, helping her adorn herself in her very best armor, making a dramatic, albeit private, spectacle.

Vivien allotted herself one brief smile.

This set of protective wear was not just a breastplate with accompanying shin and forearm sleeves. This was *full armor* (rarely worn by the Cymry, even in full combat). It encompassed torso and pelvis in the mid-section, skin-tight and v-shaped. The whole of her collar and shoulder joints were encased within complex silver steel rivets. The ridges were finned high, peaking near the level of her chin. Similarly, fins surrounded the thigh, knee joints and the length of her calves as well. The helmet was a singular piece, formed to fit tightly over the nose; its sides formed two additional fins, guarding cheek to the base of the jaw, its only opening beneath the mouth down to the center of the throat.

Her under-armor was a soft but impenetrable white leather, with thousands of silver rings threading to compose a light mail. And she bore no cloak. To look upon the Lady was to look upon a silver-skinned goddess with not so much as a finger of pink flesh.

Merlin had known, at the dawn of the Saxon Wars, that the tribes and clans must not only possess the desperate bravery that accompanies the defense of one's soil, but also a skill that differentiated them from so many other cultures that had fallen under the insatiable Long Knife of the invading Germans. He witnessed Vivien's style when the priestesses would engage in sport or ceremony, and charged her to embark upon a great experiment. Seeing the superior balance and fluidity of the female warriors made famous by Boudicca of the Iceni Tribe (but spanning back millennia before), Merlin bade Vivien create a martial art that adapted her sect's *dance* with a radical commitment to counter-fighting (for the Saxons were ever overly aggressive and Merlin sought to take advantage of this, turning the imbalance of rage into a mortal liability).

Lastly, he requested awkwardly that the method must possess no enchantment or heathen arts. The common soldier, who farmed and practiced carpentry and often knew little of Jesus (save the pomp or corruption of the bishops who bore his name) and much more about fertility and harvest gods, would embrace such practices; but the rulers, wholly committed to the Christian faith, would reject it. Although priests and priestesses to the indigenous gods were found at all battles, using the power of music and hurling enchanted missives at the Saxon menace, the rank and file soldier could hardly incorporate those arts into the official martial art of the confederate armies.

The Lady understood the times and was mindful not to make the Cymry counter-fighting *dance* 'too pagan', and she and Merlin laughed oft at how even killing methods had been politicized.

The style of the armor she wore she had passed onto her foster-son, Lancelot, who in turn passed it onto the several Royal Clans and Tribes of the Cymry.

The Round Table Fellowship decided by consensus what to wear (aside from the standard shoulder shield that fasted cloak to armor) for each battle depending upon the terrain, whether the engagement was upon water or dry land, the weather, and lastly, for what manner of message they aimed to send to the enemy. On the occasions when all the confederated armies wore *this style of armor*, accompanied by their own sigils and banners, they were a brilliant, shining sea of silver stars, ready to shed blood with flawless grace. They sent the Saxons squirming back to the coasts, or to Germania, telling tales of immortals in magical armor; killing instruments who would not easily yield their lands, cattle or daughters.

And now the Lady who had taught the Britons how to fight, and to dress for a fight, encased in her full regalia, readied for a fight of her own.

And the Adder soon arrived for that fight.

It was evident that Merlin's body and scattered garments had been, as suspected, buried or taken. He searched around *Nimue's Fountain* and the branching streams it fed, still tinted crimson. Nothing. The anti-druid then turned to the guesthouse.

The faeries had sealed every entrance so that he couldn't cowardly slay Lancelot in his slumber. Frustrated with fruitless pounding and kicking, he turned his attention on the castle, finding the great hall wide open.

Candlesticks and torches lit the hall, making it clear that either the Lady herself was in residence, or else one of her many guests was lodging there by happenstance. The Adder had a mazer to find and Giants to rouse, and whoever lit the hall knew something of the whereabouts of the Counselor of Britain's corpse and the contents of his robe. He hollered out disingenuous greetings, opting to be coy. He hollered once more, beseeching response from the master of the home. *Or the mistress.*

None make an entrance like the Lady of the Lake. Whether by climbing up the heart of a sacred lake through the roof-ceiling of her forebear's underwater cities, causing her to appear to literally *walk upon water,* or by instantaneously manifesting as a floating lily beneath the surface of a stream (using abilities to hold her breath for unnatural spans of time, on account of the traits passed down to her from her mother), always accompanied by flutes or harps or other chimes played by the water spirits who were her maidservants – always with drama and purpose she appeared.

This time the flames licked her silver skin, and the dusky sky made of her a frightful and beautiful shadow; a silver shadow on fire. The Lady of the Lake made a flaming torch.

She stood, or floated, upon a marble base atop the flat top of a spiral stairwell, a full story above her unwanted visitor.

"Is that you, Vivien?" The Wise Man saw the slenderness of the form, elsewise it could have surely been a Cymry warrior, clad for the field. At that moment her arm swiveled, and the Dynion Hysbys saw the likeness of a weapon he had recently seen spill Italian blood.

A battle dirk.

So the mother favors the same unique instrument as the son, he noted, clearly identifying Vivien, as none but Lancelot wielded such a shaft, and this person was far too small to be he.

"I am not your enemy. Merlin betrayed us all and would have stamped out our kind forever with his grace message. He aims to end religion. Merlin is your enemy; we answer to the same council, Lady!"

How she was so soon at his throat is unknowable. She neither descended the stairwell, nor did she fly. At the outrage of the traitor uttering the name of her beloved twice, she would not suffer the black-robed shaman to speak it again.

"We are Cymry. We answer to no council. We bow before no league of that which congresses in murky places, laboring shamefully in the dark to enslave men. We are a country of laws and not of men. As our sovereign, the High King himself, decrees" – she pressed the spike into the side of the neck, the pressure causing a wincing push of panicked air – "let men worship what gods they will, only that they don't kill their neighbors for it."

The Adder's walking stick had a head that was

hard onyx with an inverted and blasphemous Awen engraved over its crown. With both of Vivien's hands gripping the battle spike, he made a desperate swing towards her knees.

The fabled silver armor made this a purposeless strike, but to anger the Lady. The broken stick clacked and clapped along the stone floor, resting upon a great yellow rug.

Vivien countered with a direct thrust to the fleshy part of the intruder's right shoulder, stabbing and turning the weapon with surgical violence.

His black robe became soaked with blood, quickly.

Then she clipped his left heel. Great screams bounced through the hall, the walls protesting by throwing them back at their source.

Lancelot had used this technique hundreds of times. By taking a right arm and a left leg, no weight distribution was available, no side could be favored. As a result, the opponent, processing his plight, just stood there, ripe for a quick kill.

The Lady snatched at the nape of his robe and pulled The Adder close. Leaving her helmet on, dropping her voice with authoritative indignation, she exclaimed, "Whatever your council did to my Merlin is of no god. You will live, should you escape the vast Wood of Broceliande, to tell your master that the Council will never have that which they seek." Playing with her bleeding prey, the Lady unveiled the Cup in all its simple splendor. "Now make haste to leave this place, lest you bleed out."

And haste he made, but not before turning just beyond the gate to mumble, "I overheard much during Merlin's final initiation." Followed by a mocking shout: "Why do you help men, when you are but the child of the woeful damned? YOU ARE DAMNED!"

Undaunted by his goad, she responded. "If you have only just now learned this, your thirty-and-nine years of training must be no greater than oils and charms and marketplace tricks."

He cursed her, still in a limping and lumbering run, gushing blood.

"YOU ARE DAMNED!"

* * *

Vivien helped restore Maelgwn, caring for and spending time with him until Gwalchmai arrived to fetch away the great warrior to help him escort Gwenhwyfar ferch Ogyrfan Fawr to be queried of Meurig and Onbrawst.

Although having Maelgwn alone with Gwenhwyfar presented risk, greater was the risk that more of the Council of Nine's lapdogs would follow. *Would they leave? Or would they continue to besiege her estate until at last she was overwhelmed and the Cup of Christ lost?* In the end, she calculated that the secret order was a far greater threat than her foster-son's erratic appetites.

Thus, she begged the Hawk of May take the contents of Merlin's pouch, providing no other direction than to deliver it privily to his mother, Gwyar, who was Morgaine of the Faeries and the Lady of the Isle of Apples. Vivien gave Gwalchmai knowledge of secret and seemingly nonsensical paths to conceal his discovery without compromising speed.

Thus, Gwalchmai would bear the Grail to Morgaine.

And thus Lancelot would escort the future queen to Arthur, alone.

Vivien disappeared into exile. She was not to be seen again by the world of men, save for her foster-son, who would from time to time ensure she did well, for many years.

CHAPTER 8
The Infidelity Punisher

The raven-haired Queen Gwenhwyfar, whose tiny hands beheld the face, whose large eyes beheld their mirror, whose repaired heart beheld its equal, whispered morosely and gravely to her true love.

"Mordred. You cannot remain here. This cannot endure."

His throat undulated and his mouth became dry. Bereft of sound, his *'cry-talking'*, with broken spaces betwixt each word, could muster little protest.

Through simple deduction, the lovers would be discovered. Their capital crime exposed.

Gwyar's absence.

The undue time nursing Bedwyr, who was mending rapidly.

The return of the king.

Gwalchmai's investigative looks.

The ongoing and unrepentant treasonous acts enjoyed by the covert couple risked ruining the only other thing they coveted in this life. Even their love and passion could not blind this aim. An aim they had shared in perfect unison well before they had met: the rule of Cymru.

Rule without Arthur.

Gwenhwyfar formerly had wanted power for its own sake. To do as she pleased, when she pleased, *with whom she pleased*, minus the cords of the Christian King.

Mordred, like his mother, had at first been drawn to the darker paths of Rhiannon and Hafgan. And he fancied the dragon god Hu. From his youth, he had been obsessed with categorizing the otherworldly beings and documenting their attributes in beautiful Latin script, which he had learned of his father King Llew and his grandfather, Meirchion. Mordred had cataloged four major categories, which he grouped as:

The people from the sky or the far-off north;

Their offspring with the daughters of men;

The spirits of these offspring, which he rendered as 'demons';

Elemental spirits.

Having skill of insight and foreknowledge just as otherworldly as the creatures he sketched on scrolls and in drawings and scripts, Mordred began to disregard the pomp and awe of his native gods. Before the age of sixteen, the lad had already concluded that the pantheon of Cymreig and Goidelic deities were nothing more than the worship of demons by the fearful and the opportunistic. This he did without reading one line of Scripture. His powerful mother worshipped, or was, a *real goddess,* and he could not discuss this with her for the dread of offending her.

Also like his mother, Mordred wed into a Northern family with Roman Catholic leanings and fidelities.

He was fond of, but did not love, the fair and

pious Kwyllog ferch Caw. But through the union of the house of Cynfarch with the house of Caw, the offspring of Mordred would render the North finally stable, at last restored to the glory of those long-ago years, after Rome and before the Boar, where they had been equal in power, right and might to the Silures of the South. *And the house of Mordred even branched back to the line of Meurig through Gwyar, making a singularly unique case for a Pendragon based in the North.*

Thus, following the Catholic path, albeit nominally, was the only course. The North and their Royal Clans stabilized by religious Rome, versus the South and their Royal Clans stabilized by the primitive Church of the Britons and by the Merlin and his boy king. *And Merlin had been missing three and more years.*

And so, as Mordred suffered the silliness of the Romish priests and dabbled with his demons, an emptiness grew within, of largely unknown origin.

This abyss was replenished when King Arthur and Queen Gwenhwyfar I sent their son, the prince Amr, for fosterage and training in the northern coasts. The youths were assigned the same patrols, and instant bonds were forged. A friend closer than a brother, Mordred found joy in his drab life in the person of Amr.

Then, by chance, the sharp dagger of a soot-blackened malefactor of no significance to anyone took Amr from Mordred in a senseless and meaningless act of murder.

This brought a finality of confirmation that justice was an illusion and that men were the playthings of demons and the pets of sky creatures. Mordred drank the lie, gulping the meaninglessness of existence. *Men were as cattle, and the less miserable of the cattle were the cattle allotted rule over other cattle.*

For this cause Mordred became a dark and empty thing, positioning and posturing quietly, as an adder glides within the thrush. A man of no reputation, and overlooked by the glowing and wildly popular Gwalchmai and his other speckled and sparkling brothers – Aggravaine, Gareth and Gaheris (all who served Arthur and his Summer Kingdom with disgustingly consistent virtue and honor) – Mordred was a shadow man in the kingdoms of Cyrmu.

But for his lack of charisma, the politicians and priests would have long ago truly considered that the eldest son of Gwyar had the better claim to succeed Arthur, whose new wife had yet to give him sons.

And Simon Magus paid him no regard besides.

Embarrassed that he had even baptized himself in gold to appear as if from Heaven, to bedazzle and impress (or, if this failed, to bully and badger) the High King, a disgust for the object of his love's cuckold gestated.

If not now, then in the fullness of times will my sons qualify to replace you; the South will fall. And then I will consume my sons as a Cronos, and rule all of Britannia, and the Emerald Isles, and the Continent besides.

Even in the fantasies unfolding in his mind, there was never a thought that he could actually defeat Arthur.

Mordred removed her hands from his cheeks softly, then clasped them taut. "I will not leave your side."

"You must."

"Gwen."

"Mordred, my love." What her past had

arrested, love had wrought. In her third decade, she at last possessed what blossoms in most women by seventeen: wisdom and prudence. The sensual creature who had once sought only to consume and devour had now given way to a soft-spoken, powerful lady, desperately trapped in an unwinnable battle. She began to speak to Mordred of *endurance* and patience. Of how rulers, even as mighty as Arthur, fall to injury, lose their vitality or throne. Where Mordred would blaze the embers of civil war and leave but a smoldering heap upon which to rule, Gwyar would have him make the intentional choice to be born again; to be a charismatic, kind and heroic noble that so captivated the Tribes, the bishops and the landholders that Gwalchmai would be supplanted, and the eldest of Arthur's sister's sons would naturally be promoted to heir.

Then, should the king fall ill or suffer tragedy, there would be hope that the people would accept Mordred as a stand-in, though married, as a titular benefactor to Gwenhwyfar.

She and Mordred never quarreled, but found no consensus; when they parted they were respectfully and carefully considering the views and possibilities put forth by the other. Both knowing that they would have their field and farmhouse whenever fortune and time smiled on their infidelity. Both knowing that they would have to wear the mask of faithful spouse to Kwyllog and to Arthur.

But could so strong a love even feign a neighborly church kiss, let alone lie with another?

* * *

Fortune and time did not smile on scores of

other young lovers who entered into adultery or infidelity. The thing that was in Gwyar (or part of Gwyar) had secured an almost permanent residence in the forefront of her mind and spirit. Using her anger and confusion to take her vengeful mind perpetually under the executioner's tent, where exotic killing instruments were spread before her upon a great table in her mind's eye, she gave herself to no other occupation than luring the guilty into the forest that she, the goddess, might visit justice on them more ferocious than a priest or God Himself could construct.

She had fashioned a garment after her custom, upon which, starting at her heart and spanning the length of her torso, was sewn a black spider with a red hourglass-dyed abdomen, in the concentric knot-work style of her kind. A singular grey piece that fit all but her feet and hands. Her black hair, which she had conformed to the conservative fashions of court, was yet again a thousand grey and black marble beads, such that bead and lock were indistinguishable.

Thus the Lady of the Lake and the Lady of Avalon were self-exiled in the same vast enchanted wood of Broceliande; the one for her role in committing a murder, the other for the purpose *of* committing murder. And, at that, many murders.

Morgaine of the Faeries made use of a method of scrying that involved a large basin finished with black glass filled with still, green, spring water. Through her unmatched skill working these arts, it was most effortless for her to discover or *see* adulterers, or uncover the untoward deeds of adulteresses. Once discovered, she sent familiar spirits sheathed in the skin of Fire Salamanders to influence the minds of the lovers, enticing them with irresistible drawings to an exciting, exhilarating and forbidden indulgence of the flesh in mystical and romantic Little Britain.

With her snug little circular huts for the modest and her large privy estates for the rich, and her waterfalls and lakes, her vineyards and intoxicating apples, her flowers and sunsets and, above all, her enchanted woods, Brittany herself was a seductress; an alluring, irresistible bosom for lovers.

Morgaine's warty and crested newts (the female salamander lacked a crest, being identified by an orange stripe along her lower back or tail) slithered as unknown bedmates into where the lovers would lie, combining the newts' love juices with their treacherous emulsions. The resultant mixture would create a toxin that decreased the mind's defenses, making it moldable, lacking in discernment, subject to suggestion – especially where carnal pleasures and impulse were concerned.

The salamander would create in the lovers an unquenchable flame only to be extinguished by traveling, whether near or far, to the romps of Broceliande. The spirit within the crawling thing would whisper all through the night until, at last, at the mercy of their sin and poisoning, they would make for holiday in Little Britain, for the dark spider Morgaine.

Forgetting her station and her vows, Morgaine could see not but Gwenhwyfar ferch Ogyrfan betraying her brother, could feel not but her brother betrayed by her son. She did not often agree with Arthur's strict neutrality when it came to matters of gods and religion, nor his insistence on combatting the corruption of central overreach, hurting her deeply when he had refused to stop Rome from invading Ynys Enlli with their church and pilgrims.

But Arthur was loyal.

But Arthur respected women.

But Arthur did not go a-whoring.

But Arthur did not seek a damsel, or even a dally.

He had chosen his love and loved his choice.

Morgaine intimately respected the virtue of her brother King Arthur, the erotic hauntings of his past notwithstanding. It pained the sorceress that she herself was the one, guised in ritual veneer, within a grove, in a cave, who had robbed him of the same.

Guilt, respect, perversion and above all the failings of the mortal condition, love of Cymru bound the witch to the boy-king and she came under conviction solid as brick, inseparable as set mortar; if a terminal clash was inevitable between son and brother, Morgaine would choose brother. She favored Arthur above Mordred – though she loved them both.

And she would punish others as a proxy for her son. Using her rage in adjudication of Gwen and Mordred's high crimes upon wayward lovers, she made no grand speeches, no riddles or sleight of wordplay upon her victims ere she killed them. Simple and direct, she would cry in a whisper, "How would your spouse feel?"

And then she would add them to a stack of skeletons, a bony altar of judgment.

CHAPTER 9
All the Snakes have Driven Themselves out of Cymru

"Are you prepared to die, Lord Arthur?"

The weight of the Giant's hand upon Arthur's shoulder was as six horses tethered to the stony, domed vault of a church, all concentrated upon one joint, which crackled and shifted in protest. The Pendragon winced, and his mind gasped at the feat that lay ahead. *How do I find victory this time?* These were hard thoughts for an undefeated warrior. One direct blow from Itto Gawr would be deformity at best and at worst, and more likely, the gruesome death of the mighty ruler of the Britons.

Curiously, the Giant's query was not threatening, nor in the pitch and manner that pricks the inception of combat. It sounded rather like the deep discussions that best friends have over cider, as if the Giant was genuinely interested in Arthur's personal peace with mortality.

The Merlin had taught Arthur to always answer as a mirror, except when the opponent is angry (and then with firm confidence, salted with grace and understanding). When they are jolly, be jolly in return; when grave, recompense with gravity. When mourning, cry with those who mourn.

Following the lesson in this scenario, Arthur was contemplative. And honest.

"I am not prepared to die."

"Oh?" Itto's left hand combed at his great beard, desperate to learn more of this great man.

"Not for myself, but for those to whom I am accountable. I bear a great weight" – here the Pendragon sought an opening for humor, shifting uncomfortably and giving an audible groan – "a burden nearly as heavy as your great hand upon my tiny shoulder."

Though his face seemed to be up above the clouds and his head just below the ceiling of the firmament, Arthur was almost sure he saw a blush. And a smile.

The shy laugh confirmed the king's assumption.

"Of course, of course. I am sorry." Itto removed his hand, causing Arthur to expel great breaths of relief, at once feeling several stones lighter. "I have walked this earth since not long after Noah's Flood. I've collected beards, gotten and lost many sons, vanquished armies, won damsels and raised the horn of victory scores of times. Scores. I have seen the best of men, and men's evil worst. And I tell you, Lord Arthur, something is afoot that rivals the malevolence from before the Flood."

"And when did your walks from ancient of days bring you to Gwynedd? For during the sum of the Saxon Wars, and yet by these three and one-half years of summer, how did someone, anyone, not – well," Arthur maintained a humorous, albeit timid, tenor, *"see you?"* Arthur's neck ached from looking straight up, only to see the braided grey beard swinging down as a great rope from Heaven.

"Cymru is my homeland!" Whilst conversing, the two had come to the peak of Bwlch y Groes, upon which opened a small plain cleared of trees, with no obstacles save a few large, craggy rocks like natural borders, making a rim along the cliff of the mount.

The perfect setting for the two actors to recreate the drama of King Brutus and King Gogmagog.

Itto inhaled the view, still struck by awe after so many lifetimes enjoying the valleys spreading below. For the beauty of Cyrmu; of waterfalls and woods, of mysterious caves and caverns under the ground and yet in the waters, the winding vales and rocky gorges, the greens and blues found in no other land. Cymru brought wonderment and reverence, even to the otherworldly beings.

He continued. "I don't know where my father came from, other than that it was from somewhere called *the remote North*. As for my mother, I knew her not, only that she was a princess of striking beauty from Machynlleth, less than a morning's walk from here." Now Itto recompensed a laugh. "Or less than an hour, with the stride of these walkers." Bending them, he made a stool of a tree stump that had the circumference of the Sun, and sat. It was humid and the mighty thing sweated as pools that, when meeting with the dirt, immediately caused the dry summer ground to be as a muddy creek or farmer's trench. Ringing buckets of salty muck from his beard, he explained to Arthur things that not even Merlin had known.

"Know you how that our Isles have hundreds of stone circles and faerie rings, or in some cases Giant rings, and that the scholars and scribes rumor more here in Cymru and Eire than anywhere else the world over?"

"My friend taught me as much, aye."

"The Merlin? Of course. I shall come back to the subject of your friend. I came to learn that once, all land masses were one great breadth of earth; these were in the days of a man called Peleg, and his generation marks the time that the High God broke apart the nations. Thousands of diverse kinds of damnable things like me were either isolated, or subsequently fled here, because the Isles, when they were not Isles, were located near the northern strongholds of the Giants near the north, or center of the earth.

"As the land mass was broken up, the residue became the Blessed Isles in the Sea, upon which we now stand.

"That the stone circles are as the sands of the sea is because each of them represents a principle that threads all spirituality, and all religion: *As Above, So Below*. Every circle down here represents a formation of stars, or a tracing of their courses up there." One of Itto's six fingers pointed to the heavens. Arthur was transfigured back to his youth, when Illtud or Merlin would teach on these things. Hundreds of questions rushed into his mind, and he couldn't wait to hear more. "The Fae dance for the stars and build circles for the stars, cones of ethereal power where men ought never to tread. Giants erect gargantuan stone circles, bury their dead, and perform rituals to the very same stars."

"The legends say that Giants and the Fae are bitter rivals."

"Aye. But mark and remember the tale of Brutus and Gogmagog, Lord Arthur." Once more, the Giant pointed to the skies. "They may hate each other, but they have the same ancestry, the same stars, the same angels! And there is more." Now Itto stood, releasing another spout of sweat that muddied the surrounding dirt. "Many of these hills, in what the Romans called *the Celtic Wilds*, are where some of my kind sleep. The armies of Brutus, and other migrations of men, decimated our numbers and then, above five hundred years ago, Jesus came into and went out of the world of men."

Arthur minded not the stench and sweaty mud. He had to hear more, wishing that he and the great man towering above were enjoying cider together. The way Itto moved his hands in gestures, accompanying his oratory, impressed Arthur. Had he not wanted Arthur's beard and been moved to displace the northern princes, the monster and the king were meet to be great friends. "And what did the Lord do?!" Arthur asked, now inquisitive as a small child.

"Within about a generation of His ascension, we began to simply go to the caves, enclaves or other dark places, some as deep as the Abyss itself, and fall into long, irresistible slumber. A sleep like death, yet not dead.

"Now, I don't understand all of this, and only share what I have gathered over too many lifetimes. It would seem that we were only ever allowed to draw breath in the first place to show the power of God's Son in defeating us. Beasts for the Hero to slay. Or, from another perspective: what the Fallen Ones meant for evil, God repurposed for good. And it would seem that we were meant to sleep, that we are *reserved* for a similar future purpose as well."

Here Arthur exercised his uncanny gift of deduction.

"So, if you are awake, then…"

"Correct; the end of the world is nigh. Or someone would us have, through their arcane arts to make it as so."

"But there have been Giants and monsters, though rare, since the time of Jesus."

"I concur, Lord Arthur. We are only ever roused by some dark science or occultic arts, and these exceptions are so isolated as to be off the table as part of God's plan for the Ages. Anomalies. Moreover, some of the small descendants of our kind do walk amongst us. Most are inactive. Some engage in minor mischief, in service to the leaders of men who likewise render themselves sons of gods."

The discourse here caused Arthur to think towards his father-in-law, the Chief Ogyrfan.

Itto continued. "This 'unwilling awakening' is different, and a thousand times graver. This time, a black-robed druid brought me from the Deep. Through his spells, he put it into my mind so to see dozens more made to rise, and his enchantment drives me to kill all, even you, to devour and drink blood, making hell on earth before the Son of Man comes with His elect angels to send me unto my place.

"I think, Lord Arthur, that Merlin may have known something of the plans of these druids to bring about the end of the Age, and that calamity befell him for this cause."

The bewitchment that drove Itto to seek and kill and destroy welled, a miserable, gentile spirit with no soul, under witchcraft from the pit of Hell, driving and harassing and compelling him.

"Ask me if I am prepared to die," he beseeched the king.

"Are you, my friend Itto Gawr, prepared to die?"

Being rendered as *friend* by the one for

whom he had such regard greatly aided him in mustering the courage to finish his course. "Do you see those stones near the cliff?"

Arthur turned and then verified the outlay of the field of battle. "I do."

"When I rush upon you, I pray you have the speed of Lancelot. Roll to the side of my wounded ankle."

Arthur withdrew himself, gave ground to near the cliff, and spake these words, which live on in the songs of the bards. They memorialize the great thing done by Itto, who could have slain the king, but spared him, and thus the whole of Cymru.

The quote did something greater than exercising mercy; it gave the monster humanity.

"Itto Gawr is the bravest *man* King Arthur has *ever* known," said the Pendragon.

Hearing this, a contented and gaping smile developed under the perfect grey beard, coinciding with the very moment he made his rush upon the king. Missing the mark, he stumbled upon the stones, plunging from a height that rivaled the fall of his kinsman Gogmagog.

And thus the Giant resisted the dark power and died for the dream of Caermelyn and the hope of King Arthur, whom he had come to revere deeply.

The stanzas, poetries and ballad-songs of the bards spread rapidly throughout Cyrmu and abroad, celebrating how Arthur, far from idle in the Britons' era of tranquility, had saved the North and all of Britannia from the menace of Itto Gawr.

The Saxon slayer now the Mighty Giant Hunter.

Whereas many had prognosticated that Baeden would be the height of his star, Arthur was becoming as popular as Jesus.

But not all loved the Silure king.

That such a victory was enjoyed in the lands of Caw and Meirchion and Cynfarch *and Maelgwn* further unified some of the Ravens, whose affection for the High King, who had risked all to come champion them, intensified. However, others viewed it as an insult, a condescending example of the fact that once again the race of Silures had had to do what they could not. *A protective uncle who kills the wolves only when the village can see him pound upon his chest before all.*

And of course those who coveted the profits of war loathed his act of single combat mitigating loss of life, and expenses. And debt.

As for Maelgwn Gwynedd, he had wanted this rare moment, *the greatest warrior versus the greatest threat,* to champion his people. His credibility waxed and waned with the ebb and flow of his fractured personages and roving residences. For the first time ever, he empathized with the negative sentiments from the leaders of the Old North.

Stealing away to one of the tiny islands apart from the mainland, his bubble overcame him, resulting in his engaging in a wine-soaked orgy with flesh of his own kind (for his unbridled lust was not limited in scope to just women). Trying to slay himself afterwards with Merlin's ghostly dagger, he bled much, and slept long, but died not.

Taliesin learned of the untoward acts and chastised Maelgwn unrelentingly for his wanton thirsts and for the sake of his children, who were either bastard sons and daughters of the painted Picts or deflowered Cymry girls.

Because the bubble burst and went to its temporary abode, and not for Taliesin's calls for repentance, Maelgwn was overcome with great guilt (though he showed little emotion when alone, and none in public). Instead, he established six chapels under the Bishopric of Llandaff, and gave himself to the memorization of hundreds of additional Scripture verses to temper his flesh.

Mordred scraped himself from Gwen (for the two were as one flesh) and returned to his father's lands, determined to feign being a *good man* to rival Gwalchmai. To earn a seat at the Round Table, should one of the twenty-and-four retire or pass on, to make an unspoken case for the throne.

Gwen II faced an impossible personal and political quandary. The tribes wanted male heirs from their famed liege and their famed liege wanted daily to lie with his wife, for she was his life's love and Arthur had discovered nothing of Gwen's infidelity. Since coming to Caerleon to be queen, she had forced herself upon a dozen men, continually violating the king's bedchamber and her own body with their members. Now a part of her died each time her own husband lay with her. *Now it was adultery against Mordred, the only man she would have talk to her, let alone touch her painted body.*

Her whole life was a ruse and a deception; formerly of want, now of necessity.

But for how long? There were no wars, no invaders, and only the occasional Giant, which Arthur and Gwalchmai would quickly vanquish.

Mordred and Gwenhwyfar II wove a yarn about Gwyar being urgently called away to provide nursing for a dying kinsman of her estranged spouse so that Arthur would have no cause to investigate her abrupt exit from Caerleon. Though, during her time at court,

Gwyar and Arthur had grown closer, theirs was the kind of relationship where many moons could pass without letter or visit, then, when at last they met again, to resume as if there had been no interruption. Moreover, the distraction of finally getting to have the woman he had always wanted created a sort of fog that separated brother and sister.

And so, a year became three, and then two more, and Cymru approached the median of twenty years of peace and greatness. *Halfway through the Golden Age.* And a golden light it was, one of the too few chapters in the generations of Man where liberty, prosperity, and peace reigned. The stains of Saxon blood, of invasion, violation and constant terror, faded upon a satin of Cymreig greatness.

But, as the common person had joy in recreation, occupation and procreation, the rulers toiled with actual monsters roaming the countryside, with territorial tensions, with vain genealogies, with threats both external and of their own design. The heaven on earth was hell to maintain.

And Gwyar, now so many years a spider, had herself woven a hell of her own. She did not lure, trap and kill wayward unfaithful lovers for the sum of this time. At the first, oft; later, intermittently; at the last, seldom. Rather, she would brood and curse all that was called good for the despair that she could neither tell her brother of his harlot's treachery by her own son, nor stand with her immoral son against her righteous brother.

After some time, the days came where she simply hated infidelity, but hated solitude more. Thus the same enchantress who had once coveted her days alone on Ynys Enlli tending plants and birds, streams and orchards, sulked about, lonely, ever longing for a tea, a cider, or a walk with her sons, her brother or Vivien.

Vivien!

Mother!

The Lady of Lake.

She goes as the wind, where she listeth, but could she have remained here all these years? Broceliande was vast as it was mysterious, its breadth that of a small country. The silvery mistress had been neither seen nor even whispered of during Gwyar's years at court. Had she returned to the affairs of men or, like Gwyar, had she convicted herself of some personal crime, likely in connection to whatever conspiracy and malevolence had killed the Merlin, handing down a strong sentence of shackles of loneliness far away from all? Alone with sins and mistakes, regret her ever-companion…

If Gwyar could practice scrying to discover strangers, surely her *Sight* could discover her foster-mother.

"Merlin's pouch!" she hollered aloud, to none save an attentive audience of owls and salamanders.

The contents of the haversack were well known to Gwyar; protecting it was part of her function as Lady of Avalon, and it was now safely concealed and under her control. The worn leather that held it would now be the conduit for finding the Lady of the Lake, for surely she had touched it while giving the Cup to Gwalchmai.

It was an early winter morning when she exercised the scrying basin. The waters, once still, began to swirl, changing from green to the darkest blue. Swirling, swirling and thrice more;

then still as a looking glass it became. Clipping five tiny shavings from the strap of the pouch, she gently laid them upon the looking glass and spoke her imprecations, charging the god of forces to guide her eyes and make true their aim.

Gwyar's head jerked up from the basin, startled at her own folly.

"All this sorcery and magick, and lo, the Lady is simply home in her estate!" Gwyar laughed. At herself. "Perhaps reason and logic first before bothering the spirits, eh?" She could have sworn that the owls also mocked her with well-timed hooting.

Then her light moment became weighted, as her eyes were again drawn to the scrying bowl. Vivien's castle was still apparent, and the Lady sweeping and singing and of warm disposition as clear in vision as if she were in flesh. The scene widened, broadening further and then narrowing rapidly to fix upon a tree of oak which seemed somehow the elder of its neighbors; the ancient of the ancient oaks. *Next to?* – nay, *in* the oak was the form of a person revealed.

Gwyar peered hard. Perhaps a servant of Vivien's estate had also touched the pouch and had thus been brought into view? Perhaps it was an apparition or the incessant mischief of the Fae, who loved to bewilder and distract by making game and sport of the serious affairs of men.

Yet it was none of these things.

'Twas the form of a man – yet only in form, as he was enveloped by an orb of the whitest light.

"Merlin?" The words were an involuntary mutter, no more.

The still waters swirled, this time in reverse. Thrice and thrice again, and then still again; the scrying bowl would reveal no more.

Though the finding her was swift, the journey was slow. For the woods seemed infinite. Vast Broceliande.

When she finally approached the archway to the fore-entry, one hundred and seventy thousand petite faeries illuminated the path, lighting each of her steps and then disappearing with the next, as though fireflies with appetites for dramatic entry.

If only harps and Illtud's choirs accompanied this, she mused.

The otherworldly beings, as a swarm of bees, labored in concert to open the heavy double-doors and then burst asunder again to their places, finding perfect sockets from which to illuminate the great hall.

Standing at the base of the spiral stairway, in the self-same spot where had stood The Adder so many years ago, now stood legend's most infamous black witch, looking straight up at legend's most revered white witch; hair perfect, dress perfect, face glittering and shimmering, looking down on her foster-daughter with a smile so bright that the little faeries became jealous and dimmed, then chuckled and shone again, straining to compete.

After an embrace that stopped time and seemingly healed the world, *or at least their world,* the Lady of the Lake started.

Influenced by growing years in Brittany, she asked, "And how is Arthur's *Camelot,* daughter?" Correcting her own diction and accent, she restated, "*Caermelyn.* How is Arthur's golden fortress and glorious kingdom?"

"Camelot. I like how that feels upon the tongue," replied Morgaine. "Oh, I really like it! I feel that *Camelot* will be the word that long endures, outliving us in bardic ballads and minstrel's songs." Taking her foster-mother by both hands, she giggled. "Camelot shines, Mother, and freedom yet shines with her!" Seeing through the joy of reunion and discovering the melancholy that was in the Mistress, Morgaine sought out words of comfort to lend to the great Lady.

"You are the very foundation of Arthur's Camelot." Morgaine retained one hand, using the other to guide a stroll. "Excalibur, the Sword of Power." The little helpers, engrossed in the conversation, shone brighter still, making a similitude of the sword and emulating its legendary slashing whistle, lending drama to Morgaine's kind and edifying compliment. "Forged from the saber of angels that protected knowledge and access to eternal life when Man left his first estate, the authority and virility of the Land, whose holder is rightful king, whose granter was" – again Morgaine gave a sprawling grin, perfect white teeth emerging as the sunrise – "you, Vivien."

"And now I hear whispers that priests are the kingmakers and that the Tribes have no voice save that of the local bishops, themselves royalty with no interest but to hold power and land. And more, that the druids grow few and weak and that only the vulgar superstitions of the Dynion Hysbys hold sway."

"Well, your political fervor has not diminished," quipped Morgaine, still all beams.

More like pithy dialogue ensued for the space of about half an hour, and then the Lady of the Lake cut to the quick.

"I cannot return to Cymru, daughter."

Morgaine's rejoicing turned to tears, and the

sun set on her grin. "You cannot return, and I know not why you even left. It has been ten years."

The witches' walk had brought the two out along the stony outdoor spiral surrounding the turret of a high tower. No faeries provided light here, with only the starry onlookers above winking and giving sporadic and stingy illumination betwixt and between nighttime clouds.

"I am held hostage by an old, old man." Vivien's words were cryptic. For the residue of guilt. And for Morgaine's protection. Should she know all, she could be counted an accomplice after the deed, and her life be put in great peril (though Vivien did reckon that it would take Lancelot and a small army to vanquish the little woman, full of darkness and kindness, adorned in black from head to foot, before her).

"You are the Lady of Lake and answer to no man!" Morgaine tried the lever of feminine resilience and pride.

The trap sprang not.

Temperate and guarded, Vivien continued.

"I bargained with the only thing that had real power. The flesh betwixt a woman's legs."

Morgaine's eyebrow lifted. "Bargained for what?"

"To preserve our goddess. To ensure that she outlives Rome." Vivien looked down into the abyss of the treetops below.

The dark enchantress was becoming impatient, and now bewildered, with the scrambled discourse of her polar mistress. An interruption was offered: "Our goddess cannot die. She is eternal."

At this intentionally naïve untruth, the Lady

of the Lake pressed upon Morgaine's heart, her fingertips greeting the thing that was in, or was part of, or was, Gwyar. "My little Queen of the Faeries, you know this is not so. Many of the old gods died in the waters from above the heavens, and many more have had their flames at last exhausted." The palm joined the fingertips and pressed harder. "And some use occultic tricks to continue themselves. Only one God is eternal."

"You sound like the priests, Lady, if so be that you are referencing the Hebrew God." Gwyar's bronze eyes were brazen.

"Nay, child, they do ever pervert every detail about the Father of Lights. And herein is my great sin." Vivien paused whilst Gwyar's fuming was assuaged, desperate to know why she had lost her foster-mother for so many years. "I allowed my hatred of those men. And o, that I hate them" – lightning crackled through the night, followed by the shriek of owls – "to blind my hatred of the One they misrepresent."

"An easy snare to fall upon; I do this oft," offered Gwyar.

"I do not know the Eternal God, but for the hatred of his false emissaries, I sought to hurt one whom I knew had joined him. One whom, I allowed myself to be convinced, would destroy, not with sword or army but with word and persuasion, all religions. Even our own."

In her grace, Gwyar chose not to utter the wizard's name, her tongue holding. Barely.

"And so." Great shame intoned Vivien's words. "I struck a bargain to protect our goddess in exchange for stopping that special one from making league with this God."

"Speak plainly, I beg you." The foundation of the tower shifted.

"Our goddess will live forever, as the Church of Rome will suffer us to keep her. This was the bargain in exchange for releasing Nimue to rid of us of our newly-become common enemy."

Now the gravity and weight of the matter was known by Gwyar.

"But I repented at the course and sought to arrest the plot," she went on. "I am shackled for plotting with an old man who promised to keep my goddess alive."

"Alive by folding her into Mary."

"Yes."

At this, and at last, Vivien had shared at least the bits and pieces of her swerve from sanity so many years ago, and right before the Cymry's triumph at Mynydd Baeden, with another soul.

Now Maelgwn and Gwyar knew. Both of her foster-children. Connected by an old lie, an older love, and the future challenge of what would become of it all.

Morgaine buried her face in her hands. She had killed. She had lied; she was no better or no worse than Vivien. Error was no respecter of station or persons. The impact of Vivien's plot had a further reach: this alone was the matter. Grace wrestled against the creature within Gwyar. And grace won. She brought her head aright. Fixing the problem was paramount, nothing more. "What old man, mother?!" she demanded.

"Your grandfather."

Morgaine's countenance recovered, and hope returned in the twinkling of an eye. She gave a seemingly out of place, silly response. "My grandfather Tewdrig is long buried at his well in the village Mathern; was he not your friend?"

"You would make me say the Crone's name?" Vivien had not yet comprehended Gwyar's redirection. "Your husband's grandfather, Meirchion the Mad."

The dark little one roared in laughter. "We have exiled ourselves over folly, and you are in prison for–"

"I hardly see the humor, Gwyar–"

"Meirchion the Mad is dead, Vivien. Dead!" The sorceress then delivered the hug of hugs, followed by: "And Arthur, our just king, will reject all hearsay not delivered from the Crone's accusatory lips himself!"

"Dead lips?" Vivien dared to hope.

"Dead lips!" Morgaine affirmed.

Morgaine of the Faeries looked long at Vivien, the Lady of the Lake. Two flawed goddesses. Two brilliant women, who were more Christian in so many ways than the pseudo-Christians they loathed (for the ladies were continuously learning experientially what the Merlin had learned academically from the mysterious preacher).

"Let us make haste to win our country back," Morgaine declared.

Every gesture of Vivien's agreed. Fists pumped in the air (for she was a warrior and knight, as well as a regal and maternal figurehead for the Tribes).

As she gathered and packed her things, a query arose.

"My little daughter. You said 'we' have exiled ourselves. Why have you been long in these forests of your own accord?"

Gwyar sputtered, and muttered, "I shall tell you along the way. Along the way *home*."

CHAPTER 10
If One More of My Pagan Friends Disappears

"I will not abide lies," Arthur's voice bellowed, and the bishops to a man cowered with chin tucked to chest and left shoulder elevated, as a child squirming from the switch.

"We have summonsed him to court, but he was delayed in his coming."

The blue of the king's eyes was eclipsed by the black, becoming all pupil in a glare of disbelief conjoined with disrespect. "Delayed?" he said. And his teeth did not separate.

"He cited lack of familiarity with the roads, having not visited the vales in many years." Bedwini was Arthur's chief counselor (except for Taliesin, who was often occupied with herding the lost sheep that were Maelgwn's ongoing mischief). His voice calmed any storm, and neither friend nor foe ever had ought to say against the gentle presbyter. "If I might inquire, friend," he continued, disregarding the rickety excuse of the indicted, truant visitor, "what caused you to suspect dishonesty out of the–"

"The whelp." Arthur had to come to refer to him by this designation. And only this.

Arthur could not tell the clergy how he had been provoked to explore the *real* whereabouts of his sister, now gone for so many seasons' turnings.

His nocturnal demoness had begun to return, levitating and calling to him from above his bed. And this was how he reckoned that something was amiss with Gwyar.

The Pendragon had objectively studied the nature of his curse, and now in the fourth decade of his life, had drawn a few conclusions (though, he acknowledged, he did not comprehend the matter).

As done a hundred times over the years, his thoughts summarized his hypotheses:

Gwenhwyfar II was Arthur's one true love.

When sent away, as a mere boy, to be made king of Glamorgan and Gwent, the Tribes demanded the spring rites.

Arthur and Gwyar were the actors. He as virility, she as fertility. She was masked and painted as the vicar of both the land and the moon; Arthur, unknowingly, lay with his sister. And not just intercourse. A ritualistic act that involved every nerve-ending and created an in-between space of body and spirit.

Being so young, Gwyar became a type of replacement for Gwenhwyfar in Arthur's heart. For as a youth, his fantasies of Gwen matched the realities of the acts with Gwyar.

Gwyar was a witch, somehow, and just maybe the legendary Primal Witch from the Ancient of Days. When the Fallen Angels knew the daughters of men and got children by them, there was a first witch 'created'. She was the true Goddess above all Goddesses, by reason of her primacy and power. Too many rumors held the propensity of truth about Gwyar being one and the same with this Goddess', or more precisely, demigoddess', disembodied spirit, though Gwyar came forth innocent from Queen Onbrawst's blessed womb.

Through no fault of Gwyar's, a curse or connection tethered the siblings. Thus, for diverse reasons, Arthur felt, she would reach out to him through the apparition and recreate the forbidden deed, and remind him of their bonds, causing him to cry out to both loves of his youth in terrorized and erotic delusion.

Whether Gwyar knowingly did this or whether by the control of the vexing spirit, Arthur knew not. Gwyar was years away from court, and the king doubted he would engage her about it, were she there.

As Gwenhwyfar II had re-entered Arthur's life, the void had been filled and the visitations had ceased. Indeed, life was *heaven on earth* with his queen; yet Gwyar had begun to 'visit' Arthur again. Terrorizing and relentless, and only when Gwen did not, for this reason or that, share the king's bed.

The king's conclusion was that some trouble or peril or need had befallen his sister.

That the incompleteness was caused by a problem in his own bed and his own marriage never received a passing thought by the happy regent.

After three recurring 'visits', he decided to make the simplest of inquiries to the North.

Validation was swift and clear.

Gwyar had never been summonsed to her husband. There was no ill relative, no need for a healer or nurse. And of a certain, she had not simply decided to stay in the north with her Catholic spouse. Moreover, none in the kingdoms of Gwynedd, Rheged or Ynys Mon had seen her, for the sum of the time she had been absent from Caerleon.

Now Arthur felt burden and guilt for letting himself wander so adrift between Gwenhwyfar's legs. And when not distracted there, so preoccupied facilitating quests, slaying Giants (though none were the equal of Itto for valor, or skill, or courage) and administering his Golden Age that he had failed to long ago inquire about his sister.

A problem he would cure, with swiftness and ferocity.

Returning to Bishop Bedwini, his response was short. Vague. "It has been about five years. At some point I would need my sister, or she would need me. It was a matter of time. How much longer?"

"He approaches, Lord."

Arthur did not convene the Round Table Fellowship for discourse about Gwyar. He suspected Church involvement, and would not be triangulated by fluid versions of their accounts. And so, as had been done so many years ago, all the renowned clergy – be they of Popish or British persuasion – were convened.

He made them stand in a semi-circle in the middle of the great amphitheater of Caerleon. Like ants under a looking glass. Empty of the throngs and cheers of a chariot race, the ruckus and rants at the games of arms, or the articulate screaming of a clamorous political debate. Instead, only the howl of the wind and the rush of the Usk River provided accompaniment. These rendered the men, who thought themselves somewhat, small. And Arthur, pacing and circumambulating them, an echo following each word, immense.

Even before the guest was within range to hear them, Arthur had already lashed into them.

He was not tarrying for the whelp.

"Ten years ago, in this very spot, we won our country but lost its most precious treasure; all in the self-same night! Right here." Excalibur was thrust forcefully into the stone tiles, sparks erupting as the sword met stone. And the stone gave way. "Right here! Right here was the last place I saw my friend, my counselor, MY MERLIN!"

The whelp was now the opposite side of the bishops and priests and directly behind Arthur. The Pendragon's head swiveled and cocked with the motions of a dragon, befitting the man who bore its banner when fighting. "And I will not lose my sister over another vain theological conspiracy!"

Arthur was conflating the real conspiracy to remove Merlin (and his influence) from the king's ear with Morgaine of the Faeries' absence. A reasonable assumption, but the fuming liege had missed his mark; the Churchmen, though glad to be rid of one more heathen, were ignorant as to the cause of her supposed demise. However, so rare was it that the just and temperate king spoke in anger, let alone rage, that there was no winning by words. So each of them looked to the theatre floor, in silent innocence.

But the other invited guest was not innocent.

Cadfan, now fully installed as bishop of the Popish parish on Ynys Enlli, tried to match eyes with the visitor, tried to warn him that saying little was good, saying nothing would be better. Cadfan was unaware of a plot to displace Gwyar, but he was well aware of the connivings of the late Meirchion the Mad. And to him was the visitor intimately connected.

"Mordred."

"Lord Arthur Pendragon ap Meurig ap Tewdrig, King of all Cymru and Emperor of the world, I salute you, uncle." A bend at the waist with eyes up; by no means a full bow.

King Arthur's face was devoid of emotion, and he spoke through the pretentious salutation, giving it no regard.

"You lied."

"It was five years ago."

"Unlike men, lies do not wax old with age; like wine, they only become more potent over time."

"I was just a boy," Mordred offered.

"How old?" queried the king.

"Twenty and four," Mordred responded.

"But fourteen years younger than I. And speaking of fourteen, at that age, a full decade ere you blame youth for dishonesty, I was–"

"King of Glamorgan and Gwent, the Pendragon of all the Tribes. Lord Arthur." Mordred continued with his pretense of formality and flattery. "Second to only the Nazarene, there is but one Arthur. I am not you. I *am no Arthur.*"

"Enough!" Freeing the legendary blade from the breached floor, he gazed upon the hilt and its famous scripting. "I have but two questions, Raven." (Though Mordred was half Silure, Arthur here associated him with his paternal line, showing frustration that, yet again, problems pointed north). He sheathed Excalibur, notably in a scabbard fashioned by his sister, and stepped aggressively towards her son. Taller than the younger man, Arthur peered down into his eyes as if it was God Himself looking upon a trembling lost soul, quivering without excuse at the Judgment Day.

Mordred felt it.

Did the Saxons who fell by his sword feel it too?

Authority. Real power and authority.

The Bear of Glamorgan was not just king because some vain genealogy and the consent of the tribes had made him so. He was king *because he was a king*. A will like unto a piece of iron was upon Mordred, and he bent underneath it. That Mordred was doing as he pleased with every part of Gwenhwyfar's body now brought a terror through him, causing his pale skin to turn hues of white as the paints and dyes used upon houses.

Ghostly and slave to Arthur's will, he dropped to a knee, nearly confessing all, barely able to muster a lie.

Mordred's thoughts went unto earlier in the morning.

He had not been truant in his entrance to Caerleon.

He had not grown unfamiliar with the roads from Gwynedd to Gwent.

Far from foreign to him, he traversed them at least once a fortnight; in hours where none labored and all slept, and ever under cloak, and ever with a different steed.

He had arrived early and had audience with his life's love, the Queen of the Britons.

In a moment of sheer panic, Gwenhwyfar had deduced that Arthur's harshness over the one lie was a ruse to manifest *the real lie*, or five years of lies. That he had convened the Church, and no warriors or chieftains, rendered the matter all the more dire. Perhaps Arthur had discovered the affair and was to shame Mordred for adultery (and for treason) before God's representatives, making straight the pathway to kill him then and there. Though it was unhealed wounds of losing Merlin enraging the king, the two that lived ever under a shadow of guilt thought that this day might be their comeuppance.

They did not make love; there were no impassioned embraces or poetic meetings of the lips.

Mordred had tried, over the time of the affair, to be a better man, to earn his renown – yet his face was not yet known by any knights of significance, save his own household. Arthur grew in strength and fame and majesty, and the plan to 'endure to the end and then assert as the rightful heir' seemed as a far-off and unreachable country. Arthur was only ten-and-four years older than Mordred and, should calamity or accident not befall the Cymreig Emperor, they would both be very old together, with Arthur enjoying Gwen's bed and Mordred relegated to a hidden plaything in a child's cupboard.

If Gwenhwyfar murdered the king, then the overwhelming consent of the Tribes would promote Gwalchmai, who had already been granted Pembroke as a sub-kingdom over which to rule and practice for a broader role as Wledig, or Battle Commander, over all the kingdoms of the Britons.

This would profit the forbidden lovers in no wise.

No; Mordred must gain favor with court and amongst men so that, when Arthur fell, they would accept Mordred being steward of his kingdom, and his wife, with minimal murmuring.

So, in misery, they had suffered the waiting.

And then the emissaries of the king demanded Mordred make haste unto Caerleon, to answer charges of lying to the Pendragon regarding the whereabouts of Gwenhwyfar's ever-thorn, Morgaine of the Fairies.

Did she know?

If so, why had she not simply exposed Gwen, to whom she was no ally, and been done with it?

The couple often wondered these things. As days gave way to months and months faded into years, Morgaine's failure to make manifest the affair could now be viewed as her deliberately withholding the matter from Arthur, rendering her an accomplice. Justice delayed, seeping into advocacy of the behavior.

Or had something else befallen her?

The not knowing, blended with the summons by Arthur himself, left Mordred and Gwen just looking upon one another, with high probability that this would be the last day they would see one another. They gave themselves to love's gaze and love's stare until his departure could no longer be put off.

Gwenhwyfar implored Mordred to deny any charges of infidelity and assert the right of appeal to the Round Table, that his peers might judge the case. He would go unarmed, as he was no match with sword, fist or spear for Cymru's second greatest warrior (for only Maelgwn had more might or skill at arms than did Arthur, son of Meurig), and a confrontation would be to no profitable end.

Deny the affair, feign a thoughtful motive for the lie about his mother. This was the course.

"I love you, Mordred."

"I love you, Gwen."

And out he went, in partial contrition and partial sophistry.

To a second knee he fell, a few drops of urine escaping trouser. And with real fear.

"Your best friend Bedwyr was maimed, monsters were roaming the land, and I had no idea where my mother had gone. I wished not to add to your despair, and spared the worry by lying. I thought she would surely return soon, and when she did not, I feared greatly the snare of my own lie. To this day, I do not know what became of her. Please, lord, forgive me." The words were broken, and the contrition appeared sincere.

The subject appeared to be *the only subject*, and not a snare to delve into other matters...

Arthur grasped a handful of Mordred's curly locks. "Dark as your mother's. Rise to your feet." The Iron Bear's ferocity was only surpassed by the Iron Bear's grace. Something was deeply untrustworthy about the constitution of his sister's son, but Arthur believed him guiltless *on this matter.* Gently lifting Mordred by his hair and then delivering a brotherly wallop upon his shoulder, Arthur turned back to the gods of the villages, the deities of the cantrefs, the lords of the kingdoms, the gatekeepers of men's souls. On this day they were as grasshoppers before the son of Meurig.

He walked up and down amongst them again, pent up with ten years of not knowing what they had done to his wizard, his eyes stalking them as if to say: *He may have lied, but you made her disappear, didn't you?!*

Arthur roared a great lamentation. "Let men worship what gods they will, only that they don't kill their neighbors for it! Was this law, and the rights it contains, too grievous to bear?! Where is she?"

On many, many occasions these men had been great friends to Arthur and his family; on many more they had given authoritative pieces of advice that were more edicts than they were counsel to the king. He had signed land grants to and with many of the assembled. Dyfrig, Teilo, Cadoc, Illtud, Cadfan, Bedwini, Aiden; legends with stars as bright as Arthur's, heroes and legends in their own rights.

But on this day, Gwyar was officially missing, and answers must start with the same collective who surrounded the mystery of Merlin.

They had no answers for the sovereign. No explanation to provide. No narrative. Their mumblings and shrugs were as dry hay, their promises of innocence as stubble, and the king's anger as an all-consuming fire.

The interrogation carried on, Arthur surgically excising all facts from the time period, no stone of motive or intent not flipped on itself.

Another lamentation volleyed upward into the heavens. *"If one more of my pagan friends disappears!* Just one! I will raze every church and burn every chapel! And I say unto you that I don't think Jesus would blame me!"

The clergy understood Arthur's pain and would rebuke him not for his blasphemy. Their only objective, an objective that finally brought unity amongst the brethren, was to survive this, to limp out of the amphitheater alive, and hope to God that the witch would turn up, alive and well.

Suddenly the voice of another mighty Silure that possessed Arthur's similar innate authority, albeit in a tiny, brooding little body, filled the stadium with the shadow of its substance.

The bishops' wish was granted.

"I don't think Jesus would blame you either, brother, but unfortunately no churches will you set to the flame. For here I am." Morgaine looked upon hateful Aiden, crouched with his fellows, winked, and asked, "So, how is your arm?"

The Popish presbyter gave no pious Scripture, nor did he preach at the sorceress this time. He only gave a fearful sneer and an involuntary pestering of an old hurt.

Morgaine had no space to vex the rest of the assembly, either in jest or in earnest, as she was immediately enveloped in a great bear hug. An Iron Bear's hug. As he held his sister, the first words were peculiar.

"Merlin. Did you see him?" he asked.

"Only in visions and whispers and mists, brother." Her expression was comforting but sorrowful.

"Then hope remains," asserted the king.

"Of course."

Now Arthur surveyed the assembly. Here at the same moment were brought together his treasured sister and her son. Accustomed to strange happenings on the Blessed Isles, even a confident king knows not when to pry and when to leave be. As his next words were forming, he saw another sprinting through the west arches, making haste to join them, her stride measured but urgent (as one runs upon a hurt child and loathes having to see, but needs to see all the more).

"Gwen?" Arthur's expression was puzzled.

Gwenhwyfar, not knowing how the examination was proceeding, had lost herself to despair and was racing to save Mordred; perhaps to kill Arthur and flee, perhaps to trade her life for his own, perhaps to snatch him away and throw them into the Usk. She had no strategy, no course; she was running to save her love, no more.

A quick glimpse.

He is safe. He smiles.

Must concoct a lie, rapidly.

"My Lord, my husband – my love!"

Two men were addressed by the cunning queen, but only one understood the meaning.

Mordred crimsoned with a blush. Arthur looked upon his wife as he had ever: with absolute adoration.

"Your sister, Gwyar. She returns!" Where Hercules and the Hebrew Samson have no equals in history or legend for strength, the daughter of the Giant Ogyrfan Fawr had no rival for swift and effortless lies. She was naturally naughty, and the Faerie King had taken those natural inclinations and multiplied them a thousandfold. Even in her rebirth of true love, the old nature remained, and pivoting towards self-preserving deception was as natural to her as the lacing of a boot.

"Oh!" Arthur laughed. "My love, she is here, and still so tiny you did not see her behind my cloak." (Of course, Gwen had seen her during her gallop, only feigning receiving the news before her *hasty run*). Arthur laughed again, then finished his jest. "It is not as if she's grown taller in the past five years!"

Gwen gathered herself. "Queen Gwyar, wife of King Llew, you are most welcome home."

Gwyar measured Gwenhwyfar. And spoke not.

Arthur turned to the clergy and remembered the Merlin's lesson: *when wrong, apologize quickly and sincerely. The err can't be recovered, but you can always control how you respond.*

"Illtud, cousin, teacher and friend. I am sorry for suspecting something malicious of you. I have let a hurt from yesterday cloud the judgment of today. Please forgive me." And Arthur engaged each of the Elders, whether he liked them or not, with individual, real apologies, which left none of them with ought to say against so marvelous a king and so honorable a man.

As the Churchmen left the theatre, the tension

did not abate; rather, it simply shifted. Now in the empty stadium remained four: Gwyar and Gwen, Arthur and Mordred.

Arthur recognized instantly that Mordred, as son, must have grieved in equal measure as had the brother. "I know you greatly covet time with your mam; pray you give me a few hours, and I shall send her unto you." He then turned to his wife, the actress misted over with the fullness of disingenuous hospitality. "Gwen, please escort my nephew back into the city – perhaps have your attendants see to it that he enjoys the ancient baths – and later, we will all sup, yes?"

"Straightaway, husband." The kiss of a proud adder that had just survived the farmer's plow and fanged his ankle followed.

No. This is why I left! He has delivered his one true love into the hands of HER LOVER FOR THE AFTERNOON! Gwyar's soul screamed, but her mouth moved not.

Gwenhwyfar and Mordred exited.

* * *

"The roaming mares and wild yellow flowers call for you; to our fortress we must!" Arthur gently turned Gwyar so that their vantage allowed them to see Lodge Hill, their special place, looking down, ever protecting them. At least from enemies without.

Gwyar gave no protest. Llyn Fawr (whence Vivien had gone when returning to Cymru with Gwyar), Ynys Enlli and Lodge Hill. These were, in no special ranking, her favorite places, and though she knew not which words she would choose for her brother, she knew that any discourse would be better conducted up the old trails in the mystical stronghold. At least they could gaze across the whole of the Vale of Glamorgan, the heart and capital of the Summer Kingdom.

Instantly, they were no longer alone in the arena.

While they yet gazed towards the hills, a gentle hand alighted upon each of their shoulders. Barely present, yet each could somehow see the *color* of the fingers.

Red.

The fingers tapped and rattled first upon Arthur; next, Gwyar, followed by a greeting that matched the order of the tapping, rudely: "Blessings and Cursings upon the line of Uther Pendragon."

The mortal king spun round to face the immortal. Arthur had never met him, but legends and reports abounded.

"This arena is my stone circle, lord of the Tylwyth Teg; by what infraction or infringement do you lay charge?"

"You have the resolve of your mother, Iron Bear." The echo of the voice vibrated and rippled, as if the thing were speaking under water. *Oddly, the deepness and tone that came out of the devil reminded Arthur of Maelgwn's voice.*

The provocation agitated the Saxon Slayer, the Giant Hunter, the Undefeated Warrior, who began to unsheathe his blade. But Gwyar stayed his hand, preventing a futile enterprise.

"You know not our mother, and are being impish, which is below the station of a lord of such an ancient and noble race."

"Remarkable," the Tylwyth Teg's chief of mischief mused at the introductory missives. "The one I blessed put hand to sword and would battle me; the one I cursed did bless me with courtly edifications."

"Bless those that curse you," said Gwyar.

"And in so doing you shall leap coals upon their heads." Arthur finished the Scriptural saying. "She always was the wiser of us."

A Bible-quoting witch, a god-king overreacting all morning and having a most out-of-character day, and the most powerful of the Fair Folk standing in Caerleon in broad daylight. The spectacle was not lost on the participants. They each met eyes and enjoyed a short laugh.

"The Tylwyth Teg don't just promenade through amphitheaters in the openness of the day in this most Christian of kingdoms. What mean you by being here" – Arthur's statesmanship returned – "my Fair Lord?"

"This was my land ere it was yours, Son of Adam. Are not all interactions amongst our kind about inheritance? Do we not ever guard what you do or do not do with our islands?"

"There was a time that I could acquiesce to the logic of your premise." Arthur took caution in his tone, but posited his view with great conviction. "A time where I would have agreed that we were regrettably, at one time – millennia ago – the very invaders that we now loathe. But that is not so."

The Fae puffed his chest, his green tunic stressing at the seams. But he fiddled with his beard, and listened on.

"My new Merlin–"

"Oh, Taliesin, son of Ceridwen, a Glamorgan lad; I know him well," the Fae King interrupted.

"Yes, Taliesin provided greater insight than did *my Merlin* about the origin of otherworldly beings. He explained that Man was placed here first and was to be the sole heir of salvation and

God's agency to rule and reign upon the earth."
Here Arthur was very careful to avoid insulting
the Fae's ancestors, whom they worshiped with
absolute religious devotion. "And that your
kind share a common ancestor with my kind,
demanding that Man, or more accurately the
daughters of Man, were here first. Your kind
is very ancient but, o king, you are the original
visitors and not us."

"So Taliesin has grown bold. Your Merlin
feared he would tell you of these and other
mysteries. What else, I beseech you, Arthur
Pendragon – what else has Taliesin taught you in
your counselor's stead?"

"Oh, this and that." Arthur minimized the
matter. "He is Maelgwn's bard, but we have
had some fascinating conversations and I have
entertained his theories. Now, I in turn beseech
you: what more do you know of my Merlin? Do
you know if he lives or if he fell, how, and who
and why?"

"What gift would the Pendragon give the Fair
Folk for such knowledge? Would you dance with
us?"

"Yes."

"Arthur, stop," commanded Gwyar, upon
deaf ears.

"Would you rid the land of all iron and ore,
forever?"

"By command the mining guilds would begin
on the morrow."

"Arthur, please."

"Would you abdicate your throne?"

The answer was immediate. And immediately
'No'.

"I am king for my people and for all the Tribes,
Clans, Cantrefs and Kingdoms of Cymru and the

Isles in the Sea. I would not gain this knowledge whilst the people suffered for it."

Gwyar gave a sigh, thankful that *Arthur was still Arthur*.

"Ah, Arthur ap Meurig, son of the pious Queen Onbrawst, you are my favorite of all the Sons of Adam who have ever lived. The better part of the answers you seek reside not with me, but with your new Merlin himself. Ask Taliesin what became of your dear wizard."

Arthur knew not how to respond to this and was not given space to; the Fae King continued.

"Yes, my favorite of all the Sons of Adam. Your Golden Age must run its course, the land prospers, the people prosper, peace reigns and our Isles free from the invading Boar. It is best for all that Arthur be king until the Summer Kingdom waxes old, and then the winter shall come. You are in great peril."

Soon it was evident that the otherworldly being had come, after pricking and poking and harassing as was his manner, to warn Arthur.

"There are visitors coming who are and are not what they seem."

Arthur had been reared on riddles, being raised at the feet of the Merlin. He knew that demanding plain speech was vain, and instead listened to what was said, inferred or withheld, with the focus of an archer left with but one arrow in the quiver. He assumed that the creature was referring to emissaries from Rome, who were visiting within the month, and rumors that the Bishop of Rome would finally come to see golden Caermelyn and stately Caerleon.

"At all costs, the thing that your sister here" – an unfriendly and unflattering pointing at Gwyar – "and her foster-mother so glibly and carelessly trek about with, paying insufficient regard to its import, must not be here when they are here. Should they possess it, your kingdom will end."

"Sister, what thing?"

Now Gwyar was doing the ignoring. Instead, she protested, "But where can we take it? The Isle of Apples is under endless siege by pilgrims and her magic wanes. And if the *other treasures were found*, then all hope would be lost."

Remarkably, the unpredictable Fae King gave a reasonable response. "Merlin thought best to hide it forever in Broceliande. Now those woods are breeched. Methinks your Ynys Enlli still remains the most difficult daughter island to access from the mainland. Get thee hence back to Avalon, and try to make it your stronghold once more. Recruit maidens, rebuild, divert and misdirect the Church and the inquisitive. Move the cup between there and Llyn Fawr oft, and make this thy and thy foster-mother's occupation. Guard the Grail."

"What thing?!" Arthur demanded.

Gwyar took Arthur by the hand and stated softly, "Remember our good secret in exchange for the bad? 'Tis one of her relics, that when charged and charmed is rumored to be capable of perversion, wrath and malice."

"Or healing," the old elf added.

"Oh – the cup of Christ. Can it be? You have it, sister?"

"Vivien and I have concealed it. It is near."

"The Lady of the Lake!" Though Arthur counted her amongst his beloved *missing pagans,* there were reports that she had simply retired to Lesser Britain and that Maelgwn visited her oft. That she was active again in the affairs of men thrilled Arthur, causing him to feel partially like his wizard had returned with her. The king eschewed the warning of danger, instead brimming with excitement.

"This sounds like a–"

"Quest." The Fae King smothered the whole of his red face with his spiky fingers, partially amused. "Sons of Adam and their quests. Heed me, Arthur. Get Morgaine of the Faeries far from your Popish guests, or lose the kingdom you shall."

Lastly, the chief of the Tylwyth Teg looked upon Gwyar as a father looks upon a daughter – and in many respects, her father he was. He had *made* Morgaine, above forty years ago. Instead of retribution in kind at Onbrawst's offense with a simple changeling, ugly and insufferable, the Fae King had made something else entirely of the babe who *was Gwyar.*

Communicating only in thought that so that the king would hear him not: "I owed the Primal Witch a favor, but knew not that fate would add to black magic incest and perversion. The Morrigan hath begotten a twisted thing. He will bring winter upon our Summer Kingdom before the time." He was not greater in power than Morgaine, but was able to cause her head to turn back to road towards the city whence Mordred now made respite, surely, after finishing with the king's wife. "Had I foreseen the whelp, I would've rendered you barren. For this, I mourn for you, my child."

Tears streamed down Gwyar's cheeks.

Two abominations, part human, part devil, acting as gods – but no gods stood with the innocent and loyal king. The moment was not lost on Gwyar, and she cried a great cry.

King Arthur understood that his sister was

a peculiar, troubled and enchanted being and somehow deeply entwined with the Fae, hence her popular name amongst the tribes, and because he knew this, he knew when to abstain from pressing for information that would not be given, and if given, not be understood. Instead, he let the arcane remain such. The Fae King vanished, and Arthur said simple words.

"This time, send messengers monthly and visit oft, and I will do the same. Guard this *relic* until you feel your course is complete, and then come back to me."

"Our thoughts are aligned, brother." She embraced him and warned, "Guard your heart carefully, and let our toil continue whilst others enjoy the sun."

"As always," he mused. They shared words of love, and Morgaine departed for the Isle of Apples, concerning herself not with seeing Mordred.

CHAPTER 11
Visitors from Rome

For many seasons preceding the arrival of 'the Whelp' to Court (first to give an answer for beguiling the High King, and then, once reconciled of that matter, to make a name for himself), Arthur and Lancelot were greatly enjoying each other's company.

The offense over Arthur preferring himself versus Itto was long dormant, put far away into the corridors of Lancelot's complex and troubled mind. Skirmishes, raids, sundry quests and monsters gave the two warriors what they needed: combat.

The raids were mainly by pirates from Eire who were harassing coastal villages in the north. The clans that governed the Emerald Isles denounced the activity, and generations of intermarriage through the line of Silures ensured an iron-clad and lasting peace. To this end, Arthur recognized that the actions were wrought by criminals, individuals, and not by his neighbor nation in the western sea.

Nevertheless, the lasting peace had to be guarded with ferocious zeal, and extreme vigilance. For this cause, Arthur engaged Lancelot and Gwalchmai, rather than lesser-known guards or patrolling part-time soldiers, to send the loudest possible message abroad that examples would be made, punishment would be harsh, the behavior stamped out.

Lancelot, now in his fourth decade, was remarkably better than at the peak of his youth. More effortless, more swift, cleaner in his killing strokes; a perfect simulation of Vivien's dance, only enhanced by the strength of a demigod. He was a long man, lending him a great advantage in reach, rendering his battle spike as a spear on account of arm-span. Still cleanly shaven, still with mid-length curly raven's hair, Lancelot was *the Cymreig Warrior the Saxons feared in the night*; he and his hosts from the North were the difference in the long and long ago Saxon Wars.

He used the raiders for practice. Training with real steel. Arthur and Gwalchmai marveled at his techniques, and much fellowship, many laughs and little adventures became big memories for the troop.

Lancelot had forced himself to be more present for the Round Table Fellowship, but only when he could affirm that Gwenhwyfar II would not be at Caermelyn. On those occasions he would lie without hesitation, habitually breaking vows of honesty that were in the fiber of his identity, to protect the kingdom – *from himself.*

Gwalchmai, a young man burdened with Gwyar's observational genius and Arthur's wisdom, alone (save Taliesin) marked the patternistic behavior. And because he suspected Mordred of some malevolence with the queen, the added oddity of Lancelot's conduct doubly oppressed him. So many times, direct accusation welled but was held back, causing the sunny and shiny one sadness, gloom and pain.

Shortly after Gwyar's return (and too-soon departure, yet again), Arthur, Cai, Gwlachmai and Lancelot were about the coast, again *enjoying* quelling a small raid; twenty men of Eire and a few rogue Britons purloining cattle and harassing miners in a coastal village on Ynys Mon.

"Let's give the appearance of an army, rather than a collection of concerned citizens." Arthur beamed with excitement.

"The silver armor, red cape, tribal sigils?" Lancelot matched his king's beam.

"Precisely!"

"The special garb!" Cai was as a child about to rummage the chest for his favorite doll or plaything.

"The helmet cannot contain my hair, and it hurts," protested Gwalchmai, withholding his chuckle.

"Call the sunshine, Hawk of May" – for it had rained for four days without ceasing – "and then ride without helm," countered his happy lord.

Only criminals and villains covet actual *war*. And only baser men seek out violence. None of the Round Table Fellowship wanted war. The prolonged conflict with the invading Germans had torn at the collective soul of Cymru – multigenerational trauma that would long linger and never be forgotten.

However, all boys need to periodically fight. To engage in combat, to compete, to protect and show brawn and skill and will. Here and there, warriors must war, only to hope that they never *go to war*. And these men, who had been but boys during most of their famous twelve battles, knew this truth and, grown full of wisdom, often wondered how invincible they would be now, having the benefit of years and hard lessons. To this end, they relished the occasional raid.

Whilst they were reposing for a brief meal to discuss how to deal with the raiders and prepare for the battle, the sun broke the clouds, casting his rays of glory upon the heroes, gathered round a small fire, surrounded by ancient trees.

The Hawk of May shook his helmet off violently, making a show of it. The others gave such laughter that Cai complained that his ribs might leap from their cages. Gwalchmai glared at them, a mess of auburn hair with two eyes for a face.

"Well done, Gwalchmai!" Arthur looked upon the blue face of the firmament. He allowed the joviality to simmer and then made use of the time for more serious matters. A short discussion ensued about the task at hand. During the discourse, the Pendragon interjected.

"When we return to Caermelyn, there are two openings amongst our twenty-four by reason of retirement. It is time to consider the next generation of Round Table Knights. What of Peredur?"

All agreed to the nomination with great excitement over the upstart, who had seen no wars but possessed every quality of the special responsibility demanded by the coveted station.

"And your brother Mordred? What of him, Gwalchmai?"

"So long have I been with your House in the South, I don't know him with sufficient comfort to stand by an answer." Gwalchmai politicized the response.

"A great king you will make one day," Cai smiled at the burly but polished knight, "never giving a straight answer."

"Ha!" Arthur struck Cai upon the shoulder,

and then embraced him as they all enjoyed another portion of merriment. Then the Pendragon turned to his champion, tall as a cedar. "Your son Rhun has long been amongst our best, yet the bards say Rhufawn is the greater swordsman."

"Greater than even you!" In chorus, Gwalchmai and Cai both goaded the Lancelot.

"All good fathers desire that their sons exceed and surpass them, except in good looks," replied the Bloodhound Prince, himself fully capable of political recourse.

"Amen!" agreed Arthur. And the gaiety continued.

"In the same way that your brother Madoc lives upon the Sea, and your brothers serve the Church, my thorn begs me to not recommend Rhufawn for consideration for *our life*. He is vague and annoying about this, but I tend to heed him," said Maelgwn.

"Merlins tend to be vague and annoying. I understand." Arthur smiled and nodded.

Maelgwn knew nothing of Mordred, save that he was Gwyar's son and Gwalchmai's brother. A man with blood of North and South. In an effort to be helpful against never-ending ripples over territorial and tribal stressors, he put forth an idea. "Mordred seems to be worthy of this opportunity. Perhaps a probationary assignment? Perhaps we bring him on our next *quest or adventure*. Give him a go. Yes?"

Gwalchmai simply did not agree, nor would he ever. He discerned great evil residing within the Whelp. But the Hawk of May remained silent. A wordless and reserved protest.

"Sound thinking; this we shall do." Arthur liked the idea of the Fellowship being restored to its proper census. For twelve is the number of government. Twelve for Arthur, twelve for his champion, King Maelgwn Gwynedd. He then made an end of a horn of cider: one impressive gulp and – gone. "There is one other matter." His hand wiped some remnant of nectar from his short mustache, still colored as a sandy shore, still without grey.

"We have criminals to corral. Didn't know I was invited to a council." It was rare that Maelgwn jested, but on this day, he was just *one of four boys enjoying a moment in the sun.*

Seeing his Lancelot happy was Arthur's joy and, he knew, the ongoing salvation of Cymru. *And fleeting.* The thought was a moment of reality as the single angry cloud on a sunny day.

"Yes, yes, I shall be swift. The Church is hosting visitors." And now a moment of gravity. "From Rome."

There was an audible gasp, followed by an instant silence.

"It is an envoy of men in high places within the Church of Rome. A congregation for peace, and extension of hospitality in an effort to work out ever-growing differences, especially as it relates to the policy of baptism and church membership amongst the children living in Lloegyr." Here Arthur opted not to name the kingdom of Cedric, a thriving Germanic confederacy that was allowed to survive, on account of women and children and the values that the Cymry placed on innocent life.

However, the Native Church refused to teach them Scripture, to baptize them (in opposition to their own hard-fought and hard-won policies), or even to sup with them unless they suffered the dining party to go through a ceremonial washing.

They viewed and treated the Saxons, Jutes, Angles and Gewessi as *gentile dogs.*

The Roman Church was more opportunistic. They were converting these *dogs,* or rather, *the Boar,* by the hundreds – and rapidly.

But none of that represented Arthur's primary concern.

"Maelgwn."

"My lord?"

"As you know, men of an Italian band are deeply woven into the schemes that both sponsored my sons' plots against me and the intrigue in Brittany ten years ago, which took our great one from us."

Maelgwn gave a frustrated nod. He knew more than he could share, on account of his foster-mother.

"We have never attacked another nation. This is not the way of the Cymry. But I shall never forget this wrong. And justice do I ever seek. Continue to investigate we must. All of us must be at Caerleon; all must be vigilant. Ask questions. Probe, prod. Be good hosts, but listen to what is said and not said. By Excalibur I swear…" Arthur motioned for a second cider, treating it as the first. "If we find some cell amongst the church, some actors in the conspiracy, or that the Church itself did these things, I swear by my right as king of these Isles that attack we shall."

Maelgwn had stopped listening. Though not his intention, the words washed over him as hot oil upon a pot, not sticking, of no import. Rather, he was consumed by the test before him. The test of Gwenhwyfar. *I must lodge at Caerleon during this visit!*

"What is the duration of the visit?" he queried the king.

"Seven nights," stated King Arthur.

King Maelgwn of Gwynedd, the Lancelot who had forsaken all to serve the Iron Bear, had one week to tame thoughts and feelings that could well resurrect his bubble.

He fought flawlessly as the fully-clad Round Table Companions recreated past fame. The raiders were put to flight or to the sword. The men gasped and marveled at Maelgwn's skill. The joy of delivering justice and securing the realm brought youth and glee to the troop, transporting both Arthur and Maelgwn back to a time when they, and their two classmates, had conquered all enemies of land and sea in the kingdom of their youthful minds. A simple time of being children; boys and girls. Both sovereigns savored the moment and stole many glances at each other, redeeming the time and enjoying their small portion of the Summer Kingdom ere they returned to the trials and devils that surely awaited them back in their golden city.

* * *

Hormisdas, the Bishop of Rome, "died" in August, five hundred and twenty-three years after the Passion of the Lord.

The renowned ambassador of reconciliation had labored tirelessly for unity; unity at any cost. *There is no truth but oneness* and *endeavoring for the unity of the spirit in the bonds of peace* were the banner and sigil of his public administration.

He had healed schisms through diplomacy, stood with unwavering resolve before an emperor who had sought to discredit and destroy him, made of this foe a friend, and unified the Senate behind the Church, her councils, synods and edicts; this had strengthened waning Rome against the rising tide of the Ostrogoth and Ishmaelian Empires that had eclipsed her.

All of these achievements and maneuvers had helped position Rome to rise again, only after a different manner. Never again could she use the soldier and the sword; now she would use the vestments and the Cross to meet her aims, guilt and reward to conquer the world.

To be used for his aims. To conquer the world under his boot.

The unity, the diplomacy, the beguiling of principled men to compromise, to sell soul in order to sit under one big tent, appears good, even godly.

'Tis not so.

Unity without truth is simply the best device for gathering all of the sheep into one corral – and then slaughtering them.

Hormisdas. The Bishop of Rome. The man from Frusino with a profound accent, such that he was hard to be understood, especially when he spoke Gaelic or needed to use Cymraeg.

Hormisdas, the Bishop of Rome. While toiling and working on dominating his ecclesiastical body, too many years were passing, the sands slipping far too fast through the hourglass; his hero pawns in Less Britain and the Isles in the Sea beginning, just so, to age.

Hormisdas. Simon Magus. The leader of the Council of Nine. A man in direct congress with the Dark Lord, the Lord of the Flies and the Father of Lies. The horned and hooved one whom the Cymreig called Arddu and who went by many names; the Prince of the Power of the Air, that Dragon, the Devil, Satan.

Arddu gave Magus ruthless stripes for his lack

of progress, forcing the bishop to feign his death and develop a new scheme.

No longer would Arddu's vicar publicly rule from the direct seat of power. Too much bureaucracy and accountability rendered this illogical and inefficient. Nay. Henceforth, Simon Magus, and should the Lord tarry, his successors, would rule and reign from the shadows as *Black Popes* through the use of puppet Holy Fathers, whom they would personally promote and demote as served the ends of the Nine.

This was not accomplished without difficulty at first. Choosing the very elderly and pliable John I, the illuminated brotherhood were instantly at odds with his compromises and the intrigue in which he entangled himself amongst the politicians of Constantinople. This angered the Society, and the emperor of the Ostrogoths, who slung the old man into a dank and damp cell, leaving him to die from neglect and starvation in his own filth. Simon Magus would do better in his subsequent selection, placing Felix IV on the papal throne.

Having his new instrument in place, Magus would redouble his efforts to build up, and then destroy, the kingdoms of the Briton Arthur, elsewise Childebert. And so, ten years removed from *initiating Merlin,* he would go to the court of Arthur himself, to look in upon his top candidate to serve as vessel for the Son of Perdition, the conduit to bring about the End of Days.

He now took the part of a silent archbishop, mysteriously disfigured and confined to a mask for the cause of Christ: a part of the tapestry and dramatic scenery of Romish pageantry, barely noticeable and hardly noteworthy, save the mask.

Caution was paramount. No action must

ignite conflict with the tribes of the Cymry. Magus had spent most of his days since youth amongst the warring Boar that had toppled Rome. The viciousness of the Saxons, the wanton calamity of the Vandals, the cold cruelty of the Ostrogoths who 'ruled' at the present time over Simon's homeland (yet they all ultimately were ruled by him, who in turn was ruled by the capstone of a societal pyramid, Arddu the Horned God). None of these would be victorious over the Britons, who could not even be subdued in times past by Rome at the height of her Empire. The Britons could not, and would not, be beaten.

The irony of the People of Arthur was that they *could* conquer the world, but would not. No tribe of the Britons had ever usurped the sovereignty of another nation.

Rather, they could only be defeated through division, intrigue, subtle machinations and usurpations. And Simon's chief usurper in the Blessed Isles was the Adder, leader of the loosely-knit heathen wise men whose superstition yet controlled many of the common folk.

The Dynion Hysbys had served the Council well, rousing Giants oft and distracting the Round Table Knights by whispering of horrors, monsters and devilish threats to the realm; ever stamping as a boot upon the toes of the Summer Kingdom, ever irritating it with pricks and needles that, at any time, winter may fall.

Pertaining to Giants and phantoms, well; but pertaining to the Cup, heretofore, failure. Its guardian's keep could not be breached and, when it had been, the Cup had not been found. Rather, it had moved. Long years had passed, and the Adder was no closer to finding the Grail than finding a thimble in a wheat field.

Simon Magus was confident that he would put that commission right and recover the relic quickly.

And he wanted to know more of how the Merlin had come upon the tome, containing such a peculiar inscription, full of words that brought eternal life. And more than how, who *had given it to the old druid.*

* * *

Maelgwn wore a new road in the wild thicket on account of his pacing.

Hidden safely in a wood between Caerdydd and Caerleon, all of his selves were alone, to bring themselves under subjection and support Arthur by attending Court.

Frequently misunderstood, there was never a time when the champion of Cymru didn't *want* to be at Caerleon or Caermelyn; rather, how to perform the same and spare his mind was the matter, and his mind cared not about his wanting.

Arthur and his First Knight were truly enjoying a season likened unto their days at Illtud's before the Saxon Wars. Provided that Maelgwn could manipulate affairs to avoid Gwenhwyfar, which he could, and manipulate his bubble to leave him at peace, which he had for some time suppressed, the two enjoyed, and would continue to relish, many days of reaping their twenty years of sacrifice to win the war – reaping freedom and friendship.

But Arthur's request was wise. Was correct.

If Maelgwn, or any of Arthur's closest companions, could learn more about Rome's involvement in the seditious conspiracy to remove the king so long ago in favor of his sons, then justice might finally be wrought, the truth finally known.

The sentinel event that had been Mynydd Baeden was too grand. Too expensive. Too contrary to the nature of the Germanic Tribes. That a people who eschewed union and breathed factionism would unite under three kings and conduct the campaign that they had defied reason.

They had had help.

Nay: they had been used. An end to some unknown means.

Maelgwn believed that the Pendragon planned to give the religious overture of the meeting one to two hours for posturing over the primacy of who had the right to baptize and save men's souls and then, once annoyed by it all, to directly interrogate them about Baeden, about his sons, and about his Merlin.

Maelgwn must needs be in attendance. *Though it meant sitting in a hall near, possibly next to, her.*

He paced again.

And more pacing.

Then, suddenly, the winds shifted. A mist manifested and then a glimpse, faint and vague, of a shadowy personage peering at him through the thick fog, poised to attack.

The attacker's height and build was a mirror of Maelgwn.

The attacker's diagonal fighting stance was a mirror of Maelgwn.

The attacker's fluidity was a mirror of Maelgwn.

The mist was breaking apart and then merging again, swirling and twirling. And when it parted, the opponent could, for fleeting seconds, be seen.

The attacker's hair was a mirror of Maelgwn.

The attacker's flawless crystal eyes were a mirror of Maelgwn.

Then the weapon was brandished, picking out little dots of daylight, outlined by the mist. The battle spike, a mirror of Maelgwn's.

Seeing oneself is the greatest fear, and upon seeing it, truly seeing it, the Round Table champion, renowned for being void of fear, a hard man without tear ducts, felt the anvil of fear, the wellspring of tears. Its weight dried his mouth so that for a moment, he could neither swallow nor draw breath.

Containing the want to cry out at the specter, else his twin, only a broken whisper escaped his lips. "Maelgwn? Are you–"

"Talking to yourself, King Gwynedd?"

The mirror broke into ten thousand imperfect shards, exploding as ethereal dust. The mist gave way, revealing instead humpbacked little Taliesin, looking up at the hero with great curiosity and mirth.

"Or rather, talking to yourself *again?*" the bard snickered.

"Taliesin," rebuked Maelgwn, "you drive me to madness." A sigh followed the mystified and confused fighter, who had not ceased to think on Gwenhwyfar even as his foggy *other self* had come to slay him.

"You were expecting maybe the Bishop of Rome?" Taliesin gave a high, arching cackle. "I don't *think* he is joining the envoy but" – his arm motioned towards Maelgwn as though a shepherd's crook – "let's make haste to the city and find out."

"Never present when summonsed, always a bur when unwanted." Maelgwn meant these words, but fully knew that Taliesin was rather *present when the timing was just right* and, overcome with a coursing current of feelings that the small man had just somehow saved his life, allowed a half smile to escape towards his old thorn. His old friend.

"To Caerleon," he insisted. As they departed the thatch, the bard put his arm around the waist of Maelgwn, guiding the Bloodhound Prince as an aging father guides a grown son who has long outgrown the act but allows it anyhow, for respect and for love. (Though malformed Taliesin was younger than the Northern king.)

Seeing the ground worn, the jesting and jeering persisted. "Tilling the ground to farm?"

Maelgwn had long since calculated that the more the Taliesin goaded him, the more he already knew. Silent, he allowed the shepherd's hook around his waist, along with the goading, and the two made for Caerleon.

Compelled for a final look back to the forest, Maelgwn saw *himself* once more, peering at him from the side of a girthy tree. He quickly jumped behind it, vanishing in the twinkling of an eye.

* * *

The Church of Rome had sent twelve bishops, two archbishops (and Simon Magus in his guise accounting for one of them), and a small company of soldiers to visit the famous King Arthur at his estate in Caerleon.

The king's own brother, Prince Madoc the Sea Master, met with their vessel south of the horn of the Isles, guiding safe passage to the port of Newydd and then, transitioning from sea to river, up the winding Usk River into Caerleon.

Madoc prepared a parade upon the waters so

that the ecclesiastical guests were greeted with a shower of high-arching fiery arrows tipped with powder, clashing in the air, giving bursts of light in unusual and spectacular shapes. Hundreds of streamers of gold and great banners adorned with the Red Dragon were posted at three paces apart on either side of the river bank, making the river as a road paved and decorated with pageantry, splendor and merriment. Sculptures of art wobbled on stationary platforms that Taliesin and Madoc had engineered to float. Moreover, all the musical enchantment of the Blessed Isles was in its fullest, most prominent display. Illtud's choirs sang in unison with the rush and whistle of the river, creating a vibratory thunder of pious hymns, battlecries and love songs. Harps and horns complemented the singing, and Rome herself, even at the zenith of her external beauty and grandeur, gave no welcome that was equal to the Silures of Caerleon.

As Simon's boot met Cymry soil, the land cried out its protest. Gwyar, above the city center tending to ponies along the rim of Lodge Hill, heard Cymru's cry. Repulsed at a congress of pseudo-Christians, she gritted her teeth and made haste, descending by the path most swift into the city.

The Saints were the first to greet their Italian counterparts. Helpers (for no Cymry citizen was a servant or a slave in his own land, even if a person of lower estate or employed as the hireling of a household) brought gifts of foods and delights and fabrics and tin and copper, but Arthur forbade gifts of gold. The Catholics received the gifts with humble gratitude and exchanged brotherly kisses with all, save Magus who, limited by his mask, simply bowed.

The prominent clergy of the Britons, including both those who favored and those who opposed Rome, served as hosts. Amongst these were Dyfrig, the Evangelist of Ergyng, who also crowned Arthur; Teilo and Samson, his pupils; Illtud the Wise; Bedwini, who was Arthur's personal bishop; Cadfan, who had rooted himself on Ynys Enlli and governed the Llyn Peninsula; Dewi of Henfynyw; and Caw of the Old North, who had brought his son Gildas. He was but eleven, but had been gifted from birth to quickly master all known languages and to work in scripts from any of the tribes and kindreds upon the earth. The boy would serve as a scribe, recording the visit.

A replenishing visit to the ancient baths, and the visitors retired for the night.

Gwyar was at Gwenhywfar and Arthur's apartment, rousing them with a violent knock. The king eschewed the grump of sleepiness and favored humor.

Rubbing his eyes: "Did you kill Cai then, sister?"

"Your Steward lives."

"She is so short, brother; I often miss mice that sneak into your chamber as well." Cai hurled humor down the corridor, never far away from the one he'd pledged his life to protect.

Cai was a stoic, hard man. *The watchman of all watchmen.* His jest was so out of character that it caused the royal siblings' eyes to widen and foreheads to startle at the same time, and raucous laughter had no choice but to burst from them both at the same time.

They embraced.

A naked, immodest figure appeared in the shadow of the arched doorway. Cai, who was pleased with himself that he had been able to form a jest, had nearly joined where they were standing when he saw a flash of flesh and recoiled back into the hallway.

"I thought we agreed you would see to your orchards and bones and relics, far from here."

Gwyar's eyes met Gwenhwyfar's.

The room's hearth was not burning, for the weather was temperate, and blankets sufficed. But the moonlight revealed all of the Giant's little daughter nonetheless. Her tribal markings, decorating her body in spirals and tribal knotwork, seduced any two eyes to follow their circuits, to her navel and down to the flower, which was cleanly shorn and designed to be the ruin of men.

"My love." Arthur's visage begged his wife to consider a modicum of modesty.

She fetched a thin, silky gown and gave false eyes of wifely support.

"The Lady of Avalon goes where she will. And where she ought," Gwyar responded. "Besides, the Lady of Lake is at her turn as custodian of the Cup. Now…" She attempted to dismiss the queen and positioned her body towards her brother alone. "Will you hear me, or think you that I came banging upon your door hours before dawn for the pleasure of it?"

"By all means." Gwen was impossible to dismiss. Impossible to ignore. She placed her half-naked body in the midst of the siblings, an unspoken gesture insisting that she be part of whatever message was forthcoming.

In doing this, quite by chance, Gwen's hands brushed upon Arthur's and Gwyar's at the same time, forming a chain of contact.

'Twas but half a second in duration, and

Gwen's carnality rendered her to blind to the incident, but not so for Arthur and Gwyar.

Arthur, in the nether time between night and day where the senses are confused and gateways are opened, conjoined to his first love and his first *lover*, saw the form of his night terror rise. Only it did not come forth from Gwyar. The succubus pushed up and out of his very own chest. Beautiful. The White Phantom with flowing black hair that was at once *there and not there, wisping between the worlds*. The ancient goddess of sovereignty and war swam in and out and around the three of them, then back into the king, and once more spiraled out of Arthur's body towards the vaults above.

"Morgana," he gasped, bereft of breath. The creature was an exact composite of Gwyar and Gwen, but that it had glowing white fangs of a wolf. "Morgana!" A second gasp.

As lightning, the goddess struck straight for Arthur again, finding her mark, disappearing within his head. He fell to a knee, *the first time any foe had brought the Pendragon to a knee,* and started again to call out to her.

Meanwhile, Gwyar labored hard and, at the last moment, pulled away, breaking the conduit. Moving quickly, she conjured a binding spell in the language of Heaven and pleaded with Arthur, "Say not her other name! Brother, my love, you must not!"

The half-second ticked away, and the ordeal abated. Gwyar looked upon her brother, worried and alarmed. He did not look well. King Arthur was never sick, never lame; the comfort and rock of Cymru, the Iron Bear. To see him ill, even for a moment, gave Gwyar great pause, frightening her more than the sorcery and witchcraft and malevolence that ever accompanied her goings.

"I have a terrible ache within my head and must return to my bed. Please hasten to tell me quickly the purpose your visit, that I might retire."

Gwyar was direct. Gwen scoffed, complete with the rolling of eyes and the tapping of foot, but spake not.

"The leader of the Council of Nine, that shadow college that murdered our Merlin." She clutched both of the king's hands and pulled him closer. "He is here, in Caerleon. He is amongst the visitors from Rome."

Chapter 12
The Standoff

Ogyrfan Gawr loved his daughter. *In his own way.*
He wanted her to obtain her ambition. A reckless,
undisciplined love of libertinism, matched with
coy statesmanship and political pandering.

To be queen: achieved.

But more. To do as she pleased and have the
whole of Britannia grovel at her feet as she puffed
and proudly lorded over them: not yet achieved.

A local chieftain, his fortress was impenetrable,
set atop a gargantuan natural mound within a
plain, easily defended on all sides by superbly
drawn tracts of land that formed an expertly-
designed city. Caer Ogyrfan was the gateway
to the Midlands, and the key crossway between
north and south.

Having no particular god save Ambition,
Ogyrfan gave consistent offerings to both the
Church of the Britons and the Roman Church.
Cattle and pigs and tracts of lands he gave to
the druids and to the Dynion Hysbys. Aloof and
neutral and brooding, he paid all but was friend
to none.

And he was a Giant. He did possess the extra
fingers and toes, and wore thick black leather
gloves always so that, with time, few ever

noticed the aberration. The extra row of teeth was present as well, but only on the lower jaw and limited to half a rung. This made him jowly but not overtly deformed.

Tiny compared to Itto Gawr, Ogyrfan was identical in height to Maelgwn Gwynedd, though wider at the shoulder. A massive man; a small Giant.

His stature was on account of the dilution of angelic blood in his lineage. Ogyrfan was composed of much more man than god and as such was incredibly difficult to bewitch and activate, as Simon's identified *next monster* to harass and trouble the Summer Kingdom.

"I am the High King's father-in-law!" he bellowed. "What you ask of me is treason and would cost my Gwen the throne. And more! I will not!"

"You will." Simon had calmly removed the mask. "Tomorrow you will attack the king before all. He will slay you and increase in stature, or you will slay him, leaving an open throne. Either way, any potential ire towards Rome is distracted. Either way, our great work continues."

"I know nothing of your great work, and care for none of your politics. My daughter and I – we have our own politics."

Simon Magus ceased wasting time reasoning with the thing that was mostly man but part monster. He summonsed the Adder, already skulking around in the shadows.

"Take his will and bend it. Make him loyal unto the death. Loyal unto me."

The anti-druid nodded, setting out to do his sorcery upon the queen's father. Magus smiled, returned his face back to its mask, and retired to the guesthouse provided for him at Caerleon.

* * *

After a hearty meal to break the fast, the Roman visitors were permitted, under the careful custody of Cai and a few select men of Maelgwn's Hosts (the most elite of all fighters on the Blessed Isles), to make the short carriage ride to Caermelyn and see the famed Round Table. Little Gildas was allowed to draw and document their wonder at Merlin's creation, but they would not meet in that famed hall, not argue religion in those gilded seats. Rather, they were back to Caerleon by midday.

Returning to Arthur's estate, they convened in an ornate grange with checkered floors of marble that featured a large stage that fanned outward, then sloped down towards an open hall, where dancing and games of sport and skill were conducted.

The Cymry were seated at one long table on the stage, facing their guests, whose table was twelve steps below them. Less than subtle, the arrangement sought to check the hubris of Rome.

Simon Magus, in his guise as a crippled archbishop covering up some unknown facial deformity, was concealed from head to toe in a crimson cloak; likewise was his mask blood red. His vestments were ruddy as well, rendering him a scarlet rush, a candle of ecclesiastical peculiarity. The garb was an odd selection for one who coveted darkness and anonymity. On this day he needed to draw Arthur out, and measure him. However, he must not provoke the Bear, for if he did, the Romans would add to the bones of other invaders that now fertilized plant and tree and graveled the riverbeds. *Provoke, learn, and leave.*

The other archbishop was a very old man. Well into retirement, he had cited a deep longing to see Britannia before going into the sleep of death as the cause for his strong petition to head the envoy. As Bishop of Salona, Magus knew his politics and his military history and had discerned him harmless enough; the perfect prattler to get the bishops babbling, so that Magus could take advantage of the clamor and engage Arthur.

The archbishop had actually served for a time as western emperor for the whole of the Roman Empire several decades ago and, like Arthur's grandfather Tewdrig, had retired in favor of a religious life when spent were his political years.

Devils are smart; however, devils are not omniscient. What Magus was unaware of was that the elderly and feeble man harbored a visceral hatred of the Silures. Eighty and nine years of contempt dating back to the dusk of the Imperial Era, combined with the vanishing concern for discretion or manners that sometimes accompanies advanced age, had made him very unpredictable.

And dangerous.

Knowing none of this, Magus gingerly seated the elderly priest in the center chair at the long guest table and looked up to Arthur, Bedwini and the company of renowned Britons. He quietly spoke.

"Glycerius, ought not you ask the great Arthur of the Britons if you can bless this gathering with prayer ere we begin reason of matters plain and precious to the cause of Christ and His Holy Church?"

Honored and opportunistic, Archbishop Glycerius responded, "By your grace, you have fulfilled an old man's dying dreams."

"To it, then." Magus motioned his hand up towards the Cymreig assembly.

But the old priest's fulfillment would have to tarry as some of the guests were still assembling, the hall a loud bustle of deafening conversation and *settling in for what heated action might satisfy their itchy ears.*

Gwenhwyfar II entered, making procession to the host table. Accompanied by song from the bards, she was as a swan, gracefully dancing across the floor. Her gown was two sleeves, with the lower portion but a sophisticated woven wrap of green silk. Decorative red lacings threaded the sleeves, the small of her back and her bosom. Every jaw at once fell agape. Arthur beamed.

Four thin golden necklaces decorated her neck, several torques her wrists and sleek, perfect arms. The gold accented her speckled eyes; the most alluring eyes in all of Britannia.

Though her love for Mordred had reformed her outlook and softened her disposition, the fundamental core of her being – namely, disdain for men and thirst for power for its own sake – was starting to seep back through the cracks of external repair. The long years of pressure to give Arthur an heir and her chronic lies and façades to facilitate making love to her Mordred were *bringing back the monster.* She fought this, but the people took note… save her husband, as yet blinded by love as on the first day he had seen her.

On this day she was regal, and her authority gave great edification and confidence to the host bishops and elders, *for a strong woman supporting men always makes men stronger, and strong men as gods.*

Her eyes met with Maelgwn's.

Please don't sit here. The king of Gwynedd jiggled, desperately yearning to leap from both skin and seat.

"Please, dear wife." The king of Glamorgan and Gwent motioned for her to occupy the sole empty chair: between him and Lancelot.

Arthur, Gwenhwyfar, Lancelot; three of the four cords present.

And now, Morgaine of the Faeries.

"Cai, if you please, move a space that I might sit by my brother."

The four cords. The invincible schoolmates. At the same table, looking down upon former conquerors and potentially present conspirators; and a constant nuisance to the soul of the Isles besides. That the Cymry now condescended to the very institution that reckoned itself above the Nations and would have all men bend the knee to her ways was a relished moment. The Ostrogoths in the present generation had their way with the remnant shadow of imperial Rome, whom it behooved to behave in comely ways and sedately here in the House of Arthur, lest the Britons do the same.

Lancelot could think on none of these things. Nor could he appreciate the moment. His heart and loins burned for Gwen.

Gwen's heart and whole body ached for Mordred.

Lancelot noted her glow, and mistook its object.

The royal siblings rose above demons, pride, passion and hauntings of the past, focused as a bird of prey on matters pertaining to the preservation of the people. For this cause, Morgaine and Arthur were the greater members of the quartet.

Arthur made one more change to the seating

arrangement, asking that the lad, Gildas ap Caw, sit to his right, but for a special moment. The Iron Bear had observed that nerves and distress were overcoming the young genius and sought to encourage the boy. Though his father was a rival, *a rival approaching the measure of enemy*, Arthur had vowed never to visit the sins of the father upon the sons. Because of this principle, because Arthur treated every individual on his or her own merits, many northerners loved the Silure king, and factions were held at bay.

The situation was overwhelming Gildas: a child charged with memorializing history's mightiest empire come to visit history's most legendary king.

"Look." A great warm smile erupted from the Pendragon. "Even the bards envy you, little Gildas."

"They do?"

"Yes. Your memory and gift for understanding tongues exceeds theirs." A fatherly pat upon the head and tug of the hair. "What you can do at ten takes them a lifetime of study."

"Eleven." Kind words gave the boy confidence. Confidence to correct a king!

Arthur had completed his task, engendering a calming joy within the boy. Recalling how Caw's youngest, and most famous, son had been born the year of Mynydd Baeden, Arthur replied, "Has it been eleven years?"

The boy hugged Arthur, pulling him close with all of his might, never forgetting the kindness of the king, then scurried off quickly to his own father and a comfortable position to prepare scroll and ink.

"Eleven years of peace and liberty." Morgaine's hand gently found the king's wrist. "Let's try and make it twelve. Yes?" Her disposition beseeched

Arthur to stop suffering children and get back to dealing with the Roman Church. Arthur gave a short sigh, pursued by a shorter smile at his sister, straightened his shoulders, and allowed the congress to commence.

At last, as ready to burst as a ripe fruit, the retired emperor looked Arthur directly in the eye. "May I bless this assembly?"

"Of course." Hospitality and caution salted the response.

There was no salutation. No *thank you* offered.

"May the Lord God give the bishops of our brethren in Britannia and Eire the wisdom to bow the knee before our Holy Father, the Bishop of Rome, and cede her position and possession to the One True Church, commissioned to occupy until the Lord come!"

Magus wished for death inside his mask. For the old man had surely brought the sword upon them all.

"What is this *madness?*" It was Illtud who offered the retort. And Arthur gave him leave to continue.

Arthur was unarmed. Excalibur was displayed on the wall, well out of reach, along with one of the other swords of Britain. The sword of Caesar, raised by the king at his crowning in Londinium, accompanied the Sword of Power: a grand display and message as to the primacy and potency of Cymru. His dagger and other famed armaments were in his chamber or under the careful watch of Peredur. As the venom of religious factionism spewed so immediately, the king wondered whether he had erred in not having some means of protection, or attack, on his person. *Assassinations start after loud insults that result in a room of chaos.* Another lesson from his Merlin flooded his memories.

Archbishop Glycerius was at the ready to articulate his accusation.

"You require your princes and chieftains to pay a penance of land and cattle to your Church. In turn, you only allow princes and chieftains to enter into the clergy, thus protecting your own lands in perpetuity. It is a political mechanism. A circular fraud. A farce. A façade. A mockery of the Scriptures."

The old man was not wrong. The Church of the Britons, far older than Rome in spite of her claims, misinterpreted both Moses and John, asserting that those in ecclesiastical authority must be priests and kings. They did well to separate the two (unlike Rome), but did err in creating priest-class made wholly of immediate and strong bloodlines. This allowed frequent transfers of land, protecting Cymry soil for all times.

"And you would have all lands ceded to the Church. For you think the keys of temporal and heavenly rule are thine, yes?" Illtud fired back, yelling.

"The Bible says–"

"It has been given to me to understand that NONE OF YOU are Scriptural. It is part of your furniture, a decoration, a tool of selective misuse and no authority." Arthur winked at Taliesin, stooped in the back of the hall, forming a great and proud smile. *The Merlin would be proud too.*

"Enough theology today." The king rose. "To enjoy our rivers, bask in our baths and waterfalls, be revived by our forests, surely attempt to enjoy our women." The gathered crowd chuckled, including the bishops. "To tour our fellowship hall where all men are equal under God – only to recompense the gesture by launching into an immediate insult of our national faith. Such guile." Arthur shook his head, calming himself. "It will certainly make some story, laughing around the hearth with cider."

"I have a story for you, Celt." Glycerius used Caesar's pejorative. "I noticed that in all your hospitality and openness, you failed to take us to see the abandoned barracks of the Legionnaires, the housing of our brave soldiers in the days when we put the lash to you barbarians."

"Speak no more, Archbishop." Magus pointed his long spiny finger, motioning in vain to stop the rogue priest.

The spiny plated finger jostled a memory in Lancelot. He shifted forward but slightly.

But it was Arthur that spoke.

"Barbarian? O, Roman propaganda. My grandfather, the Pendragon King Tewdrig, told my father all about this. We taught your would-be Roman conquerors to understand Greek. Our druids taught you how to build canals, to conduct water and to live in cleanliness. As for the lash, we loaned you senators and chieftains. You were a tenuous and oft unwelcomed guest here; never a conqueror. This is the land of Bran and Caradoc. Your mythology and hubris won't be sold for truth here, Emperor."

Bedwyr, using his left hand, skated a leather-wrapped steel cup, brimming with cider, past three seated onlookers. It perfectly found rest in Arthur's palm.

"Grandfather? Yes. Let us speak on grandfathers." The delirious old priest's chest plumed, but the rest of him trembled. "I am here because of MY grandfather. For my grandfather. He was stationed HERE. He slept in your wretched barracks, pissed in your magical pools, and found your women – o, the Cymreig women that the whole of the world covets – he found them uncomely yapping dogs! You animals killed him. He fell at the tip of a Silure spear, his body never transported back to Mother Rome!"

"Perhaps you would join him?" Many Saxons had heard this particular tone, the final sounds that filled their ears ere they fell to Arthur's steel.

Unafraid, the elderly symbol of the proud but crumbled empire continued his untoward spectacle. "You will give tribute to Rome and fidelity to her Church, THE ONLY TRUE CHURCH, and to the Bishop our Father, or–"

Magus opened his armored hand. Using his unnaturally long fingers as four tethered whips, he smote the old man flush about the face. The lips split in twain, vertically. A fount instantly watered the table red and baptized the Catholic presbyters, sprinkling them with shock, spittle and much blood.

Through that massive curtain in the pagan tabernacle, I saw such a slap.

Lancelot rose so quickly it was as if he had been standing the entire time. He leaped over the long table with no more effort than a stag hops over a ditch, then majestically bounds into the deep of the forest. Also unarmed, he made for the wall, freeing the mounted Sword of Power from the hooks upon which it rested. Excalibur in hand, he rushed upon not the raging old man mourning a long dead Roman, but rather the masked villain sitting next to him.

When the Masked Man perished, there would be no answers to rest Arthur's soul, no final closure to the wound. No healing for the loss of the Merlin. And this pained Lancelot, even as he brandished the blade overhead, preparing for the terminal stroke. However, he would here make an end of the Kingdom's most dire and secret threat. The shadow menace would fall. Whatever this man and his Council of Nine were, the means by which they coerced and controlled whole nations, or their ultimate aims for mankind, the details were not relevant. They were pure evil. And the head of that snake would be severed, today. Though Arthur would not have opportunity to interrogate his great secret enemy, he would be rid of him, and Lancelot was content with that outcome.

And in killing the Masked Man, the misdeeds of Vivien would never see the light of day, her sins dying with him.

Excalibur, so sharp and wielded with Lancelot's speed, rent the sky itself, flying swiftly to visit judgment upon Simon's neck.

Judgment deferred.

A club that was as a small oak tree intercepted and deflected its course. Though the club was cut through and through by the famed blade and still found its mark, the blow was slowed, and the wound not fatal. Simon was knocked to the ground and opened, but the flesh wound was minor.

Lancelot's vision ascended slowly from where the masked priest lay to the height of the tabletop and at last, fully standing, to his eye level. Face to face and waiting for him to recompose himself was a wide and brawny form, a second club already in hand to replace the one severed and rolling away on the marble floor.

The stare was both empty and intense, filled only with malevolent intent. It belonged to the father of one whom Lancelot loved.

Ogyrfan the Giant had protected the red

Roman, and his eyes warned that he was set to execute the whole of the assembly.

Lancelot put the sword to the neck of Magus, still down, to stop the encroach of the large man, or conversely, to simply finish the task, even if the cost was absorbing a fatal blow from his newly-made foe.

Dumbfounded, Arthur's command stilled the whole of the hall.

"Lancelot, stop!" Bewilderment. "The crippled cardinal stayed the mouth of this rude collection of bones masquerading as an emperor. You launched out at the wrong masked man."

"Lancelot would not miss his aim, brother."

In a complex and closing vice, Lancelot responded to his friends, careful to conceal any indictment of his foster-mother. Haste was also demanded, given the burly opponent yet prepared to engage him.

"Lord, Gwyar." That deep and metallic voice long told in bardic song and poets' prose uttered its reply. "This man is chief of the shadow government. I saw him in the Lady of the Lake's forest so long ago. He is the one." The tip of Excalibur pressed to Simon's wound, twisting just so. Lucifer's disciple refused to reward Lancelot and cried out not.

"The one that –?"

"The one behind the mystery of Merlin, my Lord."

That the Cymry were unarmed wasn't exactly true. Although the individual guests, heroes and knights did not bring their personal arms to the peaceful accord, no leader from the days of Vortigern to the present time would allow another Night of Long Knives to occur under their watch. To this end, several leaves, shortswords of the finest craftsmanship, lightweight killing instruments designed for a quick kill in a defensive situation, were concealed in ornate, thin, hollow boxes that served as under-bases for food salvers and chargers. In a move well-rehearsed and well-practiced for such an occasion, the food dish could be lifted and gently set aside, the box unhinged, Cymry steel revealed.

Arthur gave the command, his calm matching Lancelot's answer, both of them mastering emotion, both of them assessing the whole of the room, both of them transported from assembly hall to forest, field or riverbed. Unlike in other battle settings, children and defenseless citizens abounded.

Within three seconds Bedwyr, Gwalchmai, Urien, King Meurig, Mordred, Gaheris, Cai, Peredur, Geraint, Lancelot's sons Rhun and Rhufawn, along with the Bloodhound Prince, who brandished the king's own sword, were upright. Leaves swiveling, hilts rolling in ready and anxious palms, Vivien's battle stances engaged.

Sounds of the calamity reached the troop of Roman guards, who reposed outside the hall. They and their spears forced themselves inside.

"My beloved friend, and champion of all Britannia." Arthur was calm. "In your haste to protect us from such a villain, you did err." The way the king spoke was neither condemning nor offensive towards Lancelot and was followed by, "I would have done the same thing, having discovered the one who stole Britain's Treasure." (And by this, he spake of Merlin).

Lancelot had no argument for what came next.

"Rather not to slay him. Instead, brother, arrest! Detain! Let us finally discover the truth that has so long darkened our Summer Kingdom."

In an irony of fortune, Lancelot needed not make a reply. Like a mad, diseased cow or ram, Ogyrfan, having given a few more moments of breath to the one lording over his thoughts and deeds, turned towards *his target*. Stooping into an attack pose, shoulders low and squared, he barreled into the host table, splintering it as a twig, violently knocking many to the floor, causing scrapes and wounds but no major injury. Arthur had stood and jumped backward at the onset of the assault, but the Giant was before him, *and the club was already midflight*.

Lancelot's flight was much faster than the twirling club.

"Have any more?" Lancelot cocked his head at Ogyrfan, then looked at yet another weapon rendered as wood for the hearth by Excalibur. "That's two." The champion of the Round Table wiggled two fingers, goading the attacker to assault him rather than the king.

The events were unfolding with such surreal haste that none knew whether they should kill, or *could kill*, the queen's father. While Lancelot was cultivating distraction through taunting, granting them time to think, Gwalchmai usurped the process and, wrapping his hand with a strap of leather from his belt, grasped his curved sword by the blade and struck the Giant violently upon the back of his head with the sword's hilt. Then he recovered the hilt and raised the blade high, seeking a fatal blow. *Treachery is no respecter of persons*. This was the Hawk of May's reasoning.

But now.

But now a scene that no bard could damn the tears to tell, could channel away the overmuch sorrow to utter.

Now the tip of the Sword of Power pressed into the side of Gwalchmai's neck, its bulging veins swelling at the fear, pulsating from a rapid and roaring heart. Through the droplets of sweat, Gwalchmai peered down the plane of the blade to see an oak of a man as a statue; no movement, no emotion, ready to kill.

Thinking only of his one true love, regarding neither law nor politic, Lancelot would slay Gwalchmai, or one thousand Gwalchmais, rather than suffer Gwenhwyfar to see her father slain.

Gwalchmai's sword remained at the throat of Ogyrfan.

Lancelot's sword remained at the throat of Gwalchmai.

"Gwyar, please, no." Arthur's words were for naught.

The only person in the realm, nay, any realm, that could challenge Lancelot by reason of her sorceries and her skill (and he knew as much and respected the threat) could not reach Lancelot's throat, as he was twice her height. Rather, Gwyar put a small dagger, rivaling Excalibur for sharpness and forged on the same Isle, to his kidney. She cared *for country and for her son,* and his remaining alive was best for both causes.

Gwalchmai's sword upon Ogyrfan.

Lancelot's sword upon Gwalchmai.

Gwyar's dagger upon Lancelot.

And the Roman soldiers closing in, under no obligation to delay their encroach or give space for the Briton's internal strife to reconcile itself.

Meanwhile, Magus and Glycerius used the standoff to stand and recover. Both bleeding, only one giving thought for his own life. The retired emperor, too old for combat, nonetheless attacked the mighty King Arthur.

Whilst the other Round Table Knights and Companions used hidden compartments to conceal reserve weaponry amongst lamb and beef and cakes, Cai simply kept his famed club inside his cloak – always. He tossed it to the twice-attacked-in-one-day Pendragon who, in one motion, both caught the wooden instrument and brought it hard across the Roman's jaw.

A club is light at the handle, weighted at the head. A menacing weapon. Arthur rotated explosively from his core, generating maximum torque: a colossal blow.

A dislodged eye bounced, ultimately finding rest upon a broken plate on what remained of the host table. Teeth clacked and spread over the floor. No facial structure remained; just a white face smashed, a lump of folded dough with nostrils. The bitter man was liberated of the shackles of his mortal coil, released from his hatred of the Silures by a Silure.

And so, whilst his most beloved friends were frozen in the snare, the High King of the Britons slew a Roman emperor.

Next came a command, yelled in unison by the king and his champion.

"Cai, remove the queen. Hasten her to safety!"

"At once," Cai answered them both. "Shall I send signal to Lodge Hill and rouse our soldiers?" The steward could relay a message from Caerleon up to the fortress within three minutes and the guards, using fire and mirrors, could have a hundred men at arms at the hall seven minutes after that.

Arthur looked on his men and their quandary. And upon the Romans. "No, Cai. If we manage to not kill ourselves off, we will quickly add more Romans to our soil."

Gwenhwyfar was as befuddled and bewildered over her father's behavior as any of the attendees. She had no answers, and she worried for him, but gave no protest. She glanced at him, helpless before the Hawk of May, and then kept her gaze at Mordred constant until she was out of the hall and he out of her sight.

As their leader was *busy,* the warriors furthest from the standoff, and thus nearest to the Romans, tarried not for command or instruction. Rather, *action.*

Taliesin did all to discourage Rhufawn, for he had a special affinity for Maelgwn, Gwynedd's son, but the young man could not be withheld from the fight. Indeed, becoming a marvel and spectacle to all, he *was the fight.*

Rhufawn had a similar build to his father, but was of just above average height. Where Maelgwn's hair was curly and black, his was as the sandy shores, like Arthur. The young warrior seemed to be the product of God, taking the best ingredients of the two great men and blending them into a flawless, perfect knight, gifting to the world Rhufawn ap Maelgwn, whom the bards record as Galahad, *which is a Hebrew derivative of the word Gilead, and by interpretation means 'healing balm.'*

Rhufawn, the bastard son of a Glamorgan damsel, favored the simple midnight-blue tunic worn so oft by Maelgwn, the color, when coupled with crimson, of the Silures. But he loved his father and the tribes of the north as well. For this cause, his cape was black, ensigned with a beautiful white raven. *A walking symbol of peace, unity and individuality amongst the Cymry.*

On days where he sought a shinier, statelier expression (though he was ever humble in disposition, impossible to anger, impossible to speak against), he enjoyed the gold-styled armor popular amongst the children of both Arthur and Maelgwn. When decked in gold, the lasses swooned (though endowed like his father, the boy knew no woman, vowing only to give his virginity to one wife) and the poets sang, all the while Taliesin laboring to protect him from the world.

Rhufawn had not known war. Had never known the terror of the Saxon's Long Knife, his mind not bent with the horrors of the ever-threat of ambush and torture and annihilation.

A healthy mind, but wanton for quest.

A natural warrior, he held back in training exercises, cautious and careful never to injure his opponents, his kinsmen. But natural talent is often overcome through hard work. Heeding this lesson from Taliesin, Rhufawn was a picture of *both*. Never taking the skill passed to him from Lancelot for granted, he practiced with radical commitment.

Naturally better than others, more humble, harder working.

And now a real combat situation was before him and his kinsmen and friends.

The first Roman soldier swung his spear sloppily at the young man, putting undue faith in the advantage of reach. Rhufawn not only ducked the lazy swipe but, during its flight, circled from front to back, round his opponent, slashed him in the only space between armor and spine and recoiled, watching the attacker fall paralyzed, with an agonizing death soon to follow.

He followed this, *dancing Vivien's dance* through the Romans. Always at a diagonal position, always countering, never initiating, always killing instantly. His movements were at once a tempest and a swan. As he ran one Roman through, his blade was withdrawn and already taking limb and ear from the next in one motion.

Neither clip, nor bruise, nor scrape found him. The only time he was touched was when Urien caught the lad by his tunic and chastised him, screaming, "Save us one!"

Rhufawn's singular massacre of an old invader in a new era lasted a short time.

Lovemaking and fights alike seem to last forever, but are over in minutes.

Maelgwn, though never moving from his vantage point upon Gwalchmai, whom he believed would surely strike down the queen's father minus the steel upon his throat, was able to see it all. And for him it *did* seem to last forever. The Northern king had been in battles with Rhun, a fine soldier and great young man who had already earned his own bards' songs. Thus, he was accustomed to the threat of losing that son.

But not so Rhufawn.

Maelgwn's emotions undulated as a strong spiderweb. *Fear for his safety. Dread that he now knew the stealing of another man's breath; pride over what he witnessed.*

Could it be?

Nimrod.

Hercules.

Achilles.

This was the company of fighters that Maelgwn Gwynedd kept. Invincible. Unstoppable. Grace and power personified.

But also, madness and instability.

Rhufawn had proven in his years as a boy and young man to possess none of the latter; he here showed the fullness of the former. Could it be?

Speed.

Use of balance and imbalance.

Counter-fighting skills to an extreme degree, where the opponent's next two moves could be *seen* before he began the first two.

Precise maiming skills when desired.

Killing strokes from hundreds of angles and approaches.

Fluidity.

Defense.

Could it be?

For as long as tales of valor and skill would be told and soldiers ranked, the matter would never be settled. But Maelgwn first saw his glorious son vanquish a troop as an effortless and beautiful angel delivering death with grace.

Could it be?

Yes, Galahad was greater than Lancelot. The greatest warrior to ever live.

A father's tear formed, and Maelgwn cared not to contain it.

Meanwhile, the High King was directing a battle on two fronts. He took one of the priests by the neck of his robe and demanded, "Which amongst you is a boatman? He is of the laity, the troop, or one of you?" Arthur's authority and power was delivered in Latin with the same precision and want of immediate response as when delivered in Cymraeg. "I will only ask once," he finished.

The priest, soaking his robe with urine, trembling, pointed to one of the soldiers, barely enunciating, "Sail, sail the boat."

Arthur unhanded the clergyman and threw his voice, as a javelin is hoisted through the skies at Grecian games, down the long hall. "Urien!"

The ferocious fighter paused in a kill and found the source hollering his name.

"Him." Arthur pointed and gestured frantically. "Spare him!"

But two minutes later, the Roman troop was dead. With the exception of the sailor, all had perished. All tilled at the plow by famed Round Table Knights of old, *and new.*

The civilian guests found a crack in the chaos, a collective feeling of safety, and vacated the hall. This was more dangerous than the inferior insurgency by the Italians.

Simon Magus took full advantage of the fleeing frenzy, snatching the child Gildas, who was too big to be carried and too small to push men and women aside, from his father's custody.

An evil laugh projected, louder and sharper than the king's own voice had been moments ago.

"Let's add one more knife to this tension, one more wooden piece to this game of *gwyddbwyll*. After all" – through the mask his eyes peered over the checkered floor, now a calamity of teeth and organs, broken furniture and broken bones – "we are already upon the game board, yes?" A second laugh.

"This is no game," struck back the Pendragon, taking a strong stride towards the masked priest.

"O, my king." Awe, mixed with mockery, stirred with teaching, followed. "All life is a game of *gwyddbwyll*." A short black dagger was now upon the child's neck, his pens and parchments fumbled away, his hands pushing at the priest's red robes. "Don't move, lad; not another movement." The dagger pressed. "And don't you move either."

Arthur stopped as though a statue, ceasing to tempt the villain.

The scene quieting and settling, with the fighting assuaged, begat the accusations and strained discourse amongst the chain of prisoners and prison-keepers.

"How dare you draw your sword upon my son!" Morgaine of the Faeries the first to break the silence in their deadly game.

"How dare your son attempt to kill my–"

"Your what!" Gwalchmai swelled with righteous indignation, sensing that Lancelot was primed to out himself, to snare his leg in the trap of his own adultery, and by his own words no less.

As the battle of threats and accusations proceeded, and as message had not been sent to Lodge Hill to signal for additional warriors, *other visitors were arriving.*

Lancelot captured his confession ere it fully left his lips, swallowing it back and recovering with, "My king's father-in-law. What is it you accuse me of? Use plain speech." Here, Lancelot evoked an evil and ancient technique, used by the guilty since the dawn of man. When caught in a grave and unspeakable sin, boldly dare the accuser to verbalize it, making it sound shocking and absurd, diminishing the credibility simply through its saying, though it is true.

Morgaine found her son's eyes with her own and forbade him to speak, knowing it would undo the Summer Kingdom.

Lancelot's rationalization went on. "Before we execute this man, we must understand the aberration of his action. A quiet fellow who gives alms to all and loves his daughter and her king."

"Such love manifested as an attempt to murder the king, whom you say he loves." Gwalchmai tried to corral his words, obeying his mother as he could, but alas, he could not fully. "You protect him for love of the queen, not our lord."

But Arthur had found reason in Lancelot's words, and dismissed the weight of Gwalchmai's half-concealed warning. "You are right, Maelgwn. I have seen this before. A just man atop a great hill in the north also sought to kill me. The toil in my father-in-law's eyes matches those of Itto Gawr, a just and goodly creature."

Arthur's glare turned again towards Magus.

"Somehow, Ogyrfan is bewitched and no traitor, yes?"

The Leader of the Council of Nine ignored the query.

"Gwalchmai, stand down. Mordred, would you and," Arthur found the awing Rhufawn amongst the onlookers, "this" – the enamored king wanted for words – "extraordinary young man please bind Ogyrfan and see him back to his lands? There confine him in exile until we discover how to cure the kingdom of this witchcraft. Station many soldiers there; make the arrangements and see to it swiftly. As for you," now Arthur spoke directly to the Giant who had but minutes ago made attempt on his life, "you shan't be charged with treason at this time. However, see that you tether yourself to Caer Ogyrfan, and leave not."

Then the king attended to the others. "Lancelot would not have hurt your son, Gwyar. Please." His hands made a motion to withdraw the weapon. At this point, with Gwalchmai released and Lancelot's sword no longer occupied, he could have turned and engaged the sorceress. But he counted the cost, selecting to let Arthur mediate and resolve the conflict, for he had grown up at the feet of powerful women and, to him, they were somehow different creatures entirely than maidens and farm girls, or the Picts who aided him in emptying his lusts from time to time. To him there were *goddesses and girls,* and Morgaine of the Faeries was a *goddess of goddesses.*

Arthur pleaded, repeating his motions once more. "Gwyar, he forgot himself for a moment in the chaos of confusion. He is our brother, our champion, our friend."

The sorceress drew so close that none but Lancelot could hear her. Though impossible on account of their proportions, she was in his ear.

"I have been in love too, Maelgwn." Here she spoke of the only time she had really loved a man, and that years ago foiled through Vivien's prerogative. "And I didn't let it consume and control and change me." *No, lying with your brother in ritual intercourse did that, followed by your soul shattering at the seeing of your son inside your brother's wife.* Her conscience judged her hypocrisy harshly, but she repelled those thoughts. "Get thy head out of thy loins and serve Cymru to your fullest potential." Having concluded the impassioned and maternal lecture, she at last recoiled.

Now all were free of pointed things upon their throats and vital organs.

All save little Gildas, hostage, and the sole means by which Magus might walk out of the hall alive.

"O, King Arthur, son of Meurig and Onbrawst, you cannot be defeated and your kingdom can never fail, even when conflict arises from within. Your career hath not disappointed me. I am most certain that nothing frightens you."

Her son safe and her attention fixed,

Morgaine heard the words and shrieked; candles that were unlit blazed, curtains that were closed and knotted flew open, and windows clinched and cracked. His phrases, his arrogance and false flattery. She had met this Italian before.

"Dynion Hysbys!" she cried. "Dynion Hysbys!"

"Druids in the Church of Rome? His identity you mistake." Illtud was aghast at the notion.

"And what a match I did make, little Raven." Magus looked upon Arthur and Gwyar with violating and debased expression.

King Arthur spoke to the chieftain Caw. That they had had land disputes, territorial controversies and bruised history for the whole of the Iron Bear's life was irrelevant. "Sir, your son will be safe, worry not."

Then he looked down to the frightened boy. "Gildas, be calm. Breathe. This will make some story to be added to the histories that you will memorialize for our people. Our official historian."

Gildas managed to smile through the terror and feel safe. *And this was the majesty of Arthur, the lamp in darkest times.*

"Brilliant, Briton. Brilliant." Magus stalled, confident that rescuers of his own would arrive. "What will you give me that I might refrain from opening the lad like a fish here and now?"

"You would give your life to harm a child? If Maelgwn and Gwyar are correct, you are some great one. Would that be your end? Rhufawn hasn't left with the Giant yet; I am sure he could get to you before your blade gets to my young friend."

Rhufawn's father and Urien shared a grin. That the king would threaten the priest with

Rhufawn instead of Lancelot was noteworthy, and increased Lancelot's pride o'er his boy.

"O, Arthur, if you knew my God you would know that harming a virgin male child" – he looked for words to further offend the Britons – "is not only a frequent requirement, but a great joy."

"What do you want?" The king tired of contests of words with the unwanted visitor.

"Two things." Now Magus's recourse was likewise blunt.

With one arm he strangled Gildas, using his forearm, whilst holding the dagger in the same hand. With the other he reached into the folds of his garb. "This book – from whence did it come?"

"I am Taliesin and men call me Merlin; I am Merlin, but men call me Taliesin." The hump-backed bard, with a staff to aid his gait, made straight for the Devil's own man, unafraid. "It was passed down through my family, given to my ancestor centuries ago by the one whose message you fear the most."

"So." All fell silent. "You are the one that converted the Merlin and delayed my plans. Yet, unlike the Merlin, these pseudo-Christians here" – the bishops and elders buckled that such an overtly vile thing would judge them false – "you are allowed to live, freely accessing the king, serving as the new Merlin. Why?"

"In the Body there are many members and diverse offices, as it pleases the Lord." The boy Gildas was nearly within arm's reach of Taliesin now. "My role is to look after one who will carry the truth long after the cosmic dust has rolled up our Island as a scroll and fire from Heaven discarded her. I teach individuals and influence where I can but Merlin, o, the Merlin – his voice and influence would have changed the world and filled the Body of Christ by actually saving souls and edifying saints through the gospel of the grace of God!"

A clamor and howling of heresy filled the hall.

And Magus's other guests gaining distance, soon to arrive.

"Gwyar?" Taliesin looked for aid and the sorceress obliged, causing the flames to change from shades of yellow to greens and reds and blues, rattling candlestick and curtain rod, fastening the mouths of the bishops through fear.

"And because of Merlin's mystery, which revealed how God forgave all men living in this dispensation above five hundred years ago, not imputing their trespasses against them, that salvation is a function of simply trusting that good news and being forever secured, at peace with a God that already did it all. Because neither these bishops and their works or religion, nor you and your Devil worship, can stop God's plan to reconcile heavenly places with the simple and the foolish, the beggar and the commoner, men and women of no report, because of this simple message of grace." Taliesin was a very soft-spoken man who usually used quips and humor to teach, or harassed his students with witty short allegories. Here he raised his voice, booming with righteous fury. "Because of this, *you killed the Merlin.*"

Hearing this pronouncement, Rhufawn and Mordred stopped short of the wide, arching doorways that were in the anteroom of the hall, one of two entrances to the place. Ogyrfan was bound, head dangling low in shame, confusion and externally-operated rage. Then his ear perked up, as that of a hound that hears a hare whilst hunting in the wood.

Lancelot had returned the shimmering rapier forged on Ynys Enlli to its rightful wielder.

Arthur was gazing upon its scripted hilt. The masked fiend denied nothing and the fact that Arthur was in the same room with the man, hiding behind his guise, who had killed his beloved wizard, challenged his soul to sacrifice the boy and strike Simon down. Teeth gritted, fists clenched, breathing somewhere between weeping and screaming, he managed a final question.

"And the second demand?"

"O Arthur. Your temperance and will, your mastery over passions, over self. How I will enjoy redirecting it."

"Your second demand!"

"The cup that accompanied this." Simon Magus slung the ancient text at the feet of Taliesin, improving his ability to shield himself using the dagger and the boy. "The Grail. I came to witness how you govern, to get but a glimpse of the legendary sovereign, and I came for the Grail. And the visit, the foolish emperor notwithstanding – of course most emperors are dullards and dumb – has been wildly successful, to this point."

"You won't see another sunset, yet you reckon the day a success?"

"I will outlive you, son of Meurig." Magus gave a confident response. "Now, the cup; where is it?"

The doors of the anteroom exploded open, knocking Mordred and Rhufawn back several paces and rendering Ogyrfan unconscious. Rays of light and fog filled the hall. A spectre entered.

Gracefully strolling upon the fog, she at once ascended as a dove, with pillowed sleeves and long yellow hair. She was adorned all in white, clad with silver armor. Spiraling towards the ceiling, she soared in and out amongst the long timber rafters.

But 'twas no spectre, for 'twas the Lady of the Lake.

Rhufawn's might in battle exceeding Lancelot had been the first marvel. The Lady of the Lake appearing, bearing in her very hands the Cup of Christ, was the second.

Simon Magus let Gildas loose. Into Arthur's arms he sprinted and in turn, Arthur gently guided him to Caw, who actually embraced his foe. Every witness stood silent and agape. Many swords, satchels or staffs simply dropped to the hard floor below.

The maser was borne as if by an angel, and when she tipped it down towards the watchers below, revealing the mouth of the cup, all saw through their own eyes the next world.

Rhufawn, though raised at the feet of Taliesin and grounded in his mysteries, yearned for it most. And such did it touch him that his heart thumped not for any maiden, his mind drawn away to no other thought save partaking of or *achieving the Grail.*

Taliesin noted that it vexed him.

The Roman Catholic visitors saw it.

The Primal Church of the Britons saw it.

The Round Table Fellowship present saw it.

Morgaine of the Faeries had seen it before, but never as this.

Sundry warriors, stately ladies, minor chieftains, cooks, keepers of the estate and bards looked and saw it.

Little Gildas, the historian and scribe, saw it too.

And then the Lady, as a glowing white phantom, spoke to none else but Simon Magus, the Devil's vicar upon the earth.

"They worship the creature in the stead of the Creator, and you want men to swear by this. A wicked and adulterous nation seeketh after a sign. But a sign you shall have not, and you will never have the Grail! It was given to the druids to guard, and the druids will guard it." The sound of her voice was as many rushing waters, her sermon turning unto the clergy. "And neither shall you!" She cursed the priests and vanished, the whole of the hall falling into pitch black, the silence of darkness.

Morgaine wondered if she ever she would see the Lady again. She had resurrected the purpose of their Order; she had retained her gall for the corruption of the Church, but discovered that Christ and His mother were not to blame for their deeds and had, indeed, endowed her with a sacred trust. She had become fully empowered, transfigured, and glorious. 'Twas no longer needed for the two to move the cup to and fro about the land. It was in Vivien's hands now, to keep or to destroy, to keep from the reach of the wickedness of men forever.

Simon's other expected visitors finally arrived.

Whereas the Lady of Lake had entered through the anteroom, destroying the doorway, these unwanted guests blasted through the front doors.

Two Giants. Thrice the size of Ogyrfan, with green, ghastly skin, horny brows and fanged teeth. No sooner had Urien and Cai restored some light to the hall than were the monsters upon them. Swift as four-footed beasts of the field, they barreled through the crowd. One snatched up Simon with the same effort that a child expends in snatching up a doll when it is time to clean her chamber. The other led the escape, providing a shield of flesh, absorbing sword and spear as they sprinted from the hall, adding further destruction to a place now filled with disarray and desolation. All snarls and no words, they were at once in full sprint across the fields, into the muck of the riverbeds, and gone.

Maelgwn Gwynedd thought only of Gwenhwyfar, departing at once to see her. The bubble within, no respecter of time or place or propriety, was building in him yet again.

CHAPTER 13
The Abduction of Queen Gwenhwyfar by Maelgwn

The Rescue of Queen Gwenhwyfar by Lancelot

Though lacking the Holy Grail's fame, the king had a special chalice as well. Heavy, ornate, wood inlaid with pewter; the Awen symbol sprawled the circumference of its base. Most importantly of all, the Merlin had gifted it to Arthur after the boy-king had earned his first victory in the Saxon Wars. They had enjoyed a scrumpy together so many long years ago, and with a rare but earned drunkenness, many victory cries. The poor pewter cup was dented by virtue of victorious hammerings into tables and shelves.

No longer a boy, the son of Meurig hammered it down upon a small end-table now. Scrumpy hissed, and not a few drops of the cider streamed about the surface.

Illtud, cousin to Arthur and, due to Dyfrig's advancing years, the most influential amongst the clergy, was the king's drinking companion. And his friend besides.

There was no cause for statesmanship amongst friends, not ensuing the day they had both witnessed and endured. "By Heaven and Hell, Illtud, what just happened?"

"I think I aged three lifetimes in one day!" They both laughed; the chuckle of trauma.

The king became serious, yet no less friendly. "Illtud, you maintain that education and knowledge must diffuse throughout Cymru, from beggar to prince. Moreover, that every person above twelve ought to be able to speak in Latin for commerce, to entertain strangers, and to have some Greek and Hebrew to reason the Scriptures."

"Absolutely, Lord. An educated populace has a higher propensity to eschew tyranny, being enlightened by the precepts of liberty."

Arthur swallowed hard another gulp, then replenished the scrumpy. "Then why not consider what my Merlin taught? Why preach liberty and then silence those who would take you up on the very offer you make – namely, to reason from the Scriptures? The words of the elders are at variance with your deeds."

"I know today's events have reopened your greatest wound," said Illtud. "But we did not conspire to murder your counselor. He was my friend too."

Arthur was unsatisfied by the response and responded not, opting to drink and wait for more information.

"The theology that the druid discovered, and that Taliesin the Bard champions, is not a new revelation." Illtud was respectful but continued with conviction. "Variants of it have been studied and affirmed as heresy since the times of Caradoc and his daughter Eurgaine. We find that such a mode of study slices the Scriptures like bread, selects favorable passages and ignores a balanced and holistic view of the full counsel of God. Where Taliesin would cry 'grace through faith!', we would counter with 'show me your faith by your works'."

Another swallow. "Does not their way simply maintain that consideration should be given of to whom a letter, poem or prose is speaking in the Holy Book and that audience and context matter?"

Illtud countered, "We also maintain that tradition has equal weight as Scripture, and that, when interpreted without at least some guidance by one called to teach and oversee the flock, gross error and divergent sects will emerge, fracturing the Body." Illtud proceeded to give Arthur what he coveted: direct truth. "We were going to do all to force Merlin to retire and not put his message upon your ear, lest he turn the world upside down, but by the Saviour Himself, none amongst our sect sought to injure our friend."

"You feared he might be right and you might be rendered less necessary. Or unnecessary. Would he not say that your traditions have made the word of God of no effect?"

"He might." Illtud offered candor. This pleased the king more than smokescreens and distraction.

"I don't know if Taliesin and Merlin hold the truth, or if you do, or if it lies somewhere betwixt and between. My station in this life is not to be a master of letters, but rather to secure religious liberty for every man. Even for the Romanists that we sent back to their See with tail between leg and official demands that they investigate deep corruption from within. Do you understand?"

"I do, and I agree. We let fear best us, but again, I promise–"

"I believe you, cousin. This red-robed villain is connected to the Dynion Hysbys and connected to Rome. Whether by infiltration or coercion or alliance. I find no such alliance to the druids or to our primitive Church at this point. What befell our Merlin was of fiendish design by this masked devil. We must settle the tension between the court and pulpit, and focus on his capture and deposition. Madoc will secure every port. He must not leave the Blessed Isles. We have spent the whole of our lives evicting invaders; this time every effort must be made to keep him away from his *secret society* and confined to our soil." Then Arthur eased the gravity, seasoning it with some levity. "Grace versus faith plus works we can debate another day, over much more cider – agreed?"

"Of course!"

Illtud and the king embraced. And no sooner had they embraced than there was a familiar and coordinated knock upon the king's door.

Arthur's countenance dropped as he hollered, "Cai, come. What is it?" He looked at Illtud, exclaiming, "Giants, masked red devils, Roman emperors, a demigod boy warrior and Vivien transfigured with the most precious of our Isle's relics. What else could happen today?" Equal parts smile and dismay.

"Perfectly summarized, Iron Bear. Perfectly summarized." The preacher's disposition matched his friend's.

"The Queen Gwenhwyfar," Cai panted, struggling to moisten his mouth sufficiently to form words. "Abducted. The queen abducted!"

* * *

"Unhand me!" Gwen II screeched. "You would destroy Cymru for your lust, end an era of peace for an hour of pleasure?"

Maelgwn's bubble had swelled as never before. More so than when he had murdered his uncle to have his wife, or later, arranged for his nephew's murder to bed down Rhufawn's young mother.

Discernment gone.

Temperance abandoned.

The queen was not bound, save by Maelgwn's hands, one of which eclipsed both of hers. He sat behind her, and she was pinned between the trunk of his torso, as a great muscular stone, and the saddle horn of Maelgwn's stallion.

He pressed hard against the small of her back, fully aroused. He freed his massive member from the folds of his trousers and forced her hand to reach round and stroke it.

Prior to her transformative affair with Mordred, she would have happily succumbed to his, or those of any fit and handsome lad, aggressive advances just for the intrigue and fleshly pleasure of it. But she had changed. Had *been changed* for years. Maelgwn simply knew this not. He was accosting a woman loyal to her true love. The loyal adulteress.

When she did not comply with fondling and pleasuring Maelgwn with her hand, he groaned as a dumb animal chained and just out of reach of food, and relinquished her hand. However, he left himself out of his trousers, grinding upon her bottom as they rode.

"Where will we die?" she asked, crying out to reason with the Round Table champion. "For when discovered, we shall both be put to the grave. And you know this. Arthur doth love me above all, and not even your battle dirk will prevent his sword."

Ignoring the ominous sentence of death, he answered the question. "Pictish land. The settlement of Megiel, near to the capital, Peairt. They crown kings there and view me as one of their own; they will protect our entry."

Gwenhwyfar scoffed at the tall warrior. "You would make me your Caledonian whore queen? Arthur will lay waste to the Picts, and to you–"

"Mention not his name again." The pressure from the pelvis of her abductor made the severity of the demand very serious. He could crush her, and in his current state, quite without intending to do so. She needed a different tack.

And she had help.

"When it comes time to do that which you would do–"

"Stop your mouth, wizard!" The famed low voice became a scream. A scream to none but the owls, who responded through the dark of night.

Hearing one once so dear speaking unto unknown voices, obviously originating from his own head, increased the queen's fright. She ceased talking and thought on Mordred and the few happy thoughts of a life shredded by abuse and sticky secret sins. *I have reaped what I have sowed, perhaps,* she thought. *He will be the avenging angel of the dozens of boys and men I have used. Why, in the end, would I not be likewise used?*

Megiel was in center of Alba, a four-day journey by horse or carriage; three if they continued at Maelgwn's relentless pace.

"When it comes time to do that which you would do, for the sake of your country, and for Arthur, do it

not." *The phantom voice palpable, substantive. Real. Yet not real.*

Arousal and distress caused the warrior to thirst, and thirst caused the warrior to divert his thinking from Gwenhywfar's painted body, and, being diverted, he tried to fight his bubble.

"We will camp here tonight," he stated bluntly.

They had made it as far as the midlands and were in a deep thicket, the forest itself serving as the queen's bonds. Knowing this, Maelgwn gave no thought to leaving her near their fire, that he might find a stream. Bringing them water soon afterward, indeed she had moved not.

The insane man fashioned some random rules.

"Will you give yourself to me? I'll not force myself upon you."

"With all my heart, I will not," came the reply.

Maelgwn held her through the cold night, respecting her decision, forcing himself to abstain from forcing her.

The following night brought the same exchange.

"Will you give yourself to me? I'll not force myself upon you."

"With all my heart, I will not." This time Gwen pressed the one who had pressed her. "After all these years and all the maidens you've enjoyed, your reputation as a lover spreading from the Isles to the Continent, why do you yet dote over me?" That he was respecting her rejections gave her some bravery. "Is it the simple jealousy of men, or the forbidden fruit – that you covet what you cannot have?"

Lying next to the fire, he erected himself on one elbow, the position causing the veins of his neck, thick as a python, to pop and pulsate. *There was a time that those veins alone would have driven me to disrobe and throw myself at him,* she thought. And then he uttered the secret unspoken for more than twenty and five years.

"Cannot have AGAIN, you mean, my love."

And there it was. Before the lord of the Tylwyth Teg had known and changed her, making her a weapon to trouble and disrupt the world of men, there had been Maelgwn. The troubled young man from Gwynedd, tucked away in the Southeast at Illtud's school over some great scandal. Too important to prosecute and bring to account for his actions; rather, exiled until it could be sorted. *Had she forgotten? No. Tucked away in the tiny remnant of a mostly dark heart was one room, tinier still, a room indeed that belonged yet to Maelgwn.*

"Had the Iron Bear bothered to ask me, instead of his repetitive diatribe of *seeing you first,* I would've made it known that seeing you first was not knowing you first, AND I KNEW YOU FIRST." Now tears streamed. "But curse of curses, I loved him too much to tell him."

"And this secret has undone you, my sweet." She kissed him in a friendly and maternal way, not romantically.

"I was undone before meeting you or our High King. It was but another stone to the press, another burden to bear." He pushed her away gently, then pulled her close again. "Gwenhwyfar, my" – he had no proper name for it – "impulse has not passed. You must sleep in the cold, or I will ravish you. May I ravish you?"

Softly, she declined.

"What has changed since that night ere I brought you to Caerleon? What has changed since you looked upon me three days ago?"

Now Gwen's tears arrived too.

"O, Maelgwn. You intercepted a look intended for another, and assumed it unto yourself. I am sorry. You were my first love, and I thought, devoid of hope, my last. But" – she trembled – "and I pray you not slay me, I have changed. For I am in love."

* * *

King Arthur was overwrought. A man of command, anticipation and confident control, he had become a walking corpse of helplessness. The most logical conclusion was that Giants had made off with the queen. There was no demand for ransom, no evidence of struggle, no witnesses of anything. The queen had simply vanished into the night.

The priests and elders prayed and fasted, seeking God for a vision. Not for their support of the barren queen, but rather for the wellbeing of their sovereign. Strife and wrangling and positioning for power notwithstanding, Arthur's policies had created an enduring kingdom that afforded all factions, sects and religions the *freedom* to strive and wrangle. And though they sometimes hated him in the moment, when calm were the storms of religious passion, they loved and appreciated him.

Gwyar attempted use of the Sight, to no avail.

"And Maelgwn has vanished as well." Gwalchmai's statement of fact, dripping with obvious connection, flirting with direct accusation. Again, his mother both begged and commanded him to arrest his course with unspoken pleas and desperate gestures.

"You are right," responded the red-eyed and weary king. Yet again, the blindness of love fogged his discernment. The one who could detect a ruse or perceive a dishonest eye, from merchant to priest to ambassador to fellow sovereign, neither heard nor saw any of the warnings, of late increasingly launched by his nephew. "And that is the hope of our nation. He is the hope of our nation. My Lancelot must have seen the abductors that night and given chase. He knows every forest, every crag, every fortress, every settlement, the circuit of every ancient road and modern highway. If not ambushed and slain by whomever or whatever took our queen, then he is out there, and Lancelot will save her."

* * *

"Who is he who has won your heart?" asked Maelgwn.

* * *

Mordred was brought news of the queen's abduction while reposing in his white pavilion, erected at the base of Caer Ogyrfan.

A natural first act of investigation was to validate that the queen's father, bewitched and only days removed from his attempts to assassinate the king, had not somehow managed to escape from his appointed custodians and hold his daughter captive in his formidable fortress.

The appropriate point of departure for the investigation; but of no avail. Rhufawn and Mordred were both resting, vigilant but relaxed, having rapidly rendered the fortress a home-prison for Ogyrfan Gawr, who sulked in his own chamber. Mordred's eyes clamped tight, forcing away tears that would betray him, *and betray her*. He must present himself as a concerned soldier, citizen and nephew, no more. The scales of his sorrowed response must be no greater, nor lesser, than what was meet for the situation. *Especially if Rhufwan son of Maelgwn was as observant and intelligent as he was radiant and fair.*

Worst of all, the king had charged him and Rhufwan to remain at Caer Ogyrfan until a just solution could be delivered upon the queen's father, or until the enchantment wore off. *Mordred thus knew that he was bound to midlands for a while, helpless to launch out and find his one true love.*

* * *

"It is King Arthur Pendragon, mine own husband. And none else." Gwen did not hesitate. She lied quickly. And she lied convincingly. "Ere you brought me to him, I would have let my heart go back to our time together at school. He was a fine boy and a great friend back then but he was not..." Gwenhwyfar's words were contrived but conciliatory. "He was not you."

"And after? I was the very one to deliver you to he who would replace me in your heart?" Maelgwn's mind was all splinters, and he grasped with all that he could for one of the more benign shards. "He saw you first, and finally, in the end–"

"In the end I saw him. When you and I met it was as diving into a pool, naked." Her naughty allegory gave the tall, hurt warrior a happy moment and a short laugh. "An instant shock! Followed by pleasure and joy. By contrast, loving Arthur was rather like getting up before the break of dawn, preparing a great meal, laboring to carry it up the trails and finally, with sweat upon brow and growl within belly, reaching journey's end, and feasting. It was a slow, grinding journey to know the man. Less splendor, less splash – but yes, Maelgwn, I came to love Arthur. And you know." She took him by the hand. "You love him too."

Indeed, Maelgwn did love Arthur. A love that withheld provocation by the sons of Cunedda to engage in apocalyptic civil war and wrest the paramount of the monarchy from the Silures. A love that kept Arthur on the throne in the stead of Maelgwn. A love that kept the armies of the Cymry undefeated and shining to the world, their internal squabbles notwithstanding. He loved Arthur because Arthur was all that he was not; loyal, temperate, consistent, stable. All men who have lived through an era of war are broken; all have suffered loss. Arthur had lost all of his sons and his mind was yet healthy, his character full of humor and grace. Maelgwn's sons were all well and thriving, slashing villains, achieving quests, wrestling and playing with their father. And yet their father was a mess of contradiction, sorrow, brooding and instability. Jealousy burned Maelgwn, cooled by love and respect.

Maelgwn received Gwen's words with tact and surprising grace; he offered deep apology for the abduction and for forcing himself upon her.

Then irony entered. *And irony is a cruel master, a cold trickster.*

As Maelgwn apologized and behaved himself comely, Gwenhwyfar was at instant taken back to their youth. The piece of her heart given him as a lass still glowed, a tiny ember. But tiny embers have set whole forests ablaze.

She looked on Maelgwn, his face truly as of the gods, his body as warm marble. Reminiscence and distance bring betrayal to the doorstep. And lust knocks hard upon the doorknob.

Mordred surely withholds not himself from Kwyllog in their marriage bed, and I sleep with Arthur. What is the difference?

It has been so long. Arthur has befallen no misfortune; we are no closer to Mordred upon the throne than we were after our first tryst in the field. What is the difference?

I have already lain with Maelgwn. He was my first lover. This cannot be undone, so to have him now – what is the difference?

If we cannot conjure a ruse for my abduction, he or we are as the walking dead. WHAT IS THE DIFFERENCE?

"Maelgwn. The Bloodhound Prince." She made her eyes impossibly large, her mouth as honey before a starving bear. "We are near Alba. Show me this land of the Picts and, provided it is but one time and brings no ongoing scandal, we may revisit the passion of our youth, and you may have me. But once!"

The bubble burst! This time not in relieving itself with debauchery or some erotic crime, but rather with the satisfied glory of lovemaking yet to come. Maelgwn gently mounted the lady upon his steed, making haste and pace as the wind unto the realms of the Cymry's neighbors to the north.

"Now the High King of the confederacy of the Picts is King Drest, son of Girom. Similar to our Arthur, he is a Christian man presiding over a pagan majority. He is pious, speaks seven languages, is apt with spear and bow, and, though a friend, would not play shelter to our scandal." Maelgwn felt Gwen resting upon him, this time comfortably behind him. He controlled the gallop and absorbed her weight, which was to him as a small child resting upon a parent. "Thus we must lean upon another tribe to guide our passage into Mîgeil, as discreetly as possible."

Accusations of barbarism by Roman historians volleyed against the Picts are false. Their villages and small cities were well planned to include sanitary water and waste contrivances, means of using the sun to warm homes, residential circular huts commingled with places of commerce and market, and churches and temples to old gods and the One True God. This ethnos, second only to the Cymry in rights of primacy to the Isles, was advanced and bore no resemblance to Latin tales to the contrary.

Yes, they honored their water deities, from whence they believed all life emanated, drawing on their power in warfare through smearing the woad paint their bodies over. But war paint doth not barbarism equal; neither ferocity.

Any tribe appears ferocious and barbaric when defending their farms, their churches, their homes and their daughters from the invader.

And so the little village of Mîgeil hummed of this sophisticated and ancient beauty.

"Sojourners, travelers and traders remark that Cymru is the most beautiful of all countries in the creation. But the greens up here have no equal, nor the waters so clear. Almost more–"

"Careful, my Lady; our vales and mounts stand alone–"

"Almost *equal* to the beauty of Cymru." They

laughed, Gwenhwyfar being overtaken with enamor of the place.

"Mark this, my queen," said Maelgwn. "Remember the roads, the trails, the short barge we took. Note well every part of the journey. This little fortress…" He had her look up at the single tower, a horseshoe in shape, an ornate spiral staircase twisting up its side, no gate, the only entrance near the top, beautiful and quaint apartments and chambers within. "And the chapel there to the west. These are considered my lands by the decree of the Picts who, embarrassingly" – a blush from the mighty champion of the Britons – "venerate me as a god." He shook his head, clearly disagreeing with their assessment. "If ever you are in danger, if ever you and Arthur or any of our Fellowship is in dire need to hide, to heal, or to disappear, this is the abode. These tribes will die for me and my own."

They scaled the stairwell and worked together to kindle a fire, which crackled as it matured. They rose and washed the soot from their garments, and he showed her the east from the chamber terrace, resuming the earlier discourse. "However, as with our clan and tribal rivalries, there are factions in Alba. Go not there. Ever. For they claim closer lineage to King Drest and do not favor the locals here doting over me. Avoid them. Their sigil is the skull of a seal, for they are a seafaring and hunting tribe, and no easy match in battle."

At once, Gwenhwyfar's traits seeped through her reformed exterior. Savvy and fleshly libertinism. "Maelgwn, lest you can find the head of a Giant to bag and throw across our horseback, some of these Picts must perish. Or we must. Is having me" – here she bared the top crescent of both breasts, teasing her old and would-be-again lover anew – "worth all this?"

"You must not die, for in your death dies Arthur, and in his death dies the Summer Kingdom." Maelgwn's sophistry was truthful and dark by implication.

Would that he did die, that Mordred and I could reign and love in the open of the day, or rather in the bright night of a Winter Kingdom of our own, thought Gwen.

"What ruse would you have us conjure?" he enquired.

"There was an abduction. We need an abductor. We are Pictland; clearly the Picts, whose king favors the Popish way of the Church, used the distraction of the visit to steal me away in the night, intending to demand that the mighty Arthur bow down to the Bishop of Rome, lest he fall by the sword."

Any rational person would pause greatly at the woman's ability to lie so fluidly, so without effort, *spoken as if she believed her own lies.* But the breasts of Gwen II made Maelgwn far from rational.

"But only a small faction; them!" Again Maelgwn pointed to the east of the tower. "The good and valorous chief of the Picts would denounce the acts of his own in the same way Arthur denounces cattle raiders from the house of Caw! Drest would surely stand down and give us passage for my elite hosts to crush the faction that stole you, helping my mates here, giving us breath for another day."

"Preserving the Summer Kingdom another day." Her hand was already between his legs. "Taken by Picts, rescued by the famed Lancelot, returned safely home to Caerleon." She loved him with her hand outside of his undergarment. "But not home just yet."

"Just one time," he said.

"Just one more time." She used his extreme preoccupation with their past to seduce him all the more. Moving him to a luxurious bed that was *all blankets and pillows,* she was in control.

He disrobed, and they began to kiss hard. Her eyes noted, and could not avoid, the wound where the 'V' of his muscles conjoined low on his pelvis. Not just the scar of a sloppy and poor puncture wound, but a wound atop a wound atop a wound. He paused the passionate embrace, noticed her noticing, allowing the obvious question to be posed.

"No one has breached your defenses. You are undefeated, invincible, and if the bards don't exaggerate, usually unscathed. What is this?" A gentle circumference made about the wound with her skilled fingers.

"The bards ALWAYS exaggerate." He deflected with humor.

She pressed.

"It's an old complaint, and it heals not."

"By some witchcraft?"

"Well, Gwyar and I were reared by the same foster-mother…" More nervous humor.

Knowing she would garner no further information, the task of having Maelgwn resumed. She had put herself back at Saint Illtud's. She could smell the Cymreig breeze off the shores, the sands of Ogmore beach between her toes, the fullness of young Maelgwn inside her.

But he was NOT inside her.

When it comes time to do that which you would do, for the sake of Arthur, and for Cymru, do it not.

Maelgwn was utterly naked, at the very door of fulfilling above thirty years of frustration and crazed madness.

And yet.

Instead of anger, Maelgwn cried into the night, cried from the bed within the solitary tower of Mìgeil.

"Merlin! Merlin, I need you! I cannot do this without you. Wizard! Friend! Help me!" Maelgwn had at last exhausted self-effort, coming to the end of himself.

* * *

Within the hollow of an enchanted oak, or perhaps in the hollow of the abyss itself, olden eyes did shift behind their lids. A bright light outlined a door there and not there within the tree.

* * *

I am never here when you call me and always present when unwanted, but I am never late.

Suddenly, mounted atop the daughter of the Giant, legs spread, ready to have her though the kingdom be damned, Maelgwn saw all the enemies of Arthur as if they were in the room; Caw and his impetuous sons, Meirchion the Mad, though long dead, his upstart son Mark of Cornwall, Llew ap Cynfarch, Cedric and his Gewessii. And one figure besides, shadowy and formless. A fleeting name, *Mordred*, puffed as dust, then was gone. The fall of Cymru and the sovereignty of the Blessed Isles was before him.

At the sentinel moment, Maelgwn was Lancelot. The champion of the Round Table, the first knight.

"Gwenhwyfar."

"I know, Lancelot."

Gwenhwyfar's thoughts returned to Mordred, her love. The two almost-lovers sent for a messenger to deliver tidings of the queen's rescue to Caerleon, congressed on the details that would implicate the Picts, and went unto separate beds within the tower.

In the early hours of the following morning, great pains rushed upon Lancelot, who, needing privily to combat the pain, fled into the forest, bleeding from the old wound.

CHAPTER 14
The Prophecies of Merlin

The Golden Age of King Arthur was never to last beyond twenty years.

If King Arthur was a second King David, his reign was thirty-three and seven years.

If he was a rehearsal for the heavenly kingdom on earth of Jesus Christ, also thirty-three and seven years. For the Lord came and announced His kingdom and endowed His Twelve with special powers; their ministry lasted thirty-three years prior to the *great interruption,* with seven years remaining unto the coming of the King and the ushering in of His government.

Arthur had been crowned four hundred and ninety-seven years after the birth of Christ. His famed victories during the Saxon Wars spanned twenty years, culminating in the decisive and history-altering victory at Mynydd Baeden. Thus, after that, if he be the Child of Prophecy, but twenty more were determined on him, terminating the Cymreig Golden Age in the year *Five Hundred and Thirty-Seven.*

But Merlin needed no Scriptural analysis of God's prophetic plans, neither soothsaying, neither indigenous nor tribal messianic prophecies to affirm and know this beyond disputation.

For he knew the circuits and patterns of the heavenly bodies, and they declared with a shout the lifespan of the boy-king and his gilded and glorious kingdom, commencing with the visitation of *the Red Dragon* the very year that Arthur was born.

What the stars, wandering stars and other astral bodies were, Merlin did not fully comprehend, and the nature of their composition he knew not, save that they were closely associated with gods or angels. In time, he came to understand that the heavenly hosts were made for Man; for seasons, and harvest, and travel measurements, and for signs. They declared the glory of the one unknowable creator by holding their heavenly courts within the firmament in constant pattern, day and night proclaiming the plan, purpose and grandeur of God.

But some rebelled.

These were the wandering stars, doomed to run contrary to the course of the other hosts until the Judgment Day.

Moreover, others, from time to time, broke free from their appointed routes and tried to bring devastation upon the Sons of Adam, whom they hated. Those heavenly hosts loyal to their Creator would wrestle with these and either restore them to their appointed circuit or bring them crashing to the earth, where their disembodied spirit, having been freed of its star, lay crushed in so many pieces as an egg dropped from its basket.

Men of vain sciences devoid of God, especially amongst the Greeks, called these *comets*; but Merlin and the druids, even prior to the foundation stone of Christ being laid upon the Blessed Isles in the Sea by the Princess Eurgaine, knew them to be fiery ethereal dragons. And none were more dangerous than the one that broke free of its chain, declaring the birth of the Pendragon, when Arthur was born.

Hailed with great anticipation, his coming had two meanings.

Dread and celebration.

Dread for the devastation and great loss of life the Cymry would have to endure, and celebration that the Cymry would defeat and endure his fire.

Thus the Red Dragon became the banner of the Pendragons, sharing space with the Bear as co-sigils for the royal clans of the South. Never was the dragon a heathen symbol, or a nod to the devil, as the priests would falsely accuse, but rather it was a symbol of the resilience of the Britons, ever at threat from invaders seeking to annihilate them and steal their coveted islands.

But Merlin knew the Red Dragon would come again. He was mentored in gazing upon the stars, and his knowledge of both math and astronomy had no equal. He could not know if the gods or angels would be victorious yet again when, on his next orbit over the isles, the Dragon would endeavor to hurl himself upon the earth. There was no equation of arithmetic or mapping of star patterns to know this, nor could it be divined, rather only speculated.

Only one spike of the dragon's tail had found soil the year of the birth of the king. It had caused men's eyes to melt within their faces, a plague to form within their bowels, and, where contact was direct, evaporation that left no corpse and little ash.

Merlin *believed* the Red Dragon would strike

in the Isles, in whole or in part, fifty-three years hence that awesome and dreadful first pronouncement, because he was given many prophecies.

Prophecies based upon wise speculation and understanding of the times.

Prophecies of ecstatic utterances in trances and meditations.

Prophecies using divination.

Prophecies after ingesting mushrooms, herbs or other yield of the earth that enabled a link into the world of the spirit.

In those visions, he saw that the Boar would take the sovereignty from Cymru through intrigue and cowardice (never through victory at arms). Or he saw calamity and devastation that allowed foreign migrants to simply *come ashore and colonize, unaccosted.*

His prophetic visions detailed imagery of the Boar dancing with the Raven and the Harp, and the Silures falling from their place of primacy – but surviving.

He saw a dark age like no other since the foundation of the world, where the light of liberty was all but extinguished; a thousand years of terror, ignorance and dread. All the old gods appeared as dead; an age of men and money and empty atheism or emptier rote religion reigned.

Further down the corridor of time, he saw mechanical monsters that he could describe not, neither could his mind comprehend their construction; evil inventions that could heap death upon the earth by land, sea and air.

But in the midst of the dark was found a struggling little light. The flicker of but one candle.

And the candle had a name. And the name of

the candle was Hope. And a sandy-haired young man with a blue hood and a shield upon his shoulder was the keeper of Hope. The candlestick he held in his left hand and lo, Excalibur in his right.

The Age of Arthur was not to survive the days of the king. When gone was Arthur, so too would be gone his ministry to bring hope to all men. Not hope for heaven on earth, for this belonged to God Himself, but hope that men could love their neighbors in spite of their differences, until God Himself returned. Not hope that knowledge would transform the world, as the wisdom of men is foolishness compared to the wisdom of God, but rather hope that the common man would have access to the same knowledge as the rulers and that, for some measure of the time, justice would prevail. Hope for the arts. Hope for sciences. Hope to challenge rulers lawfully; hope that the common man could live a quiet and peaceful life of liberty.

The Age of Arthur would survive as a little candle to alight a brutal and fallen world. A thousand thousand years hence, men would look back upon these heroes, their challenges, trials, failures and triumph. This was the burden of the prophecies of Merlin, and the burden of King Arthur and his Round Table Companions. They were the stewards of the flame of liberty. But that stewardship would come at great cost for all involved in its calling.

These were the prophecies and visions of the Merlin of Britain.

And with the visions, a mandate was implicit.

First, the Cymry must unite under the Pendragon for a generation, holding in ambience the infighting that had ever left them susceptible to first the Roman, and later the Long Knife.

Second, they must be undefeated. Their deeds in battle must be unblemished so that future generations amongst all tribes and nations reckoned these Britons as the standard by which all armies, and all men of valor, would be measured.

To remain undefeated against the wave upon wave of Saxon menace required Maelgwn Gwynedd. There could be no Summer Kingdom without him, for he and his hosts were greater in battle than even those famed warriors of Sparta, more elite than the renowned assassins of Persia.

Thus, third was keeping the unstable Maelgwn *stable enough* throughout the duration of the Saxon Wars, and then mitigating any damage he might do to legacy and reputation thereafter.

Fourth, to protect Arthur's gentle heart, which only ever wanted to find a love to match what he saw displayed by his parents – one of the grandest couples that ever loved.

For all the complexities of nation-building, policy-making and statecraft and through all the machinations of a country shifting from paganism to the Christian God, these four imperatives were paramount above all.

The prophecies of Merlin haunted him, being not favorable in any category.

"Fate is not written." Taliesin would challenge the troubled wizard over long talks and deep horns of cider. "Only God has foreknowledge; He alone knows the ending from the beginning."

As Merlin began to know the way of Grace from Taliesin's teaching, as he obtained what he believed to be his personal salvation, the old wizard began to doubt the veracity of the prophecies.

Becoming fully persuaded that *real and valid*

prophecies from God were centered on Israel, and only by extension and exception the Gentile kingdoms, and that they concerned Israel's reclamation of her land and her rise to reign under David and the Lord in ages to come, Merlin began to question his own visions.

He came to understand that God had but seven years remaining in His prophetic dealings with man and that over five hundred years had passed without the resumption of that week of years. As if the sundial had been paused, God was no longer dealing with man on the basis of prophecy. Rather, He was dealing with individual men on the merits of Christ's work on the Cross, regardless of Israel's position and covenants; dispensing grace to any who would, simply by faith, lay hold of eternal life. In this regard, grace had nothing to do with prophecy and prophecy nothing to do with grace.

So what of Merlin's prophecies?

The Prophets of the Old Testament Scriptures were never wrong. Never. If one detail did not come to pass, then they were marked as False Prophets and stoned to death. Far from being harsh, this was a divinely instituted protective measure between God and His People, so that they would know true Prophets from swindlers and pretenders. Many of Merlin's prophecies were slightly wrong on this or that particular (and many came to pass in precise fulfillment), and he certainly did not meet God's standards for a Prophet.

Merlin had only come to see Paul's Mystery as presented to him by Taliesin for a short time before Nimue and Simon Magus had sent him to his oaky grave. In their few discussions about the meaning of Merlin's visions (from which he had suffered from his youth) and activities as a Seer, the two drew some conclusions.

First, the Devil was the god of this world. As such, he was manipulating events and seeking to control outcomes. And thus, he could give *prophecies* to an extent, because his plan and purpose was controlling the very outcomes he was showing to those whom he was revealing, or tricking, with visions.

Second, the visions had to include much truth mixed with some lies. If the Serpent saw a great kingdom unfolding amongst the Cymry, it would behoove him to reveal as much truth as possible to beguile and entrap the Seers, leaders and visionaries. None will swallow a whole lie, but a drop of poison in otherwise clean water will render one just as dead. Thus, the greater parts of Merlin's visions were true, albeit positioned for malevolent purposes.

Additionally, some of the angelic host, ever at war with the Fallen Ones, might wink their eye at the ignorance of heathen folk who knew nothing of the Devil but worship amiss. Taliesin did not rule out that Merlin must have received some angelic or divine assistance along the way in knowing the course of his people.

Outside of these postulations, Merlin was unsure how the Council of Nine fit, if at all, into the Prince of Darkness's schemes. Though Taliesin had a greater grasp than some of how the Old Mystery School religions led to dark, murky paths, both had some hope that the Council *might* be benevolent – a secret college of men grasping the greater mysteries of godliness. As Merlin discovered firsthand, this was not so. Thus, one of his final thoughts as his lungs filled with water, his throat already closed and clamped with swelling and trauma, was that the prophecies had been Satan *showing him* what might come to pass and then endeavoring to seduce him into partaking of it.

Speculation.

All that could be known and measured was that, whether by God or by Devil, by intuition or hallucination or a combination of the same, *there was still the Red Dragon. The comet was still coming. And with him, the end of the Summer Kingdom.*

And of the magnitude of the colossal calamity coming, the only one who could warn the people remained in his oaky grave.

CHAPTER 15
No Help from the Fair Folk

Simon Magus must find the Grail. He had seen its splendor, felt its power, knew it would indeed be the very vessel from which the nations would become drunk on the outpoured wine of pseudo-peace, only then to swoon in their drunkenness into deep sleep, offering no resistance to the coming worldwide butchery of his Antichrist.

He must find it immediately.

He must immanentize the eschaton.

And if it could be immanentized, then delayed.

Always the urge to bring about the end of the world *now,* and if not now, *back to plotting and waiting.*

With or without the coveted relic, he must escape the Isles and return to Rome where he could resume his great work with the Council of Nine.

The former Emperor had wrought calamity and chaos of Simon's first firsthand view of the Pendragon. It had not gone as expected. However, calm and ever seeing the next three, nay, the next five maneuvers in advance of his opponents, he was able to make great use of the debacle.

The next immediate action was ensuring that his kinsmen, the priests of Rome, who were charged by Arthur himself to initiate a comprehensive investigation to discover and root out the secret societies corroding and corrupting their fair institution, *would never leave the Blessed Isles.* They would never reach Rome. He would. They would die here, adding more ghosts to haunt the scary British woods. He would not. They would never give report of their visit, never bear witness to the things they saw, never give testimony against the Masked Priest.

Simon met with no difficulty in achieving this. The king of the Britons, in his pathetic mercy and uncomely regard for all men, especially his enemies (who thus could never say ought against him or defame his name), had allocated twelve guards divided upon two ships, along with the boatman he had spared to escort the clergy to safe waters.

Using flat-bottomed barges designed for speed, the Cymry flanked the Roman boat, protectively escorting her from the Usk in Caerleon to the ports near Caerdydd.

Killing Arthur's brother, the Prince Madoc, was an option but was not expedient for the attention it would beget. Rather, they waited for the master at sea to break from the party, getting supplies and victuals for the less experienced sailors. An outgoing, neighborly and loving man, he sought ever toward the good of his neighbor and the care for their safe and comfortable journey.

His affable and brotherly love rendered him chatty, and a door for ambush was made ajar as he buzzed about the market, discussing winds and squalls, linens and rope, oars and oils, embracing and laughing with merchants and friends, imbibing not a few ciders.

The two Giants, now joined by two besides, crept up on the Cymry guard. Though after long fighting slain, they fought well; died well the warrior's death. But the priests mustered no physical protest and perished as whimpering dogs and no men.

The monsters made off with the bodies, burning some, eating portions of others. The ships were left tethered and calm as Madoc returned to blood splattered and pooled upon the soil, making a black mud. Brain matter and innards were strung along the reeds and tall grass, bones and jewelry garnishing the sandy pebbles of the port that the bards would come to call Penarth.

His identity contained, Simon Magus labored next on how he might return home. In the meantime, he lodged with the Adder and a select few of the Dynion Hysbys, those complicated traitors who had transgressed well past the point of return in betraying their own kind to the Prince of Darkness.

* * *

"We will search every hut, estate, fortress and castle. No closet unsearched, no bed not turned over. From the horn of the mainland to the daughter islands above Pictland, we will bring the masked villain to justice." Bishop Aiden was proud in his proclamation, believing his words would please his lord.

"What think you of the bishop's words, Mordred?"

Happy for a reprieve from guarding the chained and depressed father of his lover, exhausted from the detail, he wanted none of Arthur's politics, and less than none of his moral lessons. Alas, knowing what was wanted by way of response, his lip service formed the right words.

"I don't think we *can* do any of those things."

Arthur looked pleased, then onto Rhufawn. "And what think you?"

Here the lingering obsession was revealed. "His capture would surely lead to more knowledge about the whereabouts of the Grail. Whatever needs to be done."

Arthur was gentle but direct. "That it might, Rhufawn. But the son of my sister has spoken true. We surely will do none of those things."

"But–"

The just king's irritated hand motion stayed the bishop's tongue.

"Every citizen under his own roof is greater than the king. More powerful than the sovereign. Remember that the law rules from Caermelyn. We will not become a kingdom of raids and incursions, a government of reaction and over-reach and encroach. Our women will not be within the bath, ever anxious that their time of relaxation will be disrupted; neither will the farmer be at the plow ever with one eye on his goods being turned over, his storehouse seized."

"These things would not happen," rebutted Aiden.

"These things *always happen,* when liberty is ransomed under the banner of security. Though the Devil himself be hiding in my neighbor's home, it is not for me to encroach. This right of privacy is inalienable and is no respecter of sect, creed or god. Our State shall not do these things." Arthur loved liberty as he loved Gwenhwyfar, a love that gives all until spent – and then gives more. "We will find another way."

The Pendragon motioned. Prince Madoc entered.

"Brother. We make no changes to the law with respect to hearth and home. But the ports are a different matter. Use Merlin's fortress rings; launch signals throughout the land. Freeze the ports."

Madoc quickly realized that this would be the great work of his life. Even in Arthur's Summer Kingdom, many tribes were not fond of each other. Corrupt trade deals were made in secret rooms and other nations, offering spices and silks for tin and coal, pitting brother versus brother for gold, position and privilege. Madoc had never sought a seat at the Round Table, neither a throne nor principality. But in every way he was a king. The king of commerce. Where the import and export of goods, people and services was concerned, he was Protector and Duke of the Isles. In this regard, he was second of import only to Arthur himself.

He never questioned his older brother. Ever the response was "how?", never "why?".

"Freeze the ports." Verbalizing it frightened the prince. "For how long?"

"Until you have developed a systematic approach for ensuring that nothing leaves, nor enters, these islands without the approval of you and your designates."

"Our friends and kinsmen in Brittany will give full cooperation, as will the remnants of Lloegyr. The Scots, Picts and clans of Eire–" Here Madoc paused.

"Make your speech direct and with my authority, brother, saying unto them that King Arthur will raise the Round Table Fellowship once more, a silvery chorus of death and a song of graves and woe upon them." Arthur again confirmed his instruction. "Freeze the ports. The murderer of Merlin will not leave these Isles. We will find him" – an unkind glance upon Aiden and his opinion – "lawfully. Elsewise, he will die of old age here."

* * *

"I will not die of old age here!" One devil shouted his voice hoarse unto another devil, who answered desperation with laughter.

Conjuring the Fair Folk is rumored as impossible, yet the dark shamanism of the Adder had been able, somehow, to achieve this. Bound in a cyclone of mystical winds swirling at a great speed and rising as a funnel to the height of a small tree, the Fae was in a prison of demonic powers. Bordered in a ring of stones, he had not only been conjured but also caught. Not far from that field where Mordred and Gwen would often betray spouse, country and history, the king of the Tylwyth Teg, summonsed and held unwillingly, was before Simon Magus.

There was nothing Magus or his anti-druids could do to harm the otherworldly being. It was as the corralling of a bull with hopes that it would calm down for long enough to brand and then release it.

"Why will you not help me?! My order–"

"I owed your order, your god and the old witch a debt. Favor paid," he barked back, still cackling and dismayed that they had somehow managed to capture him in the first place.

"He is your god too, elf."

* * *

But this was not so. At least not directly. Later Christian tradition, in an effort to gather its perceived enemies into one barrel, confining them for an easy kill, created the false understanding that all spiritual beings save the Elect Angels of God are in league with Satan.

This is simply not so.

If Christendom, being full of supposed good men, is divided, then how is the kingdom of Satan, whose composition is of men and creaturekind evil and corrupt, ever to be in a state of unison and concord? If bishops of Galicia loathe bishops of Milan, then why is it assumed that oracles of Crete love the Korrigan spirits of Brittany?

This false assumption has led to ignorance, voids of compassion, tyranny and superstition.

Now the truth of the matter is this.

Many witches greatly dreaded the Devil, fearing that, if they so much as grazed the smallest twig of Mountain Ash, he would come for them (as they believed he did in the Blessed Isles every seven years) and drag them to Hell for eternal judgment.

In this regard, they viewed the Devil as God's agency, His hypocrisy of using evil to fight evil. Whether having merit or being amiss, these witches were not in league with the Devil, hating him greatly in favor of their own goddesses.

Some did not acknowledge the Christian concept of a supreme God presiding over the other gods. True polytheists, their gods came from other gods whose origins of ancient times were *intelligences* that had gathered themselves together to form gods, who formed the worlds. These were the harmless pagans who gathered mushrooms and herbs, made love without restriction or reservation, were ever kind to all, embraced their perceived duality of nature (and of nature's gods), and wanted nothing of the Christians' God, Jesus or Devil.

Still other beings were sold wholly to the Devil's scheme, feeling that the creature would somehow supplant the Creator, winning a successful rebellion in the end.

Lastly, some hoped against hope for redemption. If they helped children, fed widows, swept homes, and gave coins, would the God of Heaven and earth spare them? Would he at least let them simply cease to exist in favor of an eternity in Tartarus, or worse, the Lake of Fire?

And so, as with every son of Adam, matters of faith, of belief, of death, issues of personal eschatology and soteriology were highly individual. Yes, Satan was the god of the Tylwyth Teg because Satan's two hundred hosts originally sinned, violated creation and begat children by the daughters of men. This they did for wanton lust, but also to prevent prophecies of the Saviour, who was foretold to come of the seed of the woman. From the beginning, he manipulated the lusts and shortcomings of others to achieve his long-term ends: becoming as the Most High God. Yes, the deceived and the unbelieving were equally lost, and yes, their destiny the Devil shared... whether they hated the fallen cherub or not.

* * *

"There be gods many and lords many." The Fae continue to mock his desperate captor.

"Know you not what Arddu will do for this insolence? What infliction he will unleash upon those who betray him?"

"Yes, and how much greater the One that created *him?*"

"Oh, you fear God? Is that it?"

"For the devils believe and tremble, as says the Christian Scripture," he responded.

"The unseen and unknowable One never knew you and would cast you into the Deep, were He here to look upon you. You are a walking reminder of perversion, abomination and disappointment. Better to serve one who finds beauty in your ugliness, value in your otherworldly powers."

"Say the word again, Magus." Tired of the ruse, and inflamed at something the Devil's disciple had said, the Fae gave but a wave of his hand and a mouthful of ancient incantations. The cone of ethereal bonds burst asunder; the ring of stones resumed being just another formation of pretty and benign Cymreig rocks. The towering chief that ruled *the in between* summonsed a hundred of his mates, who surrounded the Dynion Hysbys, planting by their wiles visions of terror and fright, causing all to drop to the knees – save brave Simon Magus.

"Where is your Horned God now? 'Tis you who are in the snare." A long red finger tic-tocked left to right, chastising and lecturing without words.

Showing the same calm resolve demonstrated when but recently at the mercy of Excalibur's strident edge, Simon condescended by retort and sigh: "Which word would you like me to repeat?"

"Perversion." Here, emotion bested the king of the Fair Folk. It would seem that the residue of humanity within the Nephilim and their progeny were all the worst bits; the offal of the human condition. And the top of the refuse heap of these was *assumption*. Gifted with a broad range of powers of divination, sorcery and special knowledge but never *all-knowing*, the elf's *assumption* resulted in him gifting Magus the pathway to victory.

Perversion.

Incest between siblings.

In every culture, religion and sect, it was viewed as abomination. Cursed abomination to be avoided without exception. When royal families did it – disease and madness. Rome fell because of it, and even the ancient bloodlines that maintained their purity in an ongoing effort to rule the world were careful to diversify their inbreeding, never procreating inside the branch of first cousin. When the line would degenerate and mother would bed son, or son would have intercourse with sister, it was never to a good end.

Even the heathen and the faeries held to this. The notions of right and wrong that are memorialized for the Christian in Scripture are revealed to heathens by conscience.

"Perversion. I brought the primal witch out from her mournful wanderings in the Underworld, her anguish in the valley of the graves of her sons. Then I stole the girl-child of Onbrawst and Meurig and made her one with the mother of goddesses. A Pendragon and a Fae in one shell. So bound are the twain that they are one flesh, yet separate; one soul, yet a host and a parasite." The chief paused in contemplation. "I don't even think they know who or what they are. But I do know that when is final the Matter of Britain, Morgaine of the Faeries will survive all."

"Yes! Morgaine of the Faeries. Your finest

work, blessed be Arddu. Is this the perversion that vexes thee?"

"No! That I owed her this deed, and that she would bed her brother, forging a soul tie and a gateway to resurrect your son of perdition in him–"

Magus interrupted, further agitating the towering menace before him. "Ah, you who have violated daughters by the batch, damsels by the bundle, are bothered that the siblings would lie together? For so many years this has troubled you?" Instead of the natural fear of being squashed at the whim of a greater foe that would possess and paralyze a normal man, he was genuinely interested in the strange set of codes and ordinances that governed the perplexing ways of the olden Fae.

Here the goading and inquiries finished their course, and the assumption accidentally delivered.

"Not the deed or the ritual, but its issue that will destroy this land! I shall not help you or your Horned God expedite our demise. For all of the mystery of the Tylwyth Teg, let it be made simple for you and your conniving secret society. I simply like King Arthur more than I like you." Sometimes the faeries act in this way, and their mysteries are no deep thing but rather a pithy moment or a jovial whim. "Blessings and Cursings from the line of Pendragon. We choose the Blessing."

Brilliant and sinister Simon had stopped listening to the sermonizing of what he perceived as diatribe by the hypocritical elf.

"What issue?" he asked. "Did our schema produce not just a soul tie but a soul? *A child begotten of the boy-king and his witch sister?*"

Instantly realizing what he had done, what dark knowledge had been gifted, the red-eyed chief gave out a cry that startled stags, disrupted hares, and displaced wolves. The forest responded to his cry, crying in return.

He became vapor, and vanished. His hosts and mates burst into mushrooms and daffodils, squealing in anger and protest at the woeful exchange.

The anti-druids rose.

"Arthur will fall and Mordred will reign," they said, gleeful.

"Nay." Magus dismissed them, not so much as acknowledging those who had not been initiated into his level of sacred mysteries. Instead, he spoke to only the Adder. "Mordred will rise, in time. He will bruise Arthur's head, and Arthur will resurrect in glory. We have our villain. Nothing changes. Order these men's tongues be put to the sickle, find the Grail, and get me off this Island."

Even traitors have pride. Even rogues possess patriotism. "Prince Madoc controls the coasts and ports. The Isles are now a scroll, the ports as a lump of warm wax, and Madoc is the king's signet. None will leave unauthorized; none will arrive unawares. And surely not without some otherworldly succor, which seems to have" – the Dynion Hysbys shaman looked at the now empty faerie ring – "vanished angrily. Would you tear out the tongues of these who would harbor you? The faithful who would hide you from the High King? The Cymry abhor rudeness. It is a violation of our most ancient codes of hospitality. Sir, you are stuck."

Hubris had landed Simon Magus in a temporary vice. Seeing no other immediate option, he feigned sorrow for the directive (the taste of apology as bile in his throat) and processed his options. His mind pondered exile amongst those who had obviously grown weary of years conjuring monsters and disturbing the Summer Kingdom, all the while seeing the Catholic Church grow and the native pagan religions continue to diminish.

The threads were becoming few and thin by which he tethered the alliance between the old gods and their priests (who would be discarded when their purpose fulfilled) and the Church of Rome and their priests (who would be used to absorb and destroy all religions, forming One Church to subjugate the earth).

Honorable men see schemes quickly. Corrupt men come around. Exposure ruins the plotting of secret societies. For this cause, Simon Magus opted to say little, and to leave the custody and protection of the Dynion Hysbys.

The Masked Man made off into the forest. A scream in the thickest of Italian accents: "I must get off this island!"

CHAPTER 16
More of Taliesins Quiet Years

Simon Magus did not get off the Island.

As a vagabond and a fugitive, he slithered, as face-down, in muck and wood and thicket, in hut and hovel, winding ever north up beyond the borders of Arthur's long and brawny arm.

King Arthur was not sovereign over the Picts or the Scots; neither did he desire to be, for the Cymry never sought to rule men of other nations.

However, the Bear of Glamorgan did assert his authority over the ports, the rivers and the causeways, even unto the northernmost tips and daughter islands of Alba, even unto the horny tip of Land's End in the vassal kingdoms south of Cymru. The murderer of Merlin could hide within, but lest he grew wings and tempted Arthur's control of the air, he would find no liberty without.

A man in direct league with the Devil, Magus retained confidence in the most dire circumstances. Where all seemed lost, he simply moved onto the next opportunity. The adaptable Luciferian found refuge in the company of a wealthy landowner who, having kin in the north and the south who were ever embroiled in controversy and malicious strife over cattle and sheep and grazing lands, had given up all and became a hermit. This man had distanced himself from the tidings and gossip of the day, becoming a kind of solitary recluse. A complicated fellow, having fear of the Lord and an affinity for the Roman tradition, but also a curiosity for herbs and benign folk magic, the wanderer had abandoned wife and children, cousin and steward, the whole of his hired household and all friends.

Loathing of those who loved wealth and things more than people brought him from Glamorgan to the far north and Pictish Wilds.

Chance brought him into Caledonia.

Misfortune brought him to Simon Magus.

Having no need of garbs of concealment, Simon's mask and vestments had been put away, substituted for a simple blue robe and walking stick. The hermit was instantly enamored by the seductive knowledge of his new friend, happy to barter lodging in the Caledonian forest for lessons in herbs, in astronomy, in the mechanisms of wind and the sciences of magnetics and water. And as he valued his own privacy and seclusion, he never asked about Simon's reasons for abdication from dwelling amongst the civilized. Two hermits in the vast Pictish wood; a master and an apprentice.

In time, Simon came to corrupt the hermit's Christian name, calling him Merlin Wyllt: *the Merlin of the Wild*. This he did to mock the king who had imprisoned him. Simon had killed one Merlin in the wood and given birth to another. *And he hoped this one would engage the Fae that had shunned him, using him, if it were possible, to escape the Isles and make his return to Rome.*

Thus was the third Merlin *born.*

* * *

Lancelot had succeeded in not doing that which he would do when the opportunity was naked and spread open before him. *But would it be enough?* He continued to touch her improperly (and she gave no protest, often guiding hand or lips) during the journey home. Her heart was glad that she had not given herself to him and was fixed upon being home, with her husband's nephew, but her body could not resist the touch of one such as Lancelot. Neither could any woman's.

In the end, they contained and restrained. After the sticky fondlings and hundreds of wet, aggressive kisses and clinches that were too close, lasting too long, the infamous legends, pulsating, moist and frustrated, saw in their immediate vision the welcoming flags of the red dragon, the streamers decorating the streets of Caerleon.

They had done it. They had made it back to court without doing *it*.

A message had been sent in advance that Lancelot had rescued Gwenhwyfar ferch Ogyrfan Gawr from the Picts. The bards were already singing the tale, concocting details of the brave rescue as befitted the song or prose. Gildas had taken pen to parchment to memorialize this history that had never happened.

The welcome celebration would be grand.

During the journey home, the only thing Lancelot and Gwen did more than touch each other was rehearse the facts. Lying was natural for Gwen, but a part of Lancelot died each time he dealt in dishonesty. Not only did Merlin haunt him regarding his proclivities towards adultery, but Taliesin's voice plagued him about honesty and ethics. *Consider how this act (of debauchery or roguery) will impact your children* was deeply planted, always orbiting round in his head, thanks to the Chief Bard of Britain.

But lie he would. Expertly.

King Arthur's relief had not yet caught up with and reconciled his worry, his rage. He looked beleaguered, starved of sleep. After embracing both wife and friend he, naturally, wanted facts. Ever thoughtful of his queen, ever considering her feelings and well-being above his own, he encouraged her to leave the chapel where they were talking: "Rest, my love, you need not live through it again during Maelgwn's telling." The chapel was very near to her private apartment, and the field where she often betrayed the king with her younger consort.

"I would." Three bats of big eyes. "But I cannot leave your side, my husband; the distress is too great. I will suffer my beloved rescuer's telling of it, if only to drape upon thy arm." Beguiling Gwenhwyfar II, lying to protect two lives, and perhaps extend the life of a nation, was in perfect character; deceiving and abusing the fond feelings of a cuckolded husband, the love-blindness of the famous king.

The lie was plausible. A tribe of Picts, converted to the Roman sect, had used the distraction of the visit to abduct the queen. Their ransom? A desperate attempt to demand borderlands be declared for the Bishop of Rome and placed under Maelgwn's protection. Knowing none of the fantastic activities in the hall that day, the only abductors were but there to support and strengthen the position of their Roman allies, desperate to control the Isles.

The Bloodhound Prince offered his son, the mighty prince Rhun, to deploy Maelgwn's Hosts and a small company of soldiers to smash the offending tribe, making a decisive and swift example of them.

Arthur approved the action.

The lie was whispered, and as lies are whispered, embellished and nurtured upon lips of men everywhere. Even the tribe of Picts accused came to believe that they had committed the deed. By reason of repetition, the farce became fact. Maelgwn's Hosts easily smashed the painted warriors of Alba. Souls went to the grave on account of Lancelot and Gwenhwyfar's lies. He was celebrated as the queen's protector.

Arthur, making use of his supreme vision and wisdom, privately went to meet with King Drest of the Picts, and supped with him in Perth.

He ordered that his Round Table Companions gather as many of the Dynion Hysbys as could be found. They were directed to assemble before the Silure sovereign at water's edge, along the shore of the beach at Ogmore. With the ocean to their backs they faced twelve famed knights, helmed and armed with long spears, pressing upon them as a cook uses a long stick to plunge potatoes into the cawl, wreaking great fear of a watery death.

The Round Table Knights were a frightful sight, and the waters menacing, but Bedwyr and Urien and Cadog were a welcome end compared to the real presence of fear upon the scene, for Morgaine of the Faeries herself stood in the midst of the Round Table Knights. As she opened her tiny fists, the waves would wax; when clinched they would wane. When she lifted her dark eyes to the firmament, the skies crackled and popped; when to the ground, the sand shifted. All that witnessed this swore by their deity that the weather itself obeyed her mood.

And her mood was vengeance, driven by embarrassment.

Now what had been deduced by her brother's first wife, the *First Gwenhwyfar,* was known before all; that she had had carnal relations with her own brother during the king-making rites. That the Church would weaponize this when advantage manifested was a certainty. That she would access the seething powers of her ancient *other self* and render the shaman, or even the whole of the beach, desolate was a probability.

But something peculiar happened on the beach. In the stead of shame and political posturing, whether because Arthur himself was implicated or because the men saw the one equal in power to Lancelot rendered helpless – her countenance brought to such low depths that pity prevailed – is unknown. Where opportunity shone as the sun slowly lights a room, the curtain closed, bringing back shadows of rest, kindness and grace. Each of the knights and the bishops alike were tender-voiced and protective of the Lady of Avalon, putting her secret back in a dark and safe room as they were able to.

"Can you identify him?" asked Owain ap Urien softly.

"Take your time; they are going nowhere, my Lady." Young Peredur offered comforting words.

Morgaine the Witch buckled at the kindness, tears of frustration and thankfulness in equal measure contorting her face. Composing herself, she looked over each in the line as a hound sniffs out thieves for its master.

The men continued to help.

"Which of you are the archbishop, or high priest, or–" Urien struggled for the proper description.

His brutish and indomitable lad helped. "Who is head heathen? Identify yourself and step forward from your fellows!" he barked.

"Unlike you Christians, we have no hierarchy, no ladder of lords or tower of bureaucrats to lord over men," snapped back a black robe (although marked within their bodies in diverse knotwork, sigil and symbol, all of the Dynion Hysbys were dressed alike, with no distinguishing features of dress or vestment).

"Just the tyranny of superstition and the wiles of the Devil to frighten and control the pig farmer and the corn grower." Owain moved forward a pace, his spear now a pace closer to the head of one of the heathens. "The gods you conjure, even the most faithful pagan disdains! How long will you bind the people in fear and superstition?"

"Sounds like the Christian Church." Morgaine had to slip in one protesting jab at the obvious irony of odd bedfellows when corruption reigns. Owain's rare grin indicated that he did not agree. "He is not amongst them." She was thorough, looking for the memorably ugly teeth that had lisped at her so long ago, calling her 'little crow'. "Not amongst them, I am certain," she confirmed.

Bedwyr took the lead, shifting from an eyewitness identification scenario to a full military-style interrogation. Upon his demanding to know where they were hiding the Masked Priest, the Dynion Hysbys held fast, offering nothing upon pain of death. Innocence was easy to proclaim, given that the shadowy figure had parted from their company.

"How did a foreign leader of some secret

order come to lead you" – good-natured Bedwyr lent no humor or jest to his speech – "you who have no leader? How then did he gain position and privilege amongst you to make the very selection of the priestess who would be the proxy for *your* goddess in the spring rites that accompanied the crowning of a Pendragon? A once-in-ten-thousand-lifetimes honor, and you would have us believe that this intruder just tossed a hood about his shoulders and made himself head of your order?" With a motion of his hand, the other warriors now also advanced their spears by one pace.

"It was above thirty years ago!" the Adder answered. "We have few conferences, fewer councils and no central order. These men serve the Tribes and the old gods of stream and pool, of wind and rain. We know not how this occurred, and some of us were not yet weaned from our mother's breasts!"

"Merlin's killer chose Arthur's sister to participate in your rituals–"

"Not our rituals; the people, *your* people, demand that the king identify with the land and that the land yield its bounty in accord with the virility of the king. For this cause, the goddess chooses whom she chooses." The Adder boldly interrupted Cadog.

As the interrogation lumbered on, Morgaine actually found relief that it was now known what had happened between her and her brother at the rites. Her reaction to seeing Magus had prevented any concealment of the source of her distress. *Perhaps the burden will help him as well,* she thought.

"Some offenses do not rust over with time," she declared. "Some sins have consequences that last for a lifetime."

The Dynion Hysbys understood the double meaning of her words, but spake not of Mordred, for they yet feared Magus, and above Magus, the Horned God Arddu. Rather, they pursued the angle of perceived hypocrisy.

"This condemnation does not sound like the grace your Merlin preached. We have the greatest king in the history of the world; why cleave to this grievance? Clearly the goddess selected well, and certainly your unique union with our king has gifted him with verve unfettered!"

Morgaine ignored the whole of the vain speech. "I am not Merlin."

Many of the saints were next to her and Bedwyr upon the sandy shore. Those with fealty to the Apostolic Church of the Britons alone were permitted, with no Catholics amongst them.

"I am sorry you have not found the author of such a vile offense, my child."

Morgaine respected the kind of words of old Dyfrig. He feared her but was genuine and kind. Though she felt him misguided and mistaken, she was flattered at the words he offered in concern for the healing of her soul. She even accepted an embrace from the bishop.

As the masked villain was neither present, nor identified, Bishop Dyfrig made certain that Morgaine had completed her questions. Finding that she had, grateful that she had not used her sorcery to kill the lot of them, he revealed that King Arthur himself had commissioned him to pronounce a decree upon the wise men of the Tribes.

And this was the decree given by Dyfrig.

"By the authority of the twelve and twelve and the champion who serve Arthur, who serves Caermelyn, that shimmering city which serves the royal clans, tribes, kingdoms, cantrefs and hundreds of Cymru, to those who identify with the Dynion Hysbys, the *jealous and the hateful of the Merlin from the time in the days of Vortigern when he shamed you for the folly of your sorceries*, have been found to be in league with and conspirators both before and after the fact with the murderer of the Chief Counselor of the High King. And by his authority, and with the complete accord of both the regular druids, whom you so often impersonate, and the Primitive Church, founded here by Joseph and by Princess Eurgaine in the days of Peter and Paul themselves, we declare an end to the rituals, practices and ordinances by the Dynion Hysbys unto the time of the discovery and arrest of the murderer or unto the ninth generation of your sons' sons."

"Let men worship what gods they will–" the Adder began his protest, trying to misuse one of Arthur's oft quoted sayings.

"But you *did* kill your neighbor for it." Cai smothered the attempt to twist the king's words. "The degree violates no liberty or principle of freedom. We have cause; we have witness of this masked devil by both Maelgwn and Gwyar. Bring him to us, or you are no more. And that is the end of the matter."

Bedwyr nodded at Cai, supporting the piercing words given by the Pendragon's steward.

"The druids are dying out or converting to the new God. The people will never accept this." The Adder was resolute.

"We trust that every Cymreig citizen knows right from wrong and will understand our decision. And we will hear those who disagree, giving them freedom to voice the grievance when next, and whenever, we again at the Round Table convene," said Bedwyr.

"They will understand, provided the harvest does not fail and the Iron Bear gives the land an heir to raise Excalibur afresh when limp becomes the current Pendragon. How goes that?"

Peredur smote the Adder square upon the cheek. The twelve put the anti-druids to flight, considering it gracious that they did not put them all to the spear; but they yet needed them to hand over the masked man, to trip and lie, to be boastful or full of wine and accidentally reveal. Perhaps this extreme measure would finally bring justice, delivering judgment upon the one who had stolen the wizard from the sandy-haired boy-king.

* * *

With Simon Magus imprisoned in the Caledonian forest, world politics changed. And the world itself slowed again, into those times Taliesin the Bard called 'less weighty years', for surely one day is not equal to the next, and some seasons are indeed quiet.

Although subordinate fraternities, guilds and covert orders continued to pursue the great work of simultaneously bringing about and yet delaying the End of Days, the head of the snake was lost. And with him, finality of direction and decision. Satan's organization was run by one apostle at the top, driving paramount decisions downward through a group of nine, then of twelve, then of seventy, then of three hundred, then onto lower ranks in trade, commerce, currency, the pseudo-sciences and religion. If the Dark Lord was to raise up another Magus, he had not yet done so, nor did he intervene supernaturally to liberate his Chief Disciple from the Isles in the Sea.

Ironically, the diverse creaturekind and woeful Children of the Damned could manifest more otherworldly powers in this time than could their ancient relatives who ruled the skies. As this was the Dispensation of the Grace of God, where faith reigned, the gift of signs had ceased, and miracles of God gone too. 'Twas a doctrinal age where what men believed trumped what men saw. The powers of the Faeries, the Giants, the nymphs and elemental spirits were the leftover crumbs of a moldering slice of bread that would soon, through the process of time, become as dust and be gone, forever. Because such beings were outside of the creation, they were outside of the dispensational guidelines that governed the creation. Thus the powers of devils (which were the disembodied spirits of a Nephilim, or other like abominations against the creation) persisted, whilst the power of Fallen Angels were strictly limited to deception, excepting when they broke free of their heavenly patterns and could do direct harm unto the earth and the Sons of Adam.

And so, with Magus stuck in his little circular hut in Caledonia with his neighbor, the Wild Man of the Woods, the Church of Rome was less corrupt; the governments of Constantinople and Rome did increase in mutual respect, wars were few, and an air of production, prosperity and freedom was felt by citizens of most nations worldwide. Arthur's golden age was credited, and well deserved, but the *absence of organized and directed evil* did as much to enable men to leave quiet, peaceable lives as did *directed good and justice.*

Amongst the famed living legends at court, *the routine* resumed as well.

Lancelot could scarcely be at Caerleon or

Caermelyn and gave most of his time to missing his foster-mother, founding chapels, giving alms, and memorizing long sections of Scripture. When not about these, he secluded himself up in Gwynedd, hunting on his lands in Camlan, training with his sons, and enjoying many diverse women. His ache for Gwenhwyfar II was never assuaged and the cracks it left upon his soul were as broken glass, resulting in tiny shards broken away forever from the whole. *Shards of insanity*. During this time a daughter was born unto him, and she was called Eurgaine.

For Mordred, his *name and fame* did cultivate and grow at last during these quiet years. His deeds became noteworthy, his tongue edifying, his disposition perceived as warm by every man. Earning the adoration of his neighbors begat the softest of whispers, suggesting that perhaps the older nephew of Arthur was a perfectly fit heir to the childless king. Though not exposed to the front lines of the Saxon Wars nor battletested like the favored heir, Gwalchmai, some thought that it might behoove a peacetime ruler to *not* be hardened and haunted by war.

In his inward parts, the man had not changed. Mordred still believed that people were the playthings and cattle of superior spirits. He still wanted to be the preferred amongst the herd, he still lusted after power, and he was still reformed, or corralled, by his love for Gwenhwyfar II. Although they loved yet, circumstance required Mordred to relocate his wife, the godly and pious Kwyllog, from her lands in the north to Caerleon. His sons remained north, being at fosterage with their kinsmen of the House of Caw. And although Mordred missed his young children, their absence left only his wife to dodge and deceive when desiring to lie with the queen. *One being easier to sneak around than three.*

For Gwen, the sliver of her heart that she had given to Lancelot as a child when she also gave him her flower was an ember that could appear as choked out, smothered, or giving dying puffs. Dying but not dead, ever to be re-ignited by the subtlest breeze. The rest of her belonged to Mordred, and nothing did she reserve for her husband.

Vivien vanished after her appearance with the Cup of Christ and was not seen during the quiet years, which were five. Many questioned their own memories, though they had witnessed it firsthand, thinking the specter but a vision, a temporary fit or delusion shared by a distressed crowd. Many who heard of it secondhand came to even think it a legend or a myth. The sacred lakes and streams were still as hard glass, and not even a glimpse of the Grail was reported. Men began to forget about the relic, but Rhufawn ap Maelgwn affixed on nothing else, day and night, which grieved Taliesin.

As Vivien was transfigured, transformed, retired, or dead, Gwyar returned to Ynys Enlli, where she gave the whole of her forbidden powers to hiding the Treasures of Britain and keeping the little island's secrets and sacred groves away from Cadfan's parishioners. Though a small island, her mysticism kept the hidden parts hidden, at great toil and taxation to her health. Drawing down the Dragon's Breath, or mist, causing pilgrims to go left from the path one day and veer right from the same road the next, was not an occupation that she could sustain forever. The Fair Folk helped her at certain times, foiled her efforts at others; ever impish and under some unknowable rules of engagement were they.

Keeping her vow, however, she visited court oft, spending many fond afternoons atop Lodge Hill with Arthur. Her pattern was to visit with her brother, look in upon her son, investigate where she could to ensure that no plot was in place by the lovers to kill her brother, and then make haste and leave.

Although Arthur had Bedwyr, his closest friend, and Cai, his steward, and although both Onbrawst and Meurig, as with all Silures, were ageless, vibrant and always a supportive shadow to the sun that was their son, with Merlin gone, the two that Arthur *needed* most in his life were the two too often absent from court.

Maelgwn, because of his forbidden love for Gwenhwyfar.

Gwyar, because of her forbidden witness of Gwenhwyfar with her lover.

Druids and priestesses continued to convert to the Christian faith, and those benign orders diminished. The Dynion Hysbys sometimes conducted the rites at great peril, disobeying Dyfrig's edict. Arthur had authorized the ordinance and found it just but refused to dispatch soldiers to enforce the ban, never wanting to bring the sword of the State into the pulpit or altar of religion. However, these men *had harbored or allowed an evil murderer a place as pillar in their sect*. Thus, with each violation, Arthur would engage the local chieftains to make arrests, demand testimony, and gather information in whatever manner their local jurisdiction deemed fit. Because of this, many Dynion Hysbys were put to the sword or to the noose.

Gwenhwyfar continued to be barren, but the crops and harvests were strong, so the people suffered the dispute between the court and their wise men. Were the crops to fail and Arthur to have no son, the tribes would unite and force an abdication in favor of either Gwalchmai or Mordred. Because King Meurig had abdicated immediately upon the injury to his loins, and because Arthur had risen in his father's *fall*, endorsed even by Excalibur, the supreme symbol of virility, Meurig lived in peaceful retirement, with no fear of further superstitious or religious requirement from the masses.

Not so if Arthur, fully healthy, produced no heir AND the land gave no yield.

In this circumstance, an aging king would be offered in sacrifice, dying with his dying lands, a new king rising in his stead. The Christian faith, in five centuries of practice on the Isles, had not distinguished the rite of the Sacral King.

This was not a present danger, but the lack of a babe suckling Gwenhwyfar II gave rise to periodic gossip and grumbles. *Increasingly so.*

At times during the five more quiet years, the bishops, elders and Round Table Companions would also conference to gauge the threat or propensity for civil war. Wisdom dictated that they be vigilant, given the disunity and rivalry that tugged at the middle kingdoms and the West Country, the way two fighting sisters pull upon the legs and arms of their favorite doll. In this case *the pullers and tuggers* were the men from the Old North and the powerful Silures from the South.

Cyrmu was a loose confederacy of sovereign kingdoms. It recognized a High King and the Round Table as a "unique and special counsel", primarily on matters that impacted the borderlands between Cymru and Lloegyr to the east, Alba to the north, and the Emerald Isle to the far west, or on material threats to the people as a whole; elsewise the local kingdoms ruled themselves. And although independent kingdoms can be coopted into civil war, brilliant political marriages and a generation of peace made the notion extremely unlikely. *Almost impossible.*

For example, King Urien's mother was from Glamorgan, whilst his father hailed from the renowned line of mighty kings and queens of Gwynedd. Even if his loyalties swayed towards one parent or the other, his son Owain was fully *blended* with beloved kin, cousins and uncles from both ends of the Isle. Though a Northman by paternal descent, would he really put the spear to a Silure who might be a first cousin, or slay an elder who might be a former neighbor of his Silure grandmother?

The similitude of this wonderfully impossible strait was engineered strategically over and over again throughout the land. Gwalchmai: mother from the South, father from the North. Rhun ap Maelgwn the same, and scores more. Purebloods like Arthur, Maelgwn, Bedwyr and Taliesin were becoming a minority amongst the prominent and the powerful, which was a good thing. Prominent, powerful women had sacrificed their very hearts for the good of *the next generation.* For their selfless devotion, it was said of them: *"They lie with princes, but their marriage is to Cymru."*

A religious war had to ride atop the backs of a territorial war and thus was also unrealistic, for the same reasons. Catholics and Apostolic Britons continued to gnash and hack upon each other about baptism, the authority of the Bishop of Rome, tonsuring, how bells were to be transported, and the policy and method of converting and integrating the Germanic tribes amongst them into the Church. The sentiments and conduct were rarely friendly and ever tense – BUT the key decision-makers resided in all kingdoms and would be forced to fight their own kind, their own families.

Tensions? Yes.

Skirmishes? Plenty.

Disputes and murders? Seldom, but yes.

War? Impossible.

Except.

If Arthur perished without a direct heir and Maelgwn did not favor the selection, he could take the throne at will. His Hosts were too powerful, his reach of dread mixed with love and awe too long. This one man could turn the tide for good or for ill, resurrect regional differences and perhaps successfully pit brother versus brother.

It was rumored that Maelgwn itched to reclaim rule of his lands in Gwynedd, but there was never evidence of any ambitions beyond that, which was his right. And yet the possibility, especially during his long absences, was considered from time to time. *If the Pendragon produces not a son, the future of the Summer Kingdom rests upon the relationship between Maelgwn and Gwalchmai.*

And that relationship was strained.

Gwalchmai, whether by natural wisdom and perception or by a measure of the Sight passed onto him from his mother, perceived accurately the conflict in Maelgwn's soul over Gwenhwyfar. And *all* perceived, most accurately, *what she was.* Gwalchmai threaded the two perceptions together, weaving in his mind a vision of the future. *A future where an adulterer and adulteress might kill his king in the night and take his crown the following morning.*

As Gwyar was paralyzed to expose Gwenhwyfar for fear it would break Arthur, and having broken him, break the country, so too was her gilded and happy son ever melancholy, ever given to moods of dread over exposing Maelgwn, for the same reason. Those who loved Arthur would rather perish from within, slow and with wanton pain, than hurt their beloved king. Just and kind, undefeated in battle, fair and balanced in religion, principled in politics, the War King and the Giant Slayer. The hope of Britannia. Never, never must he know of the betrayal of she whose head rested upon a pillow but inches from his own.

And so five years passed. A half-decade more of marvelous quests, legendary adventures, pith and contentment amongst the Britons, whose hearts shone as the golden rooftops of Caermelyn and Caerleon.

Five years passed from the appearance of the Grail and the visitors from Rome.

Five remained unto the coming of the Red Dragon of Merlin's prophecy.

Then Kwyllog, wife of the traitor Mordred, took ill and died young. And Autumn fell on the Summer Kingdom.

CHAPTER 17
The False Gwenhwyfar

Seed 4 – "You put me in a vice where, behold, though I win yet will I lose."

Ogyrfan Gawr, the only Giant to have survived being *activated* by the bewitching beguilement of the Adder, did sorrowful penance for his behavior in the great hall during the Roman's visit. Though he could not control his actions, his contrition was real. An opportunist seeking security and wealth does not attack rulers, for they are his best customers. Instead, an opportunist deals in commerce, and goods, *and children*.

And this crafty brute possessed additional capital for commerce in the form of another strikingly fair daughter. A mirror image of her older sister. So uncanny was their resemblance that, though separated by two decades, one could not be distinguished from the other. Ogyrfan's second daughter was called Gwenhwyfach.

Mordred came to know the one who was as a twin to his true love whilst serving as the principal guard at a type of garrison Arthur had stationed at Caer Ogyrfan. Over long months of idle time (for Ogyrfan was of no real danger to the king, especially with Simon Magus landlocked and inactive), Mordred came to sup many times with the lass, to hunt in her father's fertile lands atop steed, and to visit the markets for trinkets or supplies for Ogyrfan's fortress and estates.

Mordred was captivated, marveling and smitten.

The eyes, the same.

The build and curves, the same.

The seductive sophistry, identical.

The sensuality and touch that could fell nations? Yet unknown.

But Mordred burned to know. With Kwyllog deceased, and with increasing access to Arthur's own ear, Mordred convinced Arthur to remove the chains upon Ogyrfan; and in return for his advocacy, Ogyrfan gave Gwenhwyfach to Mordred, making her his betrothed.

Gwenhwyfar raged.

"Your saintly wife dead not one moon and you must needs already get this wet" – she grabbed at his trousers, but not romantically – "when you can have me right here in this field, as oft as you can arrange it!" Gwen actually spat on Mordred, and then on the ground, as does a vulgar man full of too much strong drink.

"My Lady." Mordred locked up Gwen's wrist, causing her to release his privates, clutched painfully in her hand. "It is political. With my spouse dead, I could not just hover and swirl as some vulture above, waiting for your spouse to do the same. How would that look before all?"

Liars loathe the lies of other liars.

"This is about the lines upon my cheeks and sag upon my breasts."

"You are as a lass of eighteen! Stop now."

"This is as a knight putting down his old

war horse. If white, doth he not always replace it with white, and if spotted, is it not the same? You are treating me as an old war horse, or as one of Arthur's goddamned war dogs! The pup becomes a dog – get a new pup!" she seethed. "Beware the fang of this war dog, Mordred!" She whipped the back of her hand, filled with costly and jagged rings, across the Whelp's jaw, opening three gashes. Gwen had killed often. She had not the supernatural powers (save the rose betwixt her legs) of her sister-in-law, but was just as lethal. "There are games tomorrow, and the Lancelot is confirmed at court. If you lie with my sister, I will see to it that you face him at swordplay. And I will see to it that his sword is not blunted like the rest of the field. You are mine! How many long years have we endured grass and mud upon our naked arses in the stead of down and silk? You are mine!"

Mordred applied pressure to his wounds, but they yet bled in globby, chunky, circular drops.

"I am yet yours." His answer was vague. His eyes were empty.

* * *

The games were vital for fighting men, both old and young. The land had been so long at peace, and some of the Round Table Fellowship were beginning to be on the wrong side of their prime. Arthur was yet in his fourth decade, but fifty was hunting him as a pack of nearby wolves, and Lancelot had recently reached the half-century mark. These were special men, during a special time, and they aged differently. But they aged nevertheless. A twinge in the knee, a pang in the shoulder, a complaint in the lower back when rising from bed. The games were critical to make the men feel young and exercised and to combat the subtle enemy of time, which was constantly trying to remind them all that even Arthur and his twenty-four would one day lose at least one battle, that time would ultimately be the sole undefeated warrior.

But not on this day.

On this day, the warriors were brilliant. *Still brilliant.*

At archery, all possessed the eyes of the eagle, with contests amongst many masters won by the smallest measurements.

At grappling all were advanced martial artists. Locks and holds, leverage and speed; each match was as if the Cymry had invented the sport instead of the Greeks. Many jested that Zeus himself must have first visited the Isles in the Sea on account of the quality of the wrestling. The lists were careful not to match Arthur, the second-best wrestler, with the Champion of Britain. Instead, Cai met Lancelot in the final match; an epic display of force and elegance in a contrasting and well-fought dance.

The splendor of the games was second only to the noble character of the mighty men. Cool heads surpassed hot valor. None gave way to emotion; victors were humble (knowing they could just as easily fall at the next go), and the vanquished were resolute but not given to anger. The games were sport, but also training, and the participants knew this. The younger men were grappling and sparring with soldiers who had fought in the Saxon Wars. *In actual war.* When Urien or Cadoc put the staff to one's hinderside, one felt as struck by a demigod and learned much. Priceless access to greatness witnessed by fortunate few, greatness that might never be again.

The young warriors, such as Peredur and Gwrgi, deeply appreciated the lessons, the bruises notwithstanding.

Rhufwan communicated deep regret (for all would see him pitted against his father in a wondrous clash of Titans for the ages) at his absence from the games. A rumor had surfaced of a Grail sighting in a chapel in Glastenn, and he was off as hound to the scent, hunting hard.

Rhun was present, working up the lads, leading in some sibling mockery and roll of the eyes as brothers do, many having an innocent laugh over the adventures of Galahad.

But Taliesin looked at his thumb, burnt, disfigured and scarred. Taliesin laughed not.

The final event was swordplay. Head-to-head matches were fought with blunted blades and small shields that were only about the twice the circumference of the hand. These shields were designed to protect against broken knuckles or hand injuries; they were not large shields for fending off arrow or long weapon.

The combatant was not regulated regarding armor and could celebrate tribe or kingdom with ornate helm and plating, or choose simple leather cuffs and scales, or fight with bare chest as desired. Lateral slashes were executed with the flat of the blade instead of the edge so that gashes and cuts were incidental and rare, less dangerous bruises and contusions common.

Three points, defined by a clean blow to the navel, chest or head, ended the match, or an injured or overpowered contestant could yield prior to the third blow.

Bedwyr, having retired on account of the loss

of his right hand, and Illtud, who loved combat but had left such things to serve God, were judges, and their determination of a score was to be respected as final by tradition of the games.

The day's matches were contested on a large rectangular pitch near the amphitheater. Wooden benches were stacked and staggered to the east of the pitch and canopied with colored fabrics, silks and tassels, looking very much as a long half-stadium, similar in style to the chariot sprints conducted in Greece and Rome.

The most honored of guests were seated on a covered platform situated lowest to the pitch, where the clash and clank of sword and shield could actually be heard, aerial projectiles of teeth actually seen, the sweaty splash of musclebound youths actually felt.

Gwenhwyfar II, Queen Onbrawst and King Meurig were amongst the nobles watching from here. Gwenhwyfach the newcomer was seated amongst them as well. The glare of the older sister was upon the younger, without ceasing. When trumpets were blown so loudly that words were drowned, Gwen would curse the lass, though unheard. She had not reconciled the situation, had not calmed her storm from the prior day, and had all but forgotten *the long game* played by her and her love for well over a decade. She had been scorn and scorn's hell personified throughout the games, and earlier that day at home as well.

* * *

That Mordred would soon know her sister ceased not to cripple the Adulteress Queen's hypocritical heart.

Have I not changed?

Have I not been mostly good?

She screamed at God, bartering with a deity unknown to her, and she beat her fists against the air.

Worse, she carried her anger in the open of the day and volleyed it at her faithful husband. Contrary to the sum of her life, this time the *Mistress of Compartmentalization* could not separate out her segments, the slices of her trafficking in lies and diverse lives. No mask of modesty or doting wife adorned her; she was raw, nasty and rude.

And Arthur noted it.

It was impossible for him not to note it, being the object of her tirade.

She screamed about the chamber being unkempt.

She insulted the breaking of the fast, and those who had labored to prepare it.

She shrieked about misplaced bracelets.

When dessert was served, she screeched that the custard was off.

She stamped around, protesting having to sit in the summer sun at the games, which she professed were the vanity of men who refused to cease acting as boys.

And she laced Arthur with vitriol regarding his dogs.

"I will not sit and smell this shit of your mastiffs for three hours under the beating sun. Move the dogs, or move me."

King Arthur abhorred rudeness. He did not abide it in his own men when engaging each other, nor when negotiating with a foe.

"Think before reacting. When a person is taken in extreme anger, there is a matter behind the matter, and

the matter at which they yell and holler is a projection, and not the matter."

Arthur had been sixteen when the Merlin had taught him this lesson, and the king recalled clearly his response: "That's a lot of matters!" Even Merlin had laughed at his own bardic prose. But the use of unique word combinations, humor or harshness, always with love, had anchored these lessons into the core of Arthur's being, allowing him to draw from them at just the right moment – making him the greatest of kings.

Oblivious to the chronic and ongoing wrongs done unto him by Mordred, the arrival of Gwenhwyfach should have been noted as a variable, but was not. To the contrary, Arthur had become quite fond of him. Mordred wore black often, celebrating his Ravens from the North, and his presence gave Arthur a feeling of 'familiarity', most probably associated with the closeness he felt for Mordred's mother.

Pressing and pressing in his mind, he landed on another option: *Lancelot.* Away so frequently from court, and especially from Caerleon where Gwenhwyfar made her permanent home (for Arthur's residences were plenary, requiring him to lodge in diverse locations throughout the year in administration of his kingdom), the presence of the champion was the only known disruption or irregularity to the day. Arthur tried to dismiss this notion. A fog was starting to lift... slowly. Were Gwalchmai's whispers starting to creep in? Was the wisdom-filled, silent disdain of his mother at last finding fertile soil?

Women know things. They are smarter than we. Especially about other women.

The rude seductress before him suddenly caused Arthur, for the first time since they had mutually ended their marriage, to miss the company of Queen Gwenhwyfar the White, his red-headed lady, who was stately, a patriot, a Christian and maternal. A powerful, wonderful woman.

Whilst Gwen II was flirtatious, giggly, or overtly doting on the king, he could see none of the malignant sores spread over the whole of her constitution – the fester of opportunistic stink and sludge that was her character. Because she had fallen so deeply in love with Mordred, a good shell had formed about a bad egg. Acting was easy. Flawless. She could (and did) look on Arthur as if he was Mordred and engage in theatre under the name of marriage. But with the shell now cracked, the yolk did seep: a black yolk.

And this one outburst over dogs and meals and the daily happenings of every couple was able to start, albeit slowly at first, to awaken the king in the one sphere of his life where he was woefully asleep. *For the abused start to see that they are being cheated upon; if you are to cheat, be nice, ever.*

But prudence requires evidence. Thus, Arthur tucked away the concern about Lancelot for another time and took an alternative course.

"My love," he opened, countering anger with love. "Are you yet unwell because of your cycle and what happened?"

The fool hath given me easy escape! The evil queen glistened.

Arthur was referring to a potential miscarriage (of a truth, to an unknown father) that was but recent, and hard on Gwen's health. Her recovery was slow; her appetite suffered. That she would be faint and of ill disposition was not an unreasonable assumption.

Discerning that the calm king was upset at her outbursts, and underestimating his ability to see her as she was, she seized upon his suggested diagnosis. (He let her do the same to deescalate the situation, allowing him to monitor her next move. *And Maelgwn's.)*

"I deeply apologize, handsome." The actress was resurrected. "Yes, I am of foul mood, but 'tis a matter of health and not anger towards you. I love you so."

The transformation was immediate. Instantly, in her effort to restore *the fog*, she was upon her knees, loving Arthur with her mouth, making endless doting comments about his coming victories in the games, finishing him quickly so that they could enjoy banter with cider and jest ere he was off to compete.

Her efforts exceeded impressive. But Arthur was not fully fooled as they parted for the afternoon's contests.

His eye would be keen on Maelgwn.

Her foulness would resume the moment she saw Gwenhwyfach.

* * *

Maelgwn, having been away from court, had dearly missed his friends (for it was never his desire to be separated by them, but only for his madness) and his youthful verve, though he was aged fifty, was on full display during the contests of sword. He let several young aspiring warriors, thirty years or more his junior, have at him first.

The champion's objective was to teach the younger, but also not to embarrass or humiliate them, but also to win. Only the Lancelot could carry out such contradictory objectives with his grace and skill. Each opponent learned much, was allowed to fight long enough (for he could have ended each contest with a stroke or two and instead carried the lads for a few minutes apiece) to gain priceless experience, and left the day with memories that would invigorate them forever, improving their potential military careers.

And Maelgwn, the Lancelot of Britannia, shone with the sun.

Then the weather turned.

In Caerleon, the winds can hit the "river low and the hilltops high", changing the most pleasant summery day into a miserably cold wine-press of bone-chilling air. The hot day rapidly became cold.

Warm weather helps warm manners, and warm muscles are injured less.

Cold weather brings grit and grumpiness, and muscles strain and are injured more.

The whole temperament of the day seemed to change with the redirection of the weather. Combatants didn't offer a hand when their fellows fell; curse words and complaints of fouls increased, and good sportsmanship disappeared as the sun vanished behind the clouds. Saint Illtud and Bedwyr could feel the change and engaged Arthur privily, inquiring as to whether or not they should proceed, or perhaps postpone the swordplay to the following day.

During the interlude, Gwenhwyfar II called Lancelot to the platform where she was seated, in the plain view of all. The exchange looked inappropriate. Not because she was doing something untoward, but rather because she had come to her decision regarding her threat to place Mordred in the path of Maelgwn's sword.

He had done poorly in the lists, losing far

more matches than he had won. Because of this, and because of the myriad of times he had looked discreetly upon her throughout the day, saying "I promise not to touch her" with his eyes, she decided to forgo it. But she wanted Mordred to feel the threat of Lancelot's might – so she beckoned him over, only to discuss neighborly and non-essential matters.

But between Lancelot and Gwenhwyfar, nothing is neighborly and non-essential. He was still full of post-battle glow and glisten, the only warrior unfazed by the cruel winds and, forgetting himself, was *too familiar with Gwenhwyfar*, leaning in close, approaching a kiss.

"Would you betray our lord before all?!" A red-haired Round Table Knight called Gwalchmai made the accusation.

Lancelot withdrew from the Lady and ignored the son of Morgaine, instead looking to Arthur.

The only variable is you. The king was still fixed on the morning's assault by his queen, who had become all smiles at the presence of the Briton's tallest knight. Knowing that Lancelot desired him to reprimand his heir, he would not.

Morgaine was not present. Had she been there, surely she would have stopped Gwalchmai's tongue, by maternal authority, or else by sorcery. The cold weather and long hours of competition, sweat and manly pride, mixed with years of suspicion, caused the tea kettle of Gwalchmai's temperance to bubble and at last boil over.

"Do you accuse the queen?" Lancelot posed the question, whilst Arthur was stoic, and whilst a crowd gathered and constricted.

"You are our bravest and our best, yet your absence far outweighs your presence. Where a man's time is, there too is his affection."

"Then he must be wildly in love with the sheep that graze upon his hilly farm." Bedwyr volleyed humor to quell the development – to no avail.

The wind become angrier; the sunny day become vile. The throngs agitated, forming an immense half-circle of humanity around the two heroes, now pinned by the platform stage on one side, and three to four hundred souls pressing them from the other.

"Do you accuse the queen?!" Lancelot demanded a second time.

"Let the queen account to her husband. I accuse *you*."

Gwalchmai was taller than Arthur. Lancelot turned, pulling his shoulders back hard, posturing to full height, his chest plumed as a peacock, towering over the Hawk of May as a grown man in a scolding position above a small child.

Neither man had a blunted sword, as they were between matches and had their usual arms, making the incident thrice as dangerous.

The King of Gwnyedd's forearms and hands were all silver, armed in the fashion of his foster-mother. His biceps and shoulders were bare, as the day had started full of merriment and celebratory competition, and naked were his arms to bring swoons and cheers from the damsels in the stands. His breastplate was wrought of very thin metal fastened with thirty rivets upon thick leather, knotwork outlining the piece. His shins were protected, and his thighs were as his arms.

And the famous battle dirk rested in two custom leather loops along the left side of his belt. History's most accomplished killing instrument in the hands of the offended Bloodhound.

Gwalchmai was all leather scales shined with beautiful green lacquer. The lacquer was an enamel that sealed the leather and added some additional deflection and displacement on blows. Arthur's father, Meurig, made use of a dark blue enamel and had popularized the style of enamel atop leather. This kind of armor was as an extra layer of skin; fitted tight without joint or rivet, fashioned for speed and comfort, woven to be at once as a fishnet over the whole of the body but designed to 'breathe' as well.

The two curved swords, sleeping at the moment in matching green lacquered sheaths, were nearly as famous as Lancelot's battle dirk, nearly as deadly.

Neither man had a helmet.

Lancelot grumbled under his breath and looked to Arthur to intervene.

But Arthur doubted.

The queen's outlandish rudeness.

Lancelot's erratic, maddening behavior.

The *kidnapping*.

And now today's little exchange, which provoked the Hawk of May.

Arthur doubted. And Arthur remained silent.

Gwalchmai did not.

Like so many living in this transitional, and not a little confusing, era, Gwalchmai loved Jesus very much, to the extent that he understood Him. He also had no moral conflict with fluidly floating in and out of his pagan worldview. Gwalchmai was an example of tens of thousands of Britons who were 'betwixt and between'. And this was the testament to Arthur's brilliance as king. *He managed the transition, slowly.* Abrupt changes would result in rebellion, unrest, chaos and endless opportunities for the powerful to orchestrate religious wars for no god other than their bellies. It meant suffering some superstitions and customs, from both the Church and the heathen; it meant endless nuance complex decisions and directional shifts, and sometimes, it meant nearly impossible scenarios.

The Hawk of May, who was perhaps part magical creature on account of his mother, the witch-goddess Morgaine of the Faeries, or was perhaps simply a *transitional man in a transitional age*, called upon a custom as old as the Isles.

"Trial by combat!" he screamed, drawing both swords with a graceful anger. He stepped towards Lancelot, fearing not the oak tree with arms looming over him. And where he stepped, the clouds parted and rays of sun warmed him, but Lancelot remained beset by the pressing, windy and now rain-filled storm.

Lancelot now audibly appealed to the Pendragon. "If I am accused of conduct inappropriate with our queen, of the which I am surely innocent, then logic, reason and evidence should try me, not a seldom-evoked mystical custom."

Trial by combat. The belief amongst the druids held that, when one who is a warrior is accused of a great wrong and engages in such a trial, the spirit of the land would ensure that the one who was true would win versus the one who was false. That fate and right would win out over brawn and skill. The ritual did not apply to farmer or poet, and the words of the Lord were borrowed when articulating the druids' position: "*He who lives by the sword shall die by the sword.*" The intent was to mitigate false accusations, creating a healthy fear that the gods, the forces of nature, or even the Fae would help the wrongly impugned.

Arthur, the Christian Sovereign, surveyed the multitude, who was demanding that he respect the customs. He gracefully ducked behind Meurig and retched, but none saw save his mother, Queen Onbrawst, who used the breadth of her gown to screen her son, giving him the two seconds he needed to rally. Anguished in his spirit; in his mind, curious. *Is there truth behind trial by combat? And moreso, what might I learn as these men engage; what truth will fall out of their mouths?* The risk was indeed great.

King Arthur appeared in the midst of the complainant and defendant.

"I will allow it. Only that it be conducted with blunted blade, and that when either has gained an advantage near victory, he will grant mercy to the other upon my command."

The crowd loved the king's judgment. He had retained and respected custom, but modified it so that the two great men would also keep their heads. All seem pleased but Lancelot, who was crimsoned.

At this very moment, another seed plunged deep into soil, another root of offense and deepest hurt.

Yet again a seed tossed on dangerous soil. A sowing stamped with foot and watered, surely to take root. A molten anger wrought by his lifelong friend's refusal to declare him innocent. Another instance of Arthur not lending his unconditional support to his First Knight. *Your painted wife panted wet and ready before me; if you are to kill my reputation here over mere words, why did I suffer and deny myself?* Instead, regardless of outcome, Lancelot would leave the pitch the loser; a man with the public accusation of impropriety of the highest order now ever upon his head. The Tribes might love custom, might declare him divinely innocent by right of victory, but the Tribes venerated but one thing above their ancient customs… gossip.

The hot animosity that sizzled towards Arthur he would redirect towards Gwalchmai. *The son of Gwyar I will not bless to be king when gone is Arthur. Mordred will be High King if on that day I feel not like taking the diadem; elsewise Rhun or Rhufawn.* Lancelot himself was most surprised that his mind ran to politics when fury welled. He accepted the blunted sword – "I'll take two, please" – and made his way to the place designated for the trial.

Gwenhywfach took her new husband by the elbow, removing him from the main stage, endeavoring to go and stand amongst the people, closing to the fighting, curiosity needing a better vantage. Arthur saw her from the corner of his eye. Though suspicious of his spouse, and hoping against hope that the lifelong friendship between her and Maelgwn had remained as amicable siblings and not lovers, opted for edification and love in the place of the unfounded daggers that are hurtful words.

"Your younger sister looks like you," he remarked plainly.

"Some say we are twins, twenty years removed." Her response was dry.

"Similar, to be certain. But you are far more beautiful than she, my wife. I pity her."

"Oh?"

"Aye; she will ever be in the shadow of a sister more fair. Poor thing."

The one whom Gwenhwyfar loved had put her to the stables as an old mare.

The one whom she never loved revered her, preferred her and respected her.

The result was not that good sense and reason would pour in upon her, or that misplaced affection for Mordred might at least decrease. Rather, apathy towards Arthur's affections increased.

The trial by combat commenced.

Lancelot circled and waited.

Circled and waited.

He would use counter-fighting to an extreme, waging a defensive and slower strategy against his bulky red-haired opponent.

Gwalchmai had fought and bled with Lancelot during the final years of the Saxon Wars, and during countless real-combat raids. He knew the philosophical approach, and would not be goaded.

Thus, they danced.

And danced.

To stimulate action, Lancelot finally faked a looping, swooshing slice towards Gwalchmai's lead leg. Gwalchmai made a perfect blocking pose with his sword at the hip, but used two hands upon his hilt, and the strike never came. This exposed his head to Lancelot, who came forward hard, spinning and putting back of his fist hard upon Gwalchmai's mouth, splitting his lip in twain.

No stranger to his own blood, for Gwalchmai was a warrior of grit and grind, not flawless and scarless like Lancelot, he recoiled calmly and started yet again.

Years of frustration towards Lancelot helped the Hawk of May fight well above the fullness of his abilities. Like his mother, he was a patriot above all and felt that the Champion of Britain was a monumental underachiever. A man enslaved by passion and the shortcomings of the god Narcissus, ever putting personal tribulations over the public good. The shining city on the hill had many enemies but only one real threat: that it would crumble in upon itself on account of some scandal or crime of passion. *One real threat: Lancelot.*

* * *

A tremor jolted Gwyar in the center of her back, betwixt the blades of her shoulder; a supernatural flood of knowledge, a feeling of dread accompanied by the manifestation of real pain. She had once grown too accustomed to like feelings when her brother would position Gwalchmai on the front lines, or some especially precarious assignment during the Saxon Wars. But never so intensely. Never so present. A twang and a twinge would pinch when her brother would select Gwalchmai, and always Gwalchmai, to join him in the hunt for a Giant or other monstrosity of cave, wood or deep. Arthur did it for trust, for mentorship, and for love (for he greatly wanted the people to hear of Gwalchmai's deeds and achievements, that they might accept him as king).

And for the same love, she hated it. Wishing her lad ever to be safe and bringing joy to any village, warmth to any city, song and merriment to every singing tribe. These were his natural dispositions. A shaggy, auburn-curled, jolly leader of men. He possessed the best bits of grandfather Meurig and uncle Arthur, and a pinch of mother Morgaine of the Faeries. He was meant to rule one day, not to fall to the Long Knife or be eaten by some otherworldly abomination.

This danger transcended the others. *'Twas mortal.*

"I must see!"

She darted away from the small cell that had become her simple abode towards the enchanted castle she had long ago abandoned. And not by choice. She had traded marble and precious stones for thatch and mud of necessity, for Bishop Cadfan and his pilgrims were, with each passing day, closer to finding one of the little island's sacred treasures. *The treasure* that would change everything. Thus it behooved Gwyar to become as an old hag guarding a cauldron, living by her possession day and night, as a crone chasing away inquisitive children with a stick.

"My son, my son. I must see!"

Mists and enchantments were her primary instruments to keep the Catholics away. She did not frighten them. Rather, she kept them perpetually lost, perpetually unable to chart and map the small island, the surface of which was but a moderate mound with a steep, sloping opening to wood and then beach. The mystical island, called by some *Avalon,* floated as an imperfect little dumpling just beyond the outreached finger of the Llyn Peninsula. Her task was to render it as a perpetual maze, as the cornstalk labyrinths hewn for children's games during the harvest rites and festivals.

This, though, was no game. This was for the survival of her spirituality, and for the real Christians of every sect and stripe.

Distracted completely from her task as mist-weaver and path-changer, she made for a black marble scrying bowl, which was centerpiece to the upper room in the loftiest tower within the bastion. All focus went unto summonsing or becoming her *other self* and taking command of the Sight to seek out and, if possible, aid her son.

"A hawk and your keen eyes for my Hawk

and his pure soul. Help me see him." Gwyar had fetched the bird that shared her boy's namesake. Her dagger, sharper than any sword amongst the Britons save Arthur's legendary armaments, was through the hawk's neck with no effort; its blood was upon the still green waters of the scrying basin. With a physician's skill, she dissected its eyes, discarding all but the lenses, which she held in her tiny left hand. With her right hand she etched the seven-pointed star of the Fae into the rowan-wood pulpit that held her instruments, located next to the watery looking-glass.

The primal witch who dwelt in unison with her essence bore a special pain for losing children, as God Almighty, in the days of Noah, had bound her in chains and fixed her eyes open, sentencing her to watch each of her children perish as He opened the windows of the vault above, drowning them without mercy. All the while the witch had screamed her repentance to the Father, who had ceased striving with her kind. Her screams had been met with the coldest of responses. Silence. A silent heaven, far crueler than an angry hell. The Most High had charged her father, who was a Watcher, to teach men about governance and patriotism, even yet in the times before man's boundaries and habitations were apportioned. Moreover, the Watcher gave men wisdom of herb and plant, seed and silk, and the proper moderate use of the like. Her father had taken a mortal wife, who had brought her into the world. He in turn had lain with his daughter, the primal witch (though she knew not he was her father, as she had been raised an orphan, her mother dying in childbirth), begetting sons that were more god than man. Sons of double abomination.

Taking the mantle from her father-lover, the

arts she had taught the Sons of Adam were soon corrupted, developing into a forbidden body of esoteric wisdom that sinful man could not manage and, because of it, should not learn. Intended, from her perspective, for good, but always to wreak disaster and evil outcomes. In her pride she disobeyed; in her passion, she meddled.

God was right and she was wrong. The potter understood the vessel better than did the clay. *But why no mercy upon my children?*

And so, this confusion of reverence for God and Country melded with an unyielding, dominating drive to be overly protective of her young passed from her substance into Gwyar, who was relentless in her need to see Gwalchmai and his brothers safe. But not so for the oldest; the same need was not so present towards Mordred.

The meddling was passed on to Gwyar as well.

Her lenses became fused with the lenses of the hawk, empowering to her to see at great, supernaturally long, distances. The 'hawk-eyed' sorceress gazed upon the waters, setting about to scry.

Her efforts did not return void.

There in the black marble the green mirror showed her past true love, *her only true love,* steadily and increasingly dominating his bout with her son. Lancelot was punishing Gwalchmai. Where he could end the contest with minimal injury to his opponent, Lancelot would pause and go no further, allowing Gwalchmai to recuperate some strength, alongside false hope, only to punish him again. Morgaine could not see her brother, who was judging the bout; nor could she tell that the swords were blunted for training and sport. The perceived mortal danger outweighed any holistic evaluation of her vision.

Crying out to any and all gods, imploring all forces, she begged, "If Maelgwn ap Cadawalhir hath any past wound, open it; hath any weakness, manifest it! No matter how small, grant my son hope! Give my Hawk of May one ray of sun, one sliver of light, I pray!"

Meanwhile, whilst she was fully distracted, Bishop Cadfan himself found it.

* * *

Gwalchmai was losing. Losing badly. Battered, cut, ashen. By the precepts of trial by combat, he would soon have to declare Maelgwn's innocence and his allegation false. This circumstance usually resulted in the death of the accuser, but Arthur had modified the custom. He might live. Life henceforth would ever be accompanied with the shame and aggravation of knowing that an affair would crumble the Summer Kingdom. The misery of knowing that he had fallen short, the ancient custom having failed the Green Knight. Perhaps it *was* fact alone that reigned, and not who could swing a piece of steel better. A great disappointment splashed over the romantic and discouraged warrior.

As he retreated five paces and began to offer the rote words of *innocence,* it was instead Maelgwn who let out a great cry. His naked left thigh, high up near his loins, was awash in fresh blood, falling in uniform and heavy splashes as a waterfall upon his shin and calf armor, then bouncing down to the soil below.

Neither participant was to stab or poke, rather only to strike with the flat edge of the blade. Incidental cuts abounded, but this was an actual *wound*. The two had been closely engaged on a few passes in the match, but none had seen the source of this injury.

Arthur rose to speak, but Lancelot stayed his words.

"It is an old wound, my lord, the scar of which opens betimes. The Hawk did nothing afoul."

The blood brought a reminder, and the reminder was of Merlin. Lancelot was not innocent. That he had not consummated his lust in Perth did not abdicate him of hundreds of kisses and *martial eye service;* transcending the physical indiscretions, he loved the king's wife. He had caused men to die for her, neglected his mates for her, abused women for her. The blood judged him guilty. Deserving of the penalty of death, each day a borrowed and unfair day. In the very next moment, the shattered Lancelot might change his mind, might be haughty, might disagree with his own assessment, slay both Gwalchmai and Arthur, and plop the diadem upon his own crown. But in this moment, he was dripping blood and looking at a hopeless man below him. A good man. A man to whom the bards had given a place as one of Arthur's twelve. And rightly so.

Morgaine's meddling and Merlin's ghost dagger saved Gwalchmai's life.

"Iron Bear." Maelgwn humbled himself before the Pendragon. "May we please end this madness? Or would you have me bleed out right here on the field?"

But, as the Scriptures record, *jealousy is the rage of men.*

"This recurring hurt." The king's tone added the words *that none of us have ever heard of.* "How long will it take to mend?"

Surprised by the response, Maelgwn answered, "But a day or two."

"Three days will suffice." The winds remained relentless, causing Arthur's red cape to flow and flip wildly, making him look as an angry, menacing god. "This contest is finished. The Lancelot of Britannia is the victor, and by right of trial by combat, innocent of Gwalchmai's rail." The crowd warmed themselves with raucous cheers, horn and stringed instrument adding deafening praises of the mighty knight.

Because the Hawk of May had made accusation of impropriety before all, and because the test of arms had favored Maelgwn, life would henceforth forever be very different for Gwalchmai. And by extension, for the kingdom. The common man and the solider, and a few of the clergy, who lived under the old codes, traditions and manners, were forced, by their own logic, to conclude Gwalchmai as a false accuser: a sower of discord amongst the Cymry. Because of this, his star diminished somewhat, and his chance of being the popular choice to succeed King Arthur was damaged greatly. From this day, many men amongst the tribes began to pledge their swords to Mordred, the oldest of Arthur's nephews.

"This contest is finished." The king repeated himself. But Arthur was not finished. Frustrated, he settled the grumbly throng; at last they quieted. "This contest is over. But the games are not. Maelgwn is in first position, and" – the king studied the lists and results of the day, confirming how he might beguile the accused for more information – "I am in second position."

"The weather has turned vile. Let there be no more games today!" Bedwini beseeched the king.

"I said 'three days'." Arthur reprimanded his

counselor, who looked to the earth and spoke not again. "Maelgwn, heal thyself, and in three days you and I will meet here and conclude the games. That is my judgment." He turned to Gwalchmai, who required assistance from two men, firmly supporting one arm apiece, to stand. "Nephew, you fought well."

The crowd was shocked that Arthur had declared thus, but with the winds mixed with rain mixed with coming dusk (and none wore cloak or coat, for the day had begun hot, with skies blue and clear), they made haste to cottage, estate or hall. The coming championship was the sole subject of conversation and buzz for every woman and man.

But Maelgwn would have none of it. He made for the woods of Gwent immediately after dressing his wound.

Knowing he would do the same, Arthur disguised himself, and followed.

CHAPTER 18
Did You Lie with My Wife?

Breaking What Could Not Be Broken

Seed 5 – "Forty years undefeated. You take all, and would now ruin that too?"

Morgaine crushed the hawk's lenses in her hand, discarding them upon the ground. Her unholy looking-glass confirming her son lived, and without a moment to contemplate why Maelgwn would do battle with her son, or whether this would make him her enemy, or whether it was less grave – *boys must fight from time to time, after all* – she was onto the next peril. As a cat giving his chase to its own tail, back to the treasure she hastened.

The foul weather from the south had traveled northward, resulting in heavy rainfall upon Ynys Enlli. The overcast was full, with not one luminary visible in the night sky. A grey and black shell covered the whole of the isle, and the waters dashed against the shores, shrieking in symphony with the high winds.

Morgaine had been away from the hut where she served as guardian for approximately three hours. The weather had only turned in the past two. This left a one-hour window, if misfortune befell her, for a vessel to have left Ynys Enlli for the mainland. The odds were in her favor… but *ill luck comes in bunches.*

If pilgrims had found the site, but not prepared letter or messenger, nor launched to sea, then the problem could be *contained.* Gwyar would simply kill those who had found what they ought not to have sought, slay those who had seen what was meant to be concealed. *No survivors, no breach.*

At full gallop, her steed lost its footing, for the deluge mixed the dirt roads rapidly into a cake-batter-like mud and threw the sorceress. "Not so tasty as the batter we put to spoon and belly ere we put pan to oven!" she mused, her face full of the road and a little blood.

She rose quickly. Her hood was of the kind where the stretched, pointed end fell well below her lower back, designed for fashion and not function. With both hands she positioned it on her head, a wet, heavy leather cone that flopped to one side. She looked all the part of a frightful druid priestess about to do devilish deeds for the Creator God. The irony was not lost on her. She looked up to the pitch black and imagined Him, presently laughing from His throne, just above the clouds, at her. She smiled.

"At least Moses had Michael to wrestle for and hide his body. Yet the precious lady gets only devils and the bungling children of the damned for her cause. Truly, God must be a man!"

Levity gave way to horror as she finally arrived at the site: torches and many men surrounding the innocuous grave.

A sect of the druids from Glamorgan, who had seen the light of the gospel but held to many of their native traditions, had made a pact with the Blessed Lady, and with Princess Eurgaine. The relics of the Christians would be hidden amongst the druids, lest the Christians find and make idols of them, falling into corruption like God's chosen people, Israel, before them. Pagans hid Christian things so that Christians would not become as Pagans. This was the pact.

And the relics, or *treasures*, were these:

The cup, or *Holy Grail*.

The alabaster box.

The true Cross.

The second coffin of the Law (for the first had ascended into the heavens afore time).

The spear that had opened the Saviour's side.

The nails that had pierced Him.

The shroud used to wrap His precious body.

And an eighth.

The coffin of Mary, the Mother of Jesus.

Some of the relics had magical or unpredictable properties; some of them were wholly untouched, with powers unknown.

The concern over the body of Mary was not one of mysticism, but rather of history and the nature of men. Men swear by graves. They become a source of revenue to those who control them and a source of false doctrine to those who require that the presbytery come and bow down before them. Men kiss the feet of other men – more so those of other *dead* men. Mary feared that she would be venerated as a goddess, though her bones lay in a box; that an entire religion would be erected around her, appealing to all, spreading the world over, redirecting the praise and worship due the Lord alone unto the mortal woman whose womb had carried Him.

Such was the fear that the druids refused, under any condition, to disclose her location to the Church of the Britons and, over time, denied outright that she had even passed away upon Avalon. Thus, even as the bishops and elders defamed, abused and slandered the druids wherever they could, their enemies did no such thing; rather, they were protectors and guardians against the foes of all men, which are iniquity and idolatry and institutional power drunkenness.

With Vivien transfigured, and Taliesin preoccupied with politics and court and his struggles in keeping the next generation's guardian from falling into the forbidden trap of being seduced by the very thing he or she was to protect, the task fell to Morgaine, the Lady of Avalon. *Independent,* with no special affinity for any group, sect or claimant of god or goddess. A radical patriot who disagreed with much but cherished Arthur's love of liberty and religious freedom.

Perhaps it was right that it should fall to me.

But I have failed.

And, in the time of the reign of King Arthur, the Roman Catholic Church discovered the coffin of Mary, the Mother of Jesus Christ.

Shovels had already unearthed the stone coffin. A marker lay over the sarcophagus; rather than stuck upright in the ground at the head of the corpse, it was buried well beneath the earth and lay flat atop the box, per the custom of the early Saints in Cymru. The inscription read, in the Coelbren script of the bards, "Son, behold thy Mother". These were the words the Lord Jesus said unto Mary, distancing Himself from the Lady whilst He became our sin on the Cross. This was an act of love and no malice, for the Son of Man knew well that man would seek to worship her.

Cadfan the Meek had grown up to be Cadfan the Bold. Meirchion the Mad had poisoned his head with arrogance and self-importance and ill purpose, and no part of the kind, quiet-minded Christianity of Brittany remained in him. Taking full advantage of his lineage and entitlement to lands in Llyn, and by extension Ynys Enlli, he was every bit the thorn to Morgaine, Vivien and Taliesin that Meirchion and Caw had been, in their time, to Arthur and Merlin.

He was happy to let the downpour ruin his best vestments, provided he looked the part of the proud priest: the legend who had found the coffin of the Mother of God.

His time drawing breath to enjoy the fame might not survive the rainstorm, for Morgaine of the Faeries approached.

His men had torches, producing a rectangle of lights around the gravesite. She produced an illumination of her own; a purple, thick and substantive light enveloped her. She and it moved quickly, right for him. As she drew close, he could somehow see her eyes, all black to match her raven's hair, strands of which were matted against her forehead and down her cheeks, emerging as vines from the hood of her garb. Unsure of what manner of words would stop her from going right on through him with no more effort than a fox wastes on the hen pen, he opted for truth with slight.

"Lady Gwyar. None will know Mary rests here, and pilgrims will henceforth visit a façade I shall erect upon the mainland, leaving this place be. I assure thee!" He trembled, hoping the fox would hear the hen. "The pact between Meirchion and Vivien I will honor!"

The latter stopped the sorceress. The dagger was momentarily sheathed. She was not prepared to hear him, however, until her assessment was complete. Eight men and a boy – the young historian Gildas ap Caw (who lifted up Arthur in his heart with special adoration, on account of Arthur having saved the boy's life from the macabre talons of the crazed archbishop). *Jesus and Mary outweigh the loss of the lad Gildas, unfortunately,* she reasoned.

Fanning her pillowed sleeves as a great black cobra, her one question was delivered, her voice causing such terrific trembling that none could run; all were as frozen.

"Has an emissary left for Llyn with news of your *discovered treasure?*"

"No, my lady." Cadfan was frightened but coy. "Three boats have departed. Not for Cymru, but for Rome."

"Prince Madoc or his faithful stewards of the sea will stop them."

"On what grounds? What charges? What authority? Monks make pilgrimages and clerics attend sundry councils. Does not liberty still reign in our peaceful and glorious kingdom of light and summer? The masked villain who posed falsely as one of us will not be found amongst them, and to Rome they will freely go with news of the Blessed Mother, unless the sea makes an end of them." Three he had sent, knowing the likelihood that but one might reach its destination. "Would you kill the whole of Rome with your *unique* gifts to cover this truth, Gwyar?" A protective arm was now flung about the soaking and freezing young historian's shoulders. "Would you kill this boy?"

Gwyar had murdered before. Her composition and traumatic experiences caused her to loathe infidelity in any form and, if she could not contain herself by agony of will, she would give herself to judge these men and the boy here and now. However, Bishop Cadfan was correct. If the discovery had left the little island, it would reach the big island (whether he was lying about Rome made no matter), and if one spoke of it, soon so would a thousand. Her situation would not be improved by sending eight souls to the Underworld. Hearing his intentions seemed to be her best, if not only, recourse.

"What will you do with the body, priest?" she asked, bluntly.

"*The body.* I am so thankful you asked in just that manner." As he started to speak, Cadfan's eyes met Gwyar's. Seeing Death itself staring back at him, he at once discerned that wordplay and boasting was best smothered – immediately. Looking towards his boots, steadily sinking into the relentless rainy mud, he continued, with a tone and tenor of extreme caution. "Your concern about the Blessed Mother's body, with the greatest of respect, has been misplaced. There is an accord between the Lady of the Lake and my late master, Meirchion the Mad. That pact demands that we honor your goddess, though the world comes to Christ."

Gwyar knew there was deception and guile forthcoming, not knowing only what form it would take. She held her tongue.

Cadfan continued. "Where Illtud and Dyfrig would convert you all, we would rather assimilate you. You are not lost sinners doomed for a cruel, fiery hell. Rather, you are all simply departed Catholic brothers and sisters who have lost your way. Hell is a sentence served in portions and degrees, not a place of finality. We believe we can shorten your time working your way out of Hell by joining to us this side of the veil." There was little conviction behind Cadfan's discourse on Hell, and Gwyar wondered if he believed his own words. Were she pressed, Gwyar would reckon Cadfan a traditionalist, an opportunist, and an atheist.

"Instead of denouncing and forcing rejection of your goddess" – he took two contested steps in the thickening, soupy dirt away from the sorceress to deliver his next words – "we will simply appropriate her, and all goddesses in their myriad of forms, to Mary. In her will your goddess live on."

"In pretending to be kind, you would inflict cruelty and compromise upon men of all faiths! No two goddesses are compatible in characteristic, origin or purpose. None will accept that *all the gods are one God, or Goddess!*" she protested, using simple logic.

But his logic was superior, or at least more realistic. "If there is no such thing as an actual goddess, and the thousands of local deities the world over are but tribal expressions of the same *one Mother*, they will swallow the whole of our doctrine. All men want to serve a woman, to slay a dragon, to have a fair maiden, to be in the bosom of the safe harbor of a mother. We will supply all these to the faithful, in the person of Mary. She is the end of your religion."

Gwyar knew he was right, but protested just the same. "You have seen *my power!* Am I a myth or a local cultural expression?"

"Surely not. But men forget all in a generation's time. Our king is removing the land of all the Giants; the *real witches* attack villages and children and fall at his sword or axe, or else those of this or that great Round Table knight. When the supernatural prints and smudges on this land diminish, our propaganda will ensure that they all become restated as legend. You, my lady, are real today but two centuries from now will be a child's bedtime story."

The evil genius of Cadfan's presentation exceeded his levels of intelligence. He was parroting information passed down from the Masked Priest, surely.

"Even King Arthur will be a myth."

"That is treason!" Gwyar hissed.

"It is what will be. We will take the coffin of Mary to the mainland and erect a chapel there. Pilgrims will come to the chapel of Saint Mary and bow down to her *empty tomb*. Great statues and images we will erect to celebrate her. And slowly and methodically we will teach that the coffin is empty because the Mother, the *goddess*, to the tribes, hath ascended to heaven, leaving us a memorial to honor her but no body, for she lives, like the Saviour, at the right hand of the Heavenly Father."

"You will create an enterprise built on lies."

He ignored her and went on, "Your pact with the Glamorgan line of druids and the ancient promises made to Mary and Eurgaine may, of course, continue. Protect these bones; do as you will. None will believe that they are hers."

"The truth, like water, seeks its level. The truth will prevail. My brother, the greatest of all kings, will hear of this, for he loves Mary, for different reasons. He knows of the secret, and he knows of this place. Even if you overcome a little witch like me, how will you defeat Arthur ap Meurig?!"

"Did he not do the same thing at Mynydd Baeden? Did he not bear an image of Mary vague enough to be repurposed and embraced by heathens?"

"What he did was borne of respect and no guile!" she hissed.

"Nevertheless, the king faces problems and perils of his own. I doubt not that he will be much entangled in the rumors and wrangling of rival religions over bones and relics."

Cadfan's confidence was an indication that the mantle had passed from Meirchion. She surmised that he was a low-level initiate in league with the Masked Priest, who must be active from his hiding places within the Isles. Cadfan was as a breadcrumb, and for this reason, Gwyar let him live. The Church's strategy of assimilation was *a slow game* that might win the day, but not *this day*. In his boasts and revelations he had manifested his plans. He possessed a box with old scratches upon it, no more. Gwyar's only course was to stay the course.

As the tempest tendered no grace, pounding Avalon without mercy well into the early hours of the next day, the little raven managed, by herself, to labor for the whole of the night in muck and soak, in sleet and mud. She managed to reinter the earthly mother of Jesus beneath the flooring of the circular thatch hut that had recently become Gwyar's temporary home. Busy hands begat a racing brain. Her thoughts went randomly here then there as she hastened to finish the task.

First to Mary. The burden of a mother and the impossible plight that is womanhood. *To be the mother of an innocent man, to see Him slain before your very eyes. To flee beyond the fingertips of Rome, to hide from the Jews, to never have rest.*

Then to Gwalchmai. *My son, my Green Knight, the brightness of our Isle. What embarrassment and shame hath Lancelot brought to you, innocent and just now spotted and smudged by a crazy man!* The involuntary reflections increased the speed of hand and accelerated anger; unrelenting visions of Maelgwn smiting her boy joined the rains soaking and troubling her soul. Lastly, to Gwenhwyfar. The kernel and core of all that distressed Cymru. *A woman is no woman who has not known the birthing of a child. She is a well without water, a dry spring. She knows not the burden of anything save ambition.*

At last she finished, the thoughts somewhat assuaged. She looked upon the new concealed place. It was arranged with love and respect and, above all, discretion.

* * *

Both royal siblings had braved the night's summer storm.

"He makes camp at Llyn Fawr. At his foster-mother's posts, just beyond the waters."

Arthur quickly unclothed himself, throwing his soaked robes (for this time he had been guised as a bard, complete with harp and scroll) and accessories into the creel, next to a massive freestanding closet in the anteroom that joined to his and Gwenhwyfar's bedchamber. She half listened, giving the greater heed to the mud tracked in upon the floor, and the chaotic and wet greetings of Arthur's dogs, whom she rushed out of the room with intolerant and vulgar words.

She began to speak, but the king gave her no place, nor space. Replacing the disguise he had donned to follow the Lancelot with a simple flesh-colored robe and placing a circlet upon his head, though she was his only audience and the sun was not yet in his chamber, he authoritatively drew to within inches of her, and questioned the queen.

"In three days I will meet our childhood friend in a *game of sport*. Have you anything to tell me, whether in regard to the privy exchange that set my nephew at such variance, or any untoward deed or thought of past or present?"

"You have been at it all night hunting the Bloodhound. And remain yet eloquent. Yet virile, and strong. I am as innocent as the trial declared, husband," she responded.

What his heart wanted to believe, his head forbade. She was Arthur's first love, his only love. But the glow she had around *him,* the *look…* Never gave she these to Arthur. He knew that nothing revealed love so much as a lovers' quarrel. Her anger, her investment of emotion, betrayed her words to be false, though Arthur mistook what was on account of Mordred, laying Maelgwn to blame. Far from conclusive, the scales were falling, yet slow as an inchworm, from his eyes.

"Think you that I am as strong as he?" He tested the queen.

The actress, still obsessed with the probable present congress of her love with the False Gwenhwyfar, could not suffer even the briefest of exchanges of this sort.

"Oh, the two of you!" The beauty snarled, the left side of her lip raised, teeth shown as a trapped predator, giving warning before the strike. "He is stronger. Or you. You are more handsome. Or perhaps he. By my soul, I care not, for I am WEARY of you both. Ever from our youth, 'twas always the same. Will we go to our graves abiding such nonsense? Not I!" Though the aggressor, the lady retreated three steps. "Get these cursed dogs out of our room, Arthur!"

"This hatred of the pets. Is it new, or like other matters, newly revealed?" Calm words, though his heart raced as the sprinters from yesterday's games.

"I would not enumerate the things I detest, for the new day is not long enough."

Merlin had taught Arthur that extreme anger revealed one of two truths that were unfortunately negating, revealing nothing; the twin angers of innocence and guilt.

Thus, more information was needed. Information that would not be had under the current cloud of ill sentiment. In her indignation, his spouse, who was as a mouse before him, was yet intimidating; but Arthur was not subdued. He encroached further, his very breath now felt upon her forehead.

"It has been a miserable day, which has wrought hasty words. Forget not thyself, and see that you disrespect never the king, especially in his own estate."

To look upon King Arthur Pendragon when he drew upon his innate and natural authority was to look at Death itself. She suddenly felt as scores of Saxons of old had felt before Excalibur had run them through, which was a pleasant alternative to the menacing imposition of the Great Sovereign.

The actress. The politician. Seeing that she had overstepped and noting well that Arthur had transitioned office from husband to king, she forced herself to stop thinking about Mordred and Gwenhwyfach for a moment and to focus on surviving the moment. "Yes; the storm, and the moons of womanhood. Forgive me. Of course I love you alone. Please let us rest, my love." Her countenance shifted from hunter to seductress. The snarl waxed into a smile. "And yes, husband, I have always hated those damn dogs!"

They giggled, and he bade Cai put them with the horses.

The sun rose and the fair weather returned, the clear sky causing the majestic Severn to shine as a crystal river.

Surrendering to a few hours of sleep, lids too heavy to uphold, Gwen's final waking thoughts: *Mordred is having intercourse with my sister!*

* * *

Mordred was having intercourse with Gwen's sister.

Not all lovemaking is the same. Not all privy parts are a delicious counterpart. The wonderful friend Mordred had made at Caer Ogyrfan, the courtship so enticing, so alluring and confirming; the *newer Gwenhwyfar. The little sister, the 'bach' or tiny Gwen,* now beneath Mordred. His wife, his legitimate lover.

And yet.

In the very act of knowing her, with feigned looks of pleasure, the heavens themselves began to crash, the world ending in apocalyptic fashion.

She is boring.

She is not good at this.

What have I done?!

The dark magic betwixt Gwenhwyfar's thighs wrought by nature, else by the Tylwyth Teg, had ruined Mordred (and many other unfortunate souls besides) for all women, the realization thereof drowning him – not in a slow coming to terms, but as the highest tides climaxing upon hard rocks.

She is boring.

I do not like this!

What have I done?

Mordred, yet still in the act of loving, peered into the eyes of his wife, who sincerely returned his gaze with ecstatic adoration. His glance had become academic, curious, and mindful of history.

Knowing the fullness of what might come, he marveled at her. *I am looking at the one who will be the ruin of Britain.* Then he finished, and slept.

* * *

Arthur instructed Bedwyr and Cai to send word to many that the championship contest was at hand, only that the venue had changed. Both knights, uneasy, faithfully executed their charges.

Maelgwn rested under a tree, gazing upon the lake, hoping desperately to see Vivien, or the wizard, or any otherworldly being that might bewitch him to forget her and resurrect his love for him. That Arthur had allowed one swing of a blunted sword by Gwalchmai rivaled his thoughtlessness of many times afore. Denying the king of Gwynedd the chance *to defend Gwynedd,* and other hurts, boiled and boiled. And the boil produced a bubble.

Perhaps two great kings are two too many. For this cause, perhaps there can only be one. Maelgwn wrested with vivid and detailed thoughts of violence against Arthur.

And then the very object of his malicious contemplations presented itself above him, the form a familiar regal shadow. *And three hundred onlookers besides.*

"Making your leave before the final match?"

Maelgwn did not rise, but remained flat on his back beneath the tree, as a felled, dead oak fixed hard against one that was yet upright. His present foe was not Arthur; rather, the bubble.

"Yes, the match is asinine. Ought not cooling our hot heads and the more noble angels of our grace prevail?"

"You speak of the Trial by Combat," came the retort. "That was between you and the Hawk of May. Of a truth, this is in no wise related to that. Come; let us show our skills, that our peacetime warriors become not as a rusted axe and our next generation learns of your foster-mother's martial art. Let us dance her dance." Arthur's empty hand indicated the sacred lake. Lakes, mountains and waterfalls; the romance and grandeur of Cymru consolidated in one sanctified place. "A three-point match, sir."

"Nay." Maelgwn tilted his head, rather annoyed that so many boots would tread upon a spot that should only accommodate rare and discreet visitors in three or four. Instead, a hundred times as many were rendering the scene as half amphitheater bordered by a body of water. An arena comprised of men and women.

The gathering spectators included Rhufwan, returned from a fruitless questing after the Grail, and Gwyar, who had come from Ynys Enlli to the mainland by barge, then by hired carriage to Caerleon. She had not yet found Gwalchmai as she politely elbowed her way towards the front. She would find him. And she would confront Maelgwn. For she was rested, and in want of answers.

Gwalchmai and Urien, along with Peredur

and Owain, were present as well, Bishop Bedwini and Illtud and not a few noble women mixing with the crowd.

"How did you find me here?" Maelgwn continued his horizontal repose.

"You saw me on the steep; were you not of such height, our eyes would've met, though mine were shaded by a hood."

"I saw none but an old, grey-bearded Glamorgan bard braving the rain–"

Arthur produced the grey, silky deception, lifelike and remarkably realistic, and dangled it over the King of Gwynedd. Laughing and provoking, he said, "Master of disguises. With this beard in hand, and the crowd before us, we look as if we are performing theatre; I as Itto Gawr and you *as me.*" Arthur offered not levity of laughter with his jest. The intent thereof was directed to mean: *You wish you were me and I the Giant whom I slayed, championing the people you could not.*

Maelgwn rose upon an elbow, partially taking the bait. Then he recovered himself. "You and your disguises. Perhaps you, more than any of the Round Table Fellowship, understand why the chief of the secret society that vexes this land hides behind his mask as he does." Insult for insult. "Perhaps you ARE he."

Arthur gritted and ground his perfect teeth. "Rise, Lancelot. A match we will have."

Maelgwn's eyes panned round the mob. Cadog was present; Illtud appeared nervous. Queen Gwenhwyfar, in simple green gown with long brown boots suited for horseback, climbing or trudging through mud, stood amongst the damsels. *Gwenhwyfach and Mordred were not present.*

"I shall not." Standing fast, but giving the response in his familiar killing voice.

"Very well. Bedwyr." Arthur looked about for his friend.

"Yes, lord, I am here."

"Bring forth Rhufawn the Radiant, son of Maelgwn Gwynedd. As he was absent from the games and neither suffered losses nor earned wins, he will be a fair substitute. He will be his father's proxy. Go to, now; get me the lad and four blunted weapons." Then Arthur manifested *his* killing voice, glaring at his old friend. "Perhaps the son of Lancelot will learn much in fighting the High King today, and I will certainly learn much about you in felling him."

Each hero had violated unwritten boundaries, even when angered. Maelgwn intimating that Arthur was the very villain who had launched the plot resulting in his own sons' deaths, essentially *creating a reason to kill his own seed.* Arthur hinting at doing the same to Maelgwn's lad. Severe insults with thin veils and known meanings, as fiery arrows shot.

"No!" Maelgwn was on his feet so quickly that it startled Arthur, who withdrew to gather himself. The knight made quickly for the lakehouse where he had lodged. He emerged with such haste that the faeries must have dressed him, for he was fully armored save his helm. *The silver armor. The special occasion armor.* And he held no blunted sport weapon, but rather that legendary battle spike, and was at full gallop upon the king, screaming, "No! Let us stand together!"

Arthur was calm. The War King revised his request of Bedwyr, bidding him fetch Rhon, the king's enchanted spear, along with a curved shield that stood in height to an average man's torso. Excalibur remained sheathed and in

Bedwyr's custody, several yards away from the combatants.

The façade of sport had dissolved, replaced by a titanic clash. Not between Arthur and Lancelot, for their *right-minded selves* were now also as spectators. The battle between Arthur's jealousy and Maelgwn's jealousy had begun.

Maelgwn slid inside the reach of Arthur's long weapon, bringing the hook that appended the guard of his battle spike down hard on the Iron Bear's shoulder; a spraying array of blood arched high, splattering upon the spongy ground near the lake. The next maneuver would be to clip Arthur's right knee or ankle. With left shoulder and right leg debilitated, he would have no side to favor, nowhere to redistribute pain. This would result in a moment of inactivity, ensued by a violent and clean deathblow.

I have seen the steps of this dance danced scores and scores times more upon the Saxon and the Pict. Arthur had the advantage of knowing, borne of the intimacy of repetition, where Maelgwn would go. *Right knee or ankle!* In an instant, Arthur positioned his shield upon his right leg and spun away from the taller opponent's crouched striking attempt, thrusting his spear towards the Bloodhound's thigh in the same motion.

The crowd, in concert as if they were veteran members of Illtud's choir, voiced their awe, their shock. And not over the bloody wound that was the king's left shoulder.

Rhon's tip had breached the Perfect Knight's armor. Lancelot was cut!

Maelgwn Gwynedd was fifty. Maelgwn Gwynedd had been a man of sword and spear since age fourteen. Excepting the mystery of Merlin's dagger and its peculiar stab wound, and a tiny scar upon his scalp secondary to his fall in Broceliande, Maelgwn was wholly unscathed. Thirty-six years. Not a broken bone, nor a disjointed knee, nor a smashed nose. No slashes; no other scars. He was as perfect, creamy marble carving. Flawless and untouched.

By contrast, Arthur had seen two fewer winters than the Bloodhound, but his body was far more battleworn. His knees complained periodically, as did his left shoulder. He had suffered a few broken bones, and a few near kill slashes had left permanent signatures upon both his chest and back. Still, both men possessed the speed, verve and appearance of young men in their twenties.

Now Maelgwn joined his friend and opponent in bleeding.

"Do we rush upon them, tackle them, and end this?" Bedwyr asked his fellows, desperately.

"Yes," said Meurig. The old king knew that rage had displaced reason and that his son was in peril; as was Cymru, a confederacy of kingdoms, tribes, clans and cantrefs, seeing the blood of its fatherless king crimsoning the green grass. Meurig noted, and Gwen neglected to mention, that Arthur had brought a Silure death mask in his satchel. The burial helmet was all silver, save the eye sockets and outlines of the moustache and mouth, which were pure gold. The helmet was inlaid with a jeweled diadem, and ornate Latin scriptures were etched to appear as in orbit around the crown. A golden mail shirt and shiny trousers trimmed in gold were folded neatly beneath the helmet. Meurig's son was prepared to die this very day; moreover, he was controlling the action, intentionally provoking a fight under the pretext of a sport.

In the moments of hesitation as his closest

allies and friends pondered intervention, a remarkable, shocking development manifested.

Arthur was winning.

The skill of the Iron Bear in hand-to-hand combat and grappling, had no equal save that of the massive man he now enjoyed a slight advantage over. Both men disarmed of long weapon in the scrum, Arthur was mounted upon Lancelot, both legs hooked, flattening the longer man. Chest to chest upon the ground, Arthur would recoil upward, creating separation, and then bring his elbow down hard upon Lancelot's head and cheek, opening gash upon gash with each strike.

Clutched so close, words followed. The three hundred witnesses could hear that the combatants spoke, but discern their words they could not, for they were closely engaged.

"Second! I am sick of being second!" Arthur lamented. "Second in handsomeness, second to be looked upon by our fair damsels." (Now, Arthur was a noble man who did not lust after other women, nor seek their coquettish affections. But *all men* desire to be revered as handsome, and the incessant rankings in gossip, at feasts, in buzzes and hearsays, had worn upon the king's soul. *Better to be a reproach than to be the second most handsome man in the kingdom).* "Second with sword. Second in valor. Second in glory. I am" – another elbow found Lancelot's nose – "sick of being second!"

Lancelot finally caught a free-flinging wrist, locked it, and flipped Arthur. So much taller was the Bloodhound than the Iron Bear that the scene now looked as an older boy atop his infant brother, bullying him.

Arthur's defense was excellent. His jealousy,

rage, and the confidence filling him as the tide pools rapidly upon the shore, enhanced his skill, when usually such attributes imbalance a man. He blocked every shot. And now Lancelot, who was bleeding *all over Arthur*, recompensed jealousies.

"*I* am sick of being second! Second!" Another attempted crushing blow was shucked by the valiant king. "Second in decision-making, second in strategy, second in regard by the ladies." (For all women would choose to lie once with Lancelot but would, each and every one, take Arthur to husband. Pleasure for a few minutes, or romance and respect and reverence for a lifetime? Women, being smarter than men, would always choose the latter. Lancelot knew the same. Arthur, a handsome and fantastic lover in his own right, envied the taller, more godlike man, and could not see that he was the preferred choice.) Another strike went amiss. Lancelot abandoned course and stood, literally lifting Arthur with him, flinging him hard against the tree.

Lancelot's attendant ran quickly, efficiently rearming the silver knight with both his battle spike and leaf-shaped sword.

Bedwyr did the same for Arthur, but was rebuked.

"Not that sword. Fetch thou me the Sword of Power. Fetch thou me Excalibur."

But Bedwyr disobeyed, as Meurig shouted, "Will you not stop this?!"

Bedwyr followed with, "My lord. You are Arthur of the authority of the Three Swords, the possessor of the Two Swords of Britain. Wield not the sword with vanity, I beseech you."

King Arthur's eyes were now as the Red Dragon that had hailed his birth. "Bedwyr. It is not for you to determine how to bear the sword, but rather to deliver the sword. DELIVER THE SWORD."

"My lord." The trustworthy knight yielded that famed steel unto the Pendragon.

Some weeping began to replace sport-lust and curiosity.

The reality of combat, as with lovemaking, is that most sessions are very short in reality and long in legend. Actual fights typically last but a few strokes. Not so for these men.

Ten strikes given. Ten blocked or dodged. Vivien's diagonal dance executed to perfection. Spiral steps and remarkable speed; a symphony of steel.

Where the shore of lake met the high grass near where they battled was a marshy area that appeared as a stream adjoined to the lake. Tall reeds grew in the 'betwixt and between' of lake and shore and the water, in spots, rose as high as the armpits of an average man. Lancelot was pushing Arthur backwards towards the stream, where his height would give him decisive advantage, as he could stand in the waters whereas Arthur could not.

As they hacked and whacked, two figures emerged on either side of the marshy area.

Morgaine of the Faeries.

Gwenhywfar II.

Arthur stood to the north, firm upon the land.

Lancelot to the south, now in the water.

Gwen was to west, her eyes aflame as fire.

Morgaine to the east; she seemed elevated above her stature, her hair wisping about as the wind.

The four chords.

Breaking.

Gwen could here demotivate and disarm Arthur with cruel words, giving Lancelot the victory and, perhaps, Mordred a pathway to the throne.

Morgaine could use her dark magick to shift the tide for Arthur, ending the misery of the troubled beast that was Lancelot forever. *But her magick could not make Gwen return love to Arthur, or even treat him well.*

The four chords.

Breaking.

Lancelot's eyes met Gwen's. Arthur saw this, and advanced, enraged. This had been Lancelot's aim, as it drew the men deeper into the marshy waters. But Lancelot, though better on every other day, was again bested by the Pendragon's next move as Excalibur knocked Lancelot's sword cleanly from his hand, leaving him with his battle spike and no secondary weapon versus Excalibur. Arthur brought down unyielding overhand strikes, remembering the cause of the day. *Information. Truth!*

"Did you lie with my wife?" Overhand strike.

"Did you lie with my wife?" Again. Overhand strike.

"Did you lie with my wife?" Overhand strike. Again.

The volley caused Lancelot to give way and fall. His knees reached the bottom of the stream, giving Arthur the high ground. The famed battle spike was held as a broom handle by both hands above Lancelot's head, in a purely defensive pose.

"Did you lie with my wife?"

"Yes."

All sound stopped. As did Arthur. As did Lancelot.

"Adultery against the High King! This is treason!" Saint Illtud hollered as an authoritative judge and executioner.

"Nay," said Lancelot, still upon one knee, the other plunged into the bloody pink foam of the marshy stream. "Yes, I have known the queen, but queen she was not, for we were but sixteen!"

At the confirmation that Lancelot had been intimate with his life's true love, all spittle evaporated from his mouth. He could not breathe, nor control the pounding, irregular drumming of his heart.

"All of your 'I saw her first' prodding and goading and demands made it impossible to find any forum to tell you. She was MY childhood love. You are so humble in matters myriad but so arrogant on this matter. Had you but asked–"

"You withheld this from me for over thirty years!" Arthur was not addressing Lancelot alone. His statement was generalized, though his anger was acute. "Sister? Did you know? Gwenhwyfar, you withheld this as well? Were you all in league to shame your king?"

"Not to shame you, lord. To protect you," Gwyar offered, weeping.

"Rather to die under the weight of truth than to live under the false security of a lie!" Arthur, then, full of jealous rage, looked to Excalibur and spoke words ancient and powerful; words whose origins he knew not, for they formed of themselves. The Sword of Power became emerald green and the blade vibrated as if to sing a deafening song of vengeance. One more overhand strike followed, the force of which had not been matched since the foundation of the world, neither has it since.

"I SAW HER FIRST!"

Excalibur cleaved Lancelot's battle spike in twain as the famed blade made shattered glass of Lancelot's breastplate, reaching his chest, piercing flesh and bone, very near unto the heart. He reflexively slung the two shards of his battle spike into the lake and stood to counterstrike but closed his arms just as quickly, grasping his opened chest, crumpling in pain, toppling into the waters.

Excalibur also was two pieces in the stead of one.

Arthur's heart was as broken as the legendary blade. It had been made from angelic protectors of Eden, its ores now witness to two *falls*.

Llyn Fawr, the most sacred of lakes upon the Blessed Isles in the Sea, rumbled and rushed.

Lancelot, the invincible knight, lay defeated – lay dying. Undefeated no more. Arthur had broken the Bloodhound Prince; the greater had succumbed to the lesser.

Suddenly a mist emerged from the center of the lake, spiraling clockwise, filling the entire basin. Visibility became limited to shadows and forms, the summer day fighting the spontaneous shadows.

"Sister, cease," came the command.

"'Tis not I," said Gwyar.

A hooded druid appeared beneath the oak tree whence the fateful match had commenced. His robes seemed grey and he was tall, as tall as Lancelot.

For the shame of his act, Arthur had dropped the hilt and shards of the sword that had been his ever companion since gifted to him by the Lady of Llyn Fawr above three decades ago. Something caused him to turn to the druid; an eerie silence was over all. None were protesting the mist, none were chaotic over the fog. The events witnessed rendered them all yet silent, nothing remaining that could surprise them.

Then the voice came.

"You have broken what could not be broken. Hope is broken. When he could have taken the South by force, he did not; when he could have taken the queen at his whim, he did forbear, suffering himself not. You would allow Caermelyn to crumble over a youthful tumble. Little Bear, let not the sun set on your anger; yield not to wrath."

The mist and the lake and my emotions do deceive me. Arthur suffered himself not to say the name of the man, apparition, or devil that spoke unto him. *I am beside myself. This is my conscience speaking. I am beside myself. But the apparition speaks truth.*

A faint, faint whisper escaped his lips. "Merlin?"

As he turned back from the vision towards where Lancelot had slumped in collapse, laboring hard to prevent him from drowning in the stream, the fog abated, but only above Arthur and Lancelot. In the stream, another lost friend appeared.

Both Lancelot and Arthur saw her.

Contrasting Morgaine's dress, black as night, was the white gown scaled in sparkly samite, flowing in elegance, one with the water, just beneath the stream. She illuminated the marsh as a second sun. The brightness and grandeur caused Arthur to cover his eyes with blood-soaked hands. As he peeled his fingers away, he witnessed two arms fixed straight, emerging from the water, holding a sword.

"Take me up!" The voice of the shadowy druid quoted the words etched into the obverse side of Excalibur's hilt, the reverse side reading *Cast me away!* "The Lady of the Lake! Take me up! It is not thy time!" The voice begged Arthur to understand.

Slowly, and frightened, King Arthur approached the floating water spirit. The height of the stream where she held tight the sword reached well above his chest, causing him partially to swim, partially to walk.

"Take it!" the voice implored.

Delicately, the erstwhile boy-king handled what had been, for the sum of his adult life, a metal extension of himself. As he reverently put his right hand upon the hilt, the Lady's hands gently retreated from the blade and recoiled into the waters.

"How can it be?" asked the king, bewildered. For Excalibur it was! Whole, original, as if never harmed, as if newly forged. The Lady of the Lake gracefully sank into the marsh, and was then at once seen in white spots and splashes dashing away from Arthur, then beneath the surface of the lake of Llyn Fawr. Then into its center, then gone.

The fog was completely burned off by the heat of the sun, the crowd seeing their hero holding the symbol of his virility and power. They cheered and cheered the victorious king. But Arthur silenced them.

"Sister, heal him." His directive gave room neither for response or debate.

Though Arthur sorrowed greatly over the ordeal, his jealousy had not been assuaged. Every other thought was of the taller, more handsome man pleasing his exquisite wife. He wished not for Maelgwn to die, but he wished not to look upon the half portion of his misery.

Barely conscious, Maelgwn was alert enough to hear his sentence.

"Withholding the truth is the same as a lie. You are forthwith demitted from the Round Table Fellowship, unwelcome in its courts, ineligible for its adjudications. You are the champion no more. Unless it be, from time to time, to have fellowship with thy sons, see to it that you do not oft visit these lands. This is my sentence, and it will be enforced, with arms as necessary." Soft banishment, with a garnish of the value of family, was the sentence of the hurting and good king.

Taking Gwyar by the hand, he gave one more utterance. "This will not be a kingdom of secrets and lampshades and bushels. When the news is good, my people will celebrate it; when ill, my people will hear of it – and endure it. No more will we try to save people from themselves, heaping decades of lies in the process. NO MORE SECRETS."

Morgaine of the Faeries ought to have here shared that Mordred was the bastard son of the Spring Rites but, risking her relationship with her brother whom she so deeply loved – or worse, her head – she discerned that she must yet continue to shelter the king's head from truth for the sake of his heart. *For the sake of Cymru.*

Acknowledging him with her eyes, she spake not, but instructed four men to place Lancelot in her carriage, that she might take him to Avalon and heal him.

CHAPTER 19
Arthur versus Cynwyl Gawr the Last

The barge bore Lancelot to Ynys Enlli, under the care and custody of Morgaine of the Faeries.

I could kill you now for the hurts you put upon my son, report that you perished by Excalibur. But then my brother would bear the guilt of it. The sorceress recalled her dagger from his throat. Replacing the malice of steel with the soothing of herbs, she ensured that that his sleep was deep and his complaints mild. Possessing complete mastery of every herb of the field, treating him was much easier than looking upon him.

She had loved him when a lass, later revered him as warrior, was thankful to him for fifteen years of plenty and peace, but otherwise shared the collective emotion of the whole of Cymru: frustration.

Unpredictable.

Dangerous.

Volatile.

Inconsistent.

Disquieting.

These were the attributes that marked and defined the greatest knight in the history of the world from the Creation to Galahad. *Perhaps he will right your wrongs.*

His woes began on the Isle of Apples – reflection changed Morgaine's attitude by some measure – *perhaps he can find reconciliation and restoration here as well.*

The Merlin Taliesin had arrived in advance of the king's sister, greeting her warmly as her barge skidded and bobbed, docking upon Avalon's tricky port.

* * *

He nearly slayed an invincible man, a demigod amongst grasshoppers. What might the Iron Bear do unto me? Gwenhywfar the Actress conducted herself with extreme checks of her behavior. Heaping scores of apologies for not disclosing the intimacy she had shared with Maelgwn *before* her marriage to Arthur, she tried all to earn his favor and garner forgiveness.

Her years suggesting that her womb might be dry, she was now a beautiful liability, a tarnished trophy, a queen quite replaceable. Mordred had taken a young wife and had led Arthur to live under a veil of deception for fifteen years. Her situation was precarious, her disposition deflated and depressed; her instincts to survive were all that kept the lady from falling into a deep woe or removing herself from the realm of the living.

Two things saved Gwenhwyfar from divorce, or worse.

First, Arthur, though embroiled by jealousy (for he too was but a man), was no hypocrite. He possessed empathy for all, even his rivals, even his enemies, and especially his wife. Arthur's youth had deeply affected him as well; fosterage away from his parents, with whom he was very close, the spring rites to validate himself amongst the tribes, the carnal yet mystical act required of him, fighting and killing too young, fame, accountability, pressure.

I had relations with one of the four chords too, and surely I spoke not of it either. Why would I expect Gwen to do what I would not? Or, for that matter, my champion. Whether a good memory or ill, their incident shaped them. And was private. Provided that they continued not this love, nor knew one another after I wedded the queen, they are innocent. And I am wrong.

Arthur had been taught to immediately admit his transgressions, possess them, and move forward. That he could admit his wrongs in the presence of a woman differentiated him from all men who have ever lived.

Secondly, Merlin.

The quest and long-dormant hope to find the one who had taught him this lesson had been resurrected, distracting him greatly from involuntary thoughts and images of Gwen and Maelgwn doing things that poisoned his mind. No one, save perhaps Maelgwn (who was at present being nursed by Gwyar), had heard the voice, nor seen the grey druid. But Arthur was convinced. *It was his voice. Merlin was there. The fog confused the ears and distorted the eyes of the crowd. Was it a vision? Or does he live?!* An excited man with a work to do has little time to dwell upon private hurts or be governed by natural insecurities.

In light of these, the king dealt graciously with his disloyal, loathsome wife.

"We have long reigned, you and I," he opened.

She felt her kneecap knock involuntarily upon its counterpart.

"Our reign," he continued, "has had no Saxon invasions. No fear. No sending boys to marry and fight at fourteen, neither robbing the damsels of their precious youths. Art, science, enterprise, freedom. We have done well." Arthur smiled. "A question I have for you, fair Gwenhwyfar."

"Ask; I shall not answer amiss." She looked to the floor, unable to face the uncertain direction of the discourse.

"Have we Round Table Companions, we bishops and wizards, we powerful and stately women, such as you…" The good king took up a drinking horn, polished with such shine that it reflected his face. He looked upon himself for the twinkling of an eye, then gulped down his scrumpy. "Have we written enough in The Great Conversation? Woven enough in The Great Thread? Have we done all to inspire future generations to look back and to know that, for whatever short season this Summer Kingdom did endure, liberty and good can prevail? Have we lit the bright light of liberty?"

Gwen discerned that encouragement might save her neck. "One hundred or one thousand years from now, the governments of men will measure themselves by what Arthur ap Meurig achieved. You are the candle in a world ever on the brink of total darkness, the pole star that demands the clouds below him to scatter, though he be the only flicker visible on a stormy night. We have had peace on earth in our time."

"I am Arthur, the Iron Bear of Glamorgan. The War King, the Giant Slayer." A blush crimsoned his cheeks.

"You are!" she agreed.

"But you will never look upon me as you look upon him."

Not so much him as upon Mordred… but aye, never upon you.

"Not so, husband; I lo—"

"Let us not speak of love. You are innocent, and I am the fool. My mother once said that a person 'loves who they love'. What love you possess for me is eclipsed by your love for him."

Conciliatory.

"Will you put me away?"

"All things change, Gwenhwyfar. The Summer Kingdom is not buildings of gold, neither song nor merry. It is more than loving your neighbor above yourself, more than the leaders living under the very laws they subject the people to. In the end it is not even such noble things."

"What is it?"

"It is the ambassadorship of truth whilst we tarry in a fallen world. We will not make heaven on earth, neither will we replant Eden. Rather, we shall point men towards the hope of Heaven, and the promise of Eden. That is for God Himself to deliver, and He will keep His promise. Burn our estates and castles, export our gold, scorch our crops, level our chapels. All things change, all things fail. But *HOPE* never fails. We are hope."

He is going to put me away. Or worse. And abdicate!

"I will not put you away."

Tears of relief welled, this time the actress pretending not.

Arthur was direct, and crestfallen. "My heart breaks at our plight. But we must endure. The Silures must not crumble on account of such a thing. The midlands and the north are not strong enough to unite our land, and enemies are always at the door."

"A political marriage?"

"A half political marriage. I love you yet with my whole heart." Arthur sighed and laughed. "I owe Lancelot an apology. To the Isle of Apples I must go."

"Which disguise will you choose that you be not accosted on the roads, or hassled by Cai?"

They both laughed and the sorrowful moment, no less sorrowful, was eased. Arthur still operated under a heap of Gwenhwyfar's lies and deceit, but the little truth that he did know relieved her, and her disposition relieved him.

Arthur selected an old costume. One that rendered him a derelict: a beggar or thief. "I wore this years ago when traveling on a horrible assignment; a task as commissioned from Hell itself. As I made my way north I reposed, in these very garments, within a shout of your bedroom. Thoughts of you warmed me through a night of bitter cold."

"May the guise keep you hidden and the self-same thoughts keep you warm. I will be here upon your return." Gwenhwyfar embraced her husband, all the while leaping in her inward parts at the prospect of a few days with her lover. Whether in their field, the chapel or her little apartment mattered not. To see him, to peel him away from his younger lover, *or to kill him.*

Softly nestling one of her tiny hands in his, he jested: "And yes, I will take the dogs with me."

Arthur, relishing his brief moment away from the burden of the throne, selected a horse that was not his (adding to the façade), a rugged, aged but happy companion and carrier of men. He lumbered along with the war dogs, mastiffs nearly as tall as the horse, grunting and rejoicing in the change of routine.

"Don't *they* compromise the ruse, lord?" Bedwyr gave a roaring laugh, stopping King Arthur on the stone bridge that connected

Caerleon to the old roads and the valleys.

"Only within the view of these golden roofs. When wood and night become my allies, the pups will be of no consequence." Roaring laughter was matched and returned.

Bedwyr alone, as Arthur's greatest of friends, could truly distract the sovereign with pith and wit, or intellectual barbs and humor. Even as they jousted back and forth for a few minutes, Bedwyr opted not to embrace the king for the intentional musk and pungency clouding off his cloak and trousers. "You spared no detail! Even your face is blackened!"

In spite of the happy farewell, Bedwyr detected a melancholy, and was greatly alarmed. Nevertheless, he bid his friend Godspeed and departed unto his own estate, demanding that the king instantly report his return from the Isle of Apples.

The happy farewell also delayed the departure, endangering the plots of Mordred, who was making haste, rehearsed with pretended reason to look in on the queen. He also met Arthur *the beggar thief* on the way.

In the twinkling of an eye, the adulterer feigned heroism.

Quickly at the quiver, bow drawn, and from a high-ground position, the son of Morgaine of the Faeries was poised to lob arrows at the king.

"Thief!" He screeched. "You would purloin the king's own hounds? As you are in the act, I could put two in you presently, sending you to sleep in the pits of the destitute and fatherless!"

Arthur removed his cap, then used the back of his thick glove to smear off the better part of his moustache, dark as pitch and made of coarse animal hair bound with a gummy glue. Standing in direct line of a taut bow, the point of the arrow shrinking to but a dot, rebuke was offered, and no fear.

"That is NOT what our law states, Whelp." That commanding sound, which many reckoned to be how God the Father had sounded when speaking to Moses, was unmistakable, regardless of the tattered, blackened rags that covered the speaker. "By the mouth of two or three witnesses let all things be established. As a resident, or long-term *guest*, in this cantref, we detain and investigate; we do not slay first and inspect after."

"My king. Forgive me. I saw this thief with your very own dogs and I—" Mordred paused. The king had not hushed his words, neither refused to listen; rather, Mordred's own memory paralyzed him, suspending his speech.

The dirty beggar.

The garments.

The gloves.

The mannerisms too stately and measured for a derelict vagabond.

I have seen this man before!

"You wanted to impress your uncle with some brave deed of spoiling a thief in the very act. Overzealous, young man. If you are to rule when lame, retired or dead am I, you must temper passion, demoting it in favor of objective adjudication of the law. Control your feelings. Do you understand?"

The way you did when you put the Sword of Power into the chest of Cymru's Champion? Hypocrite.

"Yes, uncle. I forgot myself and will improve."

"Excellent!" Arthur seemed pleased. Full of grace, he mused, "Now I must go and fix my face."

Mordred gave a sheepish smile. "The bards

say you can trick any audience, concealing yourself amongst monk, farmer, or shipman. Or even take on the appearance of a bull or an eagle!"

"This time, the bards exaggerate not!" Arthur chortled, for he reveled in this.

"I doubt it not. Tell me, have you taken up this particular visage before – perhaps in the north?"

The eyes locked.

Sharing Morgaine in common, the eyes were the same.

Mirrored eyes speaking without words, saying in concert. *You were there the last time I wore these rags, the day Amr was slain.*

The silence was awkward. And building.

Arthur made no provision for further spectacle, tragedy or intrigue.

"I must visit King Maelgwn. The voyage will be long and I wish to make my way, privately. I bid you communicate the time of my tardy departure to Cai and to Bedwyr. And please appoint thyself unto Gwenhywfar. She enjoys your company and a visit by you and your new bride would be well received in my stead."

Half true. So wise and yet so ignorant of the doings in your own chamber.

Though the shallow and reactive voice within mocked the High King, a deeper, more contemplative voice anchored his spirit, bringing him down into an abyss of desperate fear. Mordred was a man of no moral constitution, an accomplished adulterer, pretender and sophist. For years he had betrayed the Iron Bear without repentance. Although the campaign to concoct a political career had been successful, so much so that he was known at Court as Mordred of the Golden Tongue, the list of men he had defrauded and swindled was as long as Itto Gawr's famed beard. A criminal, a lecher and more, and yet – *Even I could not kill my own children. If this man would do that to those of his own house, what might he do to me?*

The inside voice stopped mocking. And a tremble set in. Mordred hated this man more than any man ever hated; but the hate was now matched with terror.

"Mordred".

The Whelp was lost in thought and too many dark realizations.

"Mordred?"

"With great haste, Lord Arthur."

Arthur terminated the conversation, beginning his solitary journey to the Llyn Peninsula and, if the summer winds behaved, to Ynys Enlli.

Mordred the Traitor was so troubled that he lost all desire to lie with Gwenhwyfar. Instead he turned back and returned to his own place.

* * *

"I am sure they hated being tossed to and fro. Look at the poor pups."

"Taliesin!" Arthur hailed his new Merlin (although his predecessor had been reckoned as dead for above fifteen years) but embraced him not; both he and his war dogs were green from the tempestuous crossing from Porth Madwy to Ynys Enlli.

"A cider?" offered the Chief Bard.

Arthur pinched his chin, tempted, but his nausea offered a counter-response. "A cup of tea, perhaps."

After recovering himself, and marveling at how many pilgrims successfully made for the island's shore and how many perished during their personal quests, he made straightaway for Lancelot, who was convalescing in Morgaine's castle of glass.

Seeing several maidens attending the wounded knight, too long for the frame of any bed in the whole of the house, convalescing awkwardly as they doted on him, Arthur's eyes found his sister and offered a jest. "Recruiting?"

Morgaine joined her brother in a laugh at the scene. Six damsels and a fifty-year-old man whose fair looks were not only that of one twenty-and-five, but were improving as he aged. "Nurses will be needed even when your bishops and the Church have conquered these lands."

"With care such as this, I am sure your numbers will replenish threefold."

"And though 'tis my chest you ran through, I ever complain that my thigh and earlobes give complaint!"

"Lancelot!" That the complex and unstable man opened with intelligent humor that synced and cinched with the other adults greatly convinced Arthur that he was in his right mind. Sparing no moment, the king dismissed the priestesses and knelt upon a knee, placing his palm upon his friend's forehead, brushing back the curly black hair.

"You can no longer call me by that designate. I am no longer *the greater serving the lesser.* As if I ever was. You defeated me."

"Aye, with unfair advantage of a magical sword. You are the greatest of Round Table Knights; my First Knight, my Champion, my Lancelot."

"Forgive—"

Arthur interrupted. "No. Forgive me, my

friend. What happened in your youth belonged to you."

"We" – Lancelot's eyes made connection with Morgaine – "protect you from certain painful truths because our Land will fall unless you are happy and whole." Lancelot now sat aright upon the small metal framed bed. "But one lie begets another, and soon the webs of deceptions outweigh the original offense."

"Sometimes they do, sometimes they don't," offered the king.

"You did see her first. I should not have yielded to youthful lusts." Tears voiced their anguish, parading down Lancelot's chiseled and perfect jawline.

"And I put my position square in your handsome face, didn't I? Forgive me, if you can." And herein lay the greatness of King Arthur, the most noble king save the Saviour Himself: that, though brokenhearted and freshly awakened to the cold reality that Gwenhwyfar would never be to him what his mother was to his father, he sought out not his own needs but rather to mend his friend, and his friendship.

Apology and tearshed met, embraced and danced.

Then the weightiest of questions loomed, Arthur brave enough to make the query.

"What do we do now?"

Lancelot was well prepared with his answer. Honestly and sensitively, he proceeded.

"I love her, Lord Arthur." All present could feel the room shift with tension. "But I love you too. And I love Cymru." He peered at Morgaine, prayerful that the sentiment would earn him some favor.

It did.

"You have defeated me. It gave me great

perspective, great liberty and great release. It is hard to describe, but..." Lancelot now struggled for words. "I love her, and I love you. It is misery and tension and damnable pain to be at court. You have defeated me."

Where is he taking this discourse? thought the Iron Bear.

"Instead of contriving pretexts to be away and shouting my agony at trees and in caves I am going to take my defeat, and retire."

Arthur gasped. As did Morgaine. As did Taliesin.

"It gives me a legitimate cause and removes the drama, gossip and intrigue of it. The life of a monk I shall lead, and into the Holy Writ my oversized head shall go." Lancelot looked lighter, happier and different upon the honest uttering of such things.

"We need you," they all said, nearly in chorus.

"I cannot be at court. My sons you have, and they are as fleet of foot and deadly as I."

"And young," Taliesin barbed.

"We won those wars because of you. I'll not lose you," protested Arthur.

"If the Long Knife returns, or your strait is dire, I will come. Elsewise, I must retire, my friend. Visit me oft at Camlan, or at Illtud's. What have you said in no less than eight of your speeches before the armies?"

"When have you listened to any speech?"

"Shut thy mouth, bard!" Lancelot now took Arthur by the hand. "All things—"

"Change," said Arthur. "All things change."

Not to be convinced otherwise, he asked of another matter.

"Did my battle frenzy cause me to hallucinate?"

Knowing the subject, having no need of

exposition: "No, lord. I saw him too. Merlin. Or an imposter, or a ghost. No, I am sure it was he; Merlin lives! And in his breath of life is my foster-mother vindicated."

Too burdened with past hurts, the Pendragon looked only forward, a fount of undiluted grace. "Yes! Whatever troubles befell that famed pair, 'twas the hands of the Masked One that slew our wizard, and no Briton. But he is not slain; he lives!"

"My friend." Lancelot clasped Arthur 'forearm in forearm'. "I believe he does."

Here King Arthur and Lancelot said sorrowful goodbyes and intimate words that no bard knows, and if he knows, shan't utter: only that Arthur bound Lancelot to return to shimmering Caermelyn, should calamity or dire urgency require it.

Having made amends, the two men parted, both in love with one woman – who, at that very moment, paced in circumambulatory rage, smashing vessel and looking glass, renting cloth and curtain, cursing the creation that Mordred, the one *she loved*, had spurned her.

Morgaine struggled to find a sentence of discourse with her brother, so full of excitement and hope of finding his wizard was he.

As he herded the massive mastiffs into his little barge, wishing it were Madoc and not some other boatman to safely conduct him back to the Llyn Peninsula, she was at last forced to holler. "Brother, there is another matter! Hear me!"

"If problems were meat, my plate would be overly full. State the next dish."

"Our good secret in the stead of the bad."

Arthur leapt from the boat, the dogs and his sister yelping at the splashes.

"Because of the Masked Man's encroach upon our hall, most know the bad secret," he stated.

"Aye, and now the Catholics have uncovered the good. Literally."

Arthur's face became ashen. He hailed the boatman, beseeching him to wait a space of three hours so he could discuss the grave matter with his sister.

* * *

When Arthur returned home, his new reality began. He did not lie often with Queen Gwenhwyfar II. Periodically he was overcome by wanting her, for he loved her so, and she protested not, though took no pleasure in it. And there was the matter of no heir begotten of the king's seed and Gwen's womb.

Cymreig kings are selected by election often, and it is not given that the son can govern simply because his father did well. However, the line of Tewdrig and Meurig and Arthur was strong, just and long-enduring. The ease of two hundred different scenarios, all wrought with strife and friction, would be all but alleviated were there a son to take the diadem when Arthur returned to the ground, or else entered into a happy retirement.

For this cause, they periodically knew one another. However, his painted queen was two score and ten, and the tribes grumbled, aided by the needling of the scorned Dynion Hysbys.

The queen was careful not to be cold towards the king, nor overly warm. For he was tuned to her acting. The lukewarm middle made life reasonably pleasant. To stitch the heart that tore here a little, there a little, day after day, Arthur obsessed himself with finding the Merlin. A year had passed since the unpleasant match with the Bloodhound Prince, and with that year no hint of the old druid.

Arthur convened the Round Table Companions and demanded report of each of the twenty-four. No bards were to give song, neither was drink to be served. "Report, and next actions, and accountability," the king demanded, didactically.

The men were exhausted.

"We defeated the Saxon Horde, which sacked Rome, but we cannot locate two old men."

Many heads dropped, embarrassed and disappointed.

"The Masked Devil, not found. The Merlin of Britain, not found."

"Maybe the Merlin found the Masked Devil and resolved, well, half our problem," Bedwyr offered. The expression on his face could have warmed ice and caused a monk under vows of silence to bellow in giddy laughter.

It worked. Arthur laughed. "One of my theories is that Merlin lives, and is about that very enterprise. If there is anyone who knows where the adepts of secret orders hide and lurk, it is he." Arthur's countenance lightened, even casual surmising about his wizard lifting his spirits. "Forgive my curtness, brethren. For warriors, quests don't fill the void of war. Peace is difficult. The Summer is hot. Let us rest for a season. Enjoy your wives, your farms, your children."

As he was dismissing the fellowship, the guards of the hall suddenly escorted a vexed visitor, an older boy, injured, who could barely walk. The tattered messenger limped and lumbered but hastened, finally reaching the king's ear. They spoke softly, but the implication was clear and few words were needed. Gwalchmai slowly flapped his arms, crossing them at the chest, then as far back as they would go. Then he rolled his neck side to side. His curved swords were drawn with the grace of a swan and the speed of a stag. "Excalibur or Rhon, lord?"

"Rhon and Carnwenhau. The Sword of Power remains sheathed." Arthur had not used Excalibur, though magically mended and 'as new', since his battle with Lancelot at Llyn Fawr. He bore a burden of guilt at using one of the treasures of the Cymry with malice and jealousy, and believed himself yet unworthy to wield her again so soon.

"What foe hath Hell vomited up upon our peaceful kingdom?" Cai followed Gwalchmai, warming his muscles, swinging his club at the air.

The boy spoke. "A Giant. And a witch."

"Where?"

"In Caermarthen. The destruction of home and chapel is as 'tis the world ending. Many innocent lives lost. Including babes!"

Caermarthen. The very birthplace of Merlin himself. The irony lost on none, many volunteered.

Arthur embraced the shaken lad, clearly a resident suffering personal affliction from the assault. Steadying his men: "Giant hunting is not well conducted by large numbers, but rather by a small and trained troop." The king's blue eyes gleamed. "Home to your wives, friends. Cai, Gwalchmai and I shall go."

"And I," the knight insisted. Bedwyr with one hand was superior to most with two.

Caermarthen was rent in pieces; a shamble, a dung pit. In the center of the village, every shop had suffered damage such that none could conduct commerce, sell silks, eggs or other goods. Even the large glorious oak tree that honored the city's favorite son had been snapped, charred and nearly ruined. *But the base of Merlin's oak remained, and the tree would be replenished.*

It was not difficult to approximate the dwelling that the assailants had taken. Their trail, one of slime and sludge, bones and bile, painted a trail that ran to a cluster of caves not far from Caermarthen. The caves dotted the shoreline of the West Country of Cymru and had been a site of splendor, a retreat for lovers, an ancient place of worship, a spot of beauty; no more.

Henceforth the bards would call the largest of the cluster Ogof Pentywyn: the *Bone Cave.*

The cave was of the sort that had no solid floor, for the waters of the sea sought their level, creating a shallow *lake within a cave.* The rock formations jutting up from the watery bottom were as large as men and imperfectly shaped, looking as an army turned to stone mid-battle, frozen in time. The tribes took great care to ensure that the cave was illuminated and safe. In this regard, several iron torch sheathes were fastened to the walls, ropes were available to help those who slipped in the murky waters, and markings were etched into the walls, providing directions to those who might lose their way in the winding hollow.

When Arthur and his fellows reached the mouth of the cavern, dusk was upon them, but many torches rendered the place an illuminated splendor.

"They have fighting men in their company," Bedwyr remarked.

"Naye, look." Arthur pointed out that the tall humanoid shadows were indeed but rocks.

The warriors proceeded through the water, holding satchel and sword high, Arthur's famous spear picking up shards of light as he marched.

In the waters floated massive folios of Scripture, much longer and wider than even the most ornate works created by the monks. These were either a special piece of art purloined from the town chapel and desecrated, or they had been brought with the Giant and dropped or cast away in haste. The sheer size of what remained of some great tome suggested to Arthur the latter. Additionally, several more torn pages were stuck against the inner walling of the cavern. The scene reminded Arthur of what a strong-willed child does in their youth when scolded, damaging their own books and bedroom things in protest.

A tantrum occurred here. He was sure of it.

The cave narrowed, becoming, for a time, more like a tunnel broad only the shoulder-width of an average man. Arthur led the men, and as the tunnel opened he was first to see the witch.

Likewise, she saw him.

The torch light manifested the whole of her. Hideous, green. Rotted teeth and rainbow-shaped nose. A dark blue corpse beneath a hooded grey cape that was more holes than whole. She was the subject of every small child's nightmares.

And she was twice as wide as Arthur and taller than Maelgwn.

Crying in a variant of the Pictish tongue, the hag levitated above the waters and darted at Arthur. As she was too broad to breech the tunnel, the seasoned fighter simply retreated five paces, pushing his men back with him.

Crouched low, Arthur slowly turned round and spoke to Gwalchmai, who was by chance nearest him in the line of knights momentarily trapped as rats in a narrow maze. Cai filed directly behind the Hawk of May.

"Are you aware of the verse in Scripture?" he began.

"Suffer not a witch to live," quick-witted Gwalchmai whispered back.

"That verse was not written about heathens who have different beliefs to those who follow Christ."

"No?"

"No; it was written about monsters like *that*, flying around the countryside, killing the livestock and passing the children through fire. All witches are not witches. This witch is a witch and no man."

Gwalchmai comprehended. "Or woman, I think."

The men broke out in laughter at the hideousness of the devil that sought to make of them dinner (or worse) just several yards away.

"We are undefeated. We will not have our end here in some watery underground grave under the fangs of a supernatural, oversized crone! Avenge the city!" Bedwyr emboldened the troop.

"She attacks in a straight line, easy to counter. I will slay the witch. It is critical that you look not upon me. Rather, emerge from this passage and fan out, finding ground, at the ready for her companion. We know nothing of the Giant save the destruction he wrought."

Arthur drew his enchanted dagger, Carnwenhau, and emerged a second time from the mouth of the passage. Predictably, the witch was yet shrieking her Pictish imprecatory chants. Even the bravest mortal would knock at the knees seeing her. Hideous, strong as a bear and fast as hound.

But she faced the Silure War King and no mortal. King Arthur, the Bear of Glamorgan. Every thought was about preservation of his people and their season of liberty. He would live because he must live *for them*. This made him uniquely accountable and fearless.

Her speed was impressive. But he was much faster. Instead of fleeing from her attack, he used the forward and diagonal dance now, by reason of three decades of training and practice, more natural to him than drinking water or lacing his boots.

Sliding just to the right of her line of attack, Arthur countered aerial assault, stepping well inside her looping slashes with taloned hands, and caught her under her left breast, the blade plunging through her heart, clinking and redirecting as it finally notched into her backbone. Rapidly withdrawing Carnwenhau brought a fount of black, bile-like blood. Somehow, instead of falling to prostrate to the ground, she slowly descended and stood, a waterfall of blood.

"I will save the interrogation for thy partner, thou killer of babes!" Arthur made a lateral slash from his left to right, such that the follow-through of his blade hand finished wide of, and well behind, his own back.

The one monster was now in two parts, for he had cleaved the witch in twain.

The Iron Bear had not long to admire his work as Gwalchmai crashed hard upon him, knocking both warriors into the muck. Cai tumbled and crumpled a few paces away, suffering a blow to his head. The injury was not serious. Arthur's steward shook it off and stood aright, cursing at the air, preparing for another go.

Scooping sludge from his brow, the king stood and clutched Gwalchmai's hand. "Up we go. Looks like you found the Giant?" He laughed.

"That we did!" came Bedwyr's yell. "Help!"

The monster looked as a man, similar to Ogyrfan Fawr. He had a massive pot-belly and disproportionately long, slender arms that, when drooping, reached well past his feet. The appendages were all bone and muscle attached to curled, lifeless hands. They swiveled constantly at the shoulder, which were out of joint, deformed permanently from birth; designed to crush and destroy. He had no need of club or axe, for his were weapons of flesh.

The arms smashed down cyclically, looking as a waterwheel, but with the rapidity of a wasp's wings. And because of the deformity, the Giant was ever in great pain, causing him to make horrible noises.

There was limited space to fight in the cavern, and it was difficult for the knights to find range and avoid the unorthodox opponent. Thus, they were absorbing damage. Even blocking the thrashes was battering the famed mighty men. They fought well but were losing by reason of attrition, of exhaustion. Arthur could find no opening to join the fight and was constrained, having the tunnel behind and a wall of three of his fighting men before him. By fortune, he had brought his spear, giving him advantage in the circumstance. Finally, with a frustrated holler, he commanded, "Gwalchmai, move one pace to the left!"

Rhongomyniad whistled in flight; even

with the absence of air in the enclosure, the Pendragon's aim was true.

"You could've done that half an hour ago," Cai protested.

"The three of you needed the work."

The Round Table Knights appreciated the moment. Four men who had executed complex battle strategies against the Saxon hordes. Flanks and ditches, volleys and lines. Yet here they were, soaked in the stench of a seaside inlet cave, fighting monsters that reasonable people would doubt existed. *Yet better the occasional monster than a generation of invasion, terror and war.* Bedwyr jested about their sorry state, but as the men celebrated, they sensed movement.

The Giant rose, the enchanted spear lodged in his chest, disabling his right arm completely. With his left he extracted the spear, guiding it along the path of *most pain,* so that the tip came back out whence it had entered. His scream released clouds of dust, dislodged from their resting places along walls and crevices in the cavern, uninterrupted for thousands of years.

The beast wailed, then flung soggy torn pages of Scripture at the men with his working arm. Finding an artery deeper yet in the hollow, he retreated.

"Yield." Arthur directed his three to abort the chase. "I will finish this."

Cai was unable to lift his weapon. Bedwyr and Gwalchmai, bruised, beaten and cold, offered no protest. Relieved, they responded, "We will have your favorite cider waiting. This one is thine, lord."

Arthur gave chase. Alone.

The inquiry and investigation began during the pursuit. He paced quickly but there was no cause to run, for the thing's blood upon the cavern wall and pooled in black blobby botches on the watery flooring of the cave guided the way. With torch in left hand and magical dagger in right, Arthur's only complaint was the water, causing him some chill and surely ruining his boots.

"Sir," he called, recalling how respect was the most powerful agent when dealing with these sorry fellows, *all* of whom were under the dark enchantment; miserable creatures acting not of their own accord. "Sir, why are you destroying the Book of the Law? Talk to me about why you might ruin such a large, ornate and lovely work of art."

Arthur mentioned nothing of the murder and wanton destruction levied by the Giant upon Caermarthen. Neither was there judgement in his voice, only curiosity and discovery.

Additionally, Arthur added personalization. Itto and the myriad other slain otherworldly creatures had responded best when their humanity was acknowledged. The Iron Bear deployed the same tactic here.

"Sir. What are you called?"

The tactic worked.

From a hundred paces and down within the leftmost of three arteries in the hollow came the response. A voice so soft that it in no wise matched the form of its owner.

"Cynwyl," he said. "I am called Cynwyl. Are you that king? Or do I wait for another?" The sounds and echoes caused by the voice were static. The thing had stopped moving. "He said you would come."

"Aye. I am a king. Glamorgan and Gwent are my people."

"Unnecessary humility," grumped the Giant. "You are King Arthur, the High King of the Britons and Emperor of the Isles in the Sea."

"I am."

During the salutation, Arthur had closed ground and now stood before Cynwyl, within range of his monstrous strokes, yet unafraid.

"Reason with me, Cynwyl Gawr. What shall we make of all this?"

Defeated and repentant, the Giant found a stone standing out of the water and sat, the full weight of his gargantuan head falling upon his curled, deformed hand, arm bent at elbow, supporting the chin.

These beings respected the office of the real kings of the Sons of Adam. Kings that were kings indeed and not pretenders chosen by the cunning and policies of corrupt Man. Above all sovereigns they loved Arthur, though they were bewitched to harass and bring havoc to his lands. Though he slayed them, they adored him still. An awe came over them in his presence, and he had authority over them. *The Giant Hunter.*

Never much above a whisper, Cynwyl began to plainly state what had befallen him. And what had befallen Caermarthen.

The Giant inhabited this very cave, or when the Tribes were performing their ancient rites, that cave or another. Ever in the hollow hills of Cymru. Slumbering for decades at a time, he would wake to hunt stag or hare, read his Bible, then return to the groggy hibernation of the monsters reserved to be awakened at the End of Days.

To eat. To read. To sleep. And never in his unnaturally long days had he harmed mankind.

Then a Wildman of the Wood, a northern

Cymry shaman, presented himself in his cave. Cynwyl recalled that, as he had been roused, that the Wildman had protested that he was beguiled, that a conflict had ensued, that the yelling was much, and the scene confusing.

"A masked priest misused the magic of the shaman."

"For he has no power in and of himself."

"You know of this evil man?" Cynwyl asked.

"He is the thorn in my flesh – for decades ere I knew he existed. He the gold that financed the Saxon Wars and the divisive hate that feeds the Religious Wars. A shadow, a secret, a whisper. He is trapped on these Isles and clearly has found someone to serve as his agency to strike calamity within the bars of his own cage."

The Giant was engrossed in learning more of the wickedness of men. Then the tale demanded that he confess his own dark deeds. The spell had caused him to dash and slash at his Book, and then sprint into the city as a feral beast of the field, killing and destroying at random.

"The city was yours to sack. What caused you to stop?"

"A Christian druid." He fumbled at his words, the seeming oxymoron lost on neither monster nor king.

"Like Taliesin, my bard?" queried the king.

"Bring the torch closer." The deformed vine of an arm lifted high, beckoning forth the Iron Bear. "Closer."

Having no fear, but dagger ready to thrust as it must, Arthur obliged.

The light of the torch revealed the face, a large pear shape with but four or five strands of silver hair. When he had had all of his teeth there would have been two rungs; but now only pits and three yellow kernels remained. One eye wandered, as if it were a rivet with no attachment to its socket. The other eye could see but was encumbered by a heavy, drooping lid that covered all but the smallest crescent.

"No, Emperor Arthur son of Meurig. Not like your bard Taliesin of Glamorgan. Rather like his predecessor, born here."

"Merlin!" All spittle left the king's mouth, and a great lump manifested in his throat.

"He gave chase and I fled back to this cave. He saw my Book in tatters and asked about it, as you did." Cynwyl Mawr snatched up a page and arrested the conversation, straining to read, studying and contemplating.

Though the king could not bear it, feeling years of loss and hopelessness about to break, giving way to a new dawn with his old wizard, he knew that the Giant could not be rushed. At last he let the page fall as a feather upon the water. He watched it sink.

Cynwyl went on to explain that he studied Scripture for six hours each day that slumber did not possess him. And that he did so in hopes he would find the truth of what he was and, peradventure, eternal life. Concluding that he was damned, an abomination, and well outside the scope of God's creation, he hoped only to never harm a soul that the Lord would show mercy, sentencing him to some other torment besides the Lake of Fire. A woeful, sorrowful existence.

But Merlin had given him hope. He had explained that life was in the blood and the blood was passed down from the father. Through much mating, the probability of a chain of male Nephilim begetting sons only, and never a daughter to lie with a man (whose soul was redeemable), was low. Being neither a first, nor a second, but perhaps up to the eleventh generation, Cynwyl was young for his ancient race.

"Merlin shared with me grace. He said that I was a godly man, but that being godly wasn't enough. Rather that I must trust Christ alone. Whether I be salvageable or a woeful child of the damned, only God knows. And if a man, or the better part a man, then forgiven. Moreover, Merlin said that he was..." Another long pause.

"Please." Arthur could no longer contain himself. "Please tell me what else my Merlin said."

"He said that he was like me. Whether god or man, saint or monster. He shared that he and I were the same."

"And the witch? Whence came she?"

"Pict." He answered straightway. "The shaman and the masked priest brought her with them from Caledonia."

"And where did Merlin go?" Now Arthur was the one moving closer. And closer. "Is my Merlin yet in these caves?"

"No. But he said you would come. And he said he would rid Cymru of Simon Magus, the—"

"The Masked Priest!" Arthur pumped his fist excitedly. His Round Table Companions had spoken true; Merlin had joined them in the hunt.

"Then as suddenly as he appeared at the great oak in the center of the town, he vanished. I know not if he was here in the flesh, or a ghost or apparition."

"You are a godly man, Cynwyl Mawr. I too am most persuaded and amazed at this message of grace that Taliesin gave to the Merlin. I hope there is salvation for you, sir." Arthur's dagger opened the man's throat so wide that the base of the tongue was exposed. Arthur snatched at the tongue and tore the whole of Cynwyl's throat out. His wandering eye blossomed as a flower, then turned hoary; a violent but instant death. "Find your salvation or damnation in Heaven, else in the Underworld. You killed my kinsman, and must needs be removed from this land."

* * *

"How are you, men?" Arthur emerged from the cave, a minor cough developing on account of the damp and the cold.

"Is it possible that you inquire this of us when covered are you in tarry, sludge and slime? You look awful, lord!" Bedwyr gave a mighty laugh. "You sliced a witch in twain and slew a man that whipped, literally, the three of us" – even after decades of witnessing the valor and wonder of the sandy haired boy-king, the men were awestricken by their friend – "and you ask how *we* are?"

The troop found their triumphant king an oaky scrumpy while the remainder of them drank strong ale. Then they began to mourn that such death and loss could occur in the Summer Kingdom; the journey back to Caerleon was quiet, having much contemplation and little banter.

CHAPTER 20
The Madness of Maelgwn

When Arthur departed from Maelgwn, a *soft reconciliation* had been wrought between two men who loved the same woman. Some light of truth now allowed the proud warriors to at least *make the best of things*. Both men were of sufficient intelligence to know that more secrets and lies lurked. However, both men were of sufficient wisdom to not overly seek details of the same. Arthur believed to the depth of his sinew, the fiber and core, that his champion had not betrayed him *during* the fifteen years of marriage, and that left a thread of hope that they could live peaceably – finding some enjoyment themselves in the age of peace they had given to multitudes of others. Arthur further hoped that the single thread might, in time, lengthen, loop, double back and twist again and again, by the healing salve that is Time, to once again become the cord of strength and reliance that, though frayed, could never be severed. *That was the faith of Arthur.*

Moments before boarding his barge, Gwyar had made Arthur to know of the most recent insult of the Roman Church: this time desecrating the sarcophagus of Mary herself. Setting to revising and rewriting her history, laboring slowly to venerate her as a goddess and appropriate her atop all other goddesses the world over, using cultural and spiritual assimilation and annihilation in the stead of overt genocide.

Because of his radical commitment to liberty for all sects, and his refusal to allow the State to compel any man to follow one or the other, the Silure king was respected by most clergy, hated by a few, but popular with none. But now agnostic policy was impossible, for the transgression of the Roman Church was too great. Their deed had caused direct outrage, followed by official condemnation from the king. Arthur had openly fallen out with the Church. He had spent the greater part of a year handling that schism, upon his renewed quest to find his counselor, be he ghost or vision or flesh, and upon the new reality of his *situation at home.* Because of these three preoccupations, Arthur assumed that Maelgwn did well, that Gwyar and her new priestesses brought him back to full health, and that he was at the plow in Gwynedd, or at contemplative study amongst the monks and students at Saint Illtud's.

But Maelgwn did not mend as expected.

Following the friendly words, Maelgwn fell unconscious for several hours, and when awake 'twas a *sleeping feverish awakening,* followed by more sleep. It was difficult for Gwyar to discern if the overly tall warrior spilling like four great weeds over her longest bed was succumbing to the enchantment within Excalibur's blade, which had surely breeched the sternum and perhaps nicked the heart, or to illness, or to despair, pride and shame; or to the sum of all of these things.

Taliesin and Gwyar studied and pondered

upon what course of care might recover the renowned knight. Finally the Chief Bard declared, *"When the present is confused and disjointed, let it look to the past, not for judgment, but rather for answers."* As something in times past had befallen Maelgwn, by happenstance on the very isle where he lay in the dire, Taliesin and Gwyar sought to understand *that event* that it might guide resolution to *this event.*

But in order to transcend gossip, rumor and tale, to gain the fullness of *that event* required direct witness from one who had been there. Maelgwn's foster-mother.

Prior to her appearance in the streamy marsh that fed Llyn Fawr, none had seen the Lady of the Lake for years.

Taliesin, a Christian, could not endorse the means of making contact, but as Gwyar sat about to summon that witch of olden that was inside of her, *and was her,* he remarked, "We are not under the Law, but under Grace. We can do nothing against the truth but for the truth."

She enjoyed these words. Then she helped his conscience by closing the door upon the slight sage, that she might do her deeds beyond his view.

Though it exhausted her tiny body, ironically rendering her nearly as ill as the one she was seeking to save, the most powerful of all Britons met with success. Using the Sight, violating and perverting nature and its laws, she made contact with the Lady of the Lake.

She awoke, seemingly a day or more removed from the encounter, in a bed that had been prepared next to Maelgwn. As her groggy eyes were unhinged and the painful sunlight greeted her eyes, Taliesin's wit greeted her ears.

"This chamber is now more as the convalescence tent of wounded field warriors than the mystical abode of the Queen of Avalon!"

"This is why you banish him from court, isn't it?"

Maelgwn mustered a smile. "Aye. I fear not even this deathbed will free me from the dwarfish thorn. Could it be? Did you see our foster-mother?"

"Through the still waters that were as a looking glass, yes. We spoke, then I fainted and remember not since."

Taliesin had beckoned of the nine maidens to bring her a special tea, and gave her space to gather her wits. As she rallied, she waited for Maelgwn to drift back into sickly sleep, then she made known the Lady's words to the bard.

She shared how Vivien had retired to one of Cymru's myriad daughter islands that speckled the coast, and that a small but ancient castle – all but ruined by shifting shorelines and the merciless erosion caused by sand – was her abode. There, she and others guarded the Grail, desperate to keep it from Simon Magus at all costs. Because the Grail Guardians disagreed with Taliesin's theology, they viewed Rhufawn the Fair, whose obsessive love for the relic had become well known o'er the whole of the Isles and the Continent, as a desirous candidate to possess and guard it.

Vivien had gone onto say that she was aging and could not protect the Cup forever. Vivien had a mortal father, Budic I, who had been beguiled and seduced by a Korrigan. As her father was mortal, Vivien would one day sleep the sleep of death. And because her father was mortal, she had hope of resurrection. She yet learned little of the Christian God and cleaved to her goddess (who also had an origin), but hoped that her protection of the Cup that the Nazarene would sip when He returned to dine with His Twelve in the Jew's kingdom would be enough to earn her salvation.

Her concern was the Pendragon and *his twelve,* and the untoward designs on the Summer Kingdoms by dangerous foes without – and within. She made Gwyar to understand what had befallen the young Maelgwn, before the bards called him Lancelot. But first she bade Gwyar remember, above all things, to warn Arthur that Howell the Great, her kinsman and his ally, would soon need the Iron Bear to bring an army to Little Britain. For a confederacy was rising, knit of men with different tongues; a monster with many small horns under the leadership of two great horns: Childebert the Merovingian and the upstart Mark, the son of the late Meirchion the Mad. The confederacy was succored by Roman gold and strengthened with Teutonic muscle.

Gwyar recalled gasping at the news and had vowed to make her brother to know.

As for Maelgwn…

When just a boy, overtaken by the lusts of youth, he had forced himself upon his uncle's wife, and known her. The deed was discovered and, in the conflict that ensued, the uncle was slain. Some suggested murder; others maintained that the offender had committed manslaughter, defending himself.

Only an intimate circle of the influential and the powerful knew of the matter. They caused the deed to disappear, along with the innocent woman involved, violating the moral code of every Briton – that kings, queens and princes and bishops live under the very laws they required of the people. Corruption for one was corruption for all. The decision haunted otherwise principled and moral men and women. Vivien and Dyfrig and even the High King Meurig, a man devoted to justice, made exception for the boy.

This was by reason of his abilities with fist, bow, spear and sword. Not since Achilles could one dominate the field as could Maelgwn. By the age of fifteen it was evident to all that he was a legend, a god in his own time. And by reason of the loyal group of boys, *his Hosts,* as they came to be called, who surrounded him and were very near his skill. By reason of the Saxon menace. By reason of compromise and the failings of all men, the circle allied to wash away the crime.

Maelgwn was sent to train on the Continent with Vivien herself, and the two perfected her martial art. When not there, he would be tempered and controlled by the rod of the Christian Religion at Saint Illtud's. When residing in neither place, Ynys Enlli.

There he met the Merlin, who was not involved in the plot, and there he was, from time to time left to wander and explore in the sanctuary of the enchanted isle.

Peradventure one day, suffering from an intense, abnormal thirst after training, he was drawn to, and possessing no regard for sacred restrictions, profaned the Sacred Grove. There he lay with a Cymry damsel under the green canopy of its tops, loving her in its cool blue shade. As they embraced afterward, she stood with a jolt, and at once transformed before the young knight. Drums beat and horns bugled. Stringed instruments strummed. And the well-known mist filled the whole of the orchard.

The damsel now revealed herself as a radiant Fae, adorned in white apparel. Not a thumb's space upon her bosom, ribcage or arms were not filled with the ornate markings and the concentric knotwork of the Tylwyth Teg. A white owl rested upon her shoulder.

She beheld a wooden saucer filled with strong drink from a forbidden tree, sprung forth from the apple that Brutus had sought. Select druids and priestesses used some of the fruit, carefully crafting multivarietal ciders for healing and enjoyment by the Cymry. Only ever in small measures; always mixed, never whole.

Men were forbidden to enter the grove unless they be under the guidance and authority of the druids, and it was evidently by bewitchment that the boy Maelgwn had been led there in the first place. The whole of the orchard smelled of the musk of seduction, sang of lust, tasted of allure, looked as an altar of warmest pleasure.

The fermented product of the seven-seeded apple changed Maelgwn. *It radically intensified all that he already was. Plus more.*

He left the orchard with the remnants of an old war, which survived in the flesh of the fruit, now part of his blood.

The Dragon.

The Giant.

The Korrigan water spirit.

And Man.

The attributes, memories, perpetually-conflicted disposition, incompatibility, anger towards the creation itself, misery, power, strange beauty and all the good and bad of the Otherworld entered him.

Yet he remained but a man. A man poisoned by the residue of a lost and dark time.

Pleased with her work, the Fae brushed away the dark and curly locks, and kissed the tall prince upon his forehead. And vanished.

The faerie had gifted Maelgwn a curious silver cruciform featuring symbolism that represented each of the four elements that had joined to become the seven seeds. It just *was* about his neck, a simple leather strap and a pendant. None had seen the likes of the cruciform and, when spotted at sup or sport, it engendered endless assumptions by experts who caused Maelgwn to laugh, knowing nothing.

But Vivien, his mother, knew the meaning of the cross and its symbols.

"A cursed apple from a forbidden tree given him by a shining angel caused him to be this way?" Taliesin challenged.

"Sounds incredulous."

"Agreed!"

"Of course, I just spoke to a woman older than my mother whose appearance is younger than mine by means of a pool of water, and sometimes I possess the strength of five armies and can crack marble with my mind. Let's not start doubting the nature of these peculiar times now, bard."

They laughed hard at the observation.

"Does this mean he is not responsible for the ill and evil he has done?"

"We are all responsible for the ill and evil we do," Gwyar responded.

She continued Vivien's account.

The Lady of Lake went on to say that the cruciform is ever with Maelgwn, and not even Arthur knows the meaning of it. The apple was indeed his curse, but now he is inseparable from it, and in this regard, it may save and sustain him."

"Poison given to the poisoned." Taliesin

nodded, understanding. "'Tis true in nature."

"'Tis true in love."

They laughed again. The kind of chuckle that precedes peril.

"That apple has faded into legend. What if it was simply conjured by the faeries for the purpose of the ruse?" Taliesin, a man flowing with *The Awen*, or divine inspiration, given him when he achieved knowing the mysteries of God, knew not of the veracity of the legend, for this secret was hidden from even the adepts.

"You know what words Jesus gave Paul when he ascended to the third heaven but know not where reside the seven-seeded apple trees upon the island of bards?" The Sorceress playfully goaded her Christian ally.

"We all have our specialties, my lady. Is it real? Does it yet exist?"

"It is. It does." She spoke plainly. "And all who drink of it drink unto themselves death." She and the Chief Bard stood, looking down upon the sickly warrior.

Taliesin took her hand in his palms. "My dear Morgaine. Worry not. When the last stone of golden Caermelyn hath toppled and the mighty men of this epoch sleep in the ground, I believe that YOU and HE shall outlive us all. I believe this will be YOUR story to tell."

"Then I must make haste to save him," she responded.

Bishop Cadfan and his pilgrims had not breeched Gwyar's grove. It was surrounded by a great vault of green semi-transparent glass, which protected the trees and other scarce plants from the harsh, salty winds of Ynys Enlli. The original Brutus Trees, as the druids came to call them, were gone. But, through the expertise and art of grafting, they had been reborn and three of them flourished amongst Gwyar's trees, which boasted nine other Cymreig varieties besides. The seven-seeded apples were shaken, not picked, and allowed to turn in the enchanted soils prior to being pressed and fermented in woodchips within great icy steel cauldrons, which were sealed for the life-cycle of the fermentation. Once the cider, or when left in the cauldron longer, a spirit, was ready, a few drops were added to other ciders during the final stages of their cycle. It was never blended early in the process and never processed and served on its own.

But Gwyar collected a small quantity that was set aside for blending. She protected it in a drinking bladder that was very small, capped and ready to serve unto Maelgwn. The total sum was a spoonful or two, as elixir given to a sickly babe.

The cider, an accelerant, made straightway for Maelgwn's bloodstream. His blood remembered the sup and the special interaction it had shared. And the dark-painted faerie who had made use of it for the poisoning. All these quickened the Bloodhound Prince, and he woke with a feverish shout of "Gwenhywfar!"

Maelgwn lived, resurrected from the netherland between the living and the dead. He lived, but his love of Gwenhwyfar II now burned afresh, his mind seeing her markings all day, his thoughts ever upon her visage, never quite to grasp that the markings upon her were the same as those upon the elvish creature transformed from damsel so long ago.

The Champion of the Britons, the peculiar 'sometimes King of Gwynedd', divested himself once more of his hosts, who wept sorely, and his bards, who sang at him from coast to coast, and retired into extreme monasticism, spending the greater part of his days in a small chapel in Abergwaun, located in the west country of Deheubarth, which the bards would later call Pembroke. They had all witnessed him waive his rule over petty politics, land strife or when quest and desire outweighed the administration of tax and cattle. But all perceived the difference in this abeyance. Lancelot's heart had been pierced long before Excalibur pricked it.

Ironically, Gwalchmai governed the very lands of Maelgwn's abode in the role of a type of consultative governor. He did not infringe upon the local chiefs and tribal leaders, but was given an office to support them as training and practice should he one day ascend to the throne of Pendragon. After the Trial of Arms, Gwalchmai's reputation was severely damaged and the office had devalued to that of an empty title; a figurehead with no power or authority. In Cymru, the people loaned power to the rulers and, ultimately, the rulers were subject to the law. This was the heart of the light of liberty cast upon a dark world by an ancient people who refused to live under the boot of the very few reigning over the very many. When a leader fell out of favor amongst the Tribes, there was an unspoken shunning and shift of mood in the wind that typically preceded a visit by the druids or bishops, who gathered the will and directives of the people. Gwalchmai had not been deposed or asked to leave Deheubarth, but that they had lost confidence in him was a thick and ever-present reality.

Still, he did what he could to serve farmers, to assist with building villages, to train guards, to try and practice being a good leader as Arthur would have him to do.

From time to time Gwalchmai would bring food to Maelgwn, who betimes did not regard his own nutrition. The two did not like one another. Possibly they never had. But they were brothers under the codes and precepts of the Round Table, had killed Saxons together, doing things unmentionable to preserve the nation. They both knew what prolonged war did to men and they both extended a kind of cold grace, speaking of nothing save sport and weather.

Thus two of Arthur's best suffered great loss at *the games*. While Caerleon and Caermelyn were trumpets and gold and commerce and great loudness of children at play and choirs at song, the West Country was sleepy, and rainy, and grit and brood and hard labor. And also lovely and quiet. In this regard, it suited both the Hawk of May, now less bright, and the old Lancelot of Cymru and Brittany, now in service to none save his own obsessions.

Taliesin demanded that Maelgwn make himself presentable and receive his son, Rhufawn. The troubled knight loved his son deeply, so much so that each visit would cause a temporary rest from the torments of thinking on Gwenhwyfar, or upon *Arthur and Gwenhwyfar*. When the lad would return, so would the thoughts and, with them, the torments. Such was his low state that Taliesin began to wonder whether he and Gwyar had been more cruel than kind in saving him, for the poison had surely magnified his pain.

Then Rhufawn stopped visiting.

A quest for the Cup of Christ, with two other brave young and worthy knights, came the tidings. *Rhufawn has discovered the Grail Castle; trials to follow.*

Months became a year and a year became

three. And reports grew scarce.

Disdaining Taliesin's chides, Maelgwn refused to see him. Isolated in self-imposed exile but never truly alone.

For there were many Maelgwns in Maelgwn.

In the forest he would oft encounter his other selves and make combat with them, but they would always disappear the instant his blow was about to find flesh. Moreover, his other selves would audibly whisper or hiss, accusing and condemning him. This time in his own voice, that time in the voice of hag, or else that of a he-goat or some devil.

Just beyond a plot of graves that garnished the pitch outside his chapel was a great yew tree. Its sap was constant and the consistency and color of blood. Working the edges and curves of his cruciform pendant, the fallen knight gave the whole of his weight to the tree, embracing its sticky crimson issue. His black curls matted with sweat, pasted against the chiseled cheek, the broken god-man Lancelot fell upon both knees and lamented; the base of the tree and his splinters were the only audience to hear him.

I cannot kill myself, for I cannot be defeated in battle, save by the Silure.

She is my sun and my moon. The rotation of the heavens as my heart towards her. Always twirling, ever in their circuits, never to rest upon her bosom.

She regards my best friend and I regard her. She is my first love, though she were made to be his last.

Let me go down into the Deep. Disjoint my shoulders and make my knees to shake out of their places for the weight of this loss causeth me not to stand.

Violence and tremors, malice and envy and all good gone in the rage of my jealousy. And towards him it waxes.

Yet towards him it waxes not. Men will do what men will do. For we are beasts all. It kindles rather towards her. Gwenhwyfar, how I loathe thee.

Your eyes do disrobe yourself and your lips invite us to the snare. Your hair is woven of deceit and at the small of thy back are bars to the hot gates of Hades whence none return.

Where is the Christ? Does He not promise to set the captives free? Where is Rhiannon; does she not protect those who serve the sovereignty of the Cymry?

Merlin, I have done what you bade and cannot die, though I die daily. Is the kingdom worth the eternal punishment of one man? Would that the Saxons reign, that she make her bed with mine!

Can I not squash Arthur as the crawling thing, cannot my hosts devour the Silures? Their blue war paint frightens not the Ravens of the North.

Victory! But what victory to be won when she hath chosen him?

Him! Arthur the Emperor. Arthur the Temperate. Arthur the Wise. Arthur the Son of Prophecy and Messiah of his people. A man who knows not want, for he is given all by right in the stead of merit. A man who knows not to covet, for all is already his. Arthur the Just! They would make him as the Saviour Himself. But neither hath saved me!

I am more comely than thee, King Arthur. Of more brawn and girth, comelier to look upon with the eyes. Every damsel save YOURS freely giveth her life for me. And to me. You are a stalky, average fellow. You are not my equal!

But you are my greater, and I am the lesser. Beauty fades as the grass and muscle weakens year by year, but your character and command, your honesty and grace, endures forever.

You are my king; let you have what woman you will and if your choice, though the beautiful Cymry women are as the sands of the sea, be the only one I want, then it is well. I shall love you both from this pit, and all my days I shall battle the bubble that makes me a monster and the untenable love that makes me mad.

Where goes my son? Why is he not near that I might love him? He is my rock and my salvation. The flame of Arthur shall never perish, as it passes on to the son of Maelgwn. Protect my son, o Christ, and let one strand of hair be distressed under the wing of thy shadow, o Rhiannon. Let him have no regard for women, that love ruins him not, and pray ye gods and the God of Gods, that the best of me and the best of the Silure Lord combine in him, defiled not by triangles of affection and unrequited love. For we have been great; but save ye him and this and he will be threefold better.

The coasts, as they do in the West Country, brought an instant and unrelenting rain. The giant yew offered some shelter to the prostrate knight, but the storm was too great. The rush of waters cleansed him of the sap, but rendered him looking as a black salamander struggling in a soup made of blood.

CHAPTER 21
Magus Finds His Mark

In the final years of the Summer Kingdom, King Arthur was – *King Arthur.*

A cold peace at home that fell disgracefully short of his aspirations of being like his parents (who were yet as vibrant, giddy and yet stately as ever).

Open disputes and unsolvable complexities of politics with the Roman Church.

In accord with Vivien's warning by the mouth of Gwyar issued, a new threat burgeoned on the Continent, issued from the loins of a defeated and long-dead foe.

Magus not found.

Merlin, though hope was high and rumors many, remained unconfirmed as truly amongst the living.

The Dynion Hysbys brooding.

The druids worrying.

The bishops *bishopping.*

But there was no war. No Saxon menace. No invaders ruining innocence and frightening the soul of the nation. No Civil War. The Kingdoms, Royal Clans, Tribes, Cantrefs and hundreds still functioned as local principalities with Arthur as their High King and the twenty-and-four as their High Council. Cymru had long endured, approaching half a generation of prosperity and unparalleled tranquility for the common citizen.

Since the day he had cleaved the witch in twain and slain the Bible-toting menace in the dank bowels of the inlet cove of Caermarthen, a slight cough had entered Arthur's lungs, and remained. A minor and irregular complaint, it projected no indication of weakness or impotence, as the harvests were yet strong year over year.

Yet there was no direct heir. But one of Arthur's younger brothers, Frioc, dabbled in politics or in military matters, and the remainder of his kin were either devoted to the monk's robe, or else some other enterprise. His sisters had been married, quite contrary to the norms and customs of the Cymry, to northern princes for strategic purposes decades ago, and their stock produced fine nephews such as Gwalchmai and Gareth, who could bear the mantle but *were no Arthurs.*

Rhufawn, as the bastard son of a daughter of Gwent, could be promoted to Pendragon, or at minimum declared Wledig or 'Battle Commander' by the Tribes.

Then there was Mordred.

The Whelp.

Only fourteen years younger than the king, he had crystalized his reputation as a man of flattering tongue and sneaky blade. He would compliment a farmer with feigned words with the crowing of the cock and plunder the same man through corruption or legal manipulation by the setting of the sun the selfsame day. He knew Arthur had slain Amr, and Mordred knew that Arthur knew.

The son of Gwyar had left court the very day

of the uncomfortable exchange at the bridge upon the Usk River, returning to his father's lands. His fear of the Iron Bear dominated and controlled him, driving him to approximate Lancelot's lowly condition. Mordred rarely lay with Gwenhwyfach, and when he did, it was only when he could imagine her as Gwenhwyfar. On nights when he couldn't, they didn't. His affair had run nearly the sum of the Summer Kingdom, but the light of that unholy candle had been pinched, smoldering to a flicker. Gwenhwyfar periodically sent him letters. Then either sender or recipient would slay the messenger, that there be no trail of discovery. Dreading being found out and brimming with suspicion, correspondence was seldom and brief. Thus Mordred sought to make the most of an unhappy life with his pretend-Gwenhywfar whilst the authentic queen did the same with her preoccupied, inwardly distressed and outwardly perfect husband. Having neither Mordred nor Lancelot to bed rendered her miserable and cold; her only thaw the *hope* that one day Arthur would stumble from some great tower or slip into a holy well – else that Mordred might garner the gumption to overtly seize the throne.

Alas, to Arthur the challenges *behind the throne* were a light wage in exchange for the smiles of the children and the hearty embraces of farmers that the Iron Bear enjoyed every morning during his walks up to Lodge Hill.

Gwyar visited him less often and their walks grew few as she focused on raising up her nine maidens that the Roman Church might not, through their plot to elevate Mary as the new goddess, remove her faith entirely from the earth, causing it to be relegated to the corridors of the supposed superstitions of ancient man. Knowing Arthur bore too many burdens, she blamed him not but wished greatly that he would do more to aid the very vanishing sect that had gifted him his Sword of Power, validating him as king before all.

* * *

In Brittany – where Cymreig migrants had in times past settled peacefully and established a small kingdom during the Saxon Wars to protect their ports and provide for defense against pirates and invaders – the long protective reach of the Pendragon banner was vexed and torn, as diverse Germanic, Frankish and Gallic tribes, along with bitter rivals and menacing new enemies of their own kind, were encroaching upon Breton soils.

So close was the kinship between Cymru and Little Britain that corresponding 'sister cities' on the Continent bore the names of their predecessors on the Isles whence they had come. King Hoel Mawr ruled from both Kerne-Brittany and Leon-Brittany, whilst his ally King Arthur ap Meurig held court in Cernw in Gwent and also Caerleon in Cymru.

The mightiest of Hoel's foes was Childebert the Merovingian and he, tragically, was succored by one of Glamorgan's own.

Long ago when Mad Mark Meirchion had conspired to murder the Merlin of Britain, King Arthur, lacking sufficient evidence to execute him, had dispossessed the old Catholic king. The bishops studiously memorialized the transfer of his ancestral lands in south Cymru in the margins of an oversized Bible; many princes and influential landowners witnessed the document.

Though the North, with its Romanist leanings, did not follow course, Arthur made Meirchion abdicate his principalities and transfer those lands to his grandson, Urien Rheged. Meirchion was thus made a vagabond who owned nothing and died mired in shame and destitution.

Although Meirchion had been born in the south of Cymru, his religious, political and military allies resided in the Old North, as did his wife and many children. One of them, Cynfarch, begat a son, Llew, and Llew of the Old North was married to Arthur's sister, the princess Gwyar.

For this cause, and for the ripple that would rise as a tide from the North and peradventure smash and crash down upon the Midland Tribes and the Silures, Arthur chose mercy instead of the blade for Mad Mark.

The sinister old man spent the last of his days far down in the horn of the Isles amongst the Cornovii tribes. Knowing he would soon pass, he bade them raise his youngest son, Prince Mark, as their own. This they did until they witnessed the hate and corruption cursed upon the son by the father. Mark too was a *banished man* without a country.

Then Simon Magus, the imprisoned leader of the Council of Nine, found him.

From the hut that was his abode in the darkness of the Caledonian wood, the Masked One used Merlin Wyllt as his pawn – his means of divination. The recluse possessed the Sight and, with above three years of discipleship, was able to serve as the probing and scouring eyes of a hawk for Simon. Roaming the land through these forbidden means, Simon discovered a jaded lad that had done something, quite on a small scale, that thoroughly impressed the architect of the long-prophesied New Order for the Ages: confederacy.

Confederacy, save not of those of his own blood, but of those from many nations. Mark had located the discarded, the angry, the bitter and the violent from amongst the Tribes of Eire – the Picts, the Jutes, the Angles, the Saxons and some Ravens who hated *the tyrant Arthur besides.* A band of criminals, accorded of men whose native kingdoms were often at war and, where Briton and Saxon were concerned, had not been in league since the time of Vortigern the Traitor.

But this rabble was no army. Three hundred men who would be stamped underfoot without notice by the elite armies of either the Britons or the Bretons.

However, Magus saw potential. In the stead of three hundred outcasts, he saw a confederacy of six nations, and Mark as their king.

He also, at last, envisioned the means of his escape from the Isles.

Mark subdivided his three hundred into troops of twenty and, through negotiation, corruption and patience, placed his men privily into employ at posts both upon the harbors and the ports. Trade was very active, as was religious pilgrimage, making boats and barges the perfect place to hide vagrants and baser men. Prince Madoc's maritime guard meticulously searched every vessel that left or entered, but these were of no reputation. Provided Magus could convince one troop to sacrifice all to ambush and kill Madoc's men at one of the more remote, less friendly Pictish shores (for they were hot with displeasure that the Britons had intruded upon their ports for the sake of one criminal), Magus could slip away and make land on the

Continent. There, his Merovingian alternative to the Pendragon would receive and restore him.

Because Mark was a devout practitioner of Christianity after the Roman Catholic tradition, Magus was careful not to overtly use means of sorcery or devilish practices to facilitate introductions. This could prove difficult, given that Mark was either in Eire or on the Continent (circumambulating the mother island as a frightened but resolute dog circles a wolf threatening the herd), whilst Magus was in Alba. As the Merovingians shared no such opposition to occultic practices, Magus instead, through the channel of Merlin Wyllt, engaged the friendly ear of a general, who then in turn gave word to Mark of a *friend in the shadows who could help him overthrow Arthur and Hoel, and restore Mark's lands.*

Through the course of many like messages, a trust was forged with the young renegade and Magus, *the Shadow Man,* began to make Mark his pawn. Building upon his model of finding traitorous men who could be forged and molded into an *angry confederacy loyal to none save each other,* Magus taught Mark many tactics and tricks of Statecraft, and his numbers increased tenfold. A man born of any nation save the Vandals or the Visigoths (for they were the only army that could defeat the Britons, and Magus sought to not disrupt them with politics. They were to be his *final move* in creating a great war that would result in either Arthur or Childebert ascending to the dark throne of Antichrist on behalf of Simon's master, Arddu) could join their ranks.

Unpleasant to look upon just as his father had been, Mark had the ears of a donkey and a great cleft in his chin. The men followed him not for his fairness or skill with blade or spear. Rather, the allure that bound them was restoration for their sundry wrongs, real or imagined, or – for the more fully corrupted – vengeance and violence for its own sake.

Some Gewissi conscripts gave some of Mark's confederacy ongoing lodging in the far northwest of the Emerald Island, and they made a sort of settlement on the borderlands of Brittany. Magus taught Mark to have his men harass and withdraw, to garner attention and then vanish. To be a thorn and a whisper. At the same time, he bade Childebert initiate war with Hoel Mawr and his sons.

Just as a victory would be at hand for the Breton, extra brawn of no particular battle standard would manifest and sway the battle in favor of the Merovingians. Mark's confederacy of six nations was the difference, tilting all in favor of the King Childebert.

An easily dismissed rumor became first a curiosity (that Briton would fight elbow to elbow with Saxon), then it burgeoned into an urgent threat to the sovereignty, and potentially the existence of, Cymru's greatest ally. Thus Arthur requested Anwn Ddu, *the Black Knight*, who was brother to King Hoel, to join him that they might personally inquire of the matter. Anwn was husband to Arthur's sister, Anna, and he possessed knowledge of every inch of Brittany save the unknowable corridors and twists of the Broceliande forest. He was also lethal with sword and beloved by Hoel; the perfect escort for the Pendragon.

In the guise of bards adorned in simple garb, the Round Table Companions watched a small skirmish from afar. The soldiers knew not what famous men were just above them on the ridge.

The Bretons used Vivien's martial arts and, to Arthur, looked as forty Lancelots fighting in one accord in the valley below. Leaning upon the arching branch of a tree older than time, the master of disguise removed his hood and lost himself in the scene below. *All warriors miss the fight.* A rush of reminiscence, jealousy and longing for his troubled friend overcame the king. Such did his countenance shift that Anwn worried after him.

"Do you need to sit and rest, lord? May I fetch you water?"

"Cider," smiled the king, recovering back to the present. "I do well. Look how your people, my cousins, fight as one."

Then the battle before them, small in scope and number, unveiled the microcosm of the problem. Anwn and Arthur saw the fatal difficulty in fighting Mark's Six Nations Confederacy; hesitation.

The Breton made no pause when felling a Jute or putting a Saxon to flight. Not so with a Briton or a native of the Emerald Isles. Treachery and defection has ever been part of war. But not a composite army made wholly of men with no regard for their own nation. Not an army of traitors. In the marvel of it the Bretons would halt mid-stroke and beg their adversary to turn from their treachery, reminding them that their newfound allies aimed for the annihilation of all Brythonic and Goidelic peoples. In mid-sentence the Breton knight would catch an arrow to the bosom, or an axe to the gullet.

"We are not designed to kill our own kind on the field of military combat," observed Arthur. "When it is a cattle war or a land skirmish, we gnaw and devour our own, but the line is drawn when an official war with mounted horse, flanks and fire, banner and songs ensues. Our patriotism, so great a strength as 'tis..."

"...Is strength become weakness." The Black Knight finished the king's sentence.

"We must make haste back to Caermelyn and present the case for raising an army to lend aid to Hoel. The Continent hums with tension and feels as if it is on the brink of all-out war. Should Little Britain fall to this or any other abomination—"

"They would be at our doorstep next."

* * *

"A wizard sought here amongst the owls and mushrooms and heather." Merlin Wyllt smirked at Magus, who had returned from some privy preparations for his escape attempt.

"Oh?" Magus expressed little concern. "A crookbacked slight wizard with a walking stick and too many scrolls?" The Italian meant to mock Taliesin.

"Contrary. A tall Briton. Taller than any Briton I've beheld. He beseeched me cease training with you, informed me that the depths of your ill intentions reached the gates of Hell herself, and that you were a false prophet and an Antichrist. He was persuasive and had command of his words; an impressive, unusual man!"

"What else can you tell me about this sojourner that impressed you so?"

"He said that his name was already loaned to another and he called me by my Christian name, Laolkien. That would make his name—"

"Merlin." Magus dropped his satchel and stood agape. "But that's impossible."

"Nothing is impossible for the woeful

damned. At least, not during their time amongst mortals."

"No. I was there. Impossible. My Lord Arddu would have told me." Magus began to rumble. His expression became *all* concern.

"I fled politics and strife. I know not what this Merlin was, and I possess no desire to validate or disqualify any his invectives cast. My hermitage is intentional. I am far removed from Cymru and I like it so." The hermit turned and puffed up in effort to be authoritative, an effort to repossess his home. "I think it is time for you to make your escape. I think it is time for you to leave."

But the hermit spake to the air, for Magus was already gone, already mounted and riding, making his way to the designated spot for his escape – an old road above the Firth of Forth and north-east to a Pictish port.

The new *Mystery of Merlin* notwithstanding, the Council of Nine's newest iteration for immanetizing the eschaton crystalized within its leader's corrupt mind as he made for the port:

Use Mark son of Meirchion to draw Arthur to the Continent here, to the Eire there. Let the threat make the armies of the Round Table reborn. Stretch them thin and tax them with frequent travel.

Once overstretched and distressed abroad, manifest the scandal of the whelp Mordred at home. Let the Church and the heathens alike determine how to manage Arthur's firstborn son being a bastard born of incest.

Fractured and factionalized, let Merlin's long-prophesied comet come! May his tail set the Isle ablaze, furthering our Great Work!

And then, when the familiar trauma of perpetual war hath returned to the Cymry and the hope of liberty slipping as despair rises, and when the people feel as if

God Himself has predestined their fall; when their low disposition seems to have descended to ocean's floor; when they can take no more – then. Then we release the Vandal Horde. The Black Boar. Like the Iron Bear, undefeated. Two Titans. One will be fit and ready and full of verve, the other hearing its bards singing its own death songs. The Black Boar will hunt the Dragon and the Raven alike.

Arthur will be destroyed or, against hope, will rise from grievous wounds over the enemy I have yet again created for him. Judas Iscariot will rise from his place and, should we find that damned cup, place it in Arthur through the same means that Mordred was begotten.

Arthur will be Antichrist.

Else, Childebert the Merovingian will form an accord with the Vandal Horde and the Nations and simply walk onto the rubble of Caermelyn, rebuilding the Kingdom of Heaven over the grave of King Arthur.

* * *

"Whence come the greater portion of their recruits?" Arthur and Anwn ceased not to talk about the matter as their flat boat was about an hour from reaching the mainland of Cymru. The confluence was at the posterior of the Severn, and they would simply sail all the way to Caerleon, not having to step foot upon land and travel by carriage or horse until the last short leg of the journey from Caerleon to Caermelyn.

"It seemed that the greater part of their numbers were Saxon," Anwn observed.

"I agree," Arthur concurred. "Has time at last caught up with us? Are the Saxons now producing men of fighting age? That army could not *all* be the disenfranchised and the banished.

A Saxon has no regard for kin or countrymen, provided the wage is meet…"

"Conscripts," they both surmised, speaking at the same time.

"The Cymry do not invade nor encroach upon the sovereignty of another people. We protect our soil, and our just cause for doing this is that our soil is *ours,* and by extension, their soil is *theirs.*"

"Aye," the Black Knight confirmed.

"But…" Arthur paused. "In this case, although we will not invade, we will spy. I need a man who knows Brittany well and can study these men. Their dress, their dialect, their manners. Then, and I believe not that I am saying this — "

"Lord?"

"That same man must then sneak into Germania and validate whether or not these men are being exported to Gaul for the cause of bolstering this odd collective." Arthur used fingers in the air to summarize, speaking with his hands. "Find a man. Study the Germans in Gaul and Brittany. Study the Germans in Germania and the surrounding countries. Report the findings to the Round Table Fellowship. Can you find me such a man?"

"He is aged, but yes, there is such a man whose adventures qualify him for this task. Greidawl, father of your ally Gwythyr, whose vast lands span Leon, has been to Germania more than any Briton. He is your man, my lord."

"An excellent recommendation, brother-in-law. After we congress with our mates, please spend a fortnight with Anna and your children for then we, along with Bedwyr, must return again to the Continent and visit Leon, where I will personally give charges to Greidawl. I do apologize that I am removing you from hearth and home to go to and fro upon boats and vessels."

"In light of what we saw in the lands of Hoel, I think the reality of our future *is* going 'to and fro'," Anwn Ddu responded.

CHAPTER 22
Crop Failure

The year five hundred and thirty-and-five after the Incarnation of the Lord Jesus Christ was the last of what Arthur's Chief Bard referred to as the precious and priceless *quiet years* in the Summer Kingdom.

But for Arthur it was neither quiet nor restful. It was a year of travel for the sandy-haired one-time *Boy-King,* now beyond the midpoint of life. *The War King, the Giant Slayer,* now *the Traveling King.*

First, Magus did escape. He purchased the blood of nineteen of Mark's men, mostly Picts, who hacked and whacked, delivering him at long last upon a departing boat. This occurred at the very time Arthur was returning with Anwn from Little Britain. At the same time, Prince Madoc was away at sea on an expedition. Timing, poor fortune, and the use of force finally allowed the serpent to slip by the rake, through the grass, and out of the garden.

Six of Mark's men died, but for the port guards, both of Pictish and Cymreig blood, every living soul perished in the ambush. As there were no witnesses left drawing breath, Arthur himself went to investigate and deduced, based upon the scene, the evidence and the circumstance, that

Magus had made use of Mark's confederacy to make his escape from the Isles in the Sea.

The incident demanded that the Pendragon once again sup with King Drest son of Girom, once again speaking eye to eye about the grave risks associated with yet another incident that had seen Pictish souls sent to the sleep of death on account of Cymreig politics. The Pictish lord adored Arthur, but grew weary of drawing criticism and objection from his vassal tribes. When pressed, Arthur reminded the Picts through his authoritative statements to their High King that the loss of life in three score raids and one hundred skirmishes could not outweigh the blood that was upon the head of the Picts for conducting the Saxons into Gwynedd, the Old North and Powys in times past when the Saxon Wars were beginning. Moreover, the Boar would surely have turned upon their hosts and devoured the whole of Alba if not for the victory earned by the tribes of the Britons.

The Picts owed their freedom to turn to the Christian God or retain their native gods and goddesses to the Cymry king. And ultimately, they suffered some insult and encroach on account of this.

The greater sum of the year was spent making the case for the sons of Briton to die for the sons of Brittany. *We are the same sons,* argued well the High King. For nearly two decades, mothers had grown accustomed to seeing their sons grow, court, farm, play and marry. The age of manhood had slackened to eighteen; and why shouldn't it? A fourteen-year-old is a babe and no man, unless imminent and endless war and a death rate that exceeds the birth rate demands it. Only then must the boys become men, the girls mothers too soon.

Slow to be won over, Arthur and his closest

retinue traveled oft, at last gathering an army of Powys, of Deubarth, of the Midlands, of Silures and Ravens once more. Vivien and Lancelot's silver armor shone again as the undefeated Britons made ready to bring hell from above upon the Franks or other German tribes, or the renegades of Mark, as needed.

Arthur tired some from the travel, the political speeches, and the knots and tangles of promising a people that they were yet at peace whilst clearly preparing for war.

Rhun ap Maelgwn and Owain ap Urien were Arthur's strongmen from the Old North. Needing extra help, he sent for Maelgwn himself. The request went, and then remained, without response.

"Go and chastise him until he polishes his famed spike and wields it once more," Arthur commanded Taliesin.

"And remove myself from guarding the hearts and motives of Rhufawn? Even Vivien's magic is no match for his tenacity," Taliesin objected.

Arthur proposed a compromise. He suggested that Rhufawn be allowed to handle the Cup, thus satisfying his obsession, and then that it be buried with the *other relics* upon Ynys Enlli, where Gwyar herself would guard it. "Perhaps a periodic pilgrimage will tame the boy's noble lust?" offered Arthur. "If he is to be king after my passing, balance he must find."

"I don't think temperance accompanies handling the Cup of Christ. It will either consume him, that he never unhand it, or he will guard it all his days. However, none can impede him on account of his blade. His good graces alone would be all to constrain him. Thrice he has requested the company of three. Your approach may work…" Taliesin was full of doubt. And fear. "I will reason with him. Then I will go to Deheubarth and pull Maelgwn out from whatever cave he has made his dwelling place, from under whichever wood he has made his home."

"He is a special young man; have faith, Taliesin."

Gwalchmai and Mordred remained the other clear candidates for succession.

Mordred.

That Arthur had not sought him out whatsoever for inquiry (or an outright secret slaying) further proved that the king of the Britons had indeed murdered his own son, and that he knew that Mordred knew as much. Though a spineless fear of the Pendragon was ever in his bowels, Mordred became emboldened and, with Arthur ever traveling to Eire, to Alba and to Brittany as the war drums began to prattle, he began again to slither into court, causing Gwenhwyfar's bedchamber to be very active during the *last quiet year.* Moreover, Mordred kindled embers of ire amongst the Dynion Hysbys, and tested the waters of speaking against Uncle Arthur. Though they loathed Mordred's outward Catholicism, they received him and, over time, his true beliefs, his religion of *the meaningless of it all* and *keeping your head long enough to get what you want* became clearly known – and embraced.

After all, Arthur the hypocrite, while sermonizing about religious liberty, had shut down their rites. Why? Over the flimsy connection to an unproven murder of a wizard who now appeared likely not dead! *And moreso, Arthur the hypocrite, sermonizing yet more about the right to worship whatsoever gods one pleases, now openly opposes and fans public accusations against the beauty and grandeur of Rome. Why? Over a box and a shrine!*

Mordred began to garner the unspoken endorsement of the Dynion Hysbys. And, for so many tribes, whether in the remote North, Powys or Land's End, the Dynion Hysbys held captive the voice and directional will of the people.

* * *

It was winter of the year five hundred and thirty-and-five when Morgaine of the Faeries was near her birth home, tending to the harsh season's preparations at Llyn Fawr. Evening gave way to night and no star twinkled. 'Twas black as pitch.

"At some point I must question the stability of my own mind, that red eyes staring down at me – naye, through me – are as natural as being happened upon by a bunny or a house pet."

The king of the Tylwyth Teg clicked forefinger against thumb, and his hand became a torch, that the eyes could reveal the outline of a familiar and mostly unwanted elf erect as a great marble pillar before the tiny sorceress.

"Daughter," he began.

"You are not my father!" she snapped and, where a man's knees would knock out of joint for terror, started towards the otherworldly being.

"Your position is rather ambiguous, is it not? How know you that you are not a changeling and of my very loins?"

"Because you cursed the line of the Silures, not that of your own seed!"

Gasps and cackles of impress were let loose. "So wise. Still, look at you. Ambiguous, I say! But the matter of *your seed* be the purpose of my call tonight."

"Gwalchmai? Is he in danger? I had no Sight over it! What is wrong —"

"Not the Hawk of May. Rather, the son of Arthur and Morgaine."

The cruel verbalizing of it brought a rush of tears, not likely concealed by the night.

"Put your dagger away," continued the rude spirit. "I come to beg you, Morgaine of the Fae."

"What would you possibly beg of me?" She was as mouse before a moose, and the moose kept a fearful distance.

Struggling on how to form the words, he fumbled and bumbled, seeking tact that was contrary to his nature. "You must do what is contrary to nature for every mother. I know you love him without condition. I know you to be warm, to be kind — "

"Beg of me to do what!" The mouse now seemed thrice the height and double the girth of the moose.

"Kill Mordred."

"You had a direct hand in bringing him into the world of men, and now you would have me take him out of it?" Instead of the primal witch rising within and perhaps slaying the prince of elves, she was incapacitated by the very notion of the deed, grieving and shrieking at the thought of it as though it were already done. Knowing some riddle-ish explanation would ensue, she gave way to bawling and screaming *why* at the king of the Tylwyth Teg again and again. *Why? Why! Why must I do this thing?*

"We faeries live under peculiar laws and peculiar ways, daughter. It must be done lest not just your *Camelot*, but the whole of the world of men, fall."

"Is that not what you want? Why to you is that a bad thing?" she fired back.

"Man is a foolish, proud, and arrogant master

of the earth, respecting not those who ruled before, but he is far better than who will rule in the next Age. An aeon of tyranny and evil unbridled, a hammer to the head of all creaturekind." He stooped and took the tiny hands of the trembling mother. "And the abomination that *we* wrought unlocks the key to those *Dark Designs.*"

Morgaine gave the Fae the whole of her weight, which he barely noticed. "Then *you* do it."

"I cannot; neither can the Fair Folk."

"Why not?"

"We woeful and sorry damned live under peculiar laws and peculiar ways."

"No mother can put her son to the sword. I cannot bear the burden of even thinking it." Morgaine's thoughts wandered towards Queen Gwenhwyfar I. A rush of regret punished her for the cruelest of words.

The Fae King discerned those thoughts. "You must do what your brother, King Arthur the Just, had the courage to do."

"There is only one King Arthur. I will do it NOT!" She pumped her fists as small mallets upon his chest.

And at once, he had vanished. The wind swooshing over Llyn Fawr was her only company. Gwyar, who was known as Morgaine of the Faeries, wept sore knowing the time was upon her that her secret sins would soon be manifest before all. That the rightful heir, though the wrongful man, was soon to be on the move lest the Tylwyth Teg tortured her for his own amusement.

Darkness arrived early and the fullness of winter came, colder than usual, but no more than reasonable.

Arthur gave Cai a few complaints about his

knee on this day, else his shoulder on the other, his steward having none of it and showing him his own myriad of scars and dents, the two knights goading one another in an effort to remain young.

And the petulant cough that lived in Arthur's lungs roared more frequently, but no more than reasonable.

The twelfth month passed, and the year *Five Hundred and Thirty-Six arrived.*

* * *

Armies seldom attack in winter, but rogues and villains are no respecters of the weather.

Mark, son of Meirchion the Mad, dispatched above five hundred of his confederacy of the rejected and the spiteful to harass and sack Catholic churches all about the north of Gwynedd. Visiting violence on his own allies (and ensuring that neither priest nor bishop was ever present or ever harmed) would force Arthur's hand, drawing him out to either give troops and resources to protect his religious enemies or, better yet, to do nothing and lose credibility amongst the Tribes.

Conducting an atrocity against one's own people as a pretext for war or some great sacrifice of liberty is as old as the lying tongue of prince and man himself. Simon Magus had taught Mark the art, and the uncomely rogue perfected it.

But Arthur, an undefeated leader and genius of tactic and method, sniffed out the ruse.

Two thousand silver-skinned equestrians made an intentionally dramatic, slow tread through the tundra of mud and sleet that was the January soil in Gwynedd. The battle horns screamed, and the use of drum and trumpet mixed with song aided the beauty and terror of the Briton's army, against whom none could stand.

The sum of them, still mounted upon armored steeds, formed a ring of men and metal around one of the chapels, freshly ransacked, smoldering and ruined.

"You're too late!" Two clergymen emerged from the ornate wooden double doors that would not, from the shambled looks of the building, welcome the faithful on this Sunday, or the next. By happenstance, one of the men was Bishop Cadfan. Success and promotion had made the once timid boy a haughty and arrogant man. He had survived Morgaine; now he would take on her brother. "You surround the shell of a building, robbed of artifacts, relics and gold. Dereliction of duty and no regard for the Holy Church!"

Meurig, still lively as a stag, joined his son but was unarmed and in simple coat and tunic, looking the part of a druid or bard, though in reality he was but a father enjoying the field with his lad in the eventide of their years. "A tongue so full of spite ought not to wag; who but a priest would speak thus to the Pendragon of Britain?"

"The head of the dragons. The title fits the man. And look, I have the pleasure of having TWO Pendragons on the scene three hours late with the damage done and the enemy halfway to Eire, or to Mars, by now!"

At the direct and malignant conduct towards his father, Arthur himself was off his horse and eye to eye with Cadfan, whom he smote hard across the cheek, feeling the cowardly cleric crumble and cry out before him.

"Stand," Arthur commanded.

And Cadfan, his crimson arrogance trickling down from his cheek, pooling upon his collar, *stood*.

"You are not entitled for men to leave wife and child, plow and pig, to come and bleed and die for your relics."

"So you will not help us?"

"Stay thy mouth!" Arthur hollered. "You shall not tax the people, nor demand of their treasury to make yourselves fat as you dupe them with your traditions."

"There have been five attacks this month, likened unto this one," Meurig interjected; equal to his cub, this Bear was also a menace and a marvel with command of tones and words. "And we have investigated and heard report of each."

The second priest opted for the cordial approach. "Thanks be to the Lord for your assistance and protection. What evidences have you found? What cause of such outrage against the Lord's Flock?"

"Evidences." Meurig smiled. "Evidences and trends." He folded his arms, already proud of words not yet spoken. "Each time, the relics and gold are stolen with such care and lack of disruption that the marauders either are dainty as water sprites, or have complete and intimate understanding of the layout of the chapel – down to the placement of every bench and pew."

Bishop Cadfan realized he was in the presence of smarter men, and stepped back four paces, placing himself in the shadow of the double doors.

"And more," old King Meurig continued.

"May I have a go?" Arthur clutched at his father's elbow. Every mounted warrior laughed with the unison of Illtud's choir. A horn added musical accompaniment to the light moment.

"Fine," the senior sovereign grumped, and grinned.

"In each case, no bishop or clergymen are found on the scene, and only the laity are assaulted. When, EVER, is a church empty of its clergy amongst your sect? Oft times you live at the church!"

Cadfan gulped hard.

"No supposedly stolen gold, nothing of real damage save the structures themselves and a few tapestries, priests magically missing." Then the Pendragon gave his judgement. "You attack yourselves to raise a flag and rally the people falsely into war! You wanted my army?" Arthur twirled his famed spear thrice in the air and then pointed it towards Owain and Urien, a sample of mighty ones invincible and sharpened from recent and intense training. "Here we are."

"I swear it is not so, my king. 'Tis the confederacy of the son of Meirchion—"

"Meirchion, your mentor. You are the disciple of your pretend enemy!" Arthur cut off the priest hard, giving no place to his games. "Say what you will to the people. I just trust that they can discern truth." Arthur motioned for a young man of eighteen to be brought forth.

The young man brimmed with excitement and thankfulness every time fortune allowed him to be in the presence of the just and great king. With quill and vellum at the ready, the historian Gildas looked as a starving soldier before some great feast.

"Document these things, my historian." The Iron Bear hugged the boy hard.

Cadfan hissed within, as Arthur had made a close ally of a son of his most bitter rival in the North (as he had done with the sons of Maelgwn and all the line of Cunedda). Gildas ap Caw, though of the Roman sect himself, hated corruption and the abuses of power, and was happy to document the historical facts and conclusions objectively.

"The raids will cease. You will not damage roads or fences or farms, or frighten damsels and the youth in your theatre." Arthur was using the pitch and tone he used to use ere he slayed a Saxon invader. Cadfan's heart began to fail for fear, and even some of the younger knights were phantom-white with dread and awe, having had no exposure to *real military authority* in their happy lives of fat and feast and no want.

"The army is here," Arthur again asserted, making a simple hand signal that caused the circle to close as a slow vice round the church. "And you speak of relics. The coffin of the Blessed Lady. You will return it to Ynys Enlli in a fortnight, or I will raze every church of your denomination from tip to top in these Isles. You will make an idol of her no more!"

"I beg you to believe my innocence, for the raiders desecrated the shrine of the Heavenly Mother but yesterday, leaving only splinters of the box. Of course there is no body, no bones, for like the Lord, she ascended!"

Arthur now, as his sister had learned afore, realized the full magnitude of the plot to deify Mary. The false attacks were not just to bring criticism upon Arthur's increasingly harsh polices against Rome and her encroachments. More than this, they served as cover to forever control the coffin of Mary and force Arthur to either reveal that he and the Mistress of Avalon were hiding her bones from the people, or to allow the lie of her nature and essence to go forward. This was a losing prospect in either event, as men would simply worship the bones as had Israel worshiped the Brazen Serpent, the rod of Aaron, the bones of Moses should Michael make known their resting place, and so many other material things associated with the spiritual and the good. *Oh, the idolatry of man! The death toll and expense of bones and rings and cups!*

"I will make it known by policy that your doctrine is a lie."

"That is not the place of the State, lord." Cadfan found courage.

"Men can believe as they will, but Caermelyn will not remain neutral on this matter. Of your baptisms and tonsures and vestments and robes, we care not for the empty squabbles of vain men."

"You sound like the demented wizard who spewed his blasphemous words against the traditions of the Church. Meirchion was right to —"

Arthur thrust *Rhon*, his spear, down hard through the foot of Cadfan as a master fisherman, patient and still, at once strikes violently to pierce a great fish, pinning him to the ground. The spear plunged as if to the heart of the earth itself. The screams and cries of the *Man of God* and his pleas for relief moved not the Iron Bear.

"But of your lies about Mary, we will not remain neutral for as long as I have breath yet in me. I have firsthand knowledge of your lies and it is no violation of liberty for a leader, who is but a man, to share the truth of a thing with his neighbor, though he sits at a public council." Arthur gave Rhon a twist, making dust of the small bones in Cadfan's foot. "Do you maintain that these *raiders* stole the coffin, or will I have it in a fortnight?"

Knowing the punishment of Magus exceeded

the justice of Arthur, Cadfan the Crippled held taut the line of his lie. "The rebel Mark's men have it, lord, not the Church of God."

Arthur's visage added to the pain of his pierced foot caused Cadfan to swoon and fall, unconscious.

"No more raids!" the Iron Bear screamed at the inert body.

The army helped rebuild and repair damages to farm or land near the chapel, tended the wounded, and returned to Caermelyn, Arthur thinking of his Merlin without ceasing on the journey home.

* * *

"Taliesin." Arthur gazed into the hearth that gave warmth to a large hall of books and scrolls, organized from floorboard to vault. The king was at once happy and saddened to be home. "My *first Merlin* and I spent a lifetime of hours in this library, seemingly three lifetimes ago. His manifestation during the bout with Lancelot. His appearances. His supposed hunt for the Masked Priest. I heard his voice. Maelgwn heard his voice. We saw him. Or did we? Are these—"

"The illusions begotten by hope?" Taliesin offered a conclusion, knowing his lord worried that he was slipping into bereaved madness.

"Yes." Direct, full of melancholy.

"As your *current Merlin*, I say to you that too many witnesses have seen your childhood mentor and beloved friend. The Scriptures declare, in the practical wisdom, *'by the mouth of two or three witnesses, let all things be established.'*"

Arthur's countenance lifted somewhat. "Speaking of Scriptures, what does your unique theology hold regarding Merlin? Did he return from the grave? What is he? Give me your understanding, bard."

"The dead cannot contact the living. Thus, he is not an apparition. This leaves a few possibilities."

Arthur was aglow with interest, begging the Merlin Taliesin to pause his teaching that he might fetch a cider, remove his boots, repose and listen. Doing this (and it pleased Taliesin to see his sovereign allow himself to ease upon a long Roman-styled couch in the library) and clutching a simple sword, as all warriors do when they rest, he bade Taliesin continue.

The little Christian druid pointed at the weapon. "It is time to wield Excalibur again, Arthur. What is the king without his sword?"

"What is a king who strikes his ally in jealousy wrought by speculation and not fact?" Erect upon an elbow, the king became irritated, yet not angered. "Back to Merlin!"

"Well. Either Merlin survived what befell him in Broceliande, which is unlikely. Or Merlin is not a man, which seems probable, and if not a man, is not subject to the laws of man. Or, lastly, the Fae are involved. And there is no Bible for what the Fair Folk do!"

They laughed.

"If Merlin is not mortal, can he be saved?"

"The question that plagues us all, Lord Arthur. In this dispensation of the Grace of God, how will He handle the remnants of times past? I know not – only that I can only trust His grace and mercy."

"It is hard to answer the question, which plagues beggar and lord nightly, about what becomes of any of us when we pass into the sleep of death. The greater burden for me" – Arthur's throat tightened and his voice cracked – "is this. Why, if he be alive or half alive or a quarter part alive, why is he not here? Why not return, in whatever his state, to Glamorgan?"

"Drink your cider down quickly. And then have another," Taliesin insisted, and Arthur did the same. The bard, with uneven gait, bungled about in a closet, revealing a perfectly folded, stained and war-tattered battle standard. Unfolding the flag with reverence, he pointed to the Red Dragon, the symbol of victory, the sigil of peace. "Forget not Merlin's prophecies ere he came to see the Mysteries of God given us by Paul. Whether given by devil, by intuition, or by special knowledge, Merlin saw that the days of the Summer Kingdom were numbered." Taliesin made a great pause, that the statement would settle within the king, whose ears and heart were opened to hearing it by mild drunkenness.

"The comet," the rosy-cheeked Bear stated.

"Aye. You were born under its sign, and you are meant to emerge victorious from what dread might come should it return."

"You can't offer me the strong scrumpy sup and then layer upon me comments vague and broad. Plain words, *New Merlin*, speak plainly!"

The men laughed, for Arthur, a model of self-control and moderation had, in the self-same day, angrily run through a priest's foot with an enchanted spear and become drunk on potent apple spirits.

"Very well." Taliesin smiled. "I speculate. I theorize. But I do not know. Perhaps Merlin knows that he cannot stop the end of the Summer Kingdom, so he is trying to stop the end of the world. He cannot control a fiery serpent from above hurling itself upon mountain, valley and wood. But he can find and stop your adversary. He can kill the man who has funded wars and turned Silures into traitors and used whole nations as pawns to further his iniquity. If Merlin can find him, then he serves us being better out there than in here."

Somber words aided rapid sobriety. "But the Evil One escaped our grasp. Will Merlin hunt him the world over that he returns not? For I miss him sore."

"Are you not afraid of the comet?" asked Taliesin.

"We are undefeated against men and steed and steel. Giants and witches and monsters that befit children's fables have we slain in our lifetime. But against a calamity like that, I have no answer and no fear. If the sky is to fall, then let us do good and keep the light of our glorious kingdom shining bright until that day. And let our conduct be as if that day will never come, and as though it will come tomorrow."

"And you bade me speak in plain words."

The friends enjoyed another laugh.

"What about Gwenhwyfar?" Arthur posed a curious open question to the bard he had borrowed from Maelgwn.

"Lord?"

"Does Merlin *the phantom* stay away because he likes her not and cannot be around our *situation?*"

"Like you, Merlin had one great love and one great lust in his life. And like you, he struggled greatly to untangle the heart's fog that mists the senses and impedes discernment over which is which. Were he here, he would see much of himself in you. It would bother him and he would pester you with goads and riddles and unwanted advice."

"Like unto you and Maelgwn."

"Precisely!" Taliesin grinned. He traced the dragon a few times and then put away the flag. "But no, Lord Arthur, he would not stay away or forsake you on account of *her*."

"Thank you, Chief of Bards. Any other wisdom, druidic or Christian, to pass on ere I repose for the night? The hour is advanced, and I am certain that Cai wants me to sleep that he might do the same soon."

"The Catholics," Taliesin offered.

"Need I another cider ere I hear this?" said Arthur, half musingly.

"Maybe." Taliesin touched his sovereign upon the shoulder. Though younger than Arthur, Taliesin had had a paternal manner about him from his youth; he was a man full of divine inspiration, *the Awen.* "Remember the lesson that Merlin gave you about leaders and people?"

Arthur perked up, remembering it well. How Merlin had said that sometimes good people had bad leaders and other times bad people had good leaders, and that the truly special times in history were when good people were supported by good leaders. Unspoken communication ensued, then Taliesin followed with few words.

"The Catholic people are the most beautiful souls. They love the Lord, they care for the poor with devotion and sincerity; in morality there are none better, in kindness, none softer. We Britons are not evangelical. Though intensely spiritual, we are inward; they are outward. If Christ is to go to the nations, it will be because of Rome, not Britannia. Fight their corruption, but be mindful not to lose the people in the process."

King Arthur, a humble king receptive to the wisdom of others and never above reproach, absorbed the words. Many candles were spent, meeting their waxy, nubby ends, as he remained silent in the library for hours, pondering the complex problem that Magus, the Northern kings given to Church-sanctioned corruption, and the bishops presented; a canker gnawing upon his Summer Kingdom. *Be mindful not to lose the people.*

Prior to twilight he looked up, peering at the top of a great shelf, filled from floorboard to ceiling with tomes and scrolls. Filled with memories of sitting at the feet of Merlin.

"Merlin! Where are you?" he cried, his stately voice giving way to a mourning that would not abate. "I need you!"

Suddenly one scroll, provoked by chance or by magic, was dislodged from its slot and fluttered down to the floor. A folio of Scripture, penned with ink of the highest quality, scribed in ornate Latin, lighted gentle as a feather upon Arthur's feet (for he had not moved from the cushion of his chair) at the place where the Scripture read: *'And there appeared another wonder in heaven: and behold a great Red Dragon.'*

* * *

The bitter winter of the first two moons of the year ended, and spring was nigh.

* * *

The People.
The Common Man.
The cattleman.
The sower and the reaper.
The carpenter.
The miner.

These cared not about a missing wizard. They cared that they could eat. They cared not about Maelgwn Gwynedd, his bubble or his madness, and certainly not his propensity for other men's wives – especially of his kinsmen and close friends. They cared that they had eggs and milk and hay. These men, and the women that loved them, had no regard for a meddling Devil-worshipper puppeteering politicians from the shadow. They cared about the harvest, good wood and the ability to heat their homes.

But they did care about Arthur the Silure Lord and Emperor of the Isles in the Sea.

He was more than a crimson cape and blue-helmeted highborn to them. He was their hope, he was their kinsman, he was the reason the crops never failed and the hens gave eggs and the calves were fat. Remove all the dross from the golden city of Caerleon and the shimmering fortress of Caermelyn, and what remained that was of value to the common man was the crop and King Arthur. King Arthur and the crop.

Spring came.

The crop failed.

An orange haze arrived with the winds and lingered, ever filling the air, night or day. Smokey, with grit and content, yet air. A cough and an issue of blood among the weak and the young soon followed the haze. The yield of fruit and grain was the lowest in memory, even amongst the elders who had witnessed many springs, had reaped many harvests.

Mark's collection of rebels continued to harass Hoel in Britanny. Also, they hacked and carved and raided until at last they had won a lasting presence in Kernwy, a cooperative vassal kingdom and partner-state to the Silures. This gave Mark a southern position below Arthur. Though still too small to be a grave threat or resurrect the *War Years*, the thorn was growing, causing the Round Table many expeditions to the Continent (or south to the horn of the Isles). The frequent and ongoing absences resulted in a void whereby the opportunistic bishops and Dynion Hysbys could stir the people, speculating and upsetting the masses with theory and speculation over the cause of the crop failure.

The Roman Catholics blamed, of course, Arthur's sins in refusing to provide financial and military support in obedience to the needs of the Church. And not a few whispers of his taking a second wife and being smitten with impotence by an angry God found many ears in pubs and fields and times of gossip. His sins, compounded with the Cymry bishops' continued refusal to eat with, baptize or read Scripture to the Saxon tribes under Cedric in Llogyr, had brought the judgment of God, so said the priests.

Saints Illtud and Bedwini instead hurled accusation at Rome for desecrating the resting place of the Sacred Lady. This was a misplaced strategy that allowed Rome to simply state that Mary had been translated into heaven, unless the Britons could produce her body. As the Church *could not* and Gwyar *would not*, the mythos and cult of Mary blossomed even as the crops slept.

Ironically, the majority of citizens, those not princes and priests, scoffed at the superstitious jangling of both sects, yet with religious devotion cleaved unto the old gods. They turned to the Dynion Hysbys to understand the haze, the illness, and the arrested growth of fruit, vegetable and tree.

"The cough that is in our lord's chest has

manifested as a cough and diseased lung upon our land. He is sick, having no heir. Heal Arthur and heal the land."

"But he is not here! He fights the Son of Cornwall and the Franks o'er in Brittany!" The collective and recurring cry of the people.

"Then let us look to one to rule in his stead until he returns. Let us turn to the most eligible and proper heir, Mordred son of Cynfarch ap Meirchion and Gwyar ferch Meurig Pendragon. Let him unify the land as a proxy whilst our High King restores Brittany and once again frees his mighty sword from the stone, erecting it in splendor towards the Sun that it might find fertile soil and yield again." These were the words, or similar, spoken oft by the Adder. He was full of double meaning and plotting, for the people knew Mordred to be the rightful heir on account of being the son of Arthur, not the son of a Northern Chieftain. These impish anti-druids, playing games upon men as if they were the Tylwyth Teg, would insert Mordred as an "Aliteryn" or sub-king, and when the crops yet failed and plague yet scarred and sickened, they would reveal with feigned awe and dismay that they had unknowingly put forth a bastard born of incest on the throne, manifesting the *real curse* upon the land. This would force Arthur to abdicate, or worse. Mordred would be rejected as well, and Mark or a son of Caw, or even Maelgwn the Mad Exiled Hound, would ascend the throne. At last they would have revenge on the Wizard who spurned them; at last the Council of Nine or the corrupt within the Church would rule the land, leaving the Dynion Hysbys installed to mystify, regulate and control the masses on behalf of whatever wickedness reigned from high places.

And so it was, with spring vegetables scarce

and trees giving no spring bud, with children coughing blood and elderly men swooning with dehydration never to rise, that Simon Magus through his puppet Mark set about to destroy Cymru from the Continent, and the Dynion Hysbys to replace Arthur from within.

But the heathen tribal leaders miscalculated the degree to which the people loved Arthur. For those who are devoid of love can never appreciate the love extended by others.

"We will not yet entertain the proposal of Mordred as a proxy. Find another way." This was the collective command of the Tribes from Ynys Mons to Deheubarth, and all tribes and clans in between besides.

CHAPTER 23
The Red Dragon, the Sword, and the Cup

Seed 6 – "Not my son! You have now let the rituals of the tribes ruin two more lives."

The will of the people was made known to the local chieftains and princes, who in turn passed their judgment to Taliesin, who presented the news privately to Meurig, Onbrawst, Ittud, Bedwini, Dewi and Cadfan.

"First." The hunchbacked sage looked more weighty and distressed than ever, speaking as though he were carrying nine oxen. "I have convinced them to give us more time. One failed harvest and a mysterious gaseous wind shall not remove the diadem from our Pendragon!"

"How much time?" Meurig, more than any present or living, understood the verity of the ancient customs that connected High King to the output of the land.

"The fall harvest." Taliesin was ashen, grave. "A baby or a crop yield by fall."

"There are but seven months until autumn! It is one mandate and no choice!"

"I agree, my lady," responded Taliesin. "The people would have you validate that Gwenhywfar is not these past few months with child. They are being slow and diligent and hoping against hope that an heir doth grow in her belly even now."

Onbrawst was dignified in her indignance. "I have not the closeness of relationship with *our queen* to examine her fingernails, let alone her womb."

"My love, have a nursemaid accompany you; I pray you do it." Meurig was sensitive to his true love. "It is for our son. They will slay him."

At the saying of this, tears welled and ran freely from all, save Cadfan, who was as stone.

"And if there be no heir and no crop by the tenth month of the year? What then would the Cymry do with their Pendragon and" – Meurig the Cheerful's voice broke, giving lumpy and disjointed words – "my son? What then would the people do with my son, my King Arthur?"

"Will it be the nephew Mordred, or perhaps will affections return to the Hawk of May?" asked Bishop Bedwini.

"It will not be a son of Gwyar." Taliesin spoke plainly. "It will be Arthur." He panned the room, nodding and confirming, and bewildering them. "They want to keep their King Arthur as much as we do."

"Then what befalls in Autumn?" Onbrawst was understandably confused.

"A prince full of virtue and virility will draw the sword and stand as substitute, dying for the king, and the king will rise in his stead, reborn anew for another cycle of seasons."

"Are we not a nation of logic and reason?" Cadfan interjected, unable to bite his tongue. "If Arthur were to be lame and unable to lead in battle or facilitate matters of strategy and course then by all means, do a little ritual and retire him. But this ritual is nonsensical. Let us just take a firm hand and insert Mordred if and when Arthur should fall."

The bishops of the Britons did not disagree with part of Cadfan's assessment. However, the light of Christ had not penetrated the working and farming classes. Though a Christian nation in its foundational rights of man and natural law, the new faith remained yet a novelty for the rich in the minds of the agrarians who spent day and night tilling, watering, planting or hunting. Disregard for the most serious of their rites and customs would result in a refusal from them to send sons to become soldiers and knights, a refusal to sell or trade in the markets. The Cymry did not favor laws to solve problems, neither brute force or tyranny; rather, the power of abstinence, peaceful opposition and withdrawing from free markets. The power was with the people, and the slow conversion to Christ and the swap of Church superstition for Pagan was not yet.

After hearing and promptly silencing the dissenting voice, Taliesin revealed the candidate selected to *give his life that Arthur might live.*

"The slain and risen king will be Rhufawn the Fair, son of Maelgwn, the Galahad of the Isles in the Sea."

It seemed that for three minutes, even the birds of heaven and the rush of the manifold streams that treated Cymru with their song were silent. There was no sound. There was nothing to debate.

The next harvest or a babe must come.

"If the time comes, I will be the one to inform to Lancelot." Taliesin had spent the sum of

Galahad's life rearing him to replace Arthur, but not after this manner. And his whole life rebuking and spurning Lancelot, because though the new Merlin hated the sins, he loved the man.

* * *

No babe grew within the belly of Gwenhwyfar the Adulteress.

* * *

Beltane came. The cloudy orange haze had not abated; rather, matters worsened, as an ash of unknown origin swirled about for hours every day.

"It is the coals burning in the lanterns of the dragon's nostrils, is it not?" Arthur knew the answer to his own question. He and Madoc and Anwn Ddu walked along the river ports in Gwent, overseeing a plentitude of ships provisioning for departure. Taliesin with his uneven, nigh hobbled gait lagged behind.

"I believe it is, lord; the comet is slowly making its way to the earth, and his breath hides the Sun and rains poison and ash."

"So be it, bard. I am not leaving."

But the Black Knight was emphatic. "You must. We know not how much worse this will wax; the Royal Family must live, and return to reign again. Moreover, we need your leadership; Hoel —"

"I'm sorry, brother, Hoel must fight this one alone. I will not leave whilst my people choke and suffer boils and blisters and starve from this sickness." Arthur paused his promenade and waited for his counselor to join his pace. "Taliesin, what would Merlin do?"

"Merlin saw these things, and it would appear they are coming to pass. He would make you leave as Anwn bids you. You are their hope, even in exile. There is no glory in dying with them in this way."

Arthur abruptly changed the subject. He turned to his brother, the Sea Master, Prince Madoc. "Get thee hence from the Isles. We are neither conquerors nor invaders, but if there be land overrun by wild beast or Giant or creeping thing that can sustain us, find it and return unto me with tidings and findings and charts." Arthur embraced his brother hard and shared with him how much he loved him and how proud of him he was for safely guarding the entryway to Cymru for so many decades. Knowing the expedition might not include a return voyage, many fond recollections were shared, and farewells were forbidden. "Take the vessels with bolts and rivets of wood and see that supplies of iron are minimized."

Madoc obeyed, readying ships designed for long voyages. These boats could not be shaken apart by the magnetism of the vast sea or the circuits of the moon. Many thousands of men fled Cymru by way of the Usk River, which fed the sea.

"Anwn, has Greidawl returned from his mission in the Nordic lands?"

"He awaits you in Lyon, lord." The Black Knight attempted to lure the king by any means onto a barge.

"What news then? You give the report." The effort was blocked.

Anwn Ddu acquiesced and reported. "Climate change and local tyrants are causing many Geats and Danes to join King Mark upon the Continent.

They are viewed as criminals and banished men and their local tribes neither regard nor miss them. Greidawl was discovered by a young king called Beowulf. They met in single combat and Greidawl was injured. Beowulf followed Greidawl back to the cave that was made his hiding place and the Geatish King saw the mother of Greidawl, who even in her advanced age is fair, being rumored a child of the Fae."

"A fair Fae like unto her cousin Vivien she is." Arthur paused, reflected and smiled. "So these tribes of the Geats and Danes raise no army to invade Cymru?"

"Nay, lord. Mark gathers only vagabonds and desperate criminals."

"Send Greidawl back but once more to the Germanic lands, and ensure the same."

Suddenly Bedwyr appeared, upon steed. Cai was complicit in the loving but disobedient plot, and already aboard the king's ship. Arthur's hinder side was unprotected and his sword sheathed. Bedwyr leapt from his mount and tackled Arthur hard to the ground. The Black Knight controlled the wrists of the mighty king, who was eating dirt and spewing curses not befitting his office. Three more men joined, and they were needed. The struggle cost some dignity, some a few teeth, but at last King Arthur was upon a vessel meant to leave for Brittany.

Before apologies could be spoken, the Red Dragon arrived.

The sun darkened, and the moon gave not her light. The stars appeared to have fled, and only a red spike from the tail of the dragon could be seen; a red bolt of lightning contrasted against a black night (though it were yet daytime). The spike itself was taller than Cymru's tallest mountain, and it cut through the earth as a table saw finishes its final draw. Instead of sawdust and flakes of birch, the spike drew lava and rock from well beneath the surface of the earth.

The screams and confusion were deafening.

The hilltop fortress of Caermelyn *melted*. The white marble that was not thrown to the plain below was molten and became part of the mountain top; white splotches were where the gilded city had once stood.

Caerleon was on fire, yet stood.

There were no screams at first. Those who died simply vanished, consumed by the dragon. Scores were caught in the path of the spike and now part of the ash that covered the mountain. Trees were victims as well, reduced to stumps, to nubs, or to nothing.

Then the spike withdrew and the dragon flew straight up, up, towards the heavens. His ascent revealed the sun and let the living witness the devastation. Moreover, pitch and oils had begun to boil the river and pockets of flames rested upon the waters, creating lanterns, illuminating the deaths.

Now came the screams.

The rattles.

The moans of dismay.

From the river could be seen the little monastery where dwelt Queen Gwenhywfar I, and next to that, another small hall connected to the church that was used as a school. Knowing it as a safe and sturdy place, many children fled to the school.

By chance, Arthur glanced upon the monastery and caught a glimpse of the children, at risk of perishing as fires surrounded the hall, its roof giving way. The vessel had shifted from the port's bank; its tethers burned away, it began to drift. Arthur dove into the boiling water, the great cries of his kinsman and mates shouting in protest above him.

At once he appeared upon the shore, blackened, hair singed, cape ablaze, boots gashed or gone. Discarding his burning garments without breaking stride, the High King was soon upon Gwenhwyfar's cell.

Their eyes met.

But six words were spoken. "I do well! To the children!"

He did not speak, but Arthur embraced his former spouse, who felt as a skeleton in his strong arms. She vanished quickly, making haste towards her abode of old, navigating small side streets, running a labyrinth of flame and screechy chaos.

Meanwhile, he was at once inside the ancient stone structure joined to the church.

One by one he carried them to a tavern located across the bridge. It had not been stricken by the comet and was afforded some protection by the river, surrounded by a small pitch with no dry foliage to burn, nor trees to help the fires skip rooftops and devour the building.

The Red Dragon beguiled the Cymry, feigning that it was making ready to fly on to the destruction of some other country. Instead it reached its zenith, turned and plunged again towards the earth, in effortless free fall as a bird of prey.

Arthur held the last of the children in his arms; his outline was visible below a small arch in an anteroom where he might leap from the church, which was no longer the grey and brown of stone and oak but rather the whites and oranges, the blues, of angry coal. The mass of the celestial serpent rendered the summer's day pitch black once more, the tip of its tail making Gwent a wasteland. Witnesses saw a tall hooded figure absorb Arthur and the small child at the very moment that they were in turn absorbed by flame and ash. Arthur was absorbed by shadow.

* * *

As suddenly as judgment had come upon Britain, he was gone. Next came Eire, which looked as a burning lantern bobbing and rolling in the sea. Then the Dragon volleyed three-hundred-score balls of fire into the oceans, breaching the crust of the earth and the gates of the Deep. Volcanoes erupted and ash covered much of the earth. Though it was summer, a winter of ash and darkness beset the land – all lands, but especially the Isles in the Sea.

The new version of *dawn* came, and with it, some daylight. Reality was suddenly a dusk that gave way to darkness by noon time.

One thousand times one thousand Cymry were cremated by the Red Dragon.

But the luminary serpent rogue visited a death count much higher upon the Tribes of Llogyr. What twenty years of repair and replenish had begotten (for these tribes had been located nearest the Saxon Shores during the war years and were yet recovering from decades of rape, plunder and butchery) was annihilated in the space of thirteen minutes. Two thirds of the population, dead.

The northern invaders, were they organized and intending to do the same, could have walked onto the whole of the eastern half of Britannia and simply settled it as their own. Conquest by Comet. However, thanks to the might of Maelgwn, the strategy of Merlin, and the leadership of Arthur, the Germans had no present intention. They were still not ready. Twenty years was not long enough to make enough fighting-aged boys and train them for another go at the undefeated Britons.

By fortune or chance, Cedric and his small kingdom of Wessex, which had been peaceful and kept the covenants placed upon it by the Silures, was not visited by the Red Dragon, who killed with the precision of a surgeon's blade but three hundred yards from the Saxon borders.

The songs of the bards recorded how the Summer Kingdom, born in December of the year five hundred and sixteen, received its first of three great death blows in June of five hundred and thirty-six.

Merlin had predicted and dreaded that the days of the Golden Age were numbered. In accord with his visions, he had hidden well the treasures, all of which survived and were safely concealed upon Ynys Enlli, save for the Grail, which was held on an island castle that was unharmed by the serpent's assault. As for evacuating or displacing the people, this was not possible. There was no preventing what came to pass, nor adding to the years of such a gilded age; rather only the redeeming cherish of the years that they had had.

And cherish them Arthur and his noble companions did, their sins and failings notwithstanding.

His land lay dying, but the High King lived.

How he had escaped the school, and who had

shielded and then carried him to safety, was a mystery.

Arthur was conducted to a teeny daughter isle called Flat Holm, where seventy guards kept rotated watch over him day and night without ceasing.

The cantrefs were full of disease and filth without exception. Taliesin and Illtud calculated that it would take two years or more to clean and remove the ash. A country filled with satins and silks and white marble where the architecture had been a bright and clean striking contrast against the greens and romantic overcast of Cymru was now simply and impossibly *dirty.*

The water supplies were poisoned, both by the Dragon's venom and by human waste. Illtud was a master of both sanitation and the mechanisms of sea and fresh water, and set about to divert bad water and cycle in good through a complex system of dykes and purification centers. But the process would be slow and arduous.

All of the Round Table Knights had survived. All princesses, princes, and chieftains too. Like Arthur, the renowned were forbidden from stepping foot upon the mainland, even if they had to be kept away by the edge of sword, or the tip of arrow.

The concern was twofold. First that the Dragon might return to finish his ugly work. Secondly, that disease or plague would eat the living and the dead.

The leadership was thus removed whilst the Dynion Hysbys, locally, and the Church, nationally, determined what must be done.

* * *

Simon Magus and his secret college watched the Isles in the Sea burn from an exceedingly high place in Tours.

"Is this the Tribulation, and the End of Days?" asked one of the Nine.

"If Israel had received Christ, then John the Baptist would have been—" He paused, demanding that his subordinates continue to demonstrate their understanding of the principle of 'delay' found throughout the Scriptures.

"Elijah," answered another.

"Indeed." Magus beamed. "Much remains to be seen – if the wandering luminary be Wormwood, or if we look for another."

"What must occur next?"

"Taliesin's *rapture*, I suppose." A mocking laughter by each of the Nine was as crackle and pop added to the flames. "The Cup of Christ: it must fall into the hands of the daughter of Pendragon, for the ancient evil that indwells her can bring again Judas Iscariot from his place, and put him within Arthur." Simon looked hard at the smolder and ruin of the Coveted Isles. "Much to manipulate and prepare, if that peculiar place is to rise from despair and bring forth a King of Kings." His excited breaths panged off the inner metal shell of the mask. "The Holy Grail must be found."

* * *

Three months later, The Holy Grail was found.

Though this be another bard's song, Peredur was there, and his mate Gwrgi too. But 'twas Rhufawn the Fair who achieved it. *And Vivien wailed sore and vexed herself nigh unto death that she could not prevent this.*

But Rhufawn did well with the burden of it at the first. He possessed it; it did not possess him. Taliesin's dread had just begun to be tempered when word came from the druids and the Dynion Hysbys.

It is a fearful thing when all sects and denominations agree. Unison typically means bad tidings and that confusion, or error, or superstition is running unchecked. Disunity and opposition provoke thought; dissent guards against the mob, contrarianism shields liberty.

There would be no dissent here.

"This is what it means to be free, to be ruled by the Law, to be subordinate to the people. We are but stewards and no overlords." King Meurig held Taliesin as a father holds a small child who has lost a parent, *or faces the loss of a son.* Tears and sweat rushed from every pore, the ground ran damp with his sorrow, and the great senior king minded not the mess. "Your Awen allows no possibility that it might work."

"None." The Christian bard had been forged hard by the Pauline Mysteries passed down from his family, and his worldview and belief demanded that the Grail was a dead idol at best, a thing allowed to be used as a toy for Satan at worst. But as an instrument for bringing miracles, this was a thing of times past and for Israel alone; no. This was contrary to the dispensational truth found in God's word. "It is an hour of grace, which demands it be an hour of faith and belief, not signs and sight."

"And the fiery beast that laid waste to field and stream, menaced village and castle, killed with indifferent discretion. Was he not a sign?" Meurig questioned the weeping sage with all sincerity.

"No." Taliesin's answer was immediate

and authoritative. "The heavenly beings run in circuits, declaring the veracity of the Creator from before men could read or write. In the principalities and dominions above something went awry, and the hosts of heaven rebelled." More weeping. "Merlin used math to calculate the return of the wandering monster, not prophecy or sign or mysticism. Its cause is well known in that realm but to us, it was a random cataclysm. Chance."

"And God did not intervene."

"He could not."

"You flirt with blasphemy, or atheism." Meurig's voice flared.

"Grace looks like atheism, for it sees not an angel behind every sneeze, a sign under every rock. God intervenes not upon this crude matter." Suddenly, the bard clasped the brawn of Meurig's shoulder. "He has a plan for the living part of us, the *spirit*. He did not do this to us."

"And He didn't stop it either." Meurig doubted. "We have no choice, Taliesin. When I was incapacitated, they demanded that I retire. I had Arthur and he…" These words choked up the old king, leaving two men weeping. "And he has Rhufawn." Meurig gave Taliesin instruction that he find Lancelot and inform him that his son would serve as proxy in sacrificing Arthur to the land, in hopes that Arthur would rise again. The people would not wait for the Fall harvest.

Lancelot, along with Gwalchmai, were the only two Round Table Knights unaccounted for during the forced temporary exiles. Even many of the Royal Clans' animals and livestock were relocated to Brittany or to remote finger-islands unscathed by the catastrophe. Even Arthur's war dogs had been found, but the Hawk of May was rumored lost and none dared try and forcefully evacuate Lancelot.

* * *

However, the Hawk of May was not lost; he was spying on Lancelot, whom he crept upon as he slept beneath the bleeding Yew Tree, very near to the forest where he made his home.

The curls were still present, but the raven-black hair had given way to the look of polished silver coin. The eyes were yet the best of blues and the chin was still chiseled, now covered with a perfect short beard (though never cut, never trimmed, never groomed). Even as a hermit, Lancelot was magnificent.

"I hate you." Gwalchmai kicked at his wartime companion, who was in and out of sleep, or perhaps in a trance. The kick was playful, in part. "But I love you. Without you, we would speak the Saxon tongue, if we had breath to speak at all."

Lancelot rose, a towering menace, a bloodhound that durst not be provoked. "I hate you." The voice was a steel fork raking across a panel of brass. "But I love you. Without you, we would be a nation of slaves and no men. Better miserable and free than a fed slave." A moment of mutual glaring ensued. Lancelot's gaze, as steel, broke first as he caught a glimpse of Gwalchmai's wild red hair and freckled glow. Lancelot broke first, and embraced his Round Table fellow.

Crisis drives some apart; some it brings together.

"I would have killed you years ago, but—"

"Then my mother would have killed you!" Gwalchmai smiled. "You fear her."

"Precisely." The solitary warrior, oft alone save his *others*, welcomed the jostling that only men-at-arms understand. "I do fear her. Moreover" – his tone turned thoughtful – "she and I are childhood friends. Real friends. Four chords we were, inseparable. She sacrificed much, and you are here because she set aside her own needs for those of her kinsman. Never could I harm the issue of the patriot and war goddess Gwyar, for I greatly revere her. And I greatly respect you."

Here then were Gwalchmai and Lancelot reconciled, and none present to witness it. For but one positive word, one report of good gossip, would have placed Gwalchmai on the throne, with Arthur's full blessing and with Lancelot's backing. Thus would the kingdom have been salvaged; thus would the Summer Kingdom have continued.

"What has become of our Blessed Isle?" Gwalchmai moaned.

"Would that I could find my foster-mother; she would know whether or not this is the end of the Age." Lancelot looked round – the forest was filthy with ash, the air barely breathable. "Give me leave to make some preparations and return unto me again at eventide, and we will set out to find the Lady of Lake."

"A quest for two old knights?" Gwalchmai beamed, and a single shard of sun fought desperately, breaking through the chalky sky.

Lancelot nodded.

Three minutes after Gwalchmai departed, Taliesin arrived.

* * *

"A full day for guests here at the edge of the world," the tall Briton snarked.

"It is good to see you too," the short Briton rebutted.

Seeing Taliesin's disposition, his bloodshot eyes and inability to look upward, Lancelot knew the tidings were poor.

"Gwenhwyfar – is she — ?"

"The queen is safe. She was conducted to Leon in Brittany and her health is well, save that she grieves her father, whom the Dragon took."

"Was the body recovered?" Lancelot asked, hurting for his true love.

"Nay; amongst those disintegrated upon impact, a necklace charm alone remaining to indicate that it was he."

"I am very sorry to hear this." Lancelot clutched at the special cruciform about his own neck. "And Arthur?"

"He is ill, but yet has life, and has been put into exile until the air is again clean."

"The air will never again be clean," offered the king of the North.

"Our darkest days are not even yet, Maelgwn. We must endure."

Puzzled at the usually hopeful Taliesin's lack of optimism, Lancelot's questions of his random guest shifted to his children. The bard gave account of each of them, and then ran out of space for delay.

"And Rhufawn?"

"Your son, known home and abroad as the Perfect Knight, the chosen vessel, and the Galahad — " Taliesin's voice broke, and his words and thoughts became disorganized. "Arthur is sick. The Land is sick. Tribes fear starvation. Arthur is sick."

Maelgwn Gwynedd, on account of his unique and diversified upbringing, had had exposure to all the sundry religions and competing worldviews amongst the especially spiritual people of the Isles. When his madness pestered him not, he studied, and read, and studied more. More than a mountain of muscle and an insatiable male member, the complex person living as a hermit in a prison of his own sins and lusts fully understood the garbled nonsense of his former bard.

"He has achieved the Grail?"

"He has," Taliesin answered.

"And my mother?"

"We know not how it was achieved. Only that she shared our concerns for the young man and desired not these things. And is herself missing, feared taken by the Dragon."

A single sentence. A double loss. Maelgwn breathed it in, stopped breathing, and then exhaled violently. "The Lady of the Lake cannot be slain by some fire serpent; she lives."

"I hope you are right, and I believe the same." Taliesin drew some strength from Maelgwn's resolve, and verbalized what the Bloodhound Prince already knew. "Galahad has achieved the Grail, and he will heal the land, and be king." Maelgwn fully comprehended the layers of these words. "Arthur will never suffer this to be so." Taliesin did not argue the point, for he assumed that Maelgwn knew that Arthur was kept from the fullness of the ritual and would simply stop the ceremony when discovering its aim.

"When is the king-making rite?" Maelgwn asked.

"One full moon before the Autumn harvest."

"That is a fortnight hence!" Dread overcame

Maelgwn. Typically he could rapidly assemble his elite hosts, but due to the calamity, he knew not where they were. And if a military action did usurp the will of the Tribes, what then? He would save his son and lose his people? An army acting arbitrarily and contrary to the will of the people is an army of despots. Would he save his son only to deliver the lad into a life of being an outcast in his own land? Maelgwn concluded that only Arthur could stop what was coming.

* * *

Arthur knew not what was coming.

When a proxy was selected for the Slain and Risen King Rite, the dying king was not given to know anything beyond *the dying portion*. In this way, the casting-off of his old self was full and sincere. Often, the ruler would simply be told by his druids that he was being made to retire in favor of a younger successor, thus thinking that the ceremony was an abdication rather than a sacrifice.

The Dynion Hysbys and the sects of druids from Powys, from Deheubarth, and from Ynys Mon and the Old North were all of one accord about the carrying out of the rite in this manner. The minority sect of the Silures, to whom Taliesin's lineage belonged, agreed to remain silent, but abstained from participation or endorsement of the same.

But the Merlin Taliesin was tasked with delivering the message, along with Saint Illtud.

"You will abdicate your office as Pendragon."

"For Galahad?"

"Yes, lord."

"My heart hurts for Gwalchmai, but rejoices

for Galahad. It is a fine selection. May the malice that plagues us pass, and a young man lead us yet into a brighter and better iteration of our Summer Kingdom." The sockets of the ailing king's sunken eyes were blackened, his face flushed and his countenance grim. Damage had filled his lungs when he had saved the children; his left knee was badly damaged, but mainly his vexation was melancholy for the suffering of his people.

Rhufawn, who was called Galahad, was a Christian Prince and had been reared on the Pauline traditions passed on to him from his mother's line, and from Taliesin. Thus, twisting of words and deception was required to convince him to enact the ritual.

Taliesin would not participate; neither Talhaearn the Elder (a retired, older bard who had mentored both Merlin and Taliesin), but they would not condemn the ceremony either. In their silent abstinence, the officiating fell to the Adder, the most influential of the local wise men who controlled and feigned representation of the Tribes.

A seasoned liar, he used many partial truths to gain Galahad's comfort.

First, there would be a sword pulled from a stone. The sword, 'down' and in the earth, represented a king's impotence and need for renewal. The meaning of this was softened and altered, presented to Galahad as simply meaning that 'hope would be renewed' should he be able to free the sword, hold it high and present it to the ailing king.

Secondly, the actor must be in water. Water was the source of all life to the Britons and held spiritual significance of great import. Thus, a floating platform supporting a great stone would be constructed for the two participants and the Adder.

Lastly, the Cup would represent agricultural rebirth. The circle of the cup would represent the womb and its wine the placental blood of a new era. Moreover, the passing of the cup would represent fellowship, a type of oath or acceptance on behalf of the giver and receiver.

In Christian dressing, the cup was simply a vessel of healing, looking to the One who had first passed it ere He went and sacrificed Himself for His people.

Galahad could not be allowed to know that he was being made king, and Arthur could not be allowed to know that the ritual was more than an abdication. The shining prince thought he was presenting the cup and sword to an ailing king to bring hope for a return of the harvest and health (and many believed that the Grail might heal Arthur and the land as well), and the Iron Bear was made to understand that he was retiring in favor of a younger, qualified and ready man whose mother was a Silure and whose father was the greatest of all the Sons of Cunedda, that powerful line from the north.

Two actors operating on half-truths.

The darkest of pagan rituals, with a dash of Christian nomenclature and a pinch of benign symbolism, can pass for harmless without much difficulty.

The place of ritual was in Gwent, where the river passed by the very cave where Arthur had been *made king the first time*. This time, as then, many representatives and witnesses from the whole of Britain were present; the consummation of that ritual had been performed in a shadow and this one in the daylight. That first had finished with a crowning as king by the pious Bishop Dyfrig; this one would conclude with whatever the local shaman had for him. Cymru had been the first to claim Christ and the last to let go of the old gods. *A peculiar and wondrous people are we,* Arthur reckoned. For thirty and nine years he had reigned, twenty as War King, a decade and nine years as Giant Slayer. *And the sum of it as Child Executioner and Failure at Love.* The people had enjoyed the rest of peace, and the happy lethargy of plenty, but never truly the king.

Now his heart and mind were locked as behind an iron vault, scarred and numb, even to his own self, but it appeared that he welcomed the coming rest.

His only company for months had been his war dogs, the great mastiffs that were in height above some small horses, and the guardians of Flat Holm. He favored the company of the dogs, but the soldiers smelled better. *Now I understand why Gwen puts them out with the horses when I am away.* He wondered if she would be in attendance for the retirement ceremony. And his thoughts went to Mordred. Whereas criminals harbor dozens of minor secrets and sleep well, Arthur was a just and righteous man with very few secrets and slept poorly; for with secrecy it is magnitude and impact, and not quantity, that eats a man.

Will he use what he knows about Amr to promote himself, or shame me? Arthur distrusted the Whelp, and wondered if he was scheming or, like so many others, simply trying to find sustenance and clean shelter… and survive.

* * *

One moon before the harvest, at dawn, masses from every hundred, cantref, kingdom and Royal

Clan gathered about the riverbanks of Gwent. Cedric had asked permission for his Gewissi to attend, and of Picts and men of the Emerald Island there were not a few. The clergy did all to Christianize the overtly heathen event, giving sermons and promising mercy from a just and concerned God. Here the first offerings to Mary the Mother of God were encouraged, and her favor from the heavens evoked.

Arthur was directed to wear black. He wore no armor; rather, long-sleeved, simple garb and boots. Sandy hair and a simple gold circlet were the only contrasting colors in his attire.

And he was made to wear an ancient black mask that represented death. Ghastly and beautiful, it was a bearded visage of horror itself.

Simple, black, death.

A custom suit of armor had been fashioned for Galahad. The style of Vivien's metal skin was retained, then enameled with white, over and over again. Every piece, every shell, every rivet was rendered white as a dove. Gold dust was added to the enamel and a large red plume fixed to the helm, which bore the fins and traits of a Pendragon. Similar in style to a Corinthian helmet, it was only cut and soldered at the nose, revealing the whole of Galahad's face from the cheeks down. There was no mask, as Galahad possessed the face of an angel, a living mask of the ceremony.

Galahad wielded a replica of his father's battle spike, save that it too was white-enameled. The stitching of both the Ravens of the North and the Bear Claw of the south decorated his cape, also in a white thread one shade removed from the host. The three rays of the Awen, stitched in gold, collared the front chest piece of the armor.

Ornate, white, life.

Arthur was unarmed.

The participants were forbidden to speak.

All of Arthur's famed companions were present; Bedwyr, Cai, Gwalchmai, Anwn Ddu, Caradog, Gaheris, Owain, Urien, Rhun, and scores more. Each of these had been carefully given a slight variation on the course of the day's events and none knew exactly how they ought to feel, nor what would be. The common man knew they were there to witness the Sacral Rite; but the leaders had been away, and were in confusion. The orchestration of lies begat an orchestration of silence… and inaction.

Maelgwn was there too, and greatly feared. He worried for his son, but knew Arthur would find a way to do right in the situation, *in any situation,* as he always had.

But Arthur did not know what right needed to be done, and Maelgwn understood this not.

Morgaine of the Faeries looked on as well, standing next to her son, Mordred, all the while being harassed by the Tylwyth Teg who, unseen to all others assembled, pulled at her skirt, poking and tugging her, begging in concert for her to *kill the Whelp, kill him now.* For all her powers, she could not stop the mouths of the tormenting spirits, so she rebelled against them by hugging her son tighter and tighter. A man of no affection, he accepted the hug as a person accepts tea – giving surface gratitude and then leaving the cup half full.

Gwenhywfar remained yet in Little Britain, convalescing on the estate of Gwythyr ap Greidawl, an ally to the Silures likened unto King Hoel.

The morning, as had been for nearly four moons, was an orange and yellow translucent fog, a lingering poison of congested despair. The Adder would have to hasten the ritual lest he lose the support of the crowd, who would soon retreat to their homes or other shelter.

A low drum beat.

Rhythmic.

Borrowing from Illtud and Merlin's mastery of sound and its manipulation of the emotions, alertness and very directional thoughts and passions of men, the Adder's choice of musical accompaniment was the zenith of intentional drama.

The three stepped upon the platform.

Maelgwn emerged from the shade, positioning himself as close to the river as he could. Arthur saw him not.

Morgaine did the same.

"Speak the words," bade the shaman unto Galahad.

"Take," opened Rhufawn, full of the nerves of a youth giving his first public address; "this cup is the new testament in my blood, which is shed for you."

Arthur found no malice in the verse, thinking that Galahad spake of the Lord.

Galahad revealed the mazer, which he had encased in an iron egg-shaped protective case. The case was brilliant, covered in a mural of Bible scenes. The case ornate, the contents simple.

The crowd was awed, being witnesses to living history – seeing the Cup of Christ and one of the Treasures of Cymru in open display.

"If thou be the One, raise the sword." The Adder gave his line, scripted, expressions to match the drumming.

"What blade is limp and bound in the heart of the earth?" Galahad responded.

"King Arthur acts in the authority of the Three Swords, but he possesses but two. Today, for the first time in the history of our Isles, and the world, one king will possess them all."

The sword of Troy! How did the Dynion Hysbys find it? And what other treasures upon my Ynys Enlli have been breached? Morgaine tightened her fists; the still waters became unsettled.

"I be the One to restore the land." Galahad believed he said these words in the stead of Christ: an honorarium, a prayer. He knew not that he was declaring his kingship.

Arthur took no offense, for another legend was being born in his view, another boy drawing a sword. Arthur coveted not his glory at the expense of others and enjoyed the success of all – even in his supplanting.

Galahad drew the Sword of Troy. The blade had been brought to the Isles by Brutus, given him by Aeneas, who fled as the Island of the Cymry's ancestors fell in flames on account of adultery and the greed and lust of princes and demigods.

The sword was a marvel. Like Excalibur, its hilt bore ancient script, and like Excalibur, it seemed to hum or sing when wielded. As the sword was freed from the stone, the platform floated away from the shore (whether by witchcraft or whether the Adder arranged it by tethers and pullies below the platform that were set in motion by the moving of the sword is debated by the bards, and known by none).

Galahad placed the sword laterally and flat upon Arthur's outstretched arms, in a pose of *receiving*.

"You and the land are One, my lord," said Galahad. "Drink and be healed."

Arthur's hands were full, so Galahad lifted up his mask and helped his lord drink, just as the Jesus Christ had been helped to sip upon vinegar whilst on the Cross.

"Take up the sword again and drink, Galahad."

The lad did as instructed. And the power and kingship shifted to the new boy-king.

"The people would have Arthur continue as Pendragon for all seasons and all times," declared the Adder.

"Stop him!" Maelgwn was at once in the water, but the platform had gained overmuch distance and was too deep for the Bloodhound, who had to shift from running to swimming, and lacked time to reach his son.

"Rhufawn ap Maelgwn, you are forthwith king and Wledig."

"What?" The young man was confused, as the people cheered and horns and stringed instruments joined the drumming.

Then the drumming stopped.

"The king is dead!" cried out the Wise Man with evangelical heat. He then drew a sickle-shaped short knife across Galahad's throat. An instant and mortal gash; the white enamel, the stone, and the base of the platform were awash in hot red blood. "Without the shedding of blood there is no remission of sin" – the heathen mocked Scripture and Scripture's God – "long live the king! The perfect lamb has shed his blood for you, Arthur, and you are born again."

"*Long live the king!*" the mob shouted. The music resumed.

"Arthur!" Maelgwn reached the platform, his black-clad sovereign holding the dead hero Galahad in his arms.

"I knew not, I knew not!"

Suddenly the sun broke through, and the regular light of morning descended upon the river and the forest and the mouth of the cave.

"The boy achieved the Grail; Heaven accepted him and has healed our land!" The Adder basked in victory, and in real and timely actual sunlight.

Maelgwn wrested Rhufawn from Arthur and his eyes moved not from the king. His eyes were filled with rage. With hurt, with disbelief.

"I knew not," Arthur wept. "I knew not!"

Maelgwn could not slay Arthur or the devilish anti-druid, for the people rejoiced at the name of Rhufawn, which was all that remained and endured of Lancelot's son – for Galahad the Grail Guardian was no more.

CHAPTER 24
Despise Not the Wife of Thy Youth
The Seventh Seed

"Fornicating with his sister was meant only to traumatize the boy, creating a pathway into his soul, by which we could insert a spirit and possess him. That the deed brought forth a bastard maniac to be our pawn is just a delicious dividend!" No cackle can equal that cackle which is cackled in Italian. "I am so glad you have forgiven me my little *tongue* comment, and that we can again resume our Great Work, my Cymreig friend."

"And I'm glad you've graced our welcoming Isles yet again with your presence." The Adder knew well that Simon Magus hated Britannia, mostly for being made to sleep on hay and stubble, or else in mud, during his long seasons of confinement. They shared a common goal and a common enemy, but the anti-druid had no renewed affinity for the Professional Meddler in the Affairs of Men.

"Do you have one more activation spell in the workings?"

"If there be Giants left, I know not of one." The Adder was puzzled.

"No, no. We need to unleash a different monster." Magus schemed his schemed.

"Mordred?"

"Yes!"

"Not possible." The puppet protested against the puppet master.

"Why not?" Magus patronized with false patience.

"He fears Arthur. An unnatural, controlling fear that he thinks is concealed but is stained as a bright dye upon his visage at all times."

"Would the Weasel fear the Bear if he had a…" Magus, full of hubris, full of glee, playfully taunted. After much pause he revealed, "…A Bloodhound?"

"Maelgwn Gwynedd? He would put me to the sword or worse for my role in giving his son to the gods."

"The balances of power are tilted by Maelgwn Gwynedd. If the people reject Arthur and find that *he* advocated a proxy die in his stead under false pretenses when an actual heir was available… If they find he extended his reign through lies and manipulation, then will Galahad's death be in vain and his glory turned to pity or worse in the bards' songs. Then you will have your Bloodhound Prince. And with him his hosts, and with them, victory."

The Adder, seeing he was in the presence of a greater deceiver than he, acquiesced to the plan. Magus instructed him to convince Mordred to proclaim himself heir and, harvest or no, the rightful ruler in the stead of the fallen Bear of Glamorgan. Moreover, Mordred would be open and loud about being caused to live as the son of

Llew ap Cynfarch under false pretenses, as a ruse to plant yet another Royal from the South in the northern lands of Cynfarch.

Though appalled at Mordred's origins, the plotters were sure that the majority would be more disgusted with the procreators than the procreated.

It was time that Mordred transitioned from a Whelp to an usurper and traitor.

With the promise of men and succor from both the cantrefs and kingdoms of the North, and of Mark's confederacy of rebels, and of Maelgwn himself, Mordred would have hope of vanquishing the undefeated Silures.

Hope of finally having the crown.

Hope of finally having Gwenhwyfar in the open.

* * *

The harvest did come.

A glorious, bountiful harvest.

Because of the mixing of words and imagery at the Sacral Rites, the Tribes knew not whether to celebrate Rhiannon, Arianrhod, Blodeuwedd, Jesus or Mary. Thus, they celebrated each of them and, in doing that, celebrated Arddu the Deceiver unawares.

The birth pangs of the Dragon entering the atmosphere had caused the temperatures to lower in Spring, ruining the harvest; his fullness and battery of the Isles caused the temperatures to rise, bringing a temporary and false sense of plenty. In reality, the weather was erratic and the four winds, along with the circuits of the sun and moon, disjointed. But there were leeks and potatoes for cawl, and rhubarb for pies, and tiny glimpses of what had been had reappeared in less than two months' time.

Winter drew nigh, and Arthur determined to visit Hoel and to fetch his wife home from Brittany. Moreover, there were reports that Mark would harass Brittany once more before the fighting would give way to the cold. Thus, Arthur set to the channels with seven hundred upon his vessel.

And in his absence Mordred dropped the pebble of a rumor into a pond. It rippled, so he skipped a larger stone. It rippled yet more – a larger. And yet again the ripple swelled. Soon the rumor became a boulder and the subject of Arthur's bastard son a giant wave at high tide, becoming the sole subject of all discourse and gossip in every market, every Sunday assembly, every tavern and every place where men and women gather when itching are their ears.

***

"Please kill him, lady, I beg thee!"

"Why do you not cease to trouble me? I will not!" Gwyar bore the weight of sufficient burden in rehearsing her words, traveling north to confront her husband and confess that, though she had brought him many sons, his *firstborn* was in fact Arthur's. A repentant elf lacking gumption to act was the final stone stacked upon the scale. "Perhaps the only killing that need occur today is that I kill you."

The king of the Tylwyth Teg sighed. "How do you end the damned? Or destroy the accursed thing, lady?"

"Indeed," she seethed. "Which is why you and I will outlive them all, eh?" In her next breath, the elf was gone.

The northern chieftain Llew ruled a region of the Old North in conjunction with his brother, Urien. Their grandfather, Meirchion the Mad, had called the area Rheged after his territory in Glamorgan in the days when the Silures had reappropriated southern men for northern princesses that the line of Cunedda might survive. As an elderly man, Meirchion begat Mark, making the enemy of Arthur Llew's uncle (though a significantly younger man).

Urien ranked amongst Arthur's closest allies and fondest friends. Llew became poisoned with fraternal rivalry and regional envy from his youth, and was devout about the Roman way. Under pressure that felt as if at the tip of a sword, he married into the household of Meurig and begat northern sons with southern blood. A brilliant political strategy. But such maneuvers, which work well on ink and parchment, impact real people who, like Llew and Gwyar, have empty or even malicious relationships.

As soon as the children were put to fosterage, Gwyar left Llew to return to her craft (and to look after Arthur), and the couple only made appearances as were meet for public and political needs.

Still, Llew was as all men. And all men hate the notion of being lied to about matters of loins and lovers.

Gwyar entered the hall of her hilltop estate and walked, shoulders pulled back and chin up, to face Llew face-to-face, though the tip of her head only reached his navel.

Jealousy and shame beget false bravery, and false bravery impulse, and impulse begets death.

With no exchange of words, no argument, accusation, consideration or investigation, the grandson of Meirchion the Mad became mad himself and slapped Gwyar hard across the face, sending the slight Fae violently backward and to the ground.

Gwyar went down; Morgaine came up. Looming as a tower above the impulsive chieftain. The primal witch rose such that she had to stoop her back to avoid breaching the vaults of the hall. Llew had known, as he let his hand fly, that death was sure. His wife was the daughter of Meurig and Onbrawst, or Meurig and the Devil, or Onbrawst and Satan. There had ever been something wrong with her, always something otherworldly.

In the twinkling of an eye, Morgaine had recoiled and reshaped – was tiny again.

Loyalty.

Fidelity.

Honesty.

How would you feel if you were a man and the boy you raised as your own was sired by another?

Morgaine came down and Gwyar came up. She suffered the strike, a bloodied lip the fair wage for forty years of false pretense.

"I am sorry, Llew." She turned and made her leave of Rheged, departing for Ynys Enlli where she might hide the Grail. Her brother had hastily handed it to her while he and Maelgwn squirmed and slipped, scrambling in a pool of Galahad's blood, laboring in vain to stop the fount from his neck and revive the lifeless boy.

As a result, the very person who must not bear the Cup possessed the same, Simon's plan positioning and posturing by both chance and intention.

* * *

Word of Mordred's machinations had not reached Brittany by the time Arthur and his troops arrived in Leon. The weather was bitterly cold, and all bore layer upon layer of skins and caps in an effort not to freeze. Every hearth was ablaze and additional copper basins were placed throughout Gwythyr's castle, mobile fire pits that were fair to look upon, and functional besides.

Arthur saw his wife, bundled in white furs, as an adorable bunny, the flames flickering in her magical eyes, and he fell in love with her afresh.

She was indifferent to his coming, and rather enjoyed the rolling estates and Breton wines. *But she longed to see Mordred or Lancelot as an acceptable second. For this reason alone she was glad to see her escort home. And happier still when she learned that he was only come to greet her and would stay behind to lend support to Mark.*

"I heard your knee was injured and that you were restricted in breathing. Are you certain you should do this? Would that you were home instead." She kissed the king as she lied and flattered, knowing how alluring she looked, and how he looked upon her. *For often it is more attractive to conceal rather than to reveal.*

"Hard as iron and ferocious as a bear, love." Arthur used jovial wordplay with his own name.

"I see this," she remarked. "You appear as born again." These words were used to inflict a stab of pain upon Arthur, *for this is the operation of those who abuse; first with flattery, then with insult.* For she knew well that Arthur was born again; under the coming of the Red Dragon, from the bloody sacrifice of the innocent came the *new Bear* in the worldview of the tribes. Such a thought was awkward and repugnant to Arthur, the death of Galahad haunting a man who was now twice afflicted in his soul by rites and rituals.

Before he could hold his untoward spouse accountable for her subtle strokes, Gwythyr presented himself, throwing an enfolding embrace about the Pendragon.

Hoel was present as well, and these two were the foundation and backbone of Brittany. Cousins to the Cymry, but with their own cultural style and sophistication, it was *as being home but not, the same but different* for Arthur and his kinsmen. And they greatly loved the Bretons.

The discussions soon shifted to battle strategy and how that they must prepare for one more strike from Mark prior to the fullness of December causing all men to stay in the warmth of their homes. If it was not the return of the *war days*, then it was surely nigh, for the conversations, preparations and emotions surely took Arthur back to those legendary times where Saxon fell to Briton sword again and again. The threat itself invigorated the aging sovereign, who was fifty-and-three, talks of strategy causing him to miss his Merlin exceedingly.

A young woman rested her shoulders along the railing of a spiral stairway, carved of ivory, etched with knotwork and sigils, a story above those gathered in the great hall. She enjoyed the cold and allowed her yellow locks to serve as her only cap; they fell gracefully over her shoulders. A princess, aged twenty-and-three years and never wed, she governed the home and estates of her father, Gwythyr. His land holdings in Brittany were massive and she his only heiress. The people loved her and put a twist upon the name of their region; feminizing it in honor of their future queen, they called her Gwenhwyfar, the queen of Lyonesse.

Hers was a natural beauty, equal in allure yet opposite in nature to the High King's wife. Her beauty emanated from her soul and her character first, her bosom and form secondly.

Gwenhwyfar ferch Gwythyr had never met Arthur, always missing the chance, being at the market or some assembly, misfortune delaying the occasion. Like every living person, she knew of the living legend by his legends, but longed to meet the man, whom she somehow loved ere they met. She found his eyes amongst the hundreds of skins and cloaks bustling below. She looked into them, and loved him so.

But though he looked directly at her, he noticed her not, his troubled affection and affliction fixed still on Gwenhwyfar the daughter of the Giant, who was making her departure and would soon be back in Caerleon, betraying her husband with one of his own house.

Mordred grew emboldened, making passionate speeches how that his *father* had authored the ruse to keep himself on the throne in spite of the calamity that ravaged the land, how he proclaimed a false freedom erstwhile putting restrictions on the Dynion Hysbys that violated their rites, and their rights, and the same allegation made he on behalf of the Catholic Church. Moreover, he promised that he would place his sons, born of Kwyllog ferch Caw, on the throne for generations to come, finally restoring the North to a position of equality and prominence.

His seductions found willing bedfellows amongst many of the sons of Caw, and among the lines of Cynfarch, not a few. But many of those houses rejected the Whelp, seeing his treachery from the beginning.

In all, approximately two of ten from those of age and ability to fight joined unto Mordred. Sufficient to be branded an insurrection; hardly enough to ignite a revolt, or a civil war. *Maelgwn and his hosts would be needed to draw men unto Mordred, and his treachery would be quickly crushed.*

Mordred had drawn no sword, had scorched no farm, harmed not the hair of one child of Glamorgan. Thus far it had been a volley of words and accusations and no arrows.

Gwenhywfar II was overfilled with joy, singing and laughing aloud, celebrating that her paramour had finally found the stones to do what he ought to have done nearly two decades ago. *Finally! I have years of love yet to give King Mordred, though it be during the dusk of my years.* Of paramount import was that she keep great distance from the Traitor, that none suspect him at the last. They forsook engagements in their forest, avoided the farmhouse, the tiny apartment and the chapel (all places marked with the fluids of their betrayal time and again through the years).

But as her joy begat burning lust, Gwen could no longer contain herself, and took quill and ink to parchment, expressing whimsical, youthful love and naughty and explicit demands of her longing.

As Gwenhwyfar's sister, Gwenhwyfach, was wed to Mordred, she was able to use the cover of suing Mordred for peace in the stead of her husband, and for the love of her sister, to send the letter. Mordred would bring troops and would meet in public feigning discussions of good faith with the Round Table Fellows then, under the blanket of winter night, would steal away unto the bed of Gwenhwyfar.

The Deceptress informed Bedwyr and Bishop Bedwini of her course, and they found the maneuver stately and profitable, hoping that the softer words of women would quell the hotter, more impulsive aims of men.

Finding relief that she didn't have to dispose of another messenger, she sealed and released the letter.

Seven days later, one hundred of Mordred's newly formed army, mostly Ravens, met below Lodge Hill on an open plain that lay between the amphitheater and the hilltop fort. If desired, the Silures could have descended from the fort and slayed the rebels in the space of minutes. That Mordred had agreed to meet in a place of obvious and easy slaughter was an act of peaceful posturing, or overt arrogance. *Or, alternatively, that his wife had forced him to meet there.*

Bedwyr brought only fifty, Gwalchmai, Cai and Peredur amongst them.

Both armies were mounted upon steed and met 'line to line' on the pitch.

The Adder served as a dark Anti-Merlin to Mordred, and stood in the midst of the men, salivating to assist with Mordred's allegations and assertions as opportunity yielded him. But it was Gwenhywfar's meeting, so he let her speak first.

But she could utter but three words of welcome before her sister was upon her.

"Please read this aloud, sister." *Gwenhwyfach had discovered the letter.*

"Before you do that, might I speak?" A metal-skinned god interrupted.

"Lancelot!" Bedwyr rejoiced.

Mordred's own men were instantly deflated. As King Arthur had calculated that he might be long at war, and as rumor of Mordred's insurrection had reached his ears, he had evoked an old promise betwixt the strained and troubled friends.

"I too have received written charges: that I might be Protector of this kingdom whilst our lord is on the Continent. Apparently the Iron Bear finds this weasel a real threat to we Undefeated. I see it not," Lancelot goaded. "But a promise is a promise and here I be, my hosts with me." Suddenly seventy more *Lancelots* filed in behind their commander, a troop that would cause the fabled Spartans to quake, the Romans to run. The Hosts of Maelgwn were the reason the Britons had remained so long impenetrable. And they gave appearance of rest, sharpness and hunger – for battle.

As for himself, Mordred was but a doll or lifeless piece of furniture on this day. His wife had intercepted the love letter and threatened to hand deliver it to Arthur if he did not comply with the place and course of the meeting. The affair was soon to be found out; moreover, the Lancelot had joined with Arthur, despite the Adder's promises to the contrary. *We underestimated the mad knight's sense of duty and commitment to his own words.* Now Mordred was living as a dead man, moment to moment, gulping for one more, one more breath at a time.

Lancelot's arrival pleased Gwenhwyfach all the more, and she hoped to see his Hosts make a quick meal of Mordred's wretches.

"Welcome, King Maelgwn Gwynedd. I am certain our Lord Arthur is pleased to have you back in Caerleon. As I am sure my sister the queen is to be under your protective wings, my angel." Gwenhwyfach flattered *the difference maker.* "Now, sister, please take and read."

Gwenhywfar was indignant, feared nothing and, much like Simon Magus, always held out for a way out. "It is not for the High Queen to receive orders, but rather to give them."

"Read it!" her sister barked.

Gwenhywfar II repeated her stance. And then yet again the third time.

Frustrated that the Adulteress would not confess her crimes before all, Gwenhwyfach struck Gwenhywfar hard upon the jaw.

To smite a queen or king in public is an act of highest treason by the ancient laws and customs of the Cymry. The act represented more than the deed itself, and was a stroke against the king, who *was the people.* This type of rebellion wrought chaos and disorder and tyranny, and could not be abided or given place or grace.

The Adder ran to Gwenhywfach's aid, hoping to find words to defend her and regain control of the situation, *which was about Mordred shaming Arthur for his incest and lust of power and manifold sins, not the squabbles of women!* But his coming forward was mistaken as aggressive, as an assault against Bedwyr's line to follow Gwenhwyfach's blow. Perceiving the same, Cai unfastened the leather strap that fixed his double-headed battle-axe to the back plate of his armor. In but two movements the axe was in hand and the Adder was cleaved in twain, spilling his guts upon the plain.

Here then, *the slap and the slaying of the Adder* were the second death blows to the Summer Kingdom.

Bravely, but in vain, Mordred's men rushed Bedwyr's line, perceiving that they must fight desperately or perish, being put under the shadow of a military fortress in enemy lands by the foolishness of women. The battle was no battle, rather a ten minute training exercise for the Silures and their allies, the Hosts of Maelgwn. As Briton was fighting Briton, quarter was extended where possible and deaths were few. Mercy was given, and mendable broken bones took the place of death strokes. In the fracas of fighting Mordred put dagger to his own wife's back, seized the queen, and fled the battle, riding hard, harder still until he reached Arthur's very own home.

And Lancelot seized the letter, crumpled upon the frozen ground, listless as the dead lass next to it.

* * *

"It is over. Our life ends at the conclusion of this pretended abduction." Gwenhwyfar was realistic, and hopeless. Mordred had declared Arthur false and taken his own wife *prisoner,* and the people scoffed and mocked the move. Troops were assembled and besieged the chamber where he held her. Making contrived threats to put her to death, he sued Arthur to come and meet him; battle man to man, father to son.

The scandal of Arthur having a secret son by his sister had fermented and the nation wanted to hear of it from their king. Thus, they desired that he come home and face Mordred and the people.

Illtud and Bedwini distanced themselves from the situation, using the occasion to speak against heathen rites, and the druids claimed ignorance and misfortune in the stead of perversion at the selection of Gwyar to lay with her brother during his king-making. Many called for the deposing of both men due to the scandal and shame of it all, creating an open throne for this interest or that interest. At once the notion of Arthur as the *forever king* was losing its appeal, and the oldest of rivalries between north and south intensified. Smarter men than Mordred, such as Llew and Caw, could use the king's bastard as an instrument of great gain, and then discard the Whelp. And these sent emissaries and some soldiers to Caerleon, hoping to negotiate and ask for peace on his behalf, blaming his deceased wife for starting the skirmish.

Mark's latest surge quelled and, Leon-Brittany secured, Arthur braved dreadful winter seas, hastening home to his seat of power, which was occupied by another.

Rumors of the letter were confused and disjointed and fell unto Arthur's ears as written from his wife *to Lancelot*. This, and not nephew Mordred acting out as an insolent youth recently drunken at the knowledge of inheritance, dominated Arthur's every thought. Such was his rage that the frosty air and icy water was unnoticed; he could have swum across the channel, propelled by forty years of jealousy and misplaced adoration.

He stood quite alone, insisting upon solitude as the vessel cut through the waters, approaching the confluence of sea and freshwater – the inlet mouth artery that would ultimately take him to Caerleon. It was early morning, prior to the rising of the sun, and he stared upon the waves, his thoughts about Lancelot inside his wife in one instant, his approach to defeating Lancelot again in the next. Lancelot's marbled chest upon her painted frame in one thought, Arthur's spear opening the marble in the next.

He was quite alone with the racing thoughts. Then a familiar voice came, originating somehow from the rush and ebb below: *Foolish is the man who judges a matter before he heareth it,* and a moment later, *By the mouth of two or three witnesses let all things be established.*

"The cold tricks my brain. My lost wizard counsels me from the sea," he said, to no one and to any who might be eavesdropping. Still, the proverbs tempered the Iron Bear just enough that he pinched a thread of reason, a hair of patience, that would last until he was come into his own country.

'Twas Lancelot himself that met him on the bridge o'er the Usk.

Arthur's salutation was with his fists.

"You lay with my wife *AND NOT AS PUPPIES IN LOVE AT SCHOOL*; you who are Protector and First Knight, you are as my Judas Iscariot!"

"When one or more are involved in delivering a message, you can be sure that its meaning and intent will be changed thrice." Maelgwn remained calm. In this instant, Maelgwn had kept his head more so than the typically temperate and logical king. Maelgwn *knew* that it was Mordred and not he whom the queen favored, that his one true love would have neither of the *four chords*, that his heart was desperately foolish and vain. Yet he looked to Arthur's feelings, as the overmuch sadness over Galahad and the truth about Gwen and Mordred had softened the warrior, giving him introspection as substitute for power and lashing out in raw emotion.

But Arthur was in a different state. And was landing meaningful blows.

Risking injury, Lancelot did tackle and subdue the Iron Bear.

"I love the queen with all of me," he said plainly. "You know this."

"You mock me! Stand and fight, else unhand me, else strangle and slay me!" Arthur gave screaming, desperate orders.

"I touched her not. I honored thy bed, my lord!"

"I dined with the king of the Picts. I KNOW you killed men as a ruse and that you lodged with her in his lands."

Arthur was five times smarter than any man and could indeed see through any conspiracy. But he had no way of calculating that the abduction of Gwenhwyfar, that her subsequent seduction, had been arrested and that honor had been upheld. The appearance of evil was too great. Maelgwn opted for cold and abrupt honesty. He controlled the left arm and head of Arthur in a side lock, using the force of both as a type of triangle, and squeezed with heavy pressure and much leverage, forcing Arthur to listen.

"I did abduct the queen, I did take her to my stronghold in Pictland, I did frame a rival tribe and lay her kidnapping at their charge, I did lead my sons to victory and in the slaying of many painted men on account of my lies. For this, do unto me as you would according to our customs. But when the moment came that I might know her, the Merlin came, and stopped me. And I love you, and stopped myself."

Arthur was losing air, but managed to continue cursing.

Maelgwn released him and rapidly went for the crumpled letter, scribed in his wife's own hand. "Read this." Maelgwn absorbed another punch, clean to the nose. "Read this, Bear, please."

More cursing and punches.

Read it! A familiar voice descended and swirled as a cone or whirlwind about both great men. Arthur relented. And read.

After a long pause, Arthur looked towards his estate, still filthy from the calamitous debris.

"She has enchanted and bewitched you the whole of your life, hasn't she?"

"Longer than even I understand, my king."

"It is Mordred whom she loves, in the comfort of my own home, in the heart of my own lands." Arthur's face was as stone. Maelgwn had been in twelve major battles with Arthur, and more than sixty minor conflicts, and this look – this look he had never witnessed. This was Arthur's authoritative death look tenfold.

Maelgwn prayed the look was directed at Mordred and not Gwenhwyfar.

"She is a troubled creature from our youth, Bear," Maelgwn offered.

"We all have night terrors, we all wrestle with devils. She owns her actions, as do you, as do I." Arthur straightened his attire and made for his estate. "Come, Lancelot, I know a secret way into my bedchamber. I've used it for years."

"You and your disguises." A friendly, brotherly smile.

"Don't worry about a few dozen Picts, my First Knight; come with me."

Arthur *loved* his disguises, secret passages, minor escapes from the stresses of governance and simulation of other characters who suffered not from unrequited love. As a result, he knew of three different means of accessing not only the mansion that contained his and Gwen II's bedchamber, but also a covert entrance into the bedchamber itself.

Chieftains and priests and bishops had

gathered, wanting to negotiate the return of Gwenhwyfar and the voluntary surrender of Mordred. The matter was exceedingly complex. He was the king's son (if the rumors were true, and Gwyar had validated them with the brevity of her repentance towards her estranged husband) – his first son. As a result, he had rights under ancient codes and customs. He was also a traitor, a usurper, a claimant to the throne. The magnitude of the situation brought an uneasy curiosity and fascination to the assembled renowned, those given charge to manage such things.

Knowing all this, and that none were to barge in upon them too soon, Mordred put the vigor of a lifetime of lovemaking into one encounter. Their time together was at once animalistic and romantic, gentle and hedonistic, an explosion of lust and a conduit of sweet, truest love. Mordred had bound his mistress queen to a bed post, thrusting and pounding upon her from behind, exploring all that her painted body offered, when Arthur and Maelgwn burst through a secret door connected to the anterior of a large wardrobe closet.

Arthur saw her pleasure. Her satisfaction. Her involvement. Her vulnerability. Her ecstasy.

Maelgwn, on this day, was the wiser, forcing himself to look away.

Mordred pulled himself out of the queen, gathered trouser, then dagger, which he turned upon Gwenhwyfar's throat.

"Ready for more blood, father?" Pupils black, eyes black, soul black. "Step back, or you will be the widowed king."

In spite of the open betrayal and blatant encroach of living a decades of lies, Arthur loved Gwenhwyfar, as did Lancelot.

Maelgwn touched Arthur upon the forearm. "Let them run. In the end, where will they go? The law rules in Caermelyn."

"Caermelyn is fallen." Arthur transcended hurt; his visage said *butchery and revenge.*

Maelgwn did all to help. "You are Caermelyn, lord. And you yet breathe. We have survived Saxons, and Giants, and monsters indescribable. We WILL survive this scandal. You are King Arthur. She never loved either of us. Let it go. Let the law judge them."

"I must have audience with my wife," said Arthur.

"My lord?" Maelgwn responded, confused.

Arthur ignored Maelgwn momentarily. Turning to the couple before him: "You would no more harm her than would he." He pointed to his First Knight. "So go on." A judgment dwelt in Arthur's eyes that were as from God Himself. "Go on; run. What befalls you both will be far from here."

Mordred needed no further encouragement or warning, and scurried from the chamber as a rat scurries from a well-lit barn.

Arthur returned to his friend. "It was never you; it was he. The golden-armored boy who has ever coveted my crown and, now we know, my wife besides. I charge thee, best of all knights, I charge thee remain as Protector for a time yet. To Gwenhwyfar the First I must."

"As you wish, my king," Maelgwn answered, knowing he would disobey the mandate, and closely following the Iron Bear. Maelgwn was numb, but his bubble and his *others* harassed him not. On this day he was more stable than Arthur, who saw much and bore too much more.

Gwenhwyfar I's cell had survived the comet;

the adjoining school house had not. A light snowfall covered the ruin, which was but a foundation stone and four or five charred bits of wood. An aroma of despair lingered and visiting the place was not desirous, let alone abiding there. But there she abided. The crimson-haired ghost. Her lodging included a narrow, short bed with drawers built into the frame, a small table that could accommodate two children at study or tea, and a basin. In the cell a simple iron cross engraved with knotwork hung upon the east wall. These and a few gowns were the sum of the queen's possessions.

"I knew you would come," she said, her lips tightened as one concealing a great secret that everyone already knows.

"Well, you stole my sword."

"That I did." She smiled. Gwenhywfar I was full of wisdom and foresight. In the chaos of calamity, hearing though gossip that he had ceased to wield it, she had hazarded her life to retrieve, and protect, the Sword of Power.

"How did you know?" asked an inquisitive former spouse.

"Women know things."

They shared this moment and a few moments more. The subject of Llacheu and Amr was never mentioned but her grief, now twenty years on, was fresh as the morning's snowfall and just as unyielding. Finding the right moment, she took her husband by the hand. "You aren't here for Excalibur, are you, Bear? Rather a man of routine, you are here for hugs and holding, for consent's embrace."

"Yes; I come for your strength ere I..." He could not say it.

Where men falter, women have an anchor of

resolve. She made the words for him. "You must kill another son."

He broke into sobbing, more for the memory of past trauma than future duty.

The wife that Arthur had put away held him tight. She then reached below the blankets of the bed upon which they sat and revealed a long object, wrapped in white silk, tied about both ends. Loosening one end revealed the hilt.

"Kill that bastard with this, forgive yourself, and wield *your sword*, my king."

Arthur beheld Excalibur as if he were again fourteen, seeing her glow for the first time.

"In the next world, when this office is done with me and we are but man and woman, mother and father, and friends—"

"Then I will seek you out and claim you as all. You are a man just and righteous. Get thee now once more and one last time; do what only you can do."

Arthur embraced the wife of his youth once more and set out to pursue Mordred and Gwenhywfar II.

He knew exactly where they were bound and, after a few hours trailing Arthur on the path, so did Maelgwn.

Dread found Maelgwn early in the journey, for he could calculate all the outcomes, and none were good. *Mìgeil. They make for Mìgeil. She thinks it is her refuge and salvation, but knows not that Arthur discovered our lies! The Pictish king will either refuse their passage or kill them on the spot.* Maelgwn felt in his sinews that Gwen was fleeing from arrest in Caerleon to execution in Alba. *And I will stop it.*

Accompanying Arthur were Cai, Bedwyr and the Hawk of May, his *famed Giant Hunters*. And the dogs that she so loathed were leading the way.

* * *

"They venerate Maelgwn as a god, and they will protect me." Gwenhwyfar half believed her own words. "And I will protect you."

The forbidden couple knew their plight was dire, and chances of success grim. By fleeing they solidified their guilt; by fleeing they cut themselves off from Mordred's remaining loyal men; by fleeing they put themselves at the mercy of the painted warriors from Alba. After four days of hard riding and no food they arrived at the very tower where Lancelot had passed his test, where he had not done what he would have done, where loyalty to Arthur had overcome lust. *Would Arthur's loyalty to the law overcome rage?* Gwen's only aim was to extend her days, through hiding, then trial, then negotiation, then escape. Escape by way of a window or secret passage, or escape by way of a noose or blade, it mattered not. *Extend my days. Live as I please. And when I can extend them no more, escape.* She hungered; weak and dehydrated, she swooned and slumped forward on her horse.

Mordred sensed that the sentinels at the remote village gates were too complicit in giving them passage. Slender, muscular, half-naked men smeared in white paint, wearing the skins of Fisher Cats, the frightful guards were too calm, too accommodating, too easy. Assured that the safe haven was no such thing, and placing no trust in Maelgwn's year-old promises of sanctuary and safe conduct for his past lover, the bastard son of King Arthur did what was in his nature to do. Kissing his mistress, yet unconscious, upon her brow, he whispered, "Do your wiles to again manipulate your husband, and survive this if you may, my love."

Doing what cowards do, Mordred slithered away into the Caledonian Wood, preparing to battle winter as preference to Arthur's sword or Cai's club. He lit a fire for Gwen and placed her gently upon three bear skins. He made a fire and looked at her, in deep sickly sleep in the very spot where Lancelot had almost had her. He looked back once more, and vanished.

Three hours later Gwenhywfar roused to a sound she'd suffered for years. Barking. Howling. A deep but whimpering bark. A bark that sounded like the moaning words 'I love you, I love you'. Hundreds of times – nay, by the thousands – she had been forced to hear the cursed 'I love you' bark. Wits not yet gathered, she sat straight up, confused, thinking she was home.

"Arthur, else Cai, come and put these cursed dogs to the stable! Filthy wretches all, would that they were put to the butcher!"

The dogs were there, but she was not home. This she realized after her half-asleep yell had already been ejected from her lips.

"The dogs. No. He is here." Tears began to stream. She yelled for Mordred and ran to the arched windows, then onto the tower ledge. "Mordred!" she screamed and screamed and screamed. Into the December night, her cries were void. Below she saw them. The dogs. The cursed, damned dogs.

The hot breath of a man well rested, full of strength, fuller of cider and with the authority of God suddenly whispered upon her neck, clutching both of her wrists in the same action.

"Have you the Sight, mistress? Did you always know they would feast upon thy painted flesh, that they would pluck and pop and play with your copper-speckled eyes? YOU are the dog—"

"Please, no—"

"And the dog returns always to its own vomit!" Arthur used the leverage of Gwenhwyfar's wrists, turning them in on themselves; they crackled and snapped. Then he flung her from the tower as a maid tosses a bag of rubbish.

She landed far below, slamming down upon her stomach, her spine severed, resulting in paralysis, adrenaline mitigating the pain. This made her aware of when the first dog took a section of calf muscle, and when a second shook loose her foot.

Arthur's war dogs feasted on the cheating queen, the king himself looking down from above, as God looking down on Satan being cast to the bottomless pit. His obsession, his lust, his love, the object of many of the troubles that befell both the man and the kingdom, was bones and chunks below.

He saw her first.

He saw her last.

King Arthur didn't see Gwalchmai dying; rather he only heard the gurgle, and the thud.

Maelgwn had tried to stop Arthur. His battle dirk swirling and ready, he meant to clip the king behind the shoulder blade, causing a minor wound but incapacitating him with sufficient time to rescue the queen. It was a maneuver both men had executed ten score times when training or when desiring prisoners instead of corpses. There was no intent of injury.

But the Hawk of May could not discern Maelgwn's aims in the flicker of snow and sleet and minimal lighting within the small turret. He saw Maelgwn making the stabbing motion towards the Pendragon and, lacking time to draw either of his famed twin blades, threw himself between Maelgwn and Arthur.

The spike went through Gwalchmai's back. Though layered with manifold skins and coats, the killing instrument breached his heart. The blood was minimal, else hidden by his attire, and death quick. One death rattle and a free-fall to the broken, rocky floor below.

Arthur had judged Gwenhywfar by intent, and Lancelot had killed Gwalchmai by accident.

Here was delivered the third deathblow that wrought the fall of the Summer Kingdom.

Arthur drew Excalibur, and Lancelot assumed the diagonal fighting stance of the Britons. Both titans grit their teeth; the Bear versus the Bloodhound Prince.

Cai and Bedwyr, lagging but moments behind, rushed upon both men, beseeching the Picts to help them as well. At last nine men subdued the two, preventing further bloodshed. Lancelot freed his neck from the great vines that were Cai's arms and, though unable to strike out at the king, achieved a clasp of his cloak. Pulling Arthur close, so close that the tickle of spray and spittle of words was upon the king's cheeks, so near that Arthur was able to smell the salt of Lancelot's tears, Lancelot said, stoic and devoid of emotion:

"Now you will have your Civil War."

CHAPTER 25
The Winter of Magics Return

Arthur revitalized himself at the baths in Caerleon, the springs cleansing him of blood and grime, but doing naught to wash away tears or pain. After, he retired to the library, where he hoped to redeem a moment to himself to think about what lay ahead.

He fell into a familiar chair at a long reading table, the top of which was worn as a smooth stone by his very own elbows from years of childhood study. *How my Merlin made me read, then read more. But woe, there is no writ for this calamity!* He gazed upon at the scrolls, the single papyri, the bound books stacked to heights where only owls and bats could read them. *But I have read them,* he reflected.

He was not long at reflecting when the wind blew and the doors were flung open. Many parchments protested the dramatic force by rolling from the table, while three large tomes crashed upon one another, making chaos of Arthur's favorite shelf.

The king, wearing his midnight blue trousers and tunic, didn't look towards the door, assuming Cai was simply overzealous in rushing in to look upon him, as was his caring but clumsy custom. Instead, the Iron Bear remained fixed on his books, preparing to chide, utter a desperate holler, a demand for a moment of solitude.

"War King. If there is to be a war, there must be a—"

"War strategy," Arthur responded by rote.

"War strategy." The coned traveling cap of a wizard, grey and worn, was flung upon the table, spinning and landing upon Arthur's hand. A humorous jest Arthur had witnessed two hundred score times, each time followed by profound words or esoteric lessons. Dust flew. The wind rushed. Night time critters howled.

Arthur's ears had been fooled before, and his eyes, by visions he could not trust. Reluctantly, he touched the cap. 'Twas real. His posture straightened, though he felt faint; his mouth dried and his heart stopped. He touched the hat again, twisting and folding it; then he allowed himself to look.

"Merlin!"

Author Profile

Zane Newitt is an Arthurian author born on September 3rd, 1975 in Colorado, USA. *The Arthuriad Volume One: The Mystery of Merlin,* his first entry into the written genre, was released in August of 2017. An ancient and medieval history expert with an emphasis on the British Isles, the father of three enjoys travelling, speaking and teaching on an array of subjects, coaching, running a number of businesses and challenging friends and strangers alike with wit, love and unashamed irreverence tackling taboo, politically incorrect and sensitive topics - just as Merlin would do were he here today.

Publisher Information

rowanvale books

Rowanvale Books provides publishing services to independent authors, writers and poets all over the globe. We deliver a personal, honest and efficient service that allows authors to see their work published, while remaining in control of the process and retaining their creativity. By making publishing services available to authors in a cost-effective and ethical way, we at Rowanvale Books hope to ensure that the local, national and international community benefits from a steady stream of good quality literature.

For more information about us, our authors or our publications, please get in touch.

www.rowanvalebooks.com
info@rowanvalebooks.com

Printed in Great Britain
by Amazon